Straeon Cyn Cinio 2018

Straeon Cyn Cinio 2018

Casgliad o straeon byrion Pabell Lên
Eisteddfod Genedlaethol Caerdydd

Argraffiad cyntaf: 2018

ⓗ Eisteddfod Genedlaethol Cymru 2018

Rhif Llyfr Safonol Rhyngwladol: 978-0-9954987-7-8

Cyhoeddwyd gyda chymorth Cyngor Celfyddydau Cymru

Cyhoeddwyd gan Eisteddfod Genedlaethol Cymru, 40 Parc Tŷ Glas,
Llanisien, Caerdydd, CF14 5DU

Argraffwyd yng Nghymru.

Rhagair

Croeso i *Straeon Cyn Cinio* Eisteddfod Genedlaethol
Caerdydd 2018. Wedi cryn drafod a phendroni yn yr
Is-bwyllgorau Llenyddiaeth am arlwy addas ar gyfer slot
'Stori Cyn Cinio', un o ddigwyddiadau mwyaf poblogaidd
y Babell Lên yn flynyddol, penderfynwyd holi wyth
awdur oedd yn byw yng Nghaerdydd, ond â chysylltiad
â de-orllewin Cymru, a fyddent cystal â llunio stori fer
wreiddiol a fyddai'n addas i'w hadrodd yn fyw,
o gwmpas yr hanner dydd, bob dydd drwy gydol wythnos
y Steddfod, a hynny ar brif lwyfan llenyddiaeth yr Ŵyl.
Diolch i bob un a ofynnwyd am ymateb, gan gyflwyno
gwaith mor gaboledig, gwreiddiol ac unigryw. Dyma'r
canlyniad – wyth stori wahanol iawn i'w gilydd, ond
sy'n cael eu rhwydo ynghyd am eu bod yn cyfleu'r lliaws
amrywiol sy'n creu cymdeithas Gymraeg Caerdydd, a'i
pherfeddwlad ymhob cwr o Gymru. Y syniad o fedru
rhannu profiad 'byw' yr Eisteddfod â darllenwyr y
Gymraeg ble bynnag y bônt, a hynny ar ffurf cyfrol,
fu'n ysbrydoliaeth bellach i gyhoeddi'r straeon ar
ddiwedd wythnos brysur o lenydda. Hir y parhao
bwrlwm yr Eisteddfod – mwynhewch!

Diolchiadau

Hoffai aelodau Pwyllgor Llenyddiaeth lleol Eisteddfod
Caerdydd 2018 ddiolch yn ddiffuant i bawb a fu
o gymorth wrth ddod â'r gyfrol hon i fwcwl:
i Catrin Dafydd, Ceri Elen, Delyth George, Jon Gower,
Geraint Lewis, Anni Llŷn, William Owen Roberts a
Manon Rhys, am eu straeon gafaelgar, ysbrydoledig
a chofiadwy; i Bethan Mair am gydlynu a golygu'r
gyfrol, ac i Ela Mars Jones am ei gwaith dylunio hardd;
i Gyngor Celfyddydau Cymru am eu cefnogaeth ar ffurf
nawdd hael; i Elen Elis, Trefnydd a Phennaeth Artistig yr
Eisteddfod am fod mor arloesol wrth greu partneriaethau
i ddatblygu llenyddiaeth yn y Brifwyl, am gomisiynu
gweithiau llenyddol newydd a sicrhau ffordd o'u rhoi
ar gof a chadw, ac am roi llwyfan cenedlaethol proffesiynol
i gynifer o feirdd ac awduron eleni, ac i'r dyfodol.
Ar nodyn personol, hoffwn innau ddiolch i'm
cyd-aelodau ar y Pwyllgor Llenyddiaeth lleol am eu
brwdfrydedd a'u cefnogaeth ddilychwyn yn ystod y
ddwy flynedd o bwyllgora a chynllunio!

Eurgain Llŷr Dafydd
Cadeirydd Pwyllgor Llenyddiaeth Eisteddfod Caerdydd
2018

CYNNWYS

1. Trên Treherbert   Manon Rhys
2. Dŵr Poeth   Geraint Lewis
3. Y Chweched Teimlad   Ceri Elen
4. Alice yn Steddfod-land   Catrin Dafydd
5. Rebal i'r Carn   Wiliam O Roberts
6. Mrs O a Nat   Anni Llŷn
7. Diwedd y Byd   Delyth George
8. O Ddrwg i Waeth   Jon Gower

TRÊN TREHERBERT
gan Manon Rhys

Mae Dilys newydd setlo yn ei sedd, ei choffi Costa a'r *Western Mail* (y tudalen blaen wedi'i droi sha lawr) ar y bwrdd. Mae hi'n barod ar gyfer y siwrne.

Cafodd noson dda o gwsg mewn stafell chwaethus yn y Marriott, a gwledd o frecwast. Wedi'r asesiad ffafriol hwn, mae hi'n falch iddi drefnu aros yno eto, adeg yr Eisteddfod. Heddiw, mae popeth wrth fodd Dilys ofalus hyd yn hyn. Heblaw am stori flaen y *Western Mail*. Cau siop Howell's! Mae'n anodd credu. A'r golofn olygyddol yn holi pwy fydd nesa – Debenhams ynte John Lewis? Y ddwy, falle – dyna'r bygythiad. A dyna gawdel wedyn: colli statws sefydliadau pwysig, colli swyddi. Ond i Dilys a'i chenhedlaeth, bydd cau Howell's yn fwy na chau siop. Bydd yn ddiwedd cyfnod, yn arwydd arall o ddiflaniad hen fawredd y brifddinas. Ond mae atgofion Dilys yn dal eu gafael ynddi: gwynt persawr yn eich tywys drwy'r drysau troi, colur a thlysau'r cownteri gwydr, y lifft fel caetsh yn ratlan at adrannau'r dillad a'r dodrefn a'r carpedi drud ac awyrgylch chwaeth a chyfoeth yn eich denu i orwario. A chyffro te prynhawn ei phlentyndod yn y 'caffi tanfor', lle nofiai mân bysgod yn nŵr glas y ffenestri llong. A'r grotto rhyfeddol adeg y Nadolig – mae'r atgofion yn dal mor fyw...

Ond 'Dere, Dilys!' yw hi heddiw, gan mai'r antur arfaethedig sy'n mynd â'i bryd. Cychwynnodd honno eisoes: gadael y Marriott a rhuthro lawr Mill Lane gan anelu'n syth at y stesion. Prynu'r coffi, dringo at blatfform chwech y Valleys Line â'i rybudd llym: 'Dim alcohol rhwng Pontypridd a Threherbert' – sy'n amherthnasol ben bore fel hyn, gobeithio. Mae'r trên gwag yn disgwyl am ei chwmni.

Gwerthfawroga hithau wacter y *compartment*. Heb dynnu sylw neb, gall gyffroi fel croten fach pan glyw chwiban y gard a theimlo'r trên yn codi sbîd gan bwyll. A dyma hi, ar ei ffordd – am y tro cyntaf ers blynyddoedd – i ymweld â chynefin ei magwraeth.

Ymlacia wrth adael cymhlethdod canol y ddinas am ardaloedd braf Llandaf a Radur. Dilyn trywydd bwrlwm Afon Taf bob yn ail â'i phyllau llonydd. Troelli heibio i Ystum Taf a'i lilïod dŵr a'i frenin crëyr glas ar y gored. A'r olygfa honno'n haeddu 'Waw!' fach unig.

 Ymlaen drwy Drefforest a Phontypridd, sy'n foel, ôl-ddiwydiannol, fel y gellid disgwyl. Ond yn annisgwyl, wrth nesu at Drehafod a'i Barc Treftadaeth – coed. Trwch o goed mawr a balch, yn syfrdanol wyrdd. Coed sy'n teyrnasu – ie, dyna'r gair – yn dwnnel ir ar hyd y cwm.

Drwy ffenest rhith, gwêl Dilys wiwer goch yn rhedeg ras â'r trên: y wiwer ddiarhebol honno, yn ei hamser maith yn ôl, cyn difa'i chynefin gan ddiwydiant. Gallai sboncio'n llawen o gangen i gangen bob cam o'r Porth i Flaen-cwm, heb unwaith roi'i thraed ar lawr. A heddiw, mae hi'n llamu dros y rhesi coed cyfochrog â rheilffordd werdd Cwm Rhondda.

11

Ymlaen â'r trên, heibio i bentrefi'r enwau tlws. Y Porth a'r
Dinas, heibio i Drealaw a Thonypandy – pob un â'i gaeau
chwarae neu archfarchnad lle cynt y byddai corryn enfawr
o bwll glo â'i simne fawr a'i olwyn windio. Llwyn-y-pia,
wedyn. Ystrad, Pentre – a'r cwm yn lledu wrth nesu at
Dreorci dan gysgod Moel Cadwgan. A Rhydwen a'r hen
griw llengar ar ei meddwl...

A chyrraedd Ynys-wen.

Mae ei chof yn oedi yno, wrth yr ysgol fach ar fin y lein:
'Dewch glou! Trên yn dod!' Rhes o blantos, a hithau yn
eu plith, yn rhuthro dros drigain mlynedd at y ffens ar
gyfer y ddefod, 'wafo-ar-y-trên'. A hwnnw'n chwibanu ei
werthfawrogiad yn ddi-ffael.

A dyma Miss Jones, y brifathrawes, a Miss Howells, a
Mrs Edwards-y-babanod. A Mrs Ralph-y-cwc yn gwenu'n
swil o ffenest fach y gegin. Drwy ffenest dosbarth Miss
Howells, gwêl y rhesi 'Llun a Stori' lliwgar ar y waliau:
'Hunangofiant Pedol', 'Fy Nheulu i', 'Trip yr Ysgol'. A
dyma'i llun a'i stori hithau yn eu plith: 'Y Wiwer Goch'.
Drigain mlynedd yn ddiweddarach, mae'r bathodyn
'Gwobr Gyntaf' yn saff yn ei drôr trysorau.

Ond pwy yw hon yn y cefndir? Ie, y 'fenyw od': creadures
eiddil yr hen got lwyd a'r bŵtis trwm. Fe'i gwelid yn
feunyddiol yn ratlan gatiau'r iard ddwywaith, dair y dydd:
'Gwetwch rwpath yn Gwmrêg! Fi'n wilia Cwmrêg hefyd!'
Beth oedd yn ei chorddi, druan, wrth fytheirio
mewn hen iaith a ildiodd eisoes i fewnlifiad? Y wefr,
gobeithio, o gael bloeddio balchder ei Chymraeg heb

12

ofni sen a chansen ei phlentyndod. Ei gofid mawr oedd unieithrwydd trist ei hwyrion.

A sylweddolai hon, ddwywaith, dair y dydd, ei bod yn cyfarch plant y dewrion? Y rhieni a ddioddefai wawd am fynnu adfer y Gymraeg cyn ei diflaniad llwyr o strydoedd serth y cwm?

Heddiw, yn ei henaint, dymuna Dilys holi'r 'fenyw od' am hyn i gyd. Ond mae blinder yn cau'r ffenest rhith yn glep. Sha thre i'r Marriott fydd hi heno. Fory, sha thre i'w charafan yn Hafan Nolton – ei chartre, bellach, wedi iddi werthu popeth oedd o werth. Byw'n annibynnol yno yw ei nod. Ymlacio, cerdded, darllen; potsian sgrifennu, falle. Annibyniaeth: gair – cysyniad – hollbwysig iddi'r dyddiau hyn. A dyna a gaiff yn y llecyn hwnnw ganllath o'r traeth gwyn, o fewn golwg i flodau pinc y gwanwyn ar y llwybrau, yn sŵn yr heidiau adar sy'n chwyrlïo dros arfordir hardd Sir Benfro. Yno y deallodd hithau – yr Hwntw – ystyr 'Nefoedd yr Adar' hwythau'r Gogs!

Jôc ddiniwed, yn ôl ei harfer. Nid menyw'r doniolwch mawr yw Dilys, sy'n teimlo awydd, erbyn hyn, am napyn. Dyma bwyso'i phen ar nyth ei breichiau ar y bwrdd o'i blaen, fel petai yn nosbarth y babanod slawer dydd. Ac er eu bod ar fin cyrraedd stesion Treherbert, dyma gau ei llygaid. Clyw eco llais y gard yn datgan y byddai'r trên yn oedi yno am ddeng munud, cyn cychwyn 'nôl. Prin fwrw'r byffers, felly – ond câi gyfle slei i bendwmpian.

A dyna a wna, nes teimlo'r trên yn stwyrian ac yn cripian heibio i arwydd 'Diolch am alw yn Nhreherbert.

13

Cofiwch alw eto!'

Mae'n debyg mai cripian ar y trên ac i'r compartment hwn wnaethai hwythau, hefyd – y ddau lanc a'r ferch sy'n eistedd dair sedd oddi wrthi. Chlywodd hi mohonyn nhw'n cyrraedd; does dim cyfathrebu rhwng y tri, ond mae eu bysedd chwimwth yn hedfan dros eu ffôns.

Mae'r ferch yn codi'i llygaid: *'Sorry! Woken you we 'ave.'*

'No, just slumbering.'

Mae'r ferch yn gwenu. *"Pendwmping' my Gran do say. She remembers funny things in Welsh. I'm Kelly, by the way.'*

Tawelwch eto – ond wrth nesu at Ysgol Ynys-wen, mae'r tri'n gwyro at y ffenest – ac fel un, o fawr syndod i Dilys, maen nhw'n wafo, er nad oes neb yno i wafo 'nôl.

Mae'r ferch yn troi i wenu arni eto: *'Mad we are the three of us! Tha's what you are thinkin! Wavin' to a school! But we always do! Our old school it is.'*

A dyma dro Dilys i wenu: 'Ysgol Ynys-wen.'

'Correct.'

'Fy hen ysgol i – amser maith yn ôl, yn oes yr arth a'r blaidd.'

Distawrwydd. Cyn 'Wel, y jiw-jiw!' gan Kelly. Cyn cwestiwn y llencyn main: 'Beth yw "Oes yr arth a'r blaidd"?'

'Gwitho fe mas, Dymbo Darren Lewis!'

Ac mae Kelly'n gwenu ar Dilys am y trydydd tro:

'Dyma Darren, a dyma Footsie – Lloyd yw ei enw iawn.'

'A Dilys ydw i.'

'Enw anti fi. A croeso i'r clwb!' yw ymateb Darren.

'Beth am selebrêto? Sori, Dilys – dathlu!' yw cynnig Footsie.

'Reit te, ble mae'r booze?' yw'r cwestiwn cyffredinol. A'r ateb: yn y rycsac o dan y sêt. Pedwar can lager yn cael eu gosod yn glwstwr ar y bwrdd. A'r hen Dilys ofalus yn syllu'n syn arnyn nhw: 'Ond mae 'na reol! Dim alcohol rhwng Pontypridd a Threherbert!'

Chwerthin yw ymateb ei thri chyd-deithiwr, a Footsie'n wincio arni: 'Yn gwmws! Ond ble ni'n mynd i heddi, Dilys? O Dreherbert lawr trwy Ponty! Felly – does dim probs!'

'Wyt ti o ddifri?'

'Trust me, Dilys. Mae criw Cwm Rhondda'n mynd yn bloto ar Saint Mary Street weekends. Regular. Yn chwarae hafoc ar y trains sha thre. Dyna pam does dim alcohol allowed!'

'Ponty bois yn nyts hefyd. Yn shaclo cyn dod lan i clybs y cwm.'

'Dead right, Kell. Ond nawr, ar y ffordd o Dreherbert, drwy Ponty i Gaerdydd, fel ni'n mynd nawr, simple. Does dim ban. Felly . . .'

Mae Darren yn agor ei gan ag arddeliad, a'i godi'n uchel: 'Iechyd da – a twll…'

'Shurrup! A paid â dêro Darren, mun!'

'Sori, Kell.'

'Anghofia fe. Reit, iechyd da i bawb – Footsie, Darren, Dilys, Ysgol Ynys-wen ac absent friends.'

'Tidy, mun!'

Mae 'na glincian caniau, ac mae Dilys yn sipian yn ofalus.

'Chi'n hoffi Ed Sheeran, Dilys?'

'Pwy yw e, Footsie?'

'Canwr enwog. Ni'n mynd i'r gig, heno.'

Winc sydyn ar y lleill: 'Ticet sbâr 'da fi – chi'n moyn e?'

Mae Kelly'n ei lygadu – 'Bac off, Footsie! Jocan mae e Dilys! Ffyni sens o' hiwmor gyda nhw lan sha Cwmparc! So nhw cweit fel ni lawr yn y cwm! Gormod o Welsh Nash fel Darren lan 'na!'

'Cymru a Cymraeg am byth! Ontefe, Dilys?'

Yn sydyn, sylweddola Dilys fod y tri'n syllu arni. A theimla'r hen annifyrrwch. Y tyndra cyfarwydd o fod ar y cyrion, y tu hwnt i bethe, mas o bethe . . .

'Dilys, ti'n okay?'

'Odw, diolch, Kelly. A diolch i chi gyd am siarad Cymraeg â fi. Uchafbwynt 'y nhaith i heddi. Hynny a gweld y plant mas yn wafo ar y trên. Fel o'n ninne, plant . . .'

'Yn oes yr arth a'r blaidd!'

'Ie, Darren!'

Dim ond grwndi'r trên sydd i'w glywed am rai eiliadau ... Mae Kelly'n codi'i haeliau main ar y bechgyn, ac yna ar y Dilys fyfyriol . . .

'Dilys, so fe'n big deal, chi'n gwbod. Siarad Cymraeg. Mae e'n normal. Beth ni'n neud bob dydd.'

'Handi i gael jobs, mind.'

'Typical o ti, Darren! Yn cwmpo i'r hen drap. "Oherwydd y Gymraeg, mae fy mrawd yn athro yn Blaenau Gwent. A fy chwaer i ar y cyfryngau."'

'Gair da, "cyfryngau".'

'Gair gwych, Darren.'

Yr hen Ddilys nawddoglyd, ystrydebol, druan.

Wrth far y Marriott y noson honno, mae hi'n ail-fyw'r
sgwrs a fu yma ryw awr ynghynt, y sgwrs frwd,
eithafol, bwrw-bol.
'Bwrw bol? Beth yw hynny, Dilys?'
'Trafod pethe pwysig, Darren. Fel fuon ni'n neud nawr.'
'O ie! Pethe shit fel pont y Prince of Wales a legacy
Lord Tonypandy!'
'Darren! Fake Prince, a diafol Aber-fan! Shit ond pwysig!'
'Ond Kell, mae bywyd yn rhy fyr i fecso am bopeth.
Politics, plastics, ymfudwyr, yr NHS!'
'Ond mae popeth fel'na lan i ni, bobl ifanc!'
'Fi'n gwbod. A fi gyda ti rîli, Kell.'
A'r 'bwrw-bol' byrlymus yn parhau nes i bedwar rannu
cyfeiriadau e-bost. Nes i dri ymadael am eu gig.

Ym moethusrwydd unig ei stafell, mae Dilys wrthi'n
pacio'i meddyliau yn ei bag.
Drannoeth, yn fore, bydd ar ei ffordd i'w Hafan, lle bydd
'na sgyrsiau bwrw-bol galôr, a môr a thraeth a blodau ar
lwybr, ac adar uwch ei phen neu'n bolaheulo ar y creigiau.
Bydd 'na gyfle iddi ysgrifennu, garantîd. Dim 'Falle' – y
bwgan, ers blynyddoedd, a dedleins yn diflannu fel plu
eira o flaen gwynt. A phob 'Falle' yn dal i guddio yn y drôr.

Gresyn na lwyddodd i gystadlu yn Eisteddfod Caerdydd
eleni, yn enwedig gan i 'Ynni''r Fedal apelio ati'n fawr. A'r
tair beirniad, hefyd. Gresyn am hen fusnes cenedl enwau
a bod dwy o'r tair yn Gogs. A gresyn nad yw 'Cylchoedd'

Medal Llanrwst yn apelio ati.
Esgusodion un ac oll.
Mae hi'n dringo i wely cysur, yn agor y llyfr nodiadau:
'Y Coed' fydd y teitl.
Coed balch ysgolion mentrus, anturus y Gymraeg, a'i
geiriau fel gwiwerod yn sboncio bob cam o'r Porth i'r
Ynys Wen, Treherbert a Blaen-cwm.
A dyma ddechrau ar ei stori. Tidy, mun!

*Prifardd a Phrif Lenor a anwyd ac a fagwyd yn Nhrealaw,
Cwm Rhondda, yw Manon Rhys. Ei llyfr diweddaraf yw
Stafell fy Haul, Cyhoeddiadau Barddas, 2018.*

DŴR POETH
Gan Geraint Lewis

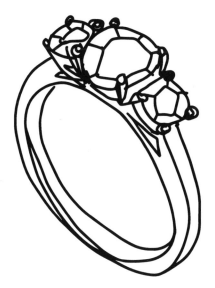

Dechreuodd e i gyd jyst dros flwyddyn yn ôl pan es i mas un pnawn canol Mehefin i redeg ar Lwybr Elái lan i Sain Ffagan. Hanner ffordd drwy'r rhedeg eisteddais ar fainc ar lan yr afon, yn anadlu'n glou fel rhyw hen gi yn y gwres. O'n i wedi blino'n lân cyn dod mas, ddim yn cysgu'n dda. A nawr o'n i'n difaru bo' fi heb ddod â dŵr gyda fi. Neu ffags. O'dd 'na olwg y diawl arna i. Traci-botyms *polyester* rhy fawr fy mrawd, crys-T 'Cymru Am Byth' Ewros 2016 yn socian. Fy ngwallt i fel nyth rhyw aderyn gwallgo. Fy wyneb yn beryglus o biws.

Wedyn dyma'r dyn yma, tua chwe deg weden i, yn dod lan ata i. Yn edrych fel yr hysbyseb 'na ar YouTube, *'the Man from Del Monte'*. Siaced *linen* wen, het Panama.

'Dyna chi haf, ynte?' meddai fe, yn pwyntio at y geiriau ar fy mronnau. 'Fuoch chi yno? Allan yn Ffrainc? Yn cefnogi Cymru?'

'Na. Aeth fy mrawd i. Anrheg o'dd hon,' ychwanegais, gan bwyntio at y crys-T.

'A. Wela i. Ifor ydw i,' meddai fe, gan estyn ei law tuag ata i. Roedd gormod o chwys ar fy llaw i ysgwyd un fe, felly wnes i jyst nodio'n gwrtais. Ac o'dd ei olwg e, ei ddannedd e'n rhy berffaith, ei lygaid glas yn disgleirio, sa' i'n gwybod, o'dd e i gyd bach yn *pervy* i weud y gwir. 'A dyma Gelert,' meddai fe, gan bwyntio at labrador du yn llamu'n sydyn tuag atom o'r llwybr.

'Victoria,' wedais i, gan ollwng ochenaid o ryddhad bod y ci'n anadlu'n fwy eithafol o gyflym na fi hyd yn oed, ac yn sgleinio'n got o chwys.

Fe eisteddodd ar bwys fi. Dyna oedd y cliw, o edrych 'nôl. Taflodd e bêl 'nôl lawr y llwybr a llamodd Gelert ar ei hôl, fel pe bai ei fywyd yn dibynnu arni.

'Dwi'n dŵad o Feddgelert yn wreiddiol' meddai fe, ''Dach chi'n gyfarwydd â'r stori?'

Nodiais i, ond wedais i ddim byd. O'n i wedi blino ar ei lais e'n barod.

'Stori drist, ynte?' parhaodd Ifor, gan fwytho pen ei labrador oedd wedi dychwelyd â'r darn pren yn ei geg.

'Ar yr aelwyd cawsoch chi'r hanes, ia? Rhyw fath o stori amser gwely, efo Mam neu Dad?'

'Dwi ddim rili yn nabod fy nhad. A doedd Mam na fe'n siarad Cymraeg. Ond gaethon ni'r stori yn yr ysgol.'

'Pa ysgol oedd honno 'lly?'

'Coed y Gof. Wedyn es i Ysgol Uwchradd Plasmawr.'

Roedd ceg Ifor yn lythrennol yn wên o glust i glust, fel pe bai ei ddannedd perffaith wedi ymestyn rownd ei fochau, fel cymeriad cartŵn. Ci hapus. Neu flaidd.

'Chwarae teg i chi. Chi a'ch tebyg ydy dyfodol y genedl. Dda ngeneth i.'

Codais i ar fy nhraed, yn barod i fynd. Yn methu diodde'r diawl nawddoglyd. Wedyn wnaeth e ryw symudiad od â'i geg, neu ei wddwg i fod yn fanwl. Fel pe bai e'n ceisio atal ei hun rhag byrpan.

'Mae'n ddrwg gen i. Dŵr poeth ofnadwy arna i. Dwi wedi cymryd moddion a thabledi, ond gwaeth mae o'n mynd, gen i ofn. Dwi fod cael *endoscopy* wythnos nesaf, i drio gweld beth

sydd o'i le. Dwi'm yn edrych ymlaen at hynny, rhaid cyfadda.'
Am y tro cyntaf roedd golwg ofnus iawn arno, ei hyder arwynebol
wedi diflannu mwya' sydyn.

'Ma' fe werth cael. Trïwch ymlacio pan roia nhw'r tiwb i lawr,
fyddwch chi'n iawn.'

''Dach chi'n swnio fel sa' chi'n dallt am be' 'dach chi'n sôn.'

'Dylen ni. Wy'n nyrs.'

A dyma fe'n edrych yn syn arna i ac yna i lawr ar y ci. Wedyn
'nôl ata' i, gan ysgwyd ei ben.'

'Victoria. Victoria? Nid Susan ydy enw eich mam, ia?'

Nodiais i eto, gan geisio cuddio fy chwilfrydedd.

'Wel, ar fy marw. Dwi'n nabod eich mam yn iawn. Mae hi'n
glanhau i mi acw, bob bore Mawrth. Ers blynyddoedd!'

O'n i'n hofran nawr, yn symud o'r naill droed i'r llall, ar dân
eisiau mynd. 'Well i fi fynd. Hwyl nawr.'

'Ia, wrth gwrs. Braf eich cyfarfod chi, Victoria. A chofiwch fi at
eich mam. Halen y Ddaear, Susan. Meddwl y byd ohoni. Halen
y Ddaear.'

Ymestynnais fy mreichiau, gan geisio cyffwrdd â'n draed, fel
rhyw fath o *token warm-up*, wnaeth achosi i Gelert ddod draw
i wynto fy mhen-ôl i. Roedd hynny'n ddigon i wthio fi i redeg
ar hyd y llwybr, heb edrych 'nôl na dweud gair arall wrth Ifor.

'Wel – am gyd-ddigwyddiad, ynte!' galwodd e ar fy ôl i.

Mae Mam a fi'n agos. Mwy fel chwiorydd rili. Rhannu popeth
gyda'n gilydd. Y noswaith honno, ar ôl i fi ddod 'nôl o'r rhedeg,
ges i fwy o hanes Ifor ganddi. Roedd hi'n meddwl bod e eithaf
swil. O'n i'n ffeindio hynny'n anodd i'w gredu. Roedd gydag e
dŷ *detached* anferth, Tŷ Madog, gwerth bron i filiwn o bunnau

ar gyrion pentref Sain Ffagan. Cyfreithiwr wedi ymddeol yn gymharol ddiweddar, ar ôl gwerthu ei gwmni ei hunan. Yn bwysicach o lawer o'm safbwynt i, gŵr gweddw oedd e. Wedi colli ei wraig rhyw ddwy flynedd ynghynt. Dim plant. Wy'n beio ci Tyrone lawr yr hewl. *Cross-breed* o ddou gi sy' 'di cael eu banio. Cyfarth trwy'r bore a finnau'n treial cysgu ar ôl shifft nos. Roedd fy mhen i'n troi erbyn amser swper. Ac ar ôl bod mas yn yr awyr iach ar hyd yr afon, clywed adar yn canu, a gwynt garlleg gwyllt yn llenwi'n ffroenau o'dd e'n *depressing* dod adre i weld graffiti newydd ar wal yn y stryd, *'Life Is Shit'*. A gorfod clywed Melanie a Bradley drws nesa'n gweiddi ar ei gilydd am y canfed tro, gan wybod bydden ni'n clywed nhw eto nes mlaen heno trwy'r wal denau a'u *kiss and make up* swnllyd. O'n i mo'yn mwy na hyn, nage jyst i fi, ond i Gwenllian y'n ferch fach i. Fy nhywysoges. Os yw merch i ficer o Drelái yn gallu bod yn Ledi, allith fy merch i fynd i ysgol Howells. Plannwyd hedyn fy syniad i ym mhen Mam y noson honno. Soniais i fod dŵr poeth cyson yn gallu datblygu'n rhywbeth lot mwy difrifol. Nawr oedd ei chyfle. Efallai ei hunig gyfle hi. Chwerthin wnaeth Mam. Hanner chwerthin wnes i, gan ddangos yn glir yn fy llygaid mod i o'r farn bod mwy na mymryn o obaith yn fy nghynllun.

Doedd ddim rhaid iddi wneud dim byd amlwg. Jyst siarad mwy gydag e. Gollwng ambell *hint* fach. Wedi'r cwbwl roedd hi bownd fod yn unig iawn i fyw mewn tŷ mor fawr ar ei ben ei hun. Ac yn ôl Mam doedd e ddim yn gweld lot o bobol chwaith, jyst hi a'r garddwr, Martin. Gelert, y labrador, oedd ei fyd e nawr. Roedd e'n chwe deg dau digon smart am ei oedran a

Mam yn bum deg dau ifanc, deniadol. Beth yw deng mlynedd amser chi oedran nhw? Dim byd. *What's not to like?*

Gaethon ni laff, meddwl am y peth. O'n i'n gwybod byddai Mam ddim yn cymryd unrhyw sylw o'n gynllun breuddwydiol. Hi oedd y person mwyaf moesol o'n i'n adnabod, o bell ffordd. Fy arwres. Wedi magu fi a'n ddou frawd hŷn ar ei phen ei hun. Ac yn fam-gu mor dda i Gwenllian. A pham fyddai unrhyw un mor foesol â Mam ag unrhyw ddiddordeb mewn rhywun oedd wedi gwneud ei ffortiwn trwy helpu cwmnïau mawr osgoi talu treth a gwneud amodau gwaith eu staff mor ddiflas â phosib? Allwch chi ddychmygu'r sioc ges i, pan ddywedodd hi, ychydig fisoedd yn ddiweddarach, bod hi mewn cariad ag Ifor Llewelyn.

I gychwyn prin roedd hi'n torri gair o gwbl ag Ifor. Wedodd hi roedd hi'n siarad llai ag ef nag erioed, rhag ofn iddo bigo lan rhyw newid ynddi. Jyst gofyn pethau ymarferol ynglŷn â'r gwaith glanhau. A oedd rhywbeth arbennig angen ei wneud? A ddylai hi ganolbwyntio mwy ar yr hwfro, drwy'r tŷ cyfan, ar draul y polisio? Neu flaenoriaethu'r ystafelloedd gwely neu olchi lloriau teils y llawr isaf? Er bod hi yno am ddwy awr bob bore Mawrth roedd hi'n amhosib gwneud bob dim bob wythnos gan fod y tŷ mor fawr.

Roedd un peth yn gyffredin i bob sesiwn *de-brief* ar nos Fawrth gyda Mam, fodd bynnag. Sef cymaint y bu Ifor yn sôn am ei wraig a fu farw, Morfudd. Wrth chwarae recordiau finyl o hen ganeuon Frank Sinatra, yn sôn am y ddau'n dawnsio tan yr oriau mân allan ar eu patio sylweddol. Neu wrth sipian gwydred o win o ardal y Loire gan sôn am eu gwyliau blynyddol yn yr ardal honno o Ffrainc gyda'i gilydd, yn nofio yn yr afonydd ac ymweld â'r gwinllannoedd gorau. Neu ei chanmol am ei gwaith gwirfoddol ar nifer o fyrddau elusennau. Fel cyfrifydd, roedd hi'n gaffaeliad i sawl cwmni bach – elusen i blant amddifad a chwmni theatr yn eu plith.

Yn ôl Mam, roedd Ifor yn amlwg yn meddwl bod yr haul yn disgleirio mas o ben-ôl y Morfudd 'ma. Roedd yn od iawn iddi hi, gan fod Mam yn cofio ei wraig fel menyw sarrug, swrth oedd yn aml yn feddw cyn amser cinio.

Cyrhaeddodd pethau'r pen wrth i Mam ollwng mỳg o eiddo Morfudd a'i dorri'n deilchion ar lawr y gegin. Un â map bach o ynys Lewis yn Yr Alban oedd e, *memento* o wyliau arbennig o braf. Ysgogodd y digwyddiad ddagrau yn Ifor, mae'n debyg, gan adael i Mam fynd adref yn gynnar, cymaint oedd ei boen. Na, doedd fy nghynllun ddim yn mynd yn dda. Ddim yn dda o gwbl.

Ond wedyn daeth tro ar fyd a ddechreuodd pethau newid i Mam. Mewn dros dri deg o flynyddoedd o lanhau ni ddwgodd hi unrhyw beth erioed, ond fyddai hi ddim yn normal os na fyddai rhyw chwilfrydedd gyda hi am gynnwys rhai o'r tai mae hi'n glanhau. Ei man gwan hi yw *jewellery* da. Wedodd hi bod hi wedi edrych ar focs *jewellery* Morfudd pan oedd hi'n fyw a bod gyda hi rhai darnau lyfli, yn cynnwys *ruby brooch* a breichled ddiemwnt.

Falle achos fy awgrymu gwreiddiol i, roedd Mam, er ei gwaethaf, wedi dechrau meddwl pa fath o fywyd fyddai hi i fod yn wraig y tŷ yn 'Tŷ Madog'. Mae'n debyg, un bore Mawrth braf yn Awst, tra oedd hi yn y brif ystafell wely, gadawodd hi i'w dychymyg

gael y gorau arni. Tynnodd hi ei menyg Marigold bant a
gwisgo hen fodrwy ddyweddïo Morfudd. Wrth iddi edrych
ar y diemwntau'n disgleirio ar ei bys fe'i synnwyd gan ei
theimladau. Nid cenfigen na rhwystredigaeth ond boddhad
dwfn; hawl, hyd yn oed.

Yna clywodd hi beswch gerllaw. Wedi rhewi yn ei hunfan,
gwelodd hi fod Ifor drws nesa iddi. Ond yn hytrach na rhoi stŵr
iddi, fe wenodd e. Yn ôl Mam, wedodd e cymaint oedd e'n hoffi'r
fodrwy. Soniodd e am ble y prynwyd hi a phryd.

Roedd Mam yn teimlo'n ofnadwy a thynnodd hi'r fodrwy oddi ar
ei bys yn syth. Gan synhwyro ei lletchwithdod, edrychodd Ifor i'w
llygaid hi a dweud y gallai hi gael y fodrwy os oedd hi mo'yn.
Atebodd Mam na allai hi byth wneud hynny ac oedd flin gyda
hi bod hi wedi tarfu ar rywbeth mor bersonol a phreifat.
Gwnaeth Ifor e'n glir iddi nad oedd e'n dal hynny yn ei herbyn
hi o gwbwl. Yn wir, roedd e'n meddwl bod y fodrwy'n ei siwtio hi.
Yn teimlo'i hun yn cochi, slipiodd Mam y fodrwy 'nôl yn y bocs
yn frysiog, gan roi ei Marigolds 'nôl ymlaen a gadael yr ystafell
er mwyn parhau â'i glanhau.

Ond pan soniodd hi wrtha i am y digwyddiad yma,
sylweddolais i, a hithau hefyd, bod yr ia rhwng Ifor a hi
o'r diwedd wedi dechrau dadmer.

P'un ai oherwydd iddo weld y ddelwedd o Mam gyda'r fodrwy
ar ei bys neu'r ffaith iddo faddau iddi am ei cham mor hawdd,
roedd hi'n glir o hyn ymlaen y byddai Ifor yn llawer mwy
hyderus yn ei chwmni. Erbyn ei sesiwn nesaf o lanhau, bu'n
ddigon hy i ofyn iddi alw yn 'Tŷ Madog' bob dydd Iau yn
ogystal â'r boreau Mawrth. Ar brynhawniau Iau byddai hi'n

gallu glanhau am awr ac yna, pe bai mor garedig â chytuno,
byddai e wrth ei fodd i'w chael hi'n gwmni iddo fe wrth iddo
gerdded ei annwyl Gelert.

Mae'n debyg ei fod e wedi dweud hyn mewn ffordd mor
charming, fel se fe'r peth mwya naturiol yn y byd i wneud,
nes bod Mam wedi cytuno'n syth, gan ychwanegu ei bod hi'n
edrych ymlaen yn barod.

Roedd eu wâc gyntaf nhw o amgylch y cae criced mawr ar y
ffordd mas o'r pentref. Er nad oedd e wedi chwarae rhyw lawer
ei hunan roedd e'n ffan brwd o'r gêm, yn mynd i gefnogi tîm
llwyddiannus Sain Ffagan yn aml. Wrth iddyn nhw gerdded y ci,
sylwodd Mam arno fe'n syllu ar rai bechgyn ifanc yn cael gwersi
bowlio ar bwys y pafiliwn. Falle taw hi oedd yn dychmygu'r peth
ond gallai dyngu fod ei lygaid yn llenwi. Roedd yn rhaid gofyn
y cwestiwn. Cael e mas o'r ffordd.

'Would you have liked to have had children, Ifor?'

Wedodd Ifor taw dyna oedd e'n difaru fwyaf yn ei fywyd. Fe,
mwy na'i wraig, a wthiodd eu gyrfaoedd yn eu blaen. Yn y
diwedd, roedd y ddau wedi dod mor gyfarwydd â bod ar ben
eu hunain gyda'r cŵn nes eu bod nhw, wel, wedi rhedeg mas
o amser, neu'r awydd, neu'r egni, doedd e ddim yn siŵr beth.
Roedd Morfudd wedi difaru mwy nag ef. Bwrodd hi'r botel
oherwydd y peth. A bu farw o fethiant yr iau ddiwrnod cyn
ei phen-blwydd yn chwe deg oed.

Wedodd Mam bod golwg welw arno fe pan wedodd e hyn,
gwedd lwydaidd dyn ag euogrwydd yn cnoi ei enaid.

Gydag amser, cawson nhw wâcs mwy dymunol gyda'i gilydd a
Gelert. Dangosodd Ifor dipyn o ddiddordeb yng ngorffennol

Mam, yn enwedig ei chyfnod hi'n ferch ifanc yn cael ei magu yn Nhrelái. Aeth Mam ag ef i un o hoff lefydd ei phlentyndod ar hyd yr afon Elái, dan bont rheilffordd, lle y treuliodd hi oriau'n chwarae yn yr afon gyda'i ffrindiau, a'i gwefreiddio gan sŵn sydyn y trenau uwch ei phen.

Ar y prynhawn arbennig hwnnw cafodd Gelert ofn sydynrwydd swnllyd y trên chwim uwch eu pennau, gan ruthro mas o'r dŵr, 'nôl i'r llwybr, mor glou ag y gallai.

Cymerodd rhyw gerddwr cyfagos dosturi dros y ci, gan fwytho ei ben yn dyner. Atgoffodd e Ifor bod clyw cŵn yn lot fwy sensitif na chlyw dynion. Diolchodd Ifor iddo fe am stopi Gelert rhag rhedeg i ffwrdd yn rhy bell a gofynnodd e i'r dyn dynnu llun ohono fe a Mam wrth ymyl y dŵr, ar y cerrig a arweiniai lawr i'r afon, gyda'r bont rheilffordd yn gefndir. Ufuddhaodd y dyn ac ar ôl iddo gerdded ychydig i ffwrdd wrthyn nhw, fe gusanodd Ifor Mam am y tro cyntaf.

Fyddai hi'n dweud nes ymlaen taw dyna oedd un o eiliadau mwyaf gwefreiddiol ei bywyd.

Roedd fy nghynllun i bendant 'nôl ar y tracs.

Roedd rhai pobol yn y pentref wedi dechrau sylwi ar y ddou ohonyn nhw'n cerdded y ci gyda'i gilydd ac roedd tafodau, yn ogystal â llygaid, yn dechrau troi. Oedd Ifor Llewelyn wedi syrthio am ei *cleaner*? A oedd hyn yn ddatblygiad da iddo fe? Neu oedd y Susan Moore hon, o Drelái mae'n debyg, jyst ar ôl ei arian e?

Fel wy'n deall roedd yr edrychiadau syn a'r tafodau cellweirus wedi effeithio ar Mam lot mwy nag Ifor. Roedd e fel se fe'n synnu fod pobol ag unrhyw ddiddordeb yn ei fywyd bach di-nod.

28

Ta beth, erbyn canol Hydref roedden nhw wedi mentro mas i'r amgueddfa werin leol gyda'i gilydd, gan ddal dwylo yn hollol agored mewn lle cyhoeddus. Ac un nos Iau, fel oedd yn bownd o ddigwydd rhywbryd, ddaeth Mam ddim adre. Arhosodd hi dros nos gydag Ifor yn Nhŷ Madog.

Tua'r adeg hyn wedodd Mam bod hi'n ei garu fe. O'n i'n falch ar ei rhan hi. Na, wir. Wrth gwrs mod i. O'n i mo'yn iddi fod yn hapus. Ond y cynllun. Y cynllun. Beth oedd wedi digwydd i'n cynllun ni? Er nad oedd unrhyw sôn wedi bod am symud mewn i fyw gydag e eto, allai'r ddau fod gyda'i gilydd am yr ugain mlynedd nesaf. Mewn gair, o'n i mo'yn gwybod sut oedd iechyd Ifor. Oedd y dŵr poeth wedi gwaethygu? O'n i'n teimlo bach yn euog yn gofyn shwt beth. O'n i mo'yn i'w salwch e fod yn waeth? Sa' i'n siŵr os allwn i fod wedi rhoi ateb onest i'r cwestiwn hwnnw. Mae'n debyg nad oedd yr *endoscopy* wedi canfod unrhyw beth o bwys. Ac ers hynny roedd e wedi cael *laryngoscopy* yn ogystal, hwnnw hefyd yn profi dim. Wedodd e bod ei ddŵr poeth wedi gwella. A chwarae teg iddo fe, rhoiodd e'r clod am hynny ar Mam. *'The best medicine in the world'* oedd e wedi galw hi. A dyna ni, felly.

Er, wy'n cofio nawr i Mam sôn ar y pryd bod ganddo beswch gwael, yn enwedig yn ystod y nos.

Roedd clywed am eu bywyd gyda'i gilydd wedi rhoi rhyw obaith newydd i mi. Nage jyst cerdded y ci o'n nhw nawr. Roedden nhw'n mynd i gyngherddau, ambell agoriad o arddangosfeydd celf a sawl perfformiad gan gwmni Opera Cenedlaethol Cymru yng Nghanolfan y Mileniwm.

O'n i'n poeni am beswch Ifor. Roedd hi'n bryd i Mam wneud ei symudiad. Yn llythrennol. Symud mewn ato fe. Wy'n cyfadde' o'n i'n pwsio'r *pace* gyda hi rili. Yn cael hi i chwarae rhan nad oedd yn dod yn naturiol iddi, yn groes graen iddi.

Roedd angen i mi ffeindio mas mwy am ei iechyd e.

Gan ddilyn fy nghyfarwyddiadau i aeth Mam i fusnesa ar i-Pad Ifor i geisio gweld a oedd unrhyw e-byst meddygol o'r ysbyty preifat lle buodd e'n cael ei brofion.

Ffeindiodd hi ddim byd o werth o ran hynny, ond wnaeth hi ganfod, er mawr syndod iddi, nifer fawr o luniau ohonof i.

Roedd rhai o'r rhain yn mynd 'nôl i'r cyfnod cyn i ni gwrdd ar y fainc 'nôl ym Mehefin. Mae'n debyg wnaeth e gyfadde 'i fod e'n gwybod yn iawn pwy o'n i pan eisteddodd e ar bwys fi. Yn wir, gan iddo wybod mod i weithiau yn rhedeg ar hyd Llwybr Elai roedd e wedi gobeithio 'bwmpo mewn' i mi, yn benodol er mwy dweud ei fod e'n meddwl y byd o Mam.

Roedd y cythraul bach wedi bod yn fy stelcian i ar-lein. Dyna lle o'n i'n meddwl taw fy 'nghynllun' i oedd e a roedd Ifor wedi bod un cam ar y blaen i fi drwy'r adeg.

Doedd ddim gwir ots gyda fi am hyn, ond pam yn y byd na wnaeth e gysylltu'n uniongyrchol gyda Mam, dweud wrthi ryw fore Mawrth wrth iddi roi *bleach* lawr y tŷ bach neu wagio un o'i *bins* e, bod e'n meddwl y byd ohoni? Wna i fyth ddeall.

O'n i yn poeni, fodd bynnag, pan wedodd Mam bo' nhw wedi cwympo mas oherwydd busnes yr i-Pad. I'r fath raddau nes bod Gelert druan wedi ffoi i gwato, gan lefain ei anfodlonrwydd o dan y ford. Nid fy neunydd ar-lein oedd asgwrn y gynnen cymaint â bod Mam wedi busnesa ar ei i-Pad o gwbwl.

Pan wnaeth hi o'r diwedd gyfadde bod hi'n becso am ei iechyd a bod hi mo'yn gweld os oedd e'n cwato rhywbeth, gwaethygu wnaeth y ffrae.

Doedd Ifor heb fod yn grac gyda Mam o'r blaen. A nawr bod hi'n ei wthio fe bach ymhellach â phob ymweliad, gan awgrymu iddi ddod draw â choginio cinio Dolig teuluol yno, a hyd yn oed yn ei atgoffa o wyliau sgïo posib yn y Flwyddyn Newydd, cynyddu fwyfwy wnaeth amheuon Ifor am ei chymhellion hi. Heb fawr o rybudd yn ail wythnos Tachwedd, daeth e â'u perthynas i ben. Wedodd e ei fod e wedi bod yn ffŵl i feddwl y byddai'r peth yn gweithio. Roedden nhw'n rhy wahanol i'w gilydd. Roedd yn flin gydag e, ond doedd Mam ddim i ddod i Tŷ Madog byth eto.

Teimlodd Mam yr ergyd i'r byw. A doedd ddim syniad gyda hi pam roedd hyn wedi digwydd mor ddisymwth. A oedd hi wedi mynd yn rhy bell? Creu'r argraff anghywir? Wnaeth e erioed ddweud hynny, ond roedd hi'n amau ei fod e'n meddwl bod hi ar ôl ei arian. Ddim yn ei garu am bwy oedd e, ond am yr hyn oedd e'n medru cynnig iddi.

Wrth gwrs, i Mam doedd hynny ddim yn wir o gwbl.

O'n i'n gwybod doedd 'na fawr o bwynt ceisio cael nhw i gymodi. Mae Mam yn fenyw browd. Ifor oedd y person cyntaf i ddangos y drws iddi mewn dros dri deg mlynedd o lanhau. No way fydde hi'n mynd 'nôl heb wahoddiad, heb ymddiheuriad.

Yn yr wythnosau wedi i'r berthynas chwalu, roedd well gyda fi glywed *action* hwyr y nos Melanie a Bradley drws nesa na'r hyn a ddeuai o wely Mam. Llefain, na – udo yn ei chwsg. Dyw 'ypset' ddim yn dechrau disgrifio fe.

Yn dilyn Nadolig hir, llawn tyndra, penderfynodd y ddwy ohonon ni i dynnu llinell dan Ifor Llewelyn a cheisio dechrau'r Flwyddyn Newydd o'r newydd.

Chi'n gallu 'neud cynlluniau, wrth gwrs. Ond weithiau dyw'r cynlluniau hynny ddim yn troi mas fel chi'n disgwyl iddyn nhw. Tarodd Mam ar draws Martin, garddwr Ifor, yn yr archfarchnad. Wedodd Martin bod Ifor wedi colli lot o bwysau a cholli ei wallt i gyd. Canser yr oesoffagws, mae'n debyg. Roedd e'n aros am fwy o ganlyniadau ac yn gobeithio nad oedd e wedi lledaenu i'r iau. Roedd Mam wedi cael ysgytwad. Yn reddfol fe brynodd hi garden Gwellhad Buan yn y fan a'r lle, un ddoniol gyda nyrs lond ei chroen yn cymryd tymheredd claf gwelw yr olwg yn ei wely. Siaradodd hi gyda fi nes perfeddion y bore yn ceisio'i gorau i feddwl beth oedd y peth iawn i wneud. O'n i mo'yn iddi alw i weld e. Ond roedd hi'n parhau yn bendant ei barn. Na, roedd rhaid parchu dymuniadau Ifor. Yn dawel bach, roedd hi hyd yn oed yn amau bod sydynrwydd cwpla'r berthynas yn rhywbeth i wneud ag Ifor yn cadw gwir gyflwr ei iechyd oddi wrthi. Drannoeth, gwthiodd Mam ei charden Gwellhad Buan trwy flwch llythyron Ifor ac fe glywodd Gelert yn cyfarth, yn driw i'r diwedd i'w feistr bregus.

Dair wythnos wedi hynny roedd e wedi marw.

Es i gyda Mam i wasanaeth yr angladd yn yr Amlosgfa. Ges i sioc i weld mor llawn oedd yr ystafell. Nifer o gydweithwyr a chyn-gleientiaid, yn ogystal â charfan swmpus o berthnasau o ogledd Cymru a Llundain.

Ar y ffordd mas, daeth un o'r perthnasau, cyfnither i Ifor, i fyny at Mam, gan ddweud wrthi nad oedd croeso iddi yn nhe'r angladd 'nôl yn y Plymouth Arms. Nodio'n gwrtais wnaeth Mam, derbyn y sarhad, yn rhy ypset i ymateb mewn unrhyw ffordd arall. Wrth i fi ddechrau protestio am hyn, daeth perthynas iau arall draw atom, gan wenu ar Mam. Roedd hi wedi clywed bod Mam yn llawn consyrn am yr hyn fyddai'n digwydd i Gelert nawr. Roedd hi am sicrhau Mam y byddai'r ci yn cael y gofal gorau ganddi hi ei hun yng ngogledd Llundain.

Aeth ychydig wythnosau heibio, gyda Mam yn cadw ei hun yn fisi gyda'i gwaith, gan dderbyn cleientiaid newydd i lanhau, hyd yn oed. O'n i'n gwybod bod hi'n meddwl am Ifor. Sut allai hi beidio? Ac yn wir roedd yna un tro arall yng nghynffon ein stori, un creulon, ond un a fwriedid yn wreiddiol, heb amheuaeth, i fod yn un caredig.

Cysylltodd cyfreithiwr Ifor. Roedd e wedi gadael rhywbeth i Mam yn ei ewyllys wedi'r cwbl. Agorodd hi amlen fawr frown, ddifrifol yr olwg, dim ond i ganfod ei charden Gwellhad Buan hi ei hun y tu fewn. Yno hefyd oedd hen fodrwy ddyweddïo Morfudd a llun o Mam ac Ifor gyda'i gilydd dan y bont rheilffordd ar Lwybr Elái. Roedd e wedi ysgrifennu nodyn ar gefn y garden mewn rhyw sgriblan rhyfedd, plentynnaidd. Mae'n rhaid bod e wedi ei ysgrifennu yn eithaf hwyr ar daith ei afiechyd terfynol. Er yn anodd ei ddatrys ar y dechrau, roedd y geiriau'n gwneud synnwyr perffaith ond poenus. *'Please forgive me Susan fach. I wanted you to remember me as I was in the photo, not for what I would become. Ifor x'*

Aeth ychydig wythnosau heibio nes i Mam ddweud wrtha' i dros swper un noson bod hi angen rhyw fath o *closure* gydag Ifor. Doedd hi ddim mo'yn ypsetio'r teulu drwy ymweld â'r garreg fach er cof amdano ar dir yr amlosgfa. Yn hytrach, roedd hi'n dymuno dathlu eiliad hyfryd gyda'r dyn y carodd hi, drwy osod tusw o flodau yn y man lle rhannon nhw eu cusan gyntaf.

Wy'n aros wrth ymyl y man hwnnw nawr. Rhyw fath o rage yrrodd fi yma. Cynddaredd. O'n i ar dân mo'yn taflu'r blodau i'r afon. Ond o'u gweld nhw'n pwyso yn erbyn carreg fawr ar lan y dŵr, wy'n methu gwneud hynny. Mae'r lilis pinc, llachar fel sêr yn y machlud oren. Mae nodyn byr yn llawysgrifen gymen Mam yn sownd wrthyn nhw.

'At least we had a few months together, Ifor bach. Though I would have liked to have been there for you. Cariad, Susan.'

Mae'r trên sy'n gwibio heibio'n swnllyd yn fy stopio rhag llefain.

Mae Geraint yn hanu o Dregaron. Bu'n ysgrifennu'n llawn-amser ers 1984. Mae e'n byw yng Nghaerdydd.'

Y CHWECHED TEIMLAD
gan Ceri Elen

Gorwedd. Sŵn y bleinds yn erbyn y ffenest. Yr awel i'w
theimlo. Ma' Caerdydd yn deffro. Diwrnod arferol:
"Betsan, dere i'r car, bach, 'na ferch dda."
A'r gath yn mewian, wrth i'r plentyn penfelyn basio,
a'r gath fel pe bai hi'n siarad.
Betsan yn bownsio'r bêl ar hyd y palmant. Sŵn plentyndod.
Ei mam yn sgwrsio gyda'r dyn ar draws y ffordd.
"Yffach, ma' ddi'n swnllyd, nagyw hi? Y gath 'na.
Glywest di ddi nithiwr? Ti'n meddwl ei bod hi'n olreit?"
"O yndi, paid â phoeni cyw. Nethon ni ei bwydo hi noson
o' blaen, meddwl ei bod hi isio bwyd. Wedyn nethon ni
ffonio'r perchennog – ma'r rhif ar ei choler hi, yli. Eniwê,
nethon ni ffonio, ac 'udodd y perchennog, ma' fel'na ma'r
gath. Cadw sŵn fatha'i bod hi'n deud storis, a mynd i rwla
gwahanol bob nos i'w deud nhw, a cal bwyd da am neud.
Ma'r perchennog yn derbyn galwad ffôn bron bob nos gan
bobl sydd wedi bwydo'r gath, ac yn meddwl bod y gath ar
goll. Ond dydi'r gath ddim ar goll. Ma'r gath yn iawn."
"Wir?"
"Ia. Ma'r gath yn wariar. *Have a good day.*"
"Ti hefyd. Da iawn Betsan. Ti'n gwd gyl."
Y Gymraeg yn troelli lawr y stryd, a'r Saesneg a'r Bwyleg,
a'r Eidaleg yn creu plethen hefo hi.

Dwi isio codi at y ffenest, a deud fy mhwt bach i:
"Wel neithiwr, nesh i godi gan feddwl bod 'na lwynog yn mynd drwy'r biniau. Do'n i ddim wedi gallu defnyddio gweddill y twrci, 'dech chi'n gweld, felly nesh i ei roi o yn y bin bwyd neithiwr. A mynd i gwely. Ac mi odd y sŵn… y gath 'na oedd o. Odd hi 'di llwyddo i dynnu'r darn twrci allan, heb dynnu dim byd arall allan. A caead y bin dal wedi cau. Dim llanast. Mae 'na rwbeth od am y gath yna."
Ond roedd Caerdydd wedi hen godi a'r bobl ar y stryd wedi mynd i'r lle nesaf yn eu diwrnod. Finnau heb ddweud gair. Y bleinds yn dal i daro yn erbyn y ffenest. A dwi angen codi. Mae swyddfa Mr Giles yn aros. Ond mae hi'n gyfforddus yn fama. Diwrnod arferol.
Dwi'n meddwl am Leila. Mi ga'i ei gweld hi heno.
Ceir yn gadael.
Y gath yn dal i fewian, yn gneud y synau mwyaf od.
A Chaerdydd yn gwenu.
Finnau'n codi.

***

Agor drws y cefn, a'r haul yn llifo mewn i'r gegin. Rhoi coffi a dŵr yn y potyn metal. Tanio'r nwy. Estyn y muesli. Sgarff Leila ar y bwrdd. Troedio i'r ardd. Sŵn y coed yn agos, sŵn y trên ymhell. Haul cynnes, cynnes. Edrych ar y ffensys, maen nhw angen eu paentio. Cau fy llygaid fel pan oeddwn i'n fachgen bach. Agor fy llygaid eto. Mae 'na bethau rhyfedd yn landio yn fy ngardd gefn weithiau. Dros y ffens maen nhw'n dod. Arwydd pren siâp calon *'all you need is love and a dog'*, dyna ddaeth wsos dwytha.

Pwy sy'n eu taflu nhw drosodd, dwi'm yn gwbod.
Ac yn sydyn dwi'n gweld Guto yn fy meddwl. Ffrind
o'r ysgol. Fflach. Dim byd mwy. Dydw i heb ei weld ers
blynyddoedd. Wedi colli cysylltiad, ddim am unrhyw
reswm. Dim ond bod hynny wedi digwydd, rhywsut.
Ac wedyn mae arogl y coffi yn dod i 'nhynnu o'm
myfyrdodau. Mewn i'r tŷ, diffodd y nwy, tywallt y coffi,
a gorffen y muesli.

***

Eistedd ac aros am y car du i ddod i nghodi. Mae swyddfa
Mr Giles tua 35 munud allan o Gaerdydd. Yng nghanol
nunlle yn y coed. Swyddfa lân. Ffenestri sy'n adlewyrchu'r
awyr a'r coed, a'r adeilad, felly, yn diflannu i mewn iddo'i
hun, i mewn i'r goedwig. Mae'r car yn cyrraedd. Dwi'n
agor y drws, a Martin yn sêt y dreifar fel arfer.
"Iawn, syr?"
"Iawn, Martin?"
A dyna ni, y pum sill boreuol, wedi'u siarad. Dim mwy.
Yn union 'run peth ag arfer.
Edrych ar y byd drwy'r ffenestri tywyll, gweld pawb.
Neb yn fy ngweld i.
Dwi'n edrych ar y geiriau o dan y bont '*everything is
connected*' – y graffiti cyfarwydd. Dwi'n meddwl am y
peth. Dwi'n gor-feddwl am y peth. A dwi'n gwrando ar
y radio yn lle. Reggae Martin yn guriad tawel, cysurus.
Ac yna, y cwsg sy'n dod bob bore rhwng 8.14 a 8.47.
Bob bore, yn ddi-ffael. Mae hwnnw'n dod eto, a'r car
yn trafeilio yn nes at swyddfa Mr Giles. Fel arfer.

***

Dwi'n deffro, agor fy llygaid a gweld y ffigwr ar y cloc yn newid o 8.46 i 8.47. Dechrau i lawr y ffordd fach tuag at y swyddfa, a gweld y magnolia ar y coed. Agor y ffenest rŵan a rhoi fy ngherdyn adnabod i Jim. A chofio am ddôl fy chwaer; Magnolia oedd enw honno. Roeddwn i wedi anghofio popeth am Magnolia tan rŵan. Mae hi'n dal i fod yn yr atic yn rhwle. Siŵr o fod. Jim yn rhoi'r cerdyn yn ôl i mi. Dwi'n sylwi ar y coed eto, a rhoi fy llaw allan i gyffwrdd â'r dail gwyrddion wrth inni ddynesu at y swyddfa. A sdopio. Dwi'n agor y drws, camu allan. Rydw i'n nodio ar Martin, yntau arnaf innau. A dwi'n troi at ddrws y swyddfa.

***

Mae hi'n dawelach yma heddiw na ddoe. Mae ffrwgwd ddoe wedi'i ddatrys, a'r pentref tu ôl i'r swyddfa yn heddychlon eto. Mae Mr Giles yn amlwg wedi cyrraedd, er mai bore Iau ydi hi. Mae'n rhaid ei fod o wedi dod i wneud yn siŵr bod y sefyllfa wedi'i setlo'n iawn. Mae o'n dda fel yna. Mae ei sgarff melyn yn hongian wrth y drws. Yndi, mae hi'n fwy heddychlon yma heddiw. Mae gen i saith o bentrefwr i'w gweld heddiw. Tri yn y bore, pedwar yn y pnawn. Dwi'n camu i mewn i'n swyddfa i. Mae'r coffi ar y bwrdd bach yn y gornel fel arfer, yn boeth, yn y potyn, a'r ager yn dianc drwy'r pig. Rhoi fy mag ar y llawr. Tywallt y coffi. Yfed. Cnoc ar y drws

***

"Bore da, Ania."

"Bore da, Macsen."

"Y drefn arferol cyn i ni ddechre."

"Wrth gwrs."

"Pam dy fod ti yma?"

"Oherwydd mod i eisiau llonydd. Cyfle i arafu. Sdopio."

"Sut ddois di o hyd i ni?"

"Gweld hysbyseb am 'Pentref Mawnog' yn y papur newydd."

"Be ydi'r telerau ynghylch gadael?"

"Gaf i adel unrhyw bryd rydw i ishe gadel."

"Diolch, Ania. Dyna hynny wedi'i wneud."

Mae hi'n chwerthin a'i dannedd hi'n wyn, wyn.

"Ti'n gweud hynna fel 'na wrth bawb, Macsen?"

"Ydw. Pawb ond Mr Giles."

Tawelwch.

"Sut mae pethau?"

Ac mae Ania'n dechrau siarad, yn cael amser i brosesu'r holl bethau hynny sydd wedi bod yn pwyso i lawr arni dros yr wythnos. A dwi'n gwrando, ar bob sill, pob ynganiad, yn gwrando...

"Wel, ti'n gwbod o'n i'n sôn am y ffeil las wthnos dwetha, y ffeil las yn ei law e..."

Mae hi'n dweud ei stori, a dwi'n gwrando ar bob gair. Yn cymryd nodiadau. Fel arfer.

***

Rŵan, mae'r ystafell yn wag. Finnau yn aros am y pentrefwr nesa. Ac mae Guto'n chwerthin. Ei wyneb o'n fflachio o mlaen i eto. Y dannedd rheini, y wên honno. Gwên

wrth i ni wylio ffwtbol. Gwên wrth i ni drafod merched.
Gwên wrth i ni drio peint am dro cyntaf. Gwên wrth i
ni ddreifio car am dro cyntaf. Yr un wên bob tro, ond yn
yr atgof yma, ryden ni mewn cae pêl droed. Haf poeth,
poeth. Ryden ni o dan y coed. Y gwybed bach, hyd yn
oed, yn dawel, wedi arafu. Rhy boeth i symud. Mae 'na
botel lemonêd o'n blaenau ni a honno'n oer. Ryden ni
wedi cadw'r botel yn yr afon ers bore 'ma. Mae o'n estyn
am y cwpanau rŵan. Cwpanau bach plastig, glas. Mae o'n
tywallt y lemonêd i'r cwpanau. A dwi'n clywed y swigod,
ac rydw i'n mynd yn fwy sychedig fyth. Wrth i'r ddiod
daro yn erbyn wal y gwpan, mae'r sŵn fel sŵn tonnau ar
y traeth – llanw'r lemonêd. Mae o'n rhoi'r gwpan i mi.
Dwi'n yfed a dwi'n teimlo'r swigod yn taro cefn fy llwnc,
a'r rheini'n oer, oer. Ryden ni'n dau yn dawel am eiliad.
Cyn iddo fo ddechrau siarad am Mrs James, yr athrawes
Maths, a'r fflach ddireidus yn ei lygaid. Mae o'n gwenu
arna i, a'i wyneb yn sgleinio yn yr haul. Mae o'n dechrau
ei antics wrth ddynwared. A dwi'n chwerthin o fy mol.
Ac wrth i mi gofio'r chwerthin hwnnw yn fy mol, dwi'n
dod yn ôl i rŵan, a dwi'n cael teimlad arall yn fy mol. Yr
ail waith i fi feddwl am Guto heddiw. Ond y tro yma, mae
o'n deimlad hefyd. Yn gwasgu. Ac wedyn y ffôn yn canu:
Mr Giles. A'r diwrnod yn cario yn ei flaen. Fel arfer.

***

Dwi'n anadlu'n ddwfn.
Chwarae'r recordiad o Ania'n siarad. Asesu, ydw i wedi
methu rhywbeth?

Dwi'n gwrando arni hi'n siarad…

"Achos o'dd Mr Ffrancon wedi gweud, ondyfe."

Dwi'n sdopio'r recordiad.

Ac am eiliad dwi'n meddwl am yr holl gyfarfodydd sydd
wedi bod heddiw, ym mhob man yn y byd, a faint o bobl
sydd wedi colli canolbwyntio, faint o'r geiriau sydd wedi
eu siarad sy'n dal i hongian yn yr awyr, wedi'u dweud,
yn meddwl eu bod nhw wedi cael eu clywed, ond heb
gael eu clywed…

Rhoi'r recordiad i chwarae unwaith eto.

"Sonia am y ffeil las eto, 'nei di?" medde fi.

Mae hi'n dechrau eto. Yn esbonio eto.

A minnau'n gwrando. Eto.

Ac mae'r diwrnod yn cario mlaen fel arfer, fel arfer.

***

Amser cinio, dwi'n mynd mewn i'r pentref tu ôl i'r
swyddfa. Pentref bach o dai gwynion ydi hwn. Pob tŷ
â'i ardd lysiau ei hun. Os ydi pobl eisiau tyfu llysiau mi
fedran nhw, os nad ydyn nhw, does dim rhaid iddyn nhw.
Yma, mae pobl yn gwneud faint maen nhw eisiau, dim
mwy, dim llai.

Dwi'n cerdded draw i ganol y pentref. Y graean dan
fy nhraed. Mae'r arogl o'r siop yn codi drwy'r awel, a
hwnnw'n fy nhynnu i'n nes. Cerdded at y drws, y gloch
yn canu. A Magi'n ymddangos. Fel arfer.

"Haia, Macsen."

"Haia, Magi."

"*Vegetarian* heddiw."

"Lyfli."

"Tisho *chips* hefo fo?"

"Ie plis, Magi."

Mae'r smotyn du o dan ei llygad yn pefrio yn yr haul.
O yndi, mae hon yn ferch dlos. A dwi wedi dal fy hun
yn meddwl amdani… yn edrych arni yn y partis gwaith…
ond mae… 'na rwbeth…bob amser wedi… mae 'na
rwbeth ar goll ynddi…

Rhyw wacter…

Rhyw dristwch…

Yr un hen sylweddoliad arferol. Yr un hen deimlad.

Mae hi'n estyn fy nghinio ata i, ei osod yn fy nwylo. Mae'r
cyfan yn dod mewn bocs bach papur. Y cyllyll a ffyrc pren.
Fel arfer.

A dwi'n mynd yn ôl i'r swyddfa, at fy ngwaith, a nghinio
yn fy llaw, fel arfer.

Mae'r diwrnod yn pasio. A'r cloc yn cyrraedd 5 o'r gloch,
a Martin yn troi i fyny eto. Dwi'n camu i mewn i'r car.
Fel arfer. Dwi'n cyrraedd adre. Dwi'n meddwl be ga'i i
swper. Nhro i i goginio heno. A ma' presenoldeb Guto'n
pwyso arna i. Yn gryfach. A dwi isio siarad hefo fo. Gyda
hynny, dwi'n clywed goriad Leila yn y drws. A dwi'n
cario ymlaen hefo'r diwrnod, fel arfer.

***

Dwi'n gorwedd yn y gwely oriau yn ddiweddarach. Ma'
Leila'n anadlu'n dawel wrth fy ymyl i. A dwi'n gorwedd yno.
Dwi isio siarad hefo Guto. Ond mae hi'n hwyr rŵan.
Dwi'n meddwl am Mr Giles.

Dwi'n meddwl am y pentrefwyr.

Dwi'n meddwl gofyn i Leila fy mhriodi i.

Dwi 'di meddwl gneud ers blynyddoedd.

Dim ond mod i ofn.

Dwi'n meddwl am y car—isio *MOT*.

Dwi'n meddwl am y ffensys sydd isio'u paentio.

Dwi'n meddwl am Mam, am Dad. Am Gwennan
fy chwaer. Am Magnolia.

Ma'r gath yn dechrau mewian ar y stryd.

Dwi'n meddwl am y feiro honno sydd ym mhoced fy
nhrowsus, a dwi isio cofio tynnu honno allan cyn i Leila
ei roi o yn y golch. Dwi'n gorwedd yno'n meddwl y gwna
i gofio gwneud hynny yn y bore.

Ond wedyn, dwi methu ymlacio…. rhaid ei wneud o rŵan.

Dwi'n codi, yn dawel, dawel.

Teimlo yn y tywyllwch am y trowsus.

Dwi'n ffendio'r trowsus. Ffeindio'r feiro.

Ei thynnu hi allan o'r boced a'i rhoi hi ar y bwrdd bach.

Dwi'n cerdded yn ôl am y gwely.

Ac wrth fynd yn nes, dwi'n taro bawd fy nhroed yn
erbyn coes y gwely.

A dwi isio sgrechian.

Ond ma' Leila'n cysgu.

Dwi'n iste ar erchwyn y gwely yn rhegi pob rheg dwi'n
ei wybod tu mewn i mhen, yn rhwbio bawd fy nhroed.

Gorwedd yn ôl i lawr.

Ac ma'r teimlad yn dod drosta i. Teimlad fel niwl yn
treiddio drwy ngwythiennau i.

Dwi'n eistedd i fyny.

Dwi'n estyn am y ffôn…

Nid rhywbeth rhesymol ydi hyn. Ma'r teimlad fel ton.
Ma'n rhaid i fi. Teimlad mwy na fi fy hun. Teimlad o
rhywle arall, rhyw fan arall, y tu allan i mi fy hun.

Ma'r rhif wedi diflannu oddi ar y ffôn.

Ma'r teimlad yn dod yn gryfach fyth. Teimlad sy'n fy
llyncu'n llwyr. Alla i ddim ei esbonio. Dim ond ei dderbyn.

Dwi'n estyn am y laptop.

Dwi'n clicio a clicio a clicio, chwilio drwy wefannau,
grwpiau cyfryngau cymdeithasol, unrhyw le.

***

Dwi ar y trên. Roedd o wedi ateb fy neges. Roedd o wedi
gofyn… o'n i awydd cyfarfod. Y bydde'n dda ganddo fo
gael siarad.

 A dyma fi ar yr *Arriva Train Wales*. Yr un arogl cyfarwydd.
Sŵn y cledrau. Enwau cyfarwydd y gorsafoedd. A
theimlad anghyfarwydd y tu mewn i mi.

Newport

Cwmbrân

Abergavenny

Ac ymlaen ac ymlaen…

Mae'r troli'n dod… a'r dyn yn gwerthu'r coffi…

Minnau'n ei brynu.

A dwi'n meddwl am Mr Giles; boi sydd mor hoff
o ddemocratiaeth, ond boi sy'n casáu trafnidiaeth
gyhoeddus. Dadl arferol.

***

Ma'r trên i Fanceinion yn cymryd yn hir. A mae gen i
neges gan Mr Giles. 'Dim problem.' Dwi erioed wedi
gwneud hyn o'r blaen, cymryd diwrnod i ffwrdd. Erioed,
ac felly dwi ddim yn gwbod ydi dim problem yn golygu
dim problem ynte ddim. Ond dyna ni. Dwi'n camu i
ffwrdd oddi ar y trên ym Manceinion Picadilly, ac yn
cerdded at y tram. Newid ym Manceinion Victoria a
thrafeilio allan o'r ddinas ar drên arall tuag at y wlad, tuag
at Hebden Bridge. Dod i sdop, ac edrych ar y siop fwyd
welais i ar y dudalen Facebook. Enw'r siop, enw'r lleoliad.
Fan hyn mae o.

Ma'r siop yn edrych yn lle twt.

Bob dim yn ei le.

Dwi'n gweld y cyfan drwy'r ffenestr.

Cawsiau.

Gwinoedd.

Bara sy'n edrych mor flasus nes mod i'n glafoerio wrth
edrych arno.

Dwi'n syllu ar y siop.

Dydi'r cymylau uwchben ddim yn symud.

A dw innau, hefyd, yn sdond.

A wedyn…

A dwi'n cerdded i mewn. Yno ar yr union eiliad, dwi'n
gweld Guto, tu ôl i'r cownter. Mae ei lygaid yn wag, yn
edrych ar y silffoedd o'i flaen. Ei ben yn gostwng, mae
o'n edrych ar ei ddwylo; ond tydio ddim yn eu gweld nhw.
Mae 'na ganhwyllau organig ar werth wrth ei ymyl –
arogl magnolia.

Dwi'n cerdded ymhellach i mewn i'r siop, a ma'
nerfusrwydd yn dod drosta i.

Dwi'n llonydd am eiliad.

Dydi Guto ddim hyd yn oed yn sylweddoli mod i yno.

"Guto?"

Mae o'n troi ei ben, ac yn edrych arna i.

A does gen i ddim syniad beth mae o'n ei feddwl.

***

Hanner awr yn ddiweddarach, ryden ni yn y caffi bach
drws nesa. Y siop wedi'i chau.

Mae 'na ddynes a chanddi *dreadlocks* blonde yn dod aton
ni, yn gwenu.

Mae hi'n gofyn yden ni'n barod i archebu.

Mae Guto'n edrych arna'i. Does ganddo ddim syniad
beth mae o ei eisiau.

Dwi'n ordro *banana milkshake* iddo fo, un mefus fi.

Mae hi'n gofyn yden ni isio unrhywbeth arall.

Dwi'n deud wrthi ein bod ni'n iawn ar hyn o bryd.

Mae hi'n diolch.

Dwi'n diolch.

Ma Guto'n fud.

Ryden ni'n eistedd yno mewn tawelwch. Ac mae hynny'n
iawn. Ar ôl sbel, mae Guto'n tynnu darn o bapur o'i
boced. Mae wedi'i blygu'n fychan, fychan, ac mae'n rhoi'r
sgwaryn yn fy llaw. Dwi'n ei droi yn fy nwylo fel *Rubik's
cube*. Yn dad-blygu'r papur, a hwnnw'n gwneud sŵn
yn y caffi tawel.

Dwi'n gweld y dyddiad.

Dyddiad heddiw.

Dwi'n gweld y symbol.

Symbol y 'sbyty.

Dwi'n gweld y neges.

A dwi'n deall pam mod i yma.

Dwi'n edrych ar Guto.

Mae o'n syllu arna i, yn 7 oed eto.

A'r ddynes *dreadlocks* yn dod gan gario'r *milkshakes* draw.

Dwi'n diolch.

Ma' Guto'n fud.

Tawelwch.

Mae'r llaeth yn felys yn fy ngheg.

Ac wedyn mae o'n siarad.

Y ddau ohonan ni'n edrych ar ein gilydd.

"Dwi'm 'di deud wrth y ngwraig na mhlant am y 'sbyty. Dim byd. O gwbl." medd Guto.

A dwi'n nodio arno.

Mae o'n gafael yn y *milkshake*, a'i yfed.

Mae o'n cymryd anadl arall. Cyn gwenu.

***

Pump o'r gloch, a dwi'n dechrau am yr orsaf, gan droi i godi llaw ar Guto. Mae yntau yn codi llaw, cyn diflannu nôl mewn i'r siop. Mi welwn ni'n gilydd eto ymhen pythefnos. Gêm Cymru yn erbyn yr Eidal. Dim byd ond peint, gwylio gêm, malu awyr, mynd adre. Fo at ei wraig a'i deulu, fi at Leila, a Mr Giles, a'r gath fach od. Dwi'n eistedd ar y trên. A'r chweched teimlad wedi ein tynnu ni at ein gilydd; nid rhywbeth rhesymol.

Rhywbeth arall, tu hwnt i ni. Rhywbeth arall, rhywbeth
dydw i'n methu ei esbonio, a rhywbeth sy'n rhoi cysur
mawr i mi. Y chweched teimlad wedi ein tynnu'n dynn
fel rhaff yn estyn drwy'r blynyddoedd. Ffrindiau bore oes.
A'r awel fel petai'n anadlu allan yn dawel, dawel. A finnau,
hefyd, yn dawel.

Ac injan y trên yn cael ei thanio.

***

Gyda hynny mae dau decst yn cyrraedd. Un gan Mr Giles
– amserlen fory, ac un gan Leila yn gofyn be dwi isio i de.
A bywyd yn cario yn ei flaen fel arfer.

*Mae Ceri Elen yn awdures ac actores, ac yn diwtor
cysylltiol yn Ysgol y Gymraeg, Prifysgol Caerdydd. Fe'i
magwyd ym Mae Colwyn.*

ALICE YN STEDDFOD LAND
gan Catrin Dafydd

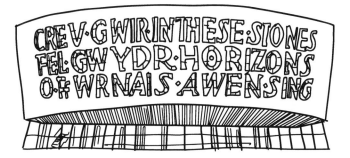

Chwaer. Pigo'r ffôn lan... pigo'r ffôn lan, ie...?

O grêt... Neges mae yn, 'te...

Oce, so neithiwr nath bywyd chwaer dau ddeg saith oed ti mynd bach yn nyts. Ac ar hyn o bryd... fi'n styc mewn fan heddlu.

Fi mor flinedig ar y foment, galle fi cysgu am gweddill y blwyddyn. Dim achos bod yr heddlu 'di aresto fi – na, achos fi heb 'di siarad cymaint â hyn o Cymraeg ers fi 'di gadael ysgol! Cymraeg 'iawn' fi'n golygu. Fi'n dweud i ti, ma'r pobol Eisteddfod ma'n nyts. Lôds o Gogs a popeth... Pobol sy'n *like* **siriysli** byw yn Cymraeg – ti'n ca'l fi? Ma' nhw'n lyfo fi pan nhw'n sylweddoli nhw'n gallu ordro hufen iâ nhw'n Cymraeg. *Like* siriysli lyfo fi. Paid ca'l fi'n rong, ma' fe actiwali eitha neis fel arfer. Dweud hwnna, o'dd y menyw 'ma ddoe reit, o'dd hi fel – "Wel, hyfryd! Siarad Cymraeg. Ac o lle 'da chi'n dŵad?" A o'dd fi fel – "Caerdydd". A o'dd hi fel – "ond o lle'n **wreiddiol**?" A o'n i fel "Pentrebane. Caerdydd". A o'dd hi fel – "A'ch rhieni?". "Abertawe". O'dd hi besicli eisiau gwybod sut dw i'n gallu siarad iaith y nefoedd ond hefyd bod yn hanner *Chinese*. Paid ca'l fi rong, fi ddim yn dweud hi'n *racist*. Jyst intrîgd. Dal heb gael un tip gan neb achos fi'n siarad Cymraeg, cofia. O wel – 'dyfal donc a dŵr y gaseg' fel o'dd Miss

Ryder arfer dweud yn Coed y Gof. Guess bydd raid fi sgrwbo lan Westi acen fi os fi rili eisiau nhw rhoi dwylo yn pocedi nhw. Ie, wrth gwrs fi'n gwbod sut i neud e. Besicli, ti jyst yn dweud 'shwmae' ar y dechrau a 'gwwwd' ar y diwedd. Ond y Gog *stuff*? Na. Fi methu neud hwnna. Ma' nhw ar planed arall... *God*, mae'n dwym mewn fan hyn. 'Croeso am y hufen ia fanila... Mwynhewch yr Eisteddfod. Mwynhewch Caerdydd. Eich priiif dinas', a gwên. Dyna *repertoire* bach fi, chwaer. Byset ti'n chwerthin pen ti bant. Cofia, fi byth yn teimlo fel gwenu – mae gyd yn act. Sdim lle i swingo pysgodyn yn y fan hufen iâ. A Mr Whippy yn y bac yn neud job da iawn o neud dim byd tu ôl y *generator*. Fi'n dweud i ti, 'so fe'n jenereto dim byd ond aer twym a darllen texts ma' dad e'n anfon draw i dweud i **fi** beth i neud. Byse fe'n neis, byse fe, bod yn disendynt i hufen iâ Rabaiottis. Ma' Whippy boi'n *sorted* am fywyd.

Ond ie, ie, ie – fi'n gallu clywed ti'n dweud e wrth wrando ar y *voicemail* – pam ar wyneb daearyddiaeth wyt ti mewn FAN HEDDLU?! So 'nai torri'r peth lawr yn fyr i ti, chwaer. Dim er mwyn fi – ma' gen i drwy'r dydd.

Dwi mewn fan heddlu.

Beth mae Mam wastad yn dweud am fi? Bod gen fi dawn dweud stori Nanna Watkins. Heddwch i'w llwch. Felly arth gyda fi, chwaer. Arth gyda fi.

Yn syml, dwi mewn fan heddlu achos, am tipyn bach neithiwr, cwympodd dy chwaer, Alice, mewn cariad.

I egluro – mae'r *vibe* yn y Steddfod 'ma yn eithaf gwahanol i beth fi wedi gweld o'r blaen achos ma' unrhyw un yn

gallu *moocho* mewn a mas a neb yn gorfod talu ceiniog.
Paid ca'l fi'n rong, os ti'n eisiau'r *big stuff* ti'n gorfod ca'l
wrist band, ond ma' lot o'r stwff – wel mae mor 'am ddim'
â'r awyr iach. Heblaw yr hufen iâ wrth gwrs. Ma' Mr
Whippy'n codi dwbwl wthnos yma. Methu beio nhw
mind – ma' *Welshies* 'da cash.
So sut wnaeth rhywun dwyn fy nghalon, rwy'n clywed ti'n
gofyn. Wel. Am hanner awr wedi pedwar ddoe wnaethon
ni rhedeg mas o hufen iâ. Roedd Mr Whippy yn y cefn yn
whipo lan ffys mawreddog achos o'dd dad e'n mynd lan
y wal ar *whatsapp* bo ni heb meddwl dod â'r *extra freezer*.
Felly doedd dim byd i'w wneud o dan y camgylchiadau
ond mynd i ymlacio yn basin Roald Dahl gyda shades ni ar.
Dyna lle roeddem... yn *chillaxo* yn y basin... pryd nath y
gang o dynion yma dod i eistedd ar bwys ni. O'n nhw'n
smart ond eitha *rowdy*. Barfiau, mwstashiau a gwisgo
t-shirts mental Cymraeg. Ar un o nhw o'dd e jyst yn
dweud – WIWER. Craco fi lan, Cymry Cymraeg, ai.
Roeddwn i'n meindio fy busnes fy hunan, gyda peint,
pan wnaeth y boi gyda'r crys-t WIWER troi ata i a dweud
– 'wel, shwmae pishyn!'. Roeddwn i'n fflabyrgastio'n syth
pin. Celt oedd ei enw. Fy gŵr... yn y dyfodol... o leia
dyna roeddwn i'n meddwl ar y pryd. Roedd e mor hardd
â gardd ... bardd fi, gweld?
Beth bynnag, cyn i fi sylweddoli beth oedd yn mynd
mlaen roedd fi a Celt yn y crowd yn gwrando ar band
rili da o'r enw Adwaith. Roedd e fel nefoedd ar y daear,
chwaer. Dawnsio bach, gwenu bach, dal dwylo bach, ticlo

palmiau ein gilydd bach... a snogo lot... fel plant ysgol.
Roedd yn hollol amêsing. Sdim wir angen dweud fod
Mr Whippy wedi mynd 'nôl i tŷ rhieni fe a bod fi wedi
aros mas drwy'r nos, oes e?!

Wrth inni eistedd gyda'n gilydd ar diwedd y nos, yn dal
llaw a teimlo fel ni wedi nabod ein gilydd ers am byth
gofynnodd Celt –

"Be tishe galw'n plentyn ni?"

"Bachgen neu merch?" Holais i.

"Gewn ni ddou."

"Rhys a Lleucu."

Ac fe wnaeth Celt nodio. A dal fy nwylo'n mwy dynn.

"Shgwla'r sêr," dwedodd e wedyn, ac fe wnaeth ni
gorwedd 'nôl ar y grisiau concrit ac edrych i fyny. Roedd
pawb arall yn dechrau gadael. Yn mynd mewn i'r dref neu
beth bynnag. Ond roedd Celt a fi yn hapus yn hollol
lle roeddem. Yn edrych lan i'r awyr ddu. Edrych ar y
sêr yn disgleirio.

"Pwy wnaeth y sêr uwchben," dechreuais canu, "y sêr
uwchben," a meddai fe, "y sêr uwchben". "Pwy wnaeth y sêr
uwchben" meddai fi a meddai Celt...

"Wyt ti'n credu yn Nuw?"

"*Too right* fi yn. Gwbod mae ddim yn ffasiynol i dweud ond
mae Hi yna."

A dyma Celt yn chwerthin. A gwenu a rhoi llaw e rownd fi.

"Ni'n deall ein gilydd, nagyn ni?" dwedodd e, "a ti'n un glefer."

Erbyn y pwynt yma, roedd hyd yn oed gwynt gwallt e'n
gwneud fi'n hapus.

"Wy'n credu bo fi 'di bod yn chwilio amdanot ti'n holl fywyd i," meddai Celt wedyn. Ac yna, daeth un o'i ffrindiau gyda barf heibio a cicio seidr dros fy sgert heb drio. Eisteddodd ni lan, a helpiodd Celt fi gael y seidr i ffwrdd.

"Sori am Gruff. Ma' fe'n *div*."

"Ti'n dweud i fi," meddais. A gwenodd Celt.

Siaradodd ni am sbel fach wedyn. Dweud ambell i beth. Fi'n egluro bod fi'n siarad Mandarin, Cymraeg a Saesneg. Bod fi'n gwerthu hufen iâ ond eisiau bod yn nyrs ac yn safio lan i neud y cwrs. Dwedodd Celt ddim llawer am ei hun ar y pryd yna, dim ond bod e'n dod o Llandys-rhywle... Mae fe'n rili propyr Cymraeg... Biwtiffwl Cymraeg. Dweud pethe fel 'isht ychan' a 'o, 'co ti, wy 'di bod yn whilo amdanot ti'. Roedd fi'n pyti yn ei law.

Ar diwedd y nos, crwydrasodd ni ar hyd y Bae. Edrych ar y Senedd. A'r Pierhead. A snogio ar bwys y dŵr. Roedd e'n propyr lysh. A pobol oedd yn siarad Cymraeg yn pasio ni. Rhai o nhw ddim ond jyst yn gallu cerdded achos roedd nhw mor feddw.

Ar diwedd y nos, aethom 'nôl i'w fflat e yn Cathays. Troi mas... bod Celt yn stiwdant... sy bach yn nyts – gan bo fi'n dau ddeg saith. Ond dyw e ddim jyst yn unrhyw stiwdant, chwaer – ma' Celt hefyd yn enwog... yn prif llenor. Besicli jiniys. Nath e ennill y Daniel Evans gwobr blwyddyn dwethaf neu rwbeth a nawr ma' fe yn yr orsedd *thingy*... O'n i'n meddwl gynta bod e'n *high* ar rwbeth pan ddwedodd e 'na, so nes i chwerthin. Ond yn ôl ffrindie fe, oedd wedi neud rownd masif o tost i ni gyd, ma' fe'n

wir. A ma' dad e'n *druid* hefyd. A ma' mam fe'n rwbeth
uchel iawn yn Merched y *Wow*. A ma' nhw gyd yn gwisgo
a deall pethe rili dwfn am Cymru ni gyd angen gwybod
am ond efo dim clem am. Stwff am coed a geiriau a....
Ond, a dwi ddim yn chwythu fy nhrwmped fy'n hunan
nawr chwaer, roedd Celt yn meddwl bo fi'n amêsing. Yn
ôl fe, rwy'n enghraifft o llwyddiant addysg Gymraeg ac
yn ryff diemwnt... Cwtshodd e lan i fi yn y gwely sengl ac
edrychais i arno gan gadael iddo llenwi fy llygaid i gyd.
Ac yna... cafon ni KO.
Beth bynnag, neithiwr oedd hwnna... deffrodd Celt bore
'ma yn mŵdi. *Hangover* oedd fi'n meddwl i fy hunan
ond aparyntli, o'dd e wedi cysgu trwy larwm e ac roedd
yr orsedd *thingy* yn cyfarfod ar y Maes i neud rhyw fath
o hud a lledrith a *blessings* neu rywbeth. Cyn i ni ca'l
cyfle am propyr *chat*, nath e neidio mas o'r gwely so 'nes
i neidio mas gyda fe – gofyn os alle fi dod... O'f fi eisiau
gweld bardd fi mewn acshyn, chwaer! O'dd Celt ddim
yn siŵr i ddechrau, o'n i'n gallu gweld yn llygaid e.
Ond nath e newid meddwl e wedyn a dweud bydde
fe'n addysg da i fi. So bant â ni! Celt a fi.
Mewn hanner awr, ro'n i'n sefyll yn y crowd masif yma
yng nghefn Canolfan y Mileniwm a Celt yn dweud i fi
bod pawb rownd fi yn llenors ac yn yr Orsedd. Peth nesaf,
roedd menyw yn sefyll o flaen fi'n hando dillad gwyn iddo
fi. "Chi ar yr Orsedd hefyd?" a nath Celt jyst chwerthin...
a dweud "Ody, wrth gwrs". So nath yr hen fenyw ticio
blwch a rhoi *sheet* i fi. Os fi'n onest, o edrych 'nôl, fi'n

recno o'dd Celt dal bach yn meddw pryd hwnna... ma' fe'n tenau o corff. Munud nesa, nes i troi rownd ac roedd Celt wedi mynd. Wedi gwneud Rosfa arno fi. O ie, fi'n cofio fe. Ma' pawb yn cofio fe.

Roeddwn i'n rili conffiwsd am beth i neud nawr achos roedd pawb arall rownd fi yn jyst roi y pethau *sheety* 'ma 'mlaen...

... Dw i'n meddwl, o edrych 'nôl, taw hwnna oedd pryd wnaeth pethau rili mynd yn rong. Achos penderfynais i roi'r *sheets* mlaen hefyd. A cyn fi gwbod be sy'n mynd mlân ma' hen ddyn yn pwsho fi ymlaen. A fi yn y ciw yma o *sheets*. Yn *sheetan* fy hunan. Os nhw'n mynd i gofyn rywbeth *druidy* nawr, fi'n cofio meddwl i fy hunan... *hell knows* beth bydd yn dod mas...

Ar un pwynt, nath dyn 'ma troi ato fi a dweud, 'Ma'r Fedal Ryddiaith yn un ddifyr 'leni dydy...?' a nes i edrych yn llygaid e, nodo a dweud, 'Ydy wir.'

O'f fi'n dechrau chwysu erbyn hyn achos i bod yn onest o'dd e'n rili dwym tu fewn y *tent / sheet thing* ac o'dd jôc bach doniol Celt yn dechrau teimlo fel syniad rili stiwpid – a ble oedd e eniwei?! Mewn bach o panic, 'nes i dechrau holi rownd amdano fe. Ond doedd neb yn gwybod dim byd amdano. Peth nesa, ro'n i'n siarad gyda'r menyw rili hyfryd yma o'r enw Dilys oedd mewn *sheet* gwyrdd a nathon ni rili bondo. Bondo gymaint mewn pum munud nes dyma fi'n penderfynu dweud y gwir i hi – 'Dilys, ma' 'na masif ff*c-yp wedi bod fan hyn... fi ddim yn *druid*.' Edrych 'nôl, dyliwn i ddim wedi trystio Dilys. Achos y peth nesa gwelais i oedd pedwar aelod o'r heddlu yn martsho tuag ataf a Dilys yn pwyntio'i bys fel menyw ar *Y Gwyll*... 'Dydy hi ddim ar yr Orsedd'. Nawr sai'n gwybod pam, a bydda i wastad yn holi fy hunan pam, ond am ryw reswm wnes i penderfynu ar y pwynt yna... i gwneud beth fyddai unrhyw *crim* da yn gwneud ar *whodunnit*. Rhedais. Rhedeg heibio rhai o'r hen dynion mewn gwyn a heibio ryw telynor. Heibio meistres y diod a'r corn hir a glas. Heibio Alex Jones. Heibio bos y *druids*. O'n i *seriously* yn teimlo fel bo fi yn *wonderland*.

Ac yna gwelais ei gwyneb. Celt. Wedyn gwelais y llawr. A teimlo yr heddlu yn cario fi ffwrdd i ochr arall y *railings*. "Pam bydd fi moyn dwyn *sheets* gwyn, offiser?" oedd fi'n cadw dweud i'r hedd-ddyn, "fi'n hefo digon adref. Mae'n nyts." Ond doedd yr heddlu ddim yn fy nghredu. Ac i gwneud pethau'n gwaeth, daeth ryw hen bardd gyda gwallt gwyn i gael sheets hi nôl a dweud i fi – "'Da chi wedi dwyn anfri ar y Steddfod".

"Ond beth am Celt?" holais. "Ei syniad ef oedd hyn."
Ac ar hynny, cafodd Celt a'i dad eu symyno draw gyda Ceidwad y Cledd. Oedd e fel rywbeth o *Game of Thrones*. "Ody hyn yn wir?" gofynnodd tad Celt o flaen yr heddlu. Chwarae gyda'i farf. "Ai dy syniad di oedd y ffwlbri hurt yma, Celt?"
Edrychodd Celt arnaf. Ei galon yn llawn cariad a'i ben yn llawn comyn sens.

"Dwi erioed wedi gweld hon o'r blaen, Dad," meddai Celt gan edrych tua'r llawr wedyn. Rwy'n gwybod pam. Mae e'n gwybod na byddai siawns iddo fod yn Brenin y Beirdd os bydd fe wedi dewis fi dros y byd Cymraeg...

Syllais arno. Fy Nghelt. A thorrodd fy nghalon. A wedyn ges i'n *chucko* mewn y fan.

Mae'r heddlu'n gwbod bo fi jyst angen mynd 'nôl i'r gwaith nawr... mae'n ridicilys. Bydd Mr Whippy ddim yn gwybod sut i weithio'r *machine* a ddim yn siarad gair o Cymraeg gyda'r cwsmeriaid. So mae pawb yn colli mas rili.

Bydd Celt ddim yn dod 'nôl i nôl fi, chwaer, rwy'n *under* dim *illusion*. Rwy'n dau ddeg saith nawr ac yn gwybod fel mae'r storis hyn wastad yn gorffen.

Mae'n siŵr fod *plan* i cael Celt i priodi ryw merch – fel *arranged marriage*. Rhyw Rhiannon neu Rhuanedd neu Gwenllïan. Ac mae hi hefyd yn bardd, fi'n siŵr ei bod. Yn gwybod pethau dwfwn.

Ond 'na'i dweud iti'r gwir, chwaer. Dim ots pwy yw hi – neithiwr, ni oedd bia'r stori. Celt ac Alice yn Steddfod-land. Roedd e'n ni'n dau ar y Roald Dahl Plass. Ac roedd e'n *class* ac yn masif.

Mae Catrin Dafydd yn awdures lawrydd. Magwyd hi yng Ngwaelod-y-garth. Enillodd ei nofel ddiweddaraf Gwales Gwobr Ffuglen cystadleuaeth Llyfr y Flwyddyn 2018.

REBAL I'R CARN
Gan William Owen Roberts

'Aeth neb erioed i nunlla trwy gadw at y rheola...'
Ond am bo fi'n cerddad rhyw bedwar cam y tu ôl iddo fo,
mi aeth ei eiria fo ar goll yn y gwynt.
'Ma'n ddrwg gen i...? *Sori*? Nes i'm clywad chi...*Be*?'
Dyma fo'n codi ei lais yn uwch a deud, 'Aeth neb 'rioed
i nunlla trwy gadw at y rheola.'
Nes i'm cynnig ateb am rhyw eiliad neu ddwy, dim ond
rhyw gnoi cil dros be oedd o newydd ei ddeud. Wedyn,
dyma fi'n holi, 'Be 'dach chi'n ddeud, Ieuan? Ma' petha
i'w torri 'di rheola?'
'Siŵr iawn...'
Cerddad ar hyd hen lwybr defaid i fyny i ben Mynydd
Rhiw oeddan ni'n dau. Wrth feddwl ei fod o bron yn wyth
deg naw oed, roedd o'n dal yn egnïol iawn, a'i goesa fo'n
rhyfeddol o gry o hyd. Ond wedyn, dyn yr awyr agorad
oedd Ieuan wedi bod erioed. Mi gafodd ei fagu mewn
oes pan oedd National Service yn dal i orfodi dynion
ifanc i mewn i iwnifform. Honno oedd y drefn 'nôl yn y
pumdegau. Doedd ganddo fo ddim mymryn o ddewis ond
gwneud yn union fel roedd pawb arall yn cael ei orfodi
i'w neud am ddeunaw mis, ac i ffwrdd â fo yn ei siwt a'i
siwtcês ar y tren o stesion Bangor tua'r ffin.
Doedd neb yn siŵr iawn fasa disgyblaeth o'r fath yn siwtio

Ieuan. Ond wedi mynd trwy *basic training* yn y baracs yn Wrecsam, er mawr syndod i bawb, mi gafodd gynnig lle yn Sandhurst. Sut a pham, medda chi? Doedd neb yn siŵr iawn, ond mi gafodd 'i longyfarch ar ei gamp gen bron pawb o'r pen yma. Achos dim ond snobs y 'sgolion preifat a stiwdants Oxford a Cambridge oedd yn 'i swagro o gwmpas fan'no. Ac a bod yn onast, doedd dim math o awydd arno fo i fynd. Roedd o'n ddigon hapus yn lle roedd o. 'Nôl Ieuan, ei dad o wnaeth ddwyn perswâd arno fo'n y diwadd, trwy fynnu y basa fo'n beth da i rywun o'i gefndir o i fynd yn swyddog, gan y basa ganddo fo fwy o gydymdeimlad hefo hogia'r werin datws. Mi gafodd o dipyn o strach cyn setlo, ond ar ôl gorffan y flwyddyn yn Sandhurst, mi gafodd gomisiwn i'r South Wales Borderers, lle roedd o ar ben ei ddigon.

Ond doedd o prin wedi bod hefo nhw am flwyddyn, prin wedi dechrau cael ei draed 'dano, pan gafodd o gynnig arall...

'Cofia di, cicio a strancio 'nes i. Os glywa i rywun yn deud 'bw', mi fydda i'n saff o ddeud 'be'. Ac os deudith rhywun 'be', mi ateba inna, 'bw'. Un felly dwi 'di bod erioed. Na, doedd gen i'm math o isio mynd...'

'Mynd i lle?'

'Berlin.'

'Berlin? Argol!'

'Fel ADC i *Commandant y British sector*.'

'Iesgob mawr, Ieuan. Joban dda?'

Rhyw chwythu'i focha fydda fo a deud yn ddi-hid,

'I rywun hefo meddwl go fawr ohono fo'i hun ella.
Ond ddim felly o'n i'n gweld hi o gwbwl....'
'Felly... be? Neuthoch chi wrthod y cynnig?'
'O'n i mewn dipyn o gyfyng gyngor, ma'n rhaid imi
gyfadda... ac ar ôl lot o boen meddwl... wsti, ma'r petha
'ma'n... rho hi fel hyn, oedd o'n ddewis anodd. Yn ddewis
anodd iawn, achos erbyn hynny, ro'n i 'di priodi Meryl
ym mis Ebrill 1951. Un peth pwysig 'nes i ddysgu trwy
briodi oedd fod yn rhaid imi fod yn llai hunanol a
dechra rhoi pobol erill yn gynta. Doedd Meryl 'rioed 'di
bod fawr pellach na Blackpool, ac oedd hi flys gweld tipyn
ar y byd... Ond dim ond am rhyw gwta chwe mis fuon
ni'n Berlin... wedyn, mi aeth hi'n llanast ym Malaya. Y
comiwnists draw 'no isio cymryd drosodd. Cofia di, gen
i gydymdeimlad 'di bod hefo'r comiwnists erioed. Roedd
fy nhad yn dipyn o sosialydd. Ac yn fy ffordd fach fy hun,
rhyw gwffio tros sosialaeth dwi wedi'i 'neud ar hyd fy oes...'
'Sut le oedd hi'n Malaya? Poeth, siŵr o fod?'
'Poeth, oedd...'
'Alla i ddychmygu...'
'Ar adega, oedd hi'n ddiawledig...'
Syllu draw tuag at Ynys Enlli oedd o, a sefyll wrth 'i ochor
o o'n i, yn gwichian wrth drio cael 'y ngwynt ata. Mae gen
i sgyfaint wan wedi bod erioed. Ac a bod yn onast, do'n
i'm yn teimlo'n hannar da. Roedd yna rhyw hen bendro
ysgafn wedi bod arna i ers ben bora, nes gwneud imi
deimlo braidd yn simsan ar fy nhraed. Ieuan fynnodd ein
bod ni'n mynd am dro i Ben Mynydd Rhiw. Doedd gen i

ddim math o isio mynd, ond mi bwysodd arna i i ddŵad
hefo fo, achos ei fod o'n teimlo mai hwn, o bosib, fydda'r
tro ola un. Doedd dim rhyfadd felly ei fod o mewn rhyw
hen hwylia digon oriog y pnawn hwnnw.

'Ty'd inni ista ar y garrag 'ma.'

A dyna naethon ni am ryw awr. Mi aeth o ati i hel
atgofion am y South Wales Borderers pan oeddan nhw
mewn lle ym Malaya o'r enw Kluang. Eu job nhw yn
fa'no oedd o'n mynd allan ar patrôl i'r jyngl a phawb wedi
baeddu'i wynab hefo *greasepaint* du, a'r Brylcreem wedi'i
olchi'n lân o'u gwalltia nhw, achos fod y gelyn yn gallu'i
ogleuo fo o bell.

'Yn fan'no nes i ddechra cicio'n erbyn y tresi, 'sti...'

'Pam fan'no?'

'Achos fod 'na benna' bach uwch 'y mhen i. Penna' bach
iawn hefyd, oedd yn meddwl eu bod nhw'n gwbod yn
well. Doedd gen i'm math o ddewis yn y diwadd ond
tynnu'n groes...'

 'Be'n union oeddach chi'n 'neud 'lly?

'Mae 'na rwbath yn'a i, 'sti... wn i'm be ydi o... nac
o lle mae o 'di dŵad... ond ma' rhai petha'n bwysicach
na cowtowio drwy'r amsar, fel tasa chdi'n ddim byd
ond pen dafad...'

'Sut naethoch chi beidio cowtowio'n Kluang 'ta?

'Yn lle mynd allan ar patrôl fesul dau neu dri... wel, nes i
roi nhroed i lawr a mynnu mod i'n mynd allan hefo wyth...'

'Be? Aethoch chi i drwbwl am hynny?'

'Trwbwl? Nefi, paid a sôn. Ges i bob math o helbul.

Ond 'na fo...ro'n i 'di sefyll i fyny iddyn nhw. Sy'm
yn beth hawdd...'
'Goelia i...'
Am bron i ddwy flynadd mi fuodd Ieuan yn cwffio yn y
jyngl ym Malaya. Ar ddiwadd y cyfnod yma, fe wnaeth
cyrnol y bataliwn awgrymu i Field Marshall Gerald
Templer ei fod o'n cael ei anrhydeddu hefo'r Military
Cross. Ac ar ôl hynny wedyn, mi fuodd o'n cwffio yn
Oman – lle gwnaeth o niwsans ofnadwy ohono fo'i hun
trwy dynnu pob math o bobol i'w ben. Wedyn yn Aden,
lle roedd o'n fwy byth o niwsans, medda fo.
'Rhei o'r petha 'nes i... Bobol bach, fasa chdi'm yn coelio...
A fasa neb byth bythoedd heddiw yn cael get-awê hefo
be 'nes i 'radag honno, cofia. A bod yn hollol onast, ma'n
syndod na ches i mo'n hel allan o'r armi...'
Ond yng nghanol y chwedegau, mi ddaeth o 'nôl adra i
Gymru, i Gaerdydd am ryw dair blynadd lle roedd o'n
dysgu hogia ifanc y Gwirfoddolwyr Cymreig. Yn anffodus
i Ieuan, mi ddigwyddodd hyn tua'r un adeg ag yr oedd
y South Wales Borderers yn cael ei lyncu gan y Welch
Regiment i ffurfio The Welch Regiment of Wales. Doedd
o'm yn hapus o gwbwl hefo'r penderfyniad yma, a wnaeth
o byth faddau i un person o Gabinet Harold Wilson –
person wnaeth o byth mo'i enwi wrtha i. Ond roedd o'n
rhefru ac yn rhuo byth a hefyd yn erbyn y person yma am
chwalu catrawd oedd wedi hen ennill ei pharch. Y fi fawr
uffernol yma oedd y person hwnnw, yn meddwl am neb
na dim ond amdano fo'i hun. Doedd dim byd yn gasach

gen Ieuan na rhywun oedd yn mynnu gwthio'i hun i'r top.
'Nes i rioed lyfu neb.'
Dwi'n cofio fo'n deud hynny fwy nag unwaith.
'A sdim byd gwaeth gen i na crafwr. Ti'n nabod fi'n ddigon
da erbyn hyn... Ti'n gwbod sut un ydw i... Dyn sy'n siarad
yn blaen. A rhywun sydd ddim ofn deud 'i ddeud, a sefyll i
fyny tros be ti'n goelio sy'n iawn. 'Na pam ma' hi'n bwysig
inni gyd ofyn y cwestiwn...'
Ro'n i ar goll braidd, ac mi fuo'n rhaid imi ofyn iddo fo
pa gwestiwn yn hollol oedd hwnnw.
'Y cwestiwn pwysica un... pwy ydw i go iawn? Ti'n
cytuno? Ti ddim, alla i ddeud wrth dy wynab di...'
'Na, na, trio meddwl ydw i...'
Dyma fo'n mynd yn ei flaen i ddeud, 'Be arall ydi'n
bywyda ni i gyd ond ffordd o ddŵad i ddysgu pwy ydan
ni? E? Dim ond mewn rhyfal ma' dyn yn dŵad i nabod
'i hun go iawn. Ma' cwffio yn testio pawb i'r pen. Wyt
ti'n gwbod pwy wyt ti, Cledwyn?'
'Am wn i...'
'"Am wn i?" Be ti'n feddwl? "Am wn i..."'
'Wel... ma' hi'n anodd inni ddeud wrtha ni'n hunan
pwy ydan ni go iawn, dydi?'
'Ydi hi? Pam?'
'Achos mai ni sy'n gofyn y cwestiwn ac yn cynnig yr atab.
Mi fedar rhywun dwyllo'i hun yn hawdd.'
'Paid â siarad yn wirion,' oedd ei atab stowt o. 'Drycha
'ma, unai wyt ti'n gwbod pwy wyt ti, ne' ti ddim. Meddwl...'
Mi wnes i ngora glas i feddwl. Ond rhyw fywyd digon

di-liw o'n i wedi'i gael. Yn enwedig o'i gymharu â bywyd rhywun fel fo. Do'n i byth wedi herio neb na dim. Do'n i erioed wedi bod yn rebal wrth reddf. Ond roedd Ieuan wedi bod trwy'r felin – a honno'n felin arw iawn. Roedd o hefyd wedi bod rownd y byd a gweld petha na allwn i ond 'u dychmygu. Roedd o wedi byw go iawn, a thrwy hynny, wedi magu cymeriad go iawn a barn glir ar bob un dim. Yn y saithdegau, 'nôl a mlaen o Ogledd Iwerddon roedd Ieuan gan fwyaf. Y fo, fwy neu lai, oedd yn gyfrifol am *operations control room* y bataliwn. Ato fo roedd pawb yn troi am ateb pan oedd petha'n dechra poethi. Hyd yn oed yn Belfast, doedd o ddim yn hapus hefo be oedd yn digwydd. Tasa fo wedi cael ei ffordd ei hun, mi fasa heddwch wedi dŵad dipyn yn gynt i Ulster na wnaeth o'n y diwadd.

Ond pan oedd o newydd droi 'i hannar cant, mi benderfynodd ei fod o'n mynd i ymddeol o'r fyddin. Roedd o a Meryl awydd treulio mwy o amsar yng nghwmni ei gilydd. Erbyn hynny, roedd o wedi dechrau chwara golff, ac roedd o'n cymryd y gêm o ddifri, ac yn awyddus i ymarfar yn gyson er mwyn gwella'i hun. Ond gwaetha'r modd, chafodd o fawr o lonydd i wneud dim byd, achos o fewn dim o dro, mi ddaeth rhywun draw i'w dŷ o'n Fulham, a mynnu mynd â fo am ginio i ryw glwb o'r enw Whites. 'Nôl Ieuan, breib oedd peth felly. Ond ar ôl pwyso a mesur y cynnig, dyma fo'n penderfynu cymryd y job, ond ddim er ei fwyn ei hun, ond er mwy gweld be alla fo neud dros bobol erill.

Ei waith o'n Whitehall oedd gwarchod lles teuluoedd –
pobol o'r armi – a oedd yn cael eu gyrru fan hyn a fan
draw i wahanol embasis ar hyd a lled y byd. 'Nôl Ieuan,
job debyg oedd ei job o'i hun cyn gadael yr armi yn
swyddogol. Am saith mis, fo oedd y *defence attache* i'r
British Consulate yn Jeddah. Ond sut bynnag roeddach
chi'n mynnu ei disgrifio hi, job tu ôl i ddesg oedd ei
job o'n y Swyddfa Dramor. A job ddiflas ar y naw oedd
hi hefyd, faswn i'n dychmygu. Ond chwara teg i Ieu,
er 'i bod hi'n job ddi-sbarc, mi sticiodd ati am dros
ddeuddag mlynadd i gyd. Erbyn y diwadd, ei unig blesar
o'n Whitehall oedd cyfarfod y Treasury Singers bob nos
Fercher. Pobol o'r Trysorlys, y Swyddfa Dramor a'r Cabinet
offis oedd yr aelodau i gyd, heblaw am Meryl, a gafodd
groeso i ymuno hefo nhw yn sgil ei gŵr, a chodi pres at
wahanol achosion da roedd y côr yn ei wneud gan fwyaf.
Wedyn, ar ôl cael ei draed yn rhydd mi werthodd y tŷ
yn Fulham a mudo 'nôl i'w hen gynefin, i dyddyn bach
ar gyrion Abardaron. Roedd cael dŵad i Ben Llŷn ugian
mlynadd yn ôl fel chwa o awyr iach, oherwydd – yn ôl
Ieuan – roedd y job yn Whitehall wedi mynd yn hollol
annioddefol. Nenwedig hefo siwtia diflas o weision
suful o'i gwmpas o, yn mynnu ei fod o'n cadw at y
rheola rownd y rîl.
Ddechra'r flwyddyn eleni mi ges i alwad ffôn gen Meryl
yn gofyn imi ddŵad draw. Roedd Ieuan wedi cael codwm
hegar ar ben y grisiau ac roedd hithau wedi methu â'i godi
fo. Erbyn i'r ambiwlans gyrraedd, roedd o wedi mynd yn

welw ac yn cwyno ei bod hi'n oer, er inni roi sawl blancad
drosto fo. Mae'n rhaid imi gyfadda ei fod o'n edrach
yn reit druenus. Ro'n i'n ama ei fod o wedi torri'i glun.
Ond wnaeth o ddim cwyno rhyw lawar. Erbyn y gyda'r
nos, roedd o wedi marw'n dawal mewn ward yn Ysbyty
Gwynedd. Roedd hi'n ddiwadd Ionawr a'r wlad drwyddi
draw wedi rhewi'n gorn a hen heth o eira dros bob man.
Mi rois i help llaw i Meryl hefo'r angladd. Ond doedd
dim rhaid inni boeni rhyw lawar achos mi ddaeth criw y
British Legion o Bwllheli i'r adwy a rhoi trefn ar y cwbwl
yn hollol ddi-lol. Mi ddaeth yna ddega draw, nes roedd
mynwant Tudweiliog yn llawn o filwyr ac o gyn-filwyr,
gweision suful, hanner dwsin o aelodau seneddol, dau
neu dri o Dŷ'r Arglwyddi a bron pawb o Glwb Golff
Morfa Nefyn, a'r Ddraig Goch yn gorwedd dros ei arch
o. O fewn ychydig ddyddiau, mi ges i gardyn neis iawn
gan Meryl yn diolch imi am fod mor ffeind wrth y
ddau ohonyn nhw.

Ar ôl yr angladd mi gyhoeddwyd teyrnged iddo fo'n y
Daily Post gan ryw ddyn o Gaergybi, a oedd hefo fo'n
Kluang. Mi gafodd Ieuan ei ddisgrifio fel *'a young officer
of outstanding initiative, skill and steady courage during
eighteen months of a most arduous campaign against
hardened communist guerillas hell-bent on destroying
that beautiful country. This won him a well-deserved
Military Cross with the highest distinction.'*

'Pwt o ddim byd...' oedd atab di-hid Ieuan am y fedal
honno. Dwi'n ei gofio fo'n dweud droeon ei fod o ar y

pryd rhwng dau feddwl i'w derbyn hi ai peidio. Ond mi wnaeth o'n y diwadd, er mwyn yr hogia na ddaeth 'nôl adra hefo fo o Malaya.

Bellach mae hi'n fis Awst.

Echnos a'th Mam a finna draw at ei fedd o. Roedd Mam am roi bloda ffresh i lawr, ond roedd rhywun wedi bod yno o'n blaena ni. Meryl, siŵr o fod. Mi fuodd hi'n driw iawn iddo fo hyd at y diwadd.

'Cradur bach,' oedd unig sylw Mam.

'Pam dach chi'n 'i ddeud o fel'na?' medda fi.

'Y cradur bach,' medda hi wedyn a sychu'i thrwyn hefo hancas cyn 'i gwthio hi i fyny'i llawas. 'Mynd yn bell ddaru o... yn bell ofnadwy hefyd... trwy neud yn union fel oedda nhw isio, siŵr o fod...'

Fuo ni'n sefyll yno am fymryn ar ôl hynny a'r gwybed yn gwingo o'n cwmpas ni. Wedyn, cyn inni'i throi hi am adra, dyma hi'n gofyn imi dynnu llun y bedd hefo'n ffôn symudol. A dyma be nes i dynnu:

'Lieutenant-Cyrnol Ieuan Vernon Davies M.C., C.B.E.' (1932 – 2018)

Fymryn yn is i lawr, roedd tri gair wedi eu naddu'n ddwfn i'r garreg: 'Rebal i'r carn.'

Mae Wiliam Owen Roberts yn ysgrifennu ers nifer fawr o flynyddoedd ac yn byw yng Nhaerdydd.

MRS O A NAT
gan Anni Llŷn

Bôrd oedd Nat, ac roedd hi'n bôrd o fod yn bôrd. Dyna
pam y gwnaeth hi ddechra'r holl beth. Roedd yn hen bryd
iddi gymryd ychydig o gyfrifoldeb dros ei diflastod.
Roedd hi newydd orffen ei choffi boreol ac yn barod i
gydio yn ei ffôn i bostio fidio cynta'r dydd.

"Hi guys! Fi jysd yn gwneud fy hun yn barod i fynd i'r
gwaith ac mae'n rhaid i fi ddweud… waw… mae ymateb
pawb i'r blog wedi bod yn anhygoel!! Diolch diolch! Fi ddim
yn gwybod beth i wneud gyda'r holl sylw! Ond cadwch
lygaid ar stories instagram fi heddiw. Bydda i'n ymateb i rai
negeseuon, ac yn rhoi syniad i chi o beth fydd ar y blog post
newydd heno! So yeah, siarad 'da chi wedynz!"

Roedd gweithio'n y cartref yn iawn. Doedd hi ddim yn
meindio o gwbwl. Doedd hi ddim yn siŵr ar y dechrau,
gan nad oedd hi wir isio bod yn ofalwraig, ond daeth cyfle
am swydd i gynorthwyo â chadw'r tŷ, ac i gymryd rôl
Swyddog Cymdeithasu, a olygai treulio hyn a hyn o amser
y dydd yn eistedd i lawr yn sgwrsio gyda'r preswylwyr, a
threfnu gweithgareddau. Roedd hynny'n siwtio Nat i'r
dim – cadw'r lle'n gyffredinol daclus, siarad am y tywydd
a threfnu ambell weithgaredd. Ac ar yr un pryd yn cael
"profiad" o'r byd gofal, i gadw'i mam yn hapus.

BING.

Daeth neges i'w ffôn – Eli Gwaith.

Hi Nat. Dwi'n really meddwl dyla ti dynnu'r blog lawr. Dwi ddim isio i chdi gael dy hun i drwbwl. Dwi ar ffordd mewn. Gweld chdi'n gwaith.x

Ochneidiodd Nat. Atebodd y tecst yn sydyn:

Mae'n iawn, sdim ishe i ti boeni. Fi ddim yn ei henwi hi... a dyw e ddim yn wir ta beth.x

Roedd Nat wedi atgoffa'i hun droeon ei bod wedi meddwl ac ystyried pethau'n iawn cyn i'r blog fynd yn fyw. Ond roedd yn rhaid iddi gyfaddef wrthi'i hun, roedd rhyw gnonyn o euogrwydd y tu mewn iddi o hyd.

Cyn gadael y tŷ, gwnaeth un fidio arall:

"Hi guys, fi 'to. Nes i anghofio atgoffa chi, os na chi 'di bod draw i ddarllen y blog, pwyywmrso.com yw'r cyfeiriad a bydda i'n rhoi blog post newydd lan heno am 8! Wedynz!"

Oedd hyn yn iawn? Yn foesol? Wel oedd, dywedodd wrthi'i hun droeon, os oedd y cyfan yn ddychmygol. Gwaith creadigol oedd o, campwaith hyd yn oed, doedd dim gwadu ei fod yn llwyddiant. Roedd pobl wrth eu bodd yn darllen am fywyd Mrs O. Y gwir amdani oedd fod Mrs O, neu Olwen, yn ddynes o gig a gwaed, yn eistedd yn y cartref o fore gwyn tan nos heb fawr i'w ddweud wrth neb. Doedd ganddi ddim teulu'n dod i'w gweld a doedd neb yn y cartref yn gwybod llawer amdani. Roedd Nat wedi eistedd gyda hi droeon yn malu awyr am y tywydd, yr ardd, *Love Island*, Brexit... wel, cymaint yr oedd hi'n gallu'i drafod ar hwnnw. Roedd

hi'n hoffi Olwen, roedd 'na rywbeth amdani. Roedd
hi'n ddynes fawr, bron yn chwe troedfedd, ac roedd ei
hysgwyddau yn llydan a chadarn fel trawst. Ond pe
bai Nat yn onest, laru wnaeth hi. Laru trio meddwl
am rywbeth i'w ddweud, laru trio cael unrhyw fath
o ymateb gan Olwen. Dechreuodd Nat ddyfalu a
dychmygu sut fywyd yr oedd Olwen wedi'w gael…
rhyw dynnu coes diniwed i ddechrau.
"Fi'n meddwl eich bod chi wedi gweithio mewn ffatri…
efallai un o'r ffatrioedd bach 'na sy'n creu nickers, fel
rheini ar *Coronation Street*," dywedodd rhyw ddiwrnod,
dim ond er mwyn gweld cysgod o wên. Ond dim.
Aeth dychymyg Nat yn ystwythach wrth i'r sgyrsiau
unochrog fynd yn eu blaenau.
"…ac er eich bod chi'n wych yn yr ysgol, yn glyfar iawn
gyda rhifau a gwyddoniaeth a pethau, aethoch chi
ddim mlân i'r coleg. Oeddech chi'n gorfod mynd
gatre i warchod… cathod… fi'n agos?" Dim. "Ydych
chi'n hoffi cathod?"
Dyna pryd y cafodd Nat y syniad. Nid agor gwarchodfa i
gathod, ond i greu blog am fywyd Olwen, wel, bywyd Mrs
O. Y bywyd yr oedd Nat yn ei ddychmygu yr oedd hi wedi
ei gael. Byddai pobl wrth eu bodd yn darllen am yr hen
ddynes dawel yma mewn cartref ond yn rhannu dirgelwch
ei bywyd cyffrous â merch ifanc annwyl fel hi. Byddai pobl
yn gwirioni ar y chwaeroliaeth hyfryd yma'n tyfu rhwng
y ddwy ar draws y cenedlaethau, meddyliodd. Byddai
hi'n datgan yn y cyflwyniad mai gwaith dychmygol yw'r

cyfan ac nad yw Mrs O yn ddynes go iawn, a bod unrhyw debygrwydd i berson go iawn yn gyd-ddigwyddiad llwyr. Roedd Nat bellach yn cerdded tuag at ddrws blaen y cartref. Roedd ei phen yn ei ffôn, roedd hi wrthi'n rhannu llun o'i hesgidiau ar Instagram, treinyrs newydd, gan ysgrifennu o dan y llun y byddai Mrs O yn "caru gweld rhain" ac ar yr un gwynt yn atgoffa pawb y bydd "…blog post newydd yn mynd lan heno am 8."

"Nat!"

Roedd Eli wrth y drws yn aros amdani.

"Plis paid gweud dim, dyw'r blog ddim yn gwneud niwed i neb… a ma'fe'n gwbl ddychmygol ta beth."

"Na… dim hynny…" roedd golwg ddifrfol ar wyneb Eli. "Mae Olwen wedi diflannu."

* * *

Roedd heddiw'n ddiwrnod rhyfedd, roedd Olwen yn teimlo'n wahanol. O'r eiliad yr agorodd ei llygaid lliw lleuad oer y bore hwnnw, roedd hi'n edrych ymlaen. Edrych ymlaen at rywbeth, ond wyddai hi ddim at beth. Cododd ac eisteddodd wrth y ffenestr yn yr ystafell fyw yn ôl ei harfer, oni bai am un manylyn. Doedd hi ddim wedi rhoi'r sliperi porffor cyffordddus am ei thraed heddiw, roedd hi wedi rhoi eisgidiau. A phan ddaeth yr amser, cododd o'i sedd a cherdded trwy'r ystafell haul, ar draws yr ardd ac allan i'r stryd. Mor rhwydd â hynny. Welodd neb mohoni, neu'n hytrach, sylwodd neb. Roedd hi wastad wedi bod yn un dda am ddflannu.

Rhywsut, roedd pob cam fel pe bai'n pwmpio rhywbeth

y tu mewn iddi. Gwrandawodd cyn croesi'r ffordd. Oedd, roedd y ddinas yn fyw, fel ac yr oedd wedi bod erioed iddi hi. Roedd haen o sŵn traffig pell fel cynfas, ac yna roedd yr artist wedi llithro'i frwsh o sŵn injan dân a sŵn lori'n bagio, drosto. Gyda sbwng cras wedyn, yr oedd wedi rhwbio sŵn tsiaen beic a bag plastig yn y gwynt. Roedd wedi bodio lleisiau yma ac acw; bloedd, chwerthiniad, dadl. Ac yna, gyda'r brwsh lleiaf erioed, rhoi'r cyffyrddiadau manwl; llwy de yn taro ochr cwpan, cot plentyn yn cael ei lusgo ar hyd y llawr, a thamaid rhydd o'r pafin yn siglo.

Cymerodd Olwen y darlun swynol hwn a'i gadw'n dawel yn un o'r rhannau gwag yn ei chof, cyn y gwichodd y goleuadau traffig, a'r dyn bach gwyrdd yn ymddangos wrth ei hochr. Roedd pawb arall i weld yn croesi, felly i ffwrdd a hi.

* * *

Roedd y staff i gyd wedi ymgynull i glywed y rheolwraig yn dweud nad oedd isio i neb boeni, na fydd hi wedi mynd ym mhell, y byddan nhw'n saff o ddod o hyd iddi. "Mae Kels, Gareth a Jac wedi mynd allan i chwilio, mae 'na heddwas ar y ffordd a Dr Morris. Nat, pan ddaw Jac yn ôl, efallai y bydde'n syniad i ti fynd allan – 'dach chi'ch dwy i weld yn dipyn o ffrindia. Diolch, cariwch ymlaen efo'ch goruchwylion bora 'ma ac mi gawn ni air efo pawb cyn bo hir."

Doedd Nat ddim wir isio crwydro'r strydoedd yn galw am Olwen fel pe bai'n chwilio am gi bach. Trôdd Eli'n wyllt ati.

"Be w't ti wedi ddeud wrth Olwen?"

"Beth? Dim byd… jysd wedi mynd am dro mae 'ddi. Garantîd newn nhw ffindo hi'n Sainsbury's yn bwyta'r *grapes* fel wnaethon nhw ffindo Mr Huws."

Rhoddodd Nat ei bawd ar ei ffôn i'w ddat-gloi.

"Be ti'n neud rŵan?" holodd Eli'n angrhediniol.

"Wel, gall hyn fod yn rhan o'r blog… Mrs O yn dianc neu rhywbeth."

"Oes rhaid i chdi fod mor… mae hyn yn siriys, Nat. Ma' isio i chdi dynnu'r blog 'na lawr, heddiw."

Llyncodd Nat ei phoer wrth wylio Eli'n martsio oddi wrthi. Clôdd ei ffôn. Roedd hi'n iawn, be ddaeth drost ei phen? Y peth cyntaf oedd wedi mynd trwy'i meddwl oedd y byddai stori am Mrs O yn dianc o'r cartref ac yn mynd ar goll ar strydoedd hunllefus y ddinas yn bennod newydd wych i'r blog. Byddai dieithriaid yn codi ofn arni, byddai ysbrydion o'i gorffennol yn ei dilyn. Byddai'r caffis coffi yn ei drysu, ac unigrwydd yn ei llyncu yn y byd dieithr tu hwnt i waliau'r cartref. Teimlodd Nat ddwrn yn ei stumog. Gam yn rhy bell? Na. Doedd Olwen ddim yn ddynes go iawn… nid Olwen… Mrs O. Doedd Mrs O ddim yn ddynes go iawn.

* * *

Teimlodd Olwen wres yn codi o'r concrid o'i chwmpas. Roedd hi'n ddiwrnod braf, ac roedd hi'n cofio ei bod wedi bod am dro yn lled-ddiweddar, ar y "diwrnod mas" yr oedd yr hogan siaradus 'na wedi'i drefnu. Ond doedd hi ddim yn cofio'r haul yn ffrwydro ar y to cragen fel yr

oedd o heddiw. Doedd hi ddim yn cofio'r prysurdeb,
yr egni oedd o gwmpas. Roedd hi'n clywed cerddoriaeth,
roedd rhyw ymdeimlad byw, egnïol iddo. Yn union fel
yr oedd hi'n cofio'r gerddoriaeth yn y caffis hwyr hynny
yr oedd hi'n eu defnyddio ar gyfer y cyfarfodydd cudd.
Mwg, dawnsio a'r wisgi afiach 'na yr oedd pawb yn
ei yfed wrth iddi lowcio dŵr i gadw'i phen yn glir.
Yn sydyn, dechreuodd y bobl o'i chwmpas ddawnsio.
Dawnsio gyda'i gilydd, yr un pryd. Pob symudiad yn
berffaith i'r curiad. Camu 'nôl, camu mlaen, clapio, troelli,
neidio, llusgo'u traed, bron iawn â'i chyffwrdd, tynnu 'nôl.
Roedd mwy a mwy yn ymuno yn y ddawns. Roeddan
nhw'n dawnsio iddi hi. Roedd hi'n dal llygaid ambell
un wrth iddyn nhw droelli o'i chwmpas. Gwalltiau'n
chwyrlïo, traed yn gwibio a'r haul yn dal i ffrwydro. Roedd
yr awyr las yn fflachio fel ffenestri trên yn mynd heibio.
Roedd hithau erbyn hyn yn gwenu, yn symud ei breichiau
rywfaint, yn ymladd i gadw'i thraed yn solat ar y llawr.
Daeth y ddawns i ben ac roeddan nhw'n cymeradwyo.
Roedd Olwen hefyd, nid yn cymeradwyo, ond yn taro'i
dwylo fel ymateb i'r cyffro roedd hi'n deimlo. Byddai'n
rhaid iddi gofio dweud wrth rywun am hyn. Efallai wrth
y ferch 'na… daro, beth oedd ei henw? Roedd y merched
ifanc 'ma'n cyflwyno'u hunain unwaith a dyna ni, roedd
yn amhosib trio cofio wedyn.
Ar yr union eiliad yr oedd Olwen yn meddwl am y ferch,
roedd rhywun wedi clicio ar ei stori Instagram Nat:
"Hi guys. Dim ond neges clou i weud diolch am yr holl

negeseuon. Mae'n amazing fod y blog wedi annog rhai o chi i sgwrsio mwy gyda mam-gus chi! Ond i ateb y rhan fwyaf... Na, dyw Mrs O ddim yn berson go iawn. Blog creadigol yw e, ond mwynhewch e fel chi moyn! Cofiwch bydd pennod newydd yn mynd lan heno a bydd e'n un arbennig Mr Menig... fi'n addo! So yeah, wedynz."

* * *

Agorodd Olwen y drws trwm i'r caffi. Camodd o'r heulwen i olau dyfnach, fel camu i ryw fyd arall. Roedd rhyw wead cyfareddol i'r golau. Mwythodd arogl cynnes ei hwyneb a sylweddolodd mai'r degau ar ddegau o flodau a phlanhigion oedd yn gyfrifol am yr awyrgylch rhyfeddol. Roedd y golau'n symud rhwng y deiliach a'r petalau fel ar antur trwy'r jyngl.

Eisteddodd Olwen wrth fwrdd go fawr. Roedd rhyw ysbryd chwit-chwat i'r lle, a'r celfi wedi'u stwffio rhwng y blodau, yn awgrymu fod yna gaffi yma'n rhywle. Roedd hi'n rhy brysur yn cael ei chyfareddu i sylwi ar y bachgen wrth ei hymyl â phapur a phensil yn ei law.

"Coffi?" holodd.

Allai Olwen ddim ateb. Daeth pwl o banig drosti, sut na welodd hi mohono'n dod tuag ati? Teimlodd ei bochau a'i brest yn poethi. Allai hi ddim siarad gydag o rhag ofn iddi ddweud rhywbeth nad oedd hi i fod i ddweud. Doedd ganddi ddim ceiniog, chwaith. Rhoddodd ei dwylo llydan ar y bwrdd a dangos eu gwacter chwyslyd.

Yn annisgwyl, plygodd y bachgen tuag ati a rhoi ei law ar ei braich.

81

"Beth am ddished fach… am ddim?"

Gwenodd Olwen arno i ddiolch. Aeth rhywbeth trwyddi, fel rhyw ysfa i grïo'n hapus braf. Efallai ei bod hi, wedi'r cyfan, wedi camu i fyd arall wrth ddod drwy'r drws trwm.

* * *

"Wyt ti'n gall?" Daeth Eli tuag at Nat. "Pennod arbennig? Plis paid â deud bo' chdi am sgwennu am hyn? Tydyn nhw dal heb ei ffeindio hi, sdi."

"Eli…ma'fe jysd wedi rhoi syniad i fi, 'na'i gyd. Mae'r blog yn rili poblogaidd, mae pobl wir wedi cymryd at Mrs O, a bydd…"

"'Di o 'motsh gen i. Ma'n rong…"

"Ma fe'n ddychmygol…"

"Dwi ddim isio dim i neud efo'r peth, na chdi."

Doedd Nat ddim yn siŵr pam fod Eli'n busnesu beth bynnag. Doedd o'n ddim i wneud â hi, dim i wneud â'r cartref, ac yn y bôn, yn ddim i wneud ag Olwen. Ysbrydoliaeth oedd hi, dyna i gyd.

Roedd Nat wedi meddwl am beth i ysgrifennu heno. Byddai Mrs O'n diflannu ond fe fyddai'r ofalwraig ifanc yn dod o hyd iddi, yn eistedd ar fainc wrth y môr yn syllu tua'r gorwel. Wedi dychryn ac yn ddryslyd, byddai hi'n dweud wrth yr ofalwraig am yr erchyllterau yr oedd wedi eu gweld… efallai fod rhywun digartref wedi ymosod arni. Efallai y byddai hi'n datgelu hanes rhyw ymosodiad arni yn y gorffennol. Byddai'r môr yn codi hiraeth am ei phlentyndod… ie, byddai'n cynnig rhywbeth gwahanol i'r penodau sydd wedi bod ar y blog yn barod.

* * *

Wedi i Olwen adael y byd blodeuog, crwydrodd tuag at
y môr. Eisteddodd. Doedd gan y môr ddim i'w ddweud
wrthi heddiw, digon oriog oedd o wedi bod â hi ar hyd
ei hoes, a dweud y gwir.

Gwyliodd y bobl yn mynd a dod am rai munudau cyn cael
ei denu gan fachgen a merch fach, tua chwe neu saith oed,
yn chwarae saethu gyda gynnau plastig. Roedd y gynnau'n
rhyfeddol o agos at y gwir, meddyliodd Olwen. Rhai tebyg
iawn oeddan nhw wedi'u defnyddio, roedd hi'n siŵr.
Dechreuodd deimlo'n annifyr wrth eu gwylio a cheisiodd
ganolbwyntio ar y môr.

Roedd ei meddwl yn rhyfeddol o glir heddiw, popeth
yn teimlo'n finiocach. Pam tybed? Efallai ei bod wedi
gwrando digon ar y ferch yn y cartref yn mwydro, ei bod
wedi llyncu peth o'r awch 'na, awch i greu stori iddi hi ei hun.
Yn sydyn, daeth llais.

"Olwen fach, 'co chi. Ni 'di bod yn becso." Llais cyfarwydd
un o'r bechgyn o'r cartref.

Gwenodd Olwen arno, roedd yn amser iddi fynd yn ei
hôl felly, yn gorfforol beth bynnag.

* * *

Roedd y diwrnod hwnnw wedi bod yn ddiwrnod
rhyfedd i Nat hefyd. Synnodd ei hun wrth fynd i
deimlo'n eitha emosiynol o weld Olwen yn dod yn
ôl tua'r cartref ar fraich Gareth. Golygfa hyfryd y bydd
hi'n ei ailgreu ar ei blog, gan osod ei hun yno yn
hytrach na Gareth, meddyliodd. Aeth o â hi yn syth

i'w hystafell gyda Dr Morris.

Yn ôl y sôn roedd hwyliau da ar Olwen, roedd hi hyd yn oed wedi dweud gair neu ddau wrth Gareth ar ei ffordd 'nôl.

"Beth ddywedodd hi 'te?" holodd Nat.

Dim ond osgoi ei llygaid ac anwybyddu'r cwestiwn wnaeth Eli. A dyna wnaeth hi bob dydd wedi'r noson honno pan welodd fod Nat wedi rhoi blog post newydd ar *pwyywmrso.com*. Doedd dim sôn am Mrs O'n crwydro o'r cartref yn y bennod, roedd yn rhaid i Eli gydnabod hynny o leiaf, ond roedd hi'n dal i gredu y dylai Nat roi'r gorau i bethau.

Wedi'r diwrnod hwnnw, teimlai Olwen yn wahanol. Gwyddai nad oedd dim byd mawr wedi digwydd iddi, ond roedd hi'n teimlo'n gryfach bob dydd. Roedd ganddi lai o ofn siarad, yn un peth, ac yn ara bach, roedd hi wedi rhoi'r gorau i drio osgoi ei hatgofion. Bechod, meddyliodd, nad oedd y ferch siaradus o gwmpas bellach, byddai wedi bod yn dda cael rhannu rhywfaint o'r gwir gyda hi.

* * *

Rai wythnosau wedi hynny, roedd *pwywmrso.com* yn mynd o nerth i nerth ac roedd gan Nat filoedd o ddilynwyr ar Instagram.

"Hi guys! Diwrnod cyffrous heddiw... bydd un o newyddiadurwyr Sass Mag yn dod i neud cyfweliad â fi!! Wna i postio lluniau, cadwch lygaid ar insta-stories fi! Bydda i'n datgelu un o gyfrinachau mawr Mrs O yn y cyfweliad!! So yeah, dydd Llun hapus!"

Roedd Nat wedi gadael ei swydd yn fuan wedi'r diwrnod yr aeth Olwen am dro. Doedd hi ddim yn gallu cario mlaen â'r blogio a theimlo beirniadaeth gyson Eli ar ei hysgwyddau. Hynny, a'r cnonyn euogrwydd 'na a deimlai. Ond cenfigennus oedd Eli, penderfynodd. Pe byddai hi wir eisiau i Nat roi'r gorau i'r blog, byddai hi wedi dweud wrth reolwraig y cartref… er nad oedd dim i'w ddweud, wrth gwrs. Beth bynnag, roedd digon o amser wedi mynd heibio erbyn hyn iddi allu rhoi'r bennod am Mrs O yn dianc o'r cartref ar y blog. Byddai'n siŵr o fod yn boblogaidd. Roedd 'na dipyn o gariad tuag at Mrs O ar y cyfryngau cymdeithasol ar hyn o bryd, a Nat yn un o'r blogwyr mwyaf poblogaidd ar y we.

Roedd hi wedi cyrraedd y caffi yr oedd y ferch o *Sass Mag* wedi'i awgrymu yn yr e-bost. Hen gaffi digon annifyr oedd e, meddyliodd. Pwy sy'n stwffio caffi i siop flodau? Doedd arni hi ddim awydd rhododendron yn ei choffi, diolch yn fawr. Ar y gair, daeth bachgen o'r un oed â hi â'i choffi iddi. Gwenodd arno'n wantan, roedd hi wedi talu digon i beidio â thrafferthu diolch iddo, meddyliodd. Rhoddodd lwyaid o siwgr yn y gwpan a'i droi. Ceisiodd baratoi ei hun at y cyfweliad. Mae'n debyg mai'r cwestiwn cyntaf fydd…
"Pwy yw Mrs O?" Cymrodd gegiad o'i choffi, llithrodd ei flas chwerw-felys i'w chrombil.

Fel mae'i henw'n ei awgrymu, hogan o Lŷn yw Anni Llŷn.
Treuliodd y blynyddoedd diweddar yn byw yng Nghaerdydd,
ond mae hi'n gweithio fel awdur, cyflwynydd ac arweinydd
gweithdai ar hyd a lled Cymru.

DIWEDD Y BYD
gan Delyth George

Estynnodd Daniel Feibl y teulu o'r silff lyfrau yn ymyl y lle
tân cyn ei blannu â chlec swnllyd ar fwrdd mawr y gegin.
'O's raid i ti neud 'na nawr?' cwynodd Enid, y llestri yn
ei llaw, ar fin dodi'r ford.
Ochneidiodd Daniel, codi'r Beibl a llusgo'i draed i
gyfeiriad y gadair esmwyth yn ymyl y lle tân lle gollyngodd
ei ben-ôl yn swnllyd i gôl y glustog fawr 'cuddio pechodau'
oedd yn ffaelu'n deg â chuddio gwich y sbrings o dan
ei bwysau. Ond prin ei fod e wedi eu clywed, heb sôn
am eu synhwyro'n crafu ar nerfau Enid, oedd wedi crefu
am gael eu gwaredu a phrynu rhai newydd, heb unrhyw
lwyddiant am nad oedd e'n gweld yr angen am newid o gwbl.
Y gwir oedd bod meddwl am waredu unrhyw beth yn
achosi gwewyr anghyffredin i Daniel, fel y gwnâi i'w
gyndeidiau o'i flaen. Crafu byw roedd y rheini wedi ei
wneud, wrth gwrs, tra'i fod e wedi ei chael hi'n haws,
rhwng sybsidi'r Cynulliad a chyfleon gwerthu i Ewrop.
Ond roedd y cyndynrwydd i hala arian wedi aros. 'Fallai
am fod atgofion hen galedi neu gybydd-dod cynhenid yn
rhan annatod o'i DNA; neu 'fallai fod rhywbeth dyfnach
y tu ôl i'r meddylfryd 'ffaelu gadael dim i fynd'. Nid dim
ond yr hen ddresel a'r bwrdd oedd wedi aros yn y ffermdy
ond yr hen soffa a'r cadeiriau esmwyth hefyd, er bod y

rheini'n ddegawdau o flynyddoedd oed! Fu yna ddim
ymdrech i ddidol a dethol o gwbl; dim ond cadw'r cyfan
yn gwmws fel roedd e. Wedi'r cwbwl, roedd hi'n anodd iawn
gwaredu dim byd a ddewiswyd gan ei fam, y byddai'n
dal i feddwl bob dydd amdani, bob dydd ers ei cholli.
Yn ddiweddar, roedd Daniel wedi gwneud mwy o feddwl
nag erioed o'r blaen, am fod daeargryn arall wedi ysgwyd
ei fyd: y bwriad i gau capel Ebenezer, rhyw filltir i lawr y
ffordd. Doedd e ddim wedi bod yn ddyn capel am y rhan
fwyaf o'i oes. Cawsai'i lusgo yno'n blentyn gan ei fam, a
wedyn fel oedolyn, o dro i dro, gan ei fod wedi dal i fyw
ym Mlaenau Isaf gyda'i rieni gydol ei oes. Ar ôl colli ei
rieni y dechreuodd fynd i Ebenezer yn gyson o'i wirfodd,
am mai yno roedd ei rieni wedi eu claddu. Mynd i gadw
cwmni iddyn nhw roedd e; mynd yno i deimlo'n agos
atyn nhw ac i liniaru rhyw gymaint ar ei alar.
O fewn dim o dro, roedd mynychu'r capel wedi tyfu'n
arfer cadarn. A thrwy daflu ei hunan i fywyd y capel a
mynd i Gymanfa Ganu'r enwad yn y cylch roedd wedi
cwrdda Enid, yr unig wejen erioed oedd wedi ennill ei
galon. Roedd pawb wedi dod i gredu mai hen lanc fyddai
Daniel am byth. Ond, a Blaenau Isaf bellach yn gragen
fawr wag ar ôl colli ei rieni, roedd e o'r diwedd yn frwd
dros briodi a symud Enid ato i Flaenau Isaf. Byddai Daniel
hefyd wedi croesawu etifedd i gario'r enw teuluol ymlaen
ac i ffarmio'r tir ar ei ôl ond, wrth i'r blynyddoedd wibio
heibio, roedd e wedi dod i dderbyn na fyddai hynny'n
digwydd. Braint, fe dybiai, oedd cael plant, nid hawl, felly

doedd e ddim hyd yn oed wedi dechrau gofyn ar bwy
roedd y bai – arno fe ynte ar Enid. Roedd e wedi ildio
i drefn natur a derbyn na fyddai etifedd yn ffarmio'r tir
ar ei ôl. Ond mater gwahanol oedd ildio i drefn dyn –
neu yn hytrach i'r dynion oedd â'u bryd ar gau drws
capel Ebenezer am y tro olaf.

'Pam yn y byd taw Ebenezer sy'n gorfod cau ac nid capel
Horeb yn y cwm nesaf?' roedd wedi gofyn yn y cyfarfod
protest a alwyd wedi'r oedfa y Sul cynt. 'Pam cau capel
ein cyndeidie ni er mwyn cadw capel rhywle arall ar agor?
Dim ond dyrnaid sy'n mynd i Horeb 'ta beth, felly pam
na allan nhw ddod aton ni?' Enynnodd ei eiriau amenio
a murmur cytundeb ymysg y dyrnaid o wrandawyr oedd
wedi dod ynghyd. 'Dyw adeilad Horeb ddim mewn tamed
gwell cyflwr na hwn,' mynnodd, gan daflu cip o'i gwmpas.
'Mae'n waeth os rhwbeth! Felly wela i ddim un rheswm
dros ddewis Horeb ar draul Ebenezer!' meddai, ei araith
yn llawn angerdd.

O'r eiliad honno, penderfynodd y gynulleidfa'n unfrydol
mai Daniel oedd y dyn i gyflwyno'u hachos gerbron
yr Undeb. A dyna a wnaeth gyda'r un tanbeidrwydd a
huodledd ag yr oedd wedi ei ddangos gerbron ei gyd-
aelodau. Ond disgyn ar dir diffaith a wnaeth ei holl
ddadleuon. Roedd Pwyllgor Meddiannau'r Undeb wedi
gwneud penderfyniad di-ildio i gau Ebenezer.

Erbyn iddo adrodd dedfryd yr Undeb wrth ei gyd-aelodau
yn Ebenezer y Sul canlynol roedd ei siom wedi ymgaledu'n
benderfyniad cadarn i frwydro ymlaen. ''Wy'n cynnig

90

'yn bod ni'n torri'n rhydd oddi wrth yr Undeb, yn eu gadael nhw ac yn sefyll ar 'yn tra'd 'yn hunain fel capel annibynnol,' cyhoeddodd a'i ben yn uchel.

Bu tawelwch syfrdan am rai eiliadau, cyn i ryw sibrwd nerfus ddilyn. A chyn pen dim, ac er mawr ddryswch i Daniel, roedd cyd-flaenor ar ei draed yn crynhoi barn y mwyafrif oedd yn barod i dderbyn dedfryd yr Undeb a chau drysau Ebenezer am byth. 'Dyna fyddai orau,' meddai hwnnw, gan daflu gwên ddyfrllyd, ymddiheurol i gyfeiriad Daniel.

'Orau', wir! Orau i bwy? meddyliodd Daniel, gan gnoi ei dafod yn dwll.

'Bradwyr. 'Na beth 'yn nhw i gyd!' pregethodd dan ei anadl wrth yrru'r landrofyr yn wyllt tuag adref hyd yr heol fach droellog, gul.

'Gan bwyll nawr, Daniel...' meddai Enid, gan afael yn reddfol yn nolen y drws.

Ond prin ei fod e wedi ei chlywed. ''Wy wedi siomi yndyn nhw i gyd. Sdim asgwrn cefen i ga'l 'da nhw, rhynton nhw!' mynnodd wedyn, gan wasgu'n drymach fyth ar y sbardun.

'Withe ma' rhaid gwbod pryd i ad'el pethe i fynd!' mentrodd Enid yn bwyllog.

'Wyt ti'n trio gweud bo nhw'n iawn?' bytheiriodd Daniel yn ôl.

'Ble ti'n meddwl gelen ni'r arian i gwiro'r capel pan fydde problem yn codi? Heb sôn am dalu'r bilie?'

'Fydde raid i bawb fynd yn ddyfnach i'w pocedi!'

'A ma'r rheini'n ddiwaelod, odyn nhw? So ti 'di clywed am y dybl-dip recession?'

'Nhw yn Horeb ddyle fod yn dod aton ni, nage fel arall,' mynnodd Daniel yn ddi-ildio, gan daro'r olwyn lywio'n galed nes bod y landrofyr yn ysgwyd yn beryglus.

'Dere i ni ga'l mynd ga'tre'n un pishyn, ife?' meddai Enid yn dawel, ei llaw yn gafael yn dynnach nag erioed yn nolen y drws.

Tawelwch llethol fu rhyngddyn nhw weddill y daith a wedyn yn y gegin ar ôl mynd adre. Sawl noson o'r wythnos roedd e wedi estyn Beibl Mawr y teulu o lwch y silff a thalu sylw anghyffredin iddo; mwy yn wir nag oedd e'n dalu i Enid erbyn hyn. Porodd ac fe borodd ynddo tan i syniad ei daro yn ei dalcen un noson.

'A' i ddim i Horeb dros 'y nghrogi!' cyhoeddodd wrth Enid.

'Ble ei di 'te? Unman?' holodd Enid yn ddigyffro.

Gwenodd Daniel yn llydan.

'Ti wedi'i gweud hi! A' i ddim i unman. Geith pobol erill ddod ata i fan hyn.'

'Beth?' Crychodd ei haeliau.

'Gewn ni oedfa yn y gegin fowr. Oedfa Blaena Isha. Ein hoedfa ni fydd hi, ac unrhyw un ddaw aton ni.'

Ysgwyd ei phen mewn penbleth wnaeth Enid. 'Ers pryd wyt ti'n bregethwr?'

'Gallwn ni ddarllen a gweddïo a chanu ambell emyn. 'Ma' llais pert 'da ti,' meddai Daniel yn frwd. 'A gallwn ni wahodd gweinidog aton ni fan hyn.'

'A talu o'n poced ni'n hunen...? A chymryd y bydde

rhywun yn barod i ddod 'ma yn y lle cynta!'

'Wy'n siŵr ffindwn ni rywun sy'n gallu meddwl tu
fas i'r bocs, ne' tu fas i'r pwlpud, ontefe?' meddai,
gan led-chwerthin yn ei gyffro.

Cyn bo hir roedd drysau Ebenezer wedi eu cau a neb yn
oedfa Blaenau Isaf, heblaw Daniel ac Enid a Bob y ci.
Darllenodd Daniel salm gyfarwydd ac fe ganodd emyn
gydag Enid â'i llais persain yn arwain y canu. Ond fflat
oedd yr oedfa; yr un gynta a'r olaf yn ffermdy Blaenau Isaf.
Cyn bo hir roedd Enid yn diflannu yn y landrofyr ar nos
Sul i oedfa Horeb yn y cwm nesaf, yn y gobaith y byddai
Daniel yn ei dilyn. Ond na, adref yn sdiwio roedd e.
'Bradwraig!' sibrydodd dan ei anadl, wrth i lwch
olwynion y landrofyr adael y clos dan gwmwl a'i adael
e yng nghwmni ei atgofion a'i feddyliau, oedd yn duo
wrth y diwrnod.

Âi Daniel yn gyson am dro i fynwent Ebenezer i roi
blodau gwyllt a dail gwyrdd ar fedd ei rieni. Câi gyfle i
fwrw'i fola wrthyn nhw ar lan y bedd. Roedd e'n teimlo'u
presenoldeb yn fwy byw yn y fynwent nag yn y ffermdy
erbyn hyn. Ond roedd pob ymweliad â'r fynwent yn achosi
poen, mwy a mwy o boen wrth iddo weld yr adeilad yn
dirywio o flaen i lygaid; y capel heb wres a'r lleithder yn
cael parti. Ofnai Daniel fod ei rieni'n ei feio fe am hynny,
eu bod nhw wedi eu siomi ynddo am beidio â rhwystro'r
fath anfadwaith. Beth os o'n nhw'n ei ystyried e yn
fradwr hefyd, am iddo golli'r frwydr?

Cyrhaeddodd ei ofnau benllanw annioddefol un diwrnod

pan sylwodd fod fandaliaid wedi peintio drws blaen y
capel ag arwyddion aflednais. Ac roedd drws y festri,
oedd eisoes wedi dechrau pydru, wedi ei dynnu oddi ar
ei golfachau gan adael yr adeilad yn gwbl agored i'r
elfennau ac i ragor o fandaliaeth.

Rhuthrodd i swyddfa'r heddlu a'i wynt yn ei ddwrn i wneud
cwyn swyddogol. Ond prin droi blewyn wnaeth yr hirlas y
tu ôl i'r cownter. Fe logiodd y gŵyn ar ei gyfrifiadur, ond
doedd e ddim am ymweld â'r safle i chwilio am unrhyw
dystiolaeth am nad oedd adeilad gwag fel'na'n flaenoriaeth
gan heddlu'r dre oedd mor brin o adnoddau erbyn hyn.
Doedd dim amdani ond dychwelyd adre i nôl ei offer a
bordio'r capel gyda'i ddwylo'i hun. Gyda phob hoelen a
gurai i'r pren teimlai ei fod yn curo hoelen arall i arch yr
hen gapel a'r hen deulu hefyd. Roedd e'n argyhoeddedig
bellach ei fod e, Daniel, hefyd, yn gyfrannog yn y brad.
Doedd e ddim wedi bod yn cysgu'n arbennig o dda ers
amser ond y noson honno, roedd ei gwsg ar chwâl yn
llwyr. A phan fachai ryw awr rwyfus fan hyn, fan draw,
câi freuddwydion erchyll lle gwelai furiau Ebenzer yn
graciau i gyd cyn chwalu'n deilchion am ei ben a diflannu
o dan y don. Dihunai Daniel wedyn yn gweiddi a
bwldagu mor aml nes i Enid fynd i gysgu i'r stafell sbâr.
'Bradwraig!' meddai Daniel unwaith eto o dan ei anadl.
'Mae'n bryd i ti fynd i weld rhywun!' awgrymodd Enid
yn dyner y bore wedyn.
'Gweld pwy?' holodd yn hurt.
Codi ei haeliau yn unig wnaeth Enid, gan gario ymlaen â'i

gorchwylion oedd yn drymach nag erioed gan fod Daniel
yn gweithio llai ac yn meddwl mwy.

'Pam wyt ti'n gadael y ffarm i fynd fel hyn?' holodd,
ar ben ei thennyn.

'Nid ar fara yn unig y bydd byw dyn,' meddai Daniel, fel
pe bai'n fwy na pharod i adael y busnes i fynd â'i ben iddo.
Ysgwydodd Enid ei phen yn ddiddeall cyn disgyn i
gadair yn swp blinedig ar ôl codi mor gynnar.

Dihangodd Daniel rhag brath ei thafod i weld sut
gyflwr oedd ar Ebenezer erbyn hyn a chael ergyd arall a'i
hysgwydodd hyd at fêr ei esgyrn. Roedd arwydd mawr
wedi ei blannu tu allan i'r capel. Nid yn unig roedd y
capel wedi ei roi ar werth ond roedd wedi ei werthu mewn
wincad gwybedyn drwy law yr asiant lleol, Prydderch
a'i fab. Rhuthrodd Daniel i'r dre ar ei union, i swyddfa'r
arwethwr i ofyn pwy oedd wedi prynu'r adeilad a pha
ddefnydd a gâi ei wneud ohono? Pan gafodd ar ddeall
bod y capel wedi ei werthu i gwmni datblygu ac adeiladu
Prydderch ei hun, cododd ei aeliau'n amheus a gofyn,
'O's hawl 'da chi neud hyn?'

Y cyfan wnaeth Prydderch oedd codi ei ysgwyddau.

'Ma'r Undeb yn hapus a ma' trwch yr aelode wedi
derbyn y drefen,' meddai, dan wenu gwên fasonaidd,
braidd, ar Daniel.

'Ond beth newch chi â'r lle?' holodd yn syfrdan.

'Amser a ddengys, Mr Lloyd!' meddai mewn goslef a
guddiai lu o gyfrinachau.

Yn hytrach na holi ymhellach, clywodd Daniel ryw
sŵn gyddfol yn dianc o'i enau, rhyw ebwch a fynegai
rwystredigaeth rhemp nad oedd modd ei gostrelu mewn
geiriau. Trodd ar ei sawdl a mynd ar ei union i fwrw'i fola
wrth ei hen gyfaill, Dic Pen-y-banc, oedd wedi ei daro'n wael.
'Daniel, dere miwn!' gorchmynnodd Megan, ei wraig.
'Ma' fe ar ddihun. Wy'n cymryd taw moyn gair bach 'da
Dic wyt ti.'
'Ie, os ga i…Shwt ma' fe?'
'Gas e nosweth fach ddiflas, ond y'n ni mor g'lonnog ag
y gallwn ni fod.'
'Ie,' meddai Daniel yn llawn edmygedd. Nid pawb fyddai
mor siriol yn wyneb cystudd mor greulon.
Trodd Megan i'w arwain i'r parlwr ble'r oedd gwely ysbyty
wedi ei roi ar fenthyg i Dic i wneud bywyd ychydig bach
yn haws i'r ddau.
'Shwt wyt ti, Dic?' holodd Daniel, gan deimlo braidd yn
ffôl yn gofyn y fath gwestiwn gan fod yr ateb yn amlwg
ym mhryd a gwedd ei hen ffrind.
'Cadw fynd, t'weld,' meddai'n dawel gan ryw hanner
pesychu, er ei bod hi'n amlwg nad oedd Dic yn mynd i
unman; ddim yn y byd hwn, beth bynnag.
'Ma' golwg…wedi…cynhyrfu arnot ti,' meddai Dic wedyn
a'i anadl yn brin.
Dechreuodd Daniel fwrw'i fola tra gwrandawodd
Dic yn astud.
'A fe ballodd e, Prydderch, weud beth o'n nhw'n mynd
i neud â'r lle ond mae'n amlwg, on'd yw hi? Ma' nhw'n

mynd i'w werthu e fel tŷ â golygfa hardd o gefen gwlad.
'Na pam taw Ebenezer o'dd yn gorfod cau a nage Horeb,
achos dyw hwnnw ddim mewn hanner cystel safle!'

'Glywes i si…' tuchodd Dic. 'Bod e, Prydderch… yn y
sêt fowr yn Horeb ers… rhyw chwe mis.'

'O'n i'n gwbod bod rwbeth yn drewi,' meddai Daniel, gan
deimlo'i bwysau gwaed yn codi. 'A fe werthan nhw i ryw
Saeson cefnog sy'n moyn djengyd o'r ddinas i brofi'r awyr
iach a llanw'r lle â'u Saesneg swanc!'

'Awyr iach,' crygodd Dic. 'O's shwt beth i' ga'l?' Tagodd a
phesychodd. 'Rhwng dip y defed… a'r dŵr … a'i lond e
o wenwyn …' pesychodd eto. 'A wedyn 'na ti lygredd…
o'r hen atomfa …'

'Ti'n iawn, Dic,' meddai Daniel, ei galon yn gwaedu
drosto. 'Ma' llygredd ym mhobman. O bob math!
Cilo ma' popeth sy'n cyfri,' ychwanegodd yn drist wrth
i'r düwch gau amdano.

Wrth wrando ar y storm o fellt a tharanau yn ysgwyd
ffenestri'r hen dŷ ffarm y noson honno, roedd Daniel yn
fwy argyhoeddedig fyth fod y Cread ei hun yn cwyno ac
yn anniddigo. Hwyrach mai rhybudd o rywbeth mwy
oedd y tywydd afreolus roedden nhw wedi bod yn ei gael
yn ddiweddar. Yn ôl rhai, roedd y ddaear yn poethi, tra bo
eraill yn gwadu. Ond beth oedd y gwir? Dim ond y Bod
Mowr oedd yn gwybod y gwir, barnai Daniel. Ac er mwyn
i'r Bod Mowr rannu'r gwirionedd hwnnw ag e, trodd at
dudalennau'r Beibl Mawr.

Tra bo'r glaw'n taranu fel cawod o fwledi yn erbyn y
ffenestri, cafodd ei hun yn darllen stori Noa a'r modd
roedd Duw wedi anfon dilyw i garthu'r byd o lygredigaeth.
Dyna'r gwirionedd roedd e wedi bod yn chwilio mor
ddyfal amdano! Roedd Duw wedi anfon y llifogydd a
welodd yr ardal yn ddiweddar fel rhybudd o'r hyn oedd i
ddod, oni bai bod dynion yn dihuno. Ond pwy oedd yn
gwrando? Neb heblaw amdano fe. Fe ofynnai am
arweiniad mewn gweddi daer.

Erbyn y bore, roedd Daniel wedi cael yr arweiniad roedd
e'n chwilio amdano ar ffurf breuddwyd. Ynddi gwelodd
ei hun yn adeiladu, nid arch, ond cwt tanddaearol, fel
byncyr adeg rhyfel, lle gallai fochel tra bod Duw yn carthu'r
byd o'r drygioni oedd ynddo, drwy ba bynnag ddull y
byddai'n ei ddewis, rhyw lif neu fom neu hyd yn oed bla.
Fe ofynnai i Enid ymuno ag e, er nad oedd e'n siŵr y dôi
hi chwaith; roedd hi wedi mynd yn ddieithr yn ddiweddar,
ers iddi fynd yn aelod mor selog yn Horeb. Fe lenwai'r cwt
â chymaint o fwyd ag y gallai, digon i bara am ddeugain
dydd a deugain nos. Byddai'n siŵr o gael cyngor ar y we
ar sut i godi adeilad diogel a ble i brynu'r deunyddiau.
Beth oedd yr ots am y gost? Cydiodd yn ei Feibl a dechrau
darllen yn uchel fel roedd Enid yn dod i mewn o'r clos
ar ôl bod yn gweithio ers oriau.

'Ewch i mewn trwy y porth cyfyng. Canys eang yw y porth
a llydan yw y ffordd sydd yn arwain i ddistryw;
a llawer yw y rhai sydd yn myned i mewn trwyddi.'

Edrychodd Enid yn syn arno. Ac yna'n syfrdan pan ofynnodd,

'A ddei di gyda fi drwy borth cyfyng y cwt tanddaearol
fydda i'n 'i adeiladu i gadw ni'n dou'n saff tra bydd Duw
yn carthu'r byd o'i lygredigaeth, fel nath e yn amser Noa?'

'A ti'n mynd i fynd â'r da i gyd i'r cwt hefyd? Heb sôn am
Bob y ci!?' meddai'n goeglyd.

Pendronodd Daniel am eiliad neu ddwy. 'Fe werthwn
ni'r stoc,' mynnodd.

'A'r ffarm?' holodd Enid yn obeithiol.

'Na, allwn ni ailafel yn y ffarm pan fydd y storom wedi cliro!'

'Yn dy ben di ma'r storom,' meddai Enid yn bigog, cyn
troi i wneud brecwast i un.

'Dy golled di fydd hi,' atebodd Daniel. 'Ond 'na fe, ti'n
ddigon hapus i fynd gyda'r llif, on'd wyt ti?' meddai, gan
ryfeddu at ei ffraethineb ei hun.

Aeth Daniel ati'n ddiwyd, heb boeni am ofyn caniatâd
gan neb i adeiladu'r cwt tanddaearol. Beth oedd y pwynt?
Fallai na fyddai Cyngor Tref na Dosbarth ar ôl wedi i'r
dinistr daro. Wedi'r cwbl, llond llaw o bobl lygredig oedd
yn rhedeg llefydd fel'na beth bynnag, felly beth yr ots am
eu barn nhw. Palodd y ddaear yn ffyrnig a gosod trawstiau
i ddal y to. Chwysodd waed i greu'r ddihangfa berffaith.
Yna, pan oedd yn hapus â diogelwch y cwt, llenwodd ef
â bwyd sych, bareli dŵr a thabledi puro dŵr i wneud yn
siŵr fod ganddo ddigon i'w yfed. Pan oedd e'n ffyddiog
fod y bibell awyru'n gweithio'n iawn, gadawodd y ffermdy
a mentro i'r cwt er mwyn cau'r drws ar y byd.

Y noson honno, yn y cwt, fe gysgodd fel twrch, cysgu'n

well nag roedd e wedi ei wneud ers tro. Drannoeth treuliodd y diwrnod yn darllen yng ngolau gwan y gannwyll ac yn hepian bob yn dipyn. Pan ddihunai, ac edrych ar ei watsh, doedd e ddim yn siŵr ai nos neu ddydd oedd hi, oedd doedd fawr o ots am hynny chwaith. Teimlai'n flinedig tu hwnt ag ystyried nad oedd e'n gwneud fawr ddim heblaw symud cam neu ddau, estyn bwyd neu ddiod a phori yn y Beibl. Llithrodd y dyddiau'n wythnosau, yn fisoedd efallai, doedd e ddim yn siŵr gan ei fod wedi colli pob trac o amser.

Yna un bore, barnodd ei fod wedi laru braidd ar y muriau cyfyng roedd e wedi eu codi o'i gwmpas. Tybed oedd hi'n ddiogel iddo ddod o'r cwt? Doedd ganddo ddim syniad sut fyd oedd ar y tu fas erbyn hyn. Penderfynodd droi at stori Noa unwaith eto i weld a gâi'r ysbrydoliaeth roedd ei angen arno yn y fan honno. Toc, fe'i cafodd. Roedd angen iddo chwilio am arwydd fod y byd yn ddiogel. Yn raddol, llusgodd ei gorpws gwanllyd at y drws ac ymdrechu i'w agor. O'r diwedd, ar ôl gwthio a thynnu a chwysu'n stecs, llwyddodd i wthio'i ben i olau dydd.

Y peth cynta a welodd ar ôl i'w lygaid gynefino â'r goleuni llachar, oedd dail gwyrdd ar y coed uwchben. Doedd yna ddim llif na chemegion wedi dinistrio natur beth bynnag. Blinciodd yn galed cyn edrych o'i gwmpas i weld fod porfa fras wedi tyfu dros y clos. Yna edrychodd ar y ffermdy a gweld rhyw olwg fach drist ar y lle, a'r drws wedi'i gau'n dynn. Llusgodd ei gorpws, gam wrth gam, tuag ato er mwyn chwilio am Enid.

'Enid, Enid!' gwaeddodd a churo ar y drws, ond heb gael ateb. Teimlad rhyfedd oedd cael ei gloi mas o'i garte ei hun. Os nad oedd Enid yn y ffermdy, ym mhle'r oedd hi? Doedd dim golwg o'r landrofyr, chwaith. Os oedd Daniel am fynd i chwilio am arwydd o fywyd, fe fyddai'n rhaid iddo gerdded.

Llusgodd ei goesau gwan, oedd mor stiff â phrocer ar hyd yr heol nes cyrraedd o'r diwedd safle hen gapel Ebenezer. Blinciodd unwaith eto. Gallai weld fod yr hen adeilad ar ei draed, ond edrychai'n wahanol iawn i sut yr edrychai cynt. Nid yr Ebenezer a gofiai oedd yr adeilad hwn. Ac nid capel oedd e, chwaith. Cartref oedd hwn. Camodd at y drws a dyrnu arno, yn marw o syched, yn wan fel pluen ac yn marw o eisiau bwyd. Roedd ei farf hir yn cosi'n ddifrifol yn y gwres. Chwiliodd yn ei ben am ryw eiriau Saesneg y byddai arno'u hangen i siarad â'r bobl o bell fyddai'n siŵr o fod yn berchen ar y lle. O'r diwedd, gwelodd, drwy drugaredd, gil y drws yn agor a dechreuodd ofyn, 'Could I please …?' cyn tagu a phesychu.

Erbyn hyn, roedd y drws ar agor led y pen ac o'i flaen safai menyw roedd e'n credu ei fod yn ei hadnabod.

'Enid …' mentrodd yn grug, gan flincio a rhwbio'i lygaid yn galed yn y golau llachar.

'Daniel …?' meddai'n syfrdan.

'Beth wyt ti'n neud fan hyn?' holodd Daniel.

'Fan hyn ma' 'nghartre i nawr,' atebodd Enid yn dyner.

'Ond…shwt allet ti ffwrdo hwn?' dechreuodd, cyn gweld wyneb lled-gyfarwydd arall yn llenwi'r drws, yn rhoi ei

fraich am ganol Enid a'i thynnu ato a gwenu gwên
fasonaidd ar Daniel.

'Prydderch!' sibrydodd yn gras.

Prydderch ac Enid. Ei Enid e!

Os nag oedd hi'n ddiwedd y byd ar y cwm ac ar Gymru,
roedd hi yn ddiwedd y byd ar Daniel.

*Brodor o Gefneithin, Sir Gâr, yw Delyth George sydd bellach
yn byw yng Nghaerdydd. Cyhoeddodd ddwy nofel, Gwe o
Gelwyddau ar gyfer oedolion, a Tebyg at ei Debyg? ar gyfer yr
arddegau. Mae hefyd wedi sgriptio ar gyfer rhaglenni teledu
yn cynnwys Pobol y Cwm ac Y Palmant Aur.*

O DDRWG I WAETH
gan Jon Gower

Roedd yr archdderwydd, Caswallon o Ferthyr, yn gynddeiriog. Ei ben yn borffor fel betys am fod ei bwysau gwaed reit lan i'r entrychion meddygol oherwydd y sefyllfa. Gallai gael *embolism* yn y fan a'r lle. Yn grac? Na. Yn grac a thri chwarter? Oedd, o oedd.

'Yffach gols ma' hyn yn mynd i droi'r Ŵyl mewn i siop siafins. Os 'ych chi'n cario mlaen 'da'r cynlluniau hynod ddwl yma bydd gen i ddim dewis ond ymddiswyddo'n syth. A byddaf yn mynd at y cyfryngau – coeliwch chi fi – er mwyn datgan y glir bod Trefnydd yr Eisteddfod Genedlaethol wedi troi'r wythnos bwysicaf yng nghalendr y genedl Gymraeg yn syrcas. Na, yn waeth na hynny, yn syrcas crap. Heb nag eliffant na chlown na rhyw foi o Rwsia mewn pants rhy dynn yn cerdded ar raff uwch eich pen. Am ffars! Beth sydd yn eich pen chi, Iestyn? Odych chi wedi mynd yn gyfan gwbl dwlali bost?'

'Mae'n flin gen i'ch bod chi wedi eich hypseto gymaint, Archdderwydd, ond y gwir yw bod 'na lot llai o arian ar gael nawr bod Brexit wedi dod â Phrydain i'w phengliniau, ac roedd Cymru fach yn ddigon tlawd cyn chwalfa ariannol dau ddeg un. Ond os yw arian yn brin, rhaid i ni fod yn fwy dyfeisgar ac yn hynod fwy creadigol. Gŵyl greadigol yw hi...'

'Dwi'n gwybod ni Iestyn. Paid bod yn nawddoglyd nawr...'

'Dwi'n bod yn bragmatydd. R'yn ni'n edrych am nawdd mewn ffordd greadigol. Does 'na ddim ceiniog goch yn dod o'r Llywodraeth ddim mwy. Dim yw dim. Felly does dim dewis 'da ni... Nid yw'r Llywodraeth yn medru fforddio talu am ysbytai, felly maen nhw wedi cefnu ar nifer fawr o'i pholisïau a'i haddewidion ac mae cyrraedd y miliwn o ran siaradwyr y Gymraeg wedi mynd i'r bin.'

'Ond y ddawns flodau? "Sponsored by Dutch Tulips of Amsterdam." Bydd Mrs Jones Llanrug yn gynddeiriog.'

'Beth sy'n bod ar hynny?'

'Ma' nhw eisiau lluniau mawr o tiwlips yn gefnlen i'r llwyfan.'

'Bydd hynny'n bert, Archdderwydd. Dod â sblash o liw ychwanegol i'r defodau... Rhai melyn a coch. Ugain troedfedd o uchder. Bydd yn gefnlen ddramatig.'

'Os 'ych chi eisiau gwerthu tiwlips. Ynte tiwlipiaid?'

'Tiwlipau. Ma' nhw yn flodau trawiadol.'

'A pheidiwch dweud, bydd y dawnswyr bach yn gwisgo lan fel tiwlipau? Odw i'n iawn?'

'Wel, mae'n rhaid i'r noddwyr gael rhywbeth 'nôl am eu harian.'

'Y ddawns flodau yw hi, nid dawns y blydi tiwlips. Byddai Iolo Morganwg yn troi yn ei fedd.'

'Chi'n gwybod, rwy'n credu byddai Iolo yn eistedd lan yn ei fedd ac yn dechrau clapo. Byddai fe'n hoffi'r syniad oherwydd ei fod e mor swreal.'

'Mae'n well na rhai o'r syniadau ddaeth gerbron, y math aeth yn syth i'r bin.'

'Y twba sbwriel.'

'Reit.'

'Iawn.'

Byddai'r Archdderwydd ac Iestyn yn chwarae'r em ping pong ieithyddol hon bob tro y byddent yn cwrdd, yr Arch yn chwifio baner ceidwadaeth a gwarchodaeth iaith tra bo Iestyn yn tanlinellu pwysigrwydd gweld yr iaith yn esblygu, yn newid gyda'r oes, yn hytrach na chael ei rhewi fel cleren mewn asbig. Ni fyddai'r Arch yn hoffi'r trosiad hwnnw, gan ei fod yn gyfieithiad llythrennol o 'like a fly in aspic', ond, fel mynnai Iestyn, dyna roedd e'n feddwl. Cleren. Mewn asbig.

'Ac am faint ma'r cytundeb yma gyda Dutch Tulips of Amsterdam fod i bara?'

'Dim ond pum mlynedd.'

'Pum mlynedd? Pum mlynedd! Esgusodwch fi os dwi'n tagu i farwolaeth ar y ffaith anhygoel hon. Pum mlynedd o'r dawnswyr bach yn gwisgo lan fel tiwlips. A faint mae'r cwmni 'ma'n talu am yr anrhydedd o weld yr holl diwlips yma'n cael hys-bys ar lwyfan y Brifwyl? Mil o bunnoedd? Dwy fil o bunnoedd?

'Hanner miliwn Ewro. Dros y cyfnod, hynny yw.'

'Wela' i.'

Setlodd y tawelwch. Safodd y ddau ddyn fel tasen nhw wedi'u parlysu.

Doedd neb yn cofio'r Archdderwydd yn mynd yn dawel

o'r blaen. Gallai drafod telynegion gyda'i geg yn llawn
Scotch Egg a gallai ddyfynnu barddoniaeth o fore gwyn
tan nos, hyd yn oed tra'n gyrru car, ond roedd y ffigwr
sylweddol hwn – echel ein diwylliant, bardd gorau ei
genhedlaeth – wedi troi'n fud fel mynach yn Fietnam.
Hanner miliwn. Cyndyn oedd i ddweud hyn ond
roedd sicrhau'r math hynny o arian yn gamp.

Arhosodd Iestyn, ar bigau'r drain, gan dybio, am fod yr
Archddwerwydd yn prosesu'r rhifau, na fyddai hynny'n
aros felly'n hir. Cliriodd yr Arch ei lwnc.

'Iawn, 'te. Bydd rhaid i ni dderbyn y newidiadau.
Mae'n swm sylweddol. Da iawn.'

Yn y gornel cofnododd Kevin y drafodaeth a'r ffordd
roedd gwreichion yn tasgu. Mae'n anodd i hanesydd
fyw drwy gyfnod hanesyddol heb fod eisiau ymyrryd
mewn rhyw ffordd ac, yn achos Kevin Price, nid oedd yn
dymuno gwybod am yr hanes hwnnw o gwbl, heb sôn
am fyw drwyddo. Kevin oedd croniclwr yr Eisteddfod
ddyddiau 'ma, olynydd y cawr hwnnw o Langennech,
Hywel Teifi Edwards, wrth iddo geisio deall gwleidyddiaeth
fewnol, ac arwyddocâd diwylliannol yr Ŵyl. Ac roedd
Kevin bellach yn croniclo dyddiau du, wrth i gymylau
lliw inc setlo dros y pafiliwn ac wrth i'r Steddfod fynd
i drafferth ryfedd oherwydd nawdd. Wedi sgrifennu'r
cofnod am y cyfarfod diweddar rhwng yr archdderwydd
a'r trefnydd i drafod nawdd o'r Iseldiroedd, ac yntau'n
gwybod, oherwydd iddo siarad gyda'r gŵr oedd yn codi
arian i'r Ŵyl, bod mwy o newyddion felly i ddod. Lot,

lot mwy. Oherwydd roedd y dyledion yn pentyrru
a'r gost o gynnal y Brifwyl yn codi'n ddyddiol bron,
wrth i chwyddiant yn y byd ôl-Brexit godi a chodi a
chodi. Ysgrifennodd ar ei liniadur cledr-llaw y geiriau
anhanesyddyddol hyn… "Nid dyddiau du ond dyddiau
hynod ddu, fel pe bai'r cofiadur yn arbrofi 'da crac cocên
am y tro cyntaf ac yn dihuno mewn bola buwch neu ar
waelod pydew neu ogof ddiwaelod." Ie, nid trafferthion
mawr ond trafferthion enfawr, oll yn cael eu storio yn
ei gyfrifiadur maint cledr llaw wrth i Kevin groniclo.
Iddo ddeall y sefyllfa'n iawn, roedd yn rhaid mynd
'nôl i ddiwrnod y penderfyniad tyngedfennol. Yn yr
hen ddyddiau, fyddai neb yn disgwyl i Lys yr Orsedd
bleidleisio o blaid derbyn nawdd gan William Hill The
Bookmakers, a hynny er mwyn trefnu gamblo ar y prif
gystadlaethau, ond oherwydd effaith hirdymor Brexit,
roedd arian yn hynod, hynod brin ac felly bu'n rhaid
derbyn nawdd o lefydd na fydden nhw'n disgwyl o gwbl
flynyddoedd yn ôl, y math o lefydd fyddai'n gwneud i
Crwys ac Elfed a Gwenallt droi yn eu beddau. Megis
newid yr enw. Yr enw, cofiwch chi.
Yn dilyn sgandalau enwi Stadiwm y Mileniwm yn
Stadiwm y Principality ac yna yn 2026 unwaith 'to
i'r Poundstretchers Stadium, a chan gofio'r seremoni
rwysgfawr i enwi Pont Hafren ar ôl yr hen frenin Carlo
– the King Charles Anglo-Welsh Bridge – bu'n rhaid i'r
Eisteddfod Genedlaethol dderbyn arian sylweddol, dim
llai na miliwn o bunnoedd, ar yr amod ei bod yn newid yr

enw i Greggs the Bakers Welsh National Show, gafodd ei dalfyrru gan y papurau tabloid megis y *Mirror* a'r *Sun* i'r Welsh Nash o fewn chwinciad. Ac fe werthwyd hawliau enwi eraill oedd yn gysylltiedig â'r Steddfod i nifer o gwmnïau eraill hefyd. Trodd y Babell Lên yn The Waterstones Literary Tent.

"Nid *tent* mo'r Babell Lên!" gwaeddodd mynychwyr selog y Babell, wrth iddynt hwy gynnal protest, ond ni lwyddasant â chadw'r fangre rhag cael ei bedyddio gan y llyfrwerthwyr a'u llyfr siec. Llosgodd sawl aelod o'r Orsedd eu gwisgoedd seremonïol yn fyw ar raglen *Prynhawn Da*, ond aeth y stynt yn angof ar ôl i'r tân gynnau yn y stiwdio, gan adael i'w gwylwyr weld yr injan dan yn cyrraedd reit ynghanol y gystadleuaeth, a fflamau'n tasgu lan tua'r camerâu.

Ond aeth pethau o ddrwg i waeth. Fel petasai hynny'n bosib mewn gwirionedd. Roedd hyn yn gyson gyda newid y rheol Gymraeg, wnaeth achosi rhwyg nid yn unig o fewn Senedd yr Orsedd ond drwy'r Gymdeithas Gymraeg yn gyfan gwbl; y to ifanc gyfan-gwbl ddwyieithog yn hapus â'r drefn, ac yn ei gweld fel ffordd o groesawu yn hytrach nag amddifadu cynulleidfa, tra bo'r bobl hŷn yn dadlau'n gryf dros ei chadw hi'n ŵyl Gymraeg, gan ofyn os nad oedd hi'n bosib cadw'r Ŵyl yn uniaith Gymraeg, pa obaith cadw'r winllan rhag sathriadau'r moch? Moch Seisnig megis Tamworths neu Berkshires neu Gloucester Old Spots, yn trwfflan drwy'r winllan gan fwyta gwreiddiau pob peth.

Dyna'r broblem gyda moch – eu diffyg parch tuag at
wreiddiau, tuag at wareiddiad.

Ond arian enillodd y dydd, oherwydd fel roedd Kevin
wedi esbonio yn ei ddadansoddiad, roedd arian yn brin
iawn, a'r Deyrnas Unedig wedi troi'n Deyrnas Ranedig
tu hwnt, nawr bod yr Alban annibynnol yn cael aros yn
Ewrop a Gogledd Iwerddon ar ei ffordd yn glir i uno
gyda'r Weriniaeth i greu un Ynys Werdd. A Chymru fach,
wel…gwinllan a ddifrodwyd yw Cymru fy ngwlad.

Aeth blwyddyn arall heibio, a chyfarfodydd y Trefnydd
a'r Archdderwydd yn dechrau dilyn patrwm chwedl felly.
Cyfarfod, yna rhyw sialens fawr yn ystod treigl y flwyddyn
ac yna cytundeb i gwrdd unwaith yn rhagor. Ond y tro
hwn ni allai'r Arch gredu'r syniad, i gynnal yr Ŵyl yn sir
Benfro. Er, nid Sir Benfro oedd yn achosi'r anghrediniaeth,
o na. Y ffaith ei bod hi'n mynd i ddigwydd nid ar y tir mawr
ond ar ynysoedd Sir Benfro, ac ar ben hynny, ym mis Medi.
'Mis Medi, Iestyn. Ma'r Steddfod wastad yn digwydd yn
wythnos lawn gyntaf mis Awst. Byth yn newid, Iestyn.
'Na beth yw traddodiad hirhoedlog. Ac mae traddodiad
yn bwysig. Allwch chi adeiladu ar draddodiad, mae e
fel craig, tra bo newydd-deb yn rhywbeth bas, rhywbeth
dros-dro, fel adeiladu pyramid ar y tywod.' Cyndyn oedd
Iestyn i ddweud fod yr Eifftiaid wedi codi pyramidiau ar
y tywod, ond gallai weld o liw croen yr Archdderwydd –
ei fochau 'run lliw â grawnwin Sauvignon – taw nid
nawr oedd yr amser i ddweud hynny a gwneud i'w
bwysau gwaed fynd lan nes i'w benglog fostio fel balŵn.

'Allwn ni ddim newid dyddiadau'r Eisteddfod i fis Medi. Pam, yn enw'r tad?'

'Oherwydd yr adar.'

'Peidiwch â dweud ein bod ni'n dibynnu ar dymhor nythu Adar Rhiannon nawr.'

Credai'r Arch bod ganddo jôcs da, ond nid oedd hyn yn wir.

'Oherwydd bydd yr adar sy'n nythu ar Sgogwm a Sgomer wedi gadael erbyn hynny… y llurs, y gwylog ac adar drycin Manaw.'

'A pham 'yn ni hyd yn oed yn ystyried y fath Ŵyl anghonfensiynol?'

'Oherwydd mae cwmni olew yn fodlon noddi'r bali lot.'

'Ma' hynny fel derbyn arian gan Beelzebub yntydi?'

Edrychodd Iestyn yn syn.

'Y diafol, enw arall ar y diafol."

Diolch byth fod y tywydd wedi bod yn dda, a bod pob cyngor sir wedi rhoi caniatâd i ysgolion ddechrau 'nol wythnos yn hwyrach wedi gwyliau'r haf er mwyn gadael i bawb fynychu'r Ŵyl, a bod gweld baneri'r Ŵyl yn chwifio yn awel gref yr Iwerydd yn wych, a phawb, gan gynnwys synics mwya'r cyfryngau, yn synnu i weld bod y trefniadau i gludo pobl 'nôl a blaen ar gychod fferi oedd wedi hwylio draw yn unswydd o Albania er mwyn gwneud, wedi gweithio fel watsh.

Dyma'r tro cyntaf i'r Babell Lên neu'r Literary Tent godi yng ngerddi goleudy, a thawelodd Cymdeithas Edward Llwyd dipyn ynglŷn â thwpdra cynnal rhywbeth fel hyn ar warchodfa natur genedlaethol, ar ôl i'w haelodaeth ddyblu erbyn y dydd Mercher a threblu erbyn y dydd Iau. Nid oedd yn bosib cynnal cyngherddau gyda'r nos yn y Pafiliwn oherwydd y llanw a'r trai a pheryglon cael pobl yn ddiogel oddi ar y fferi gan ddefnyddio'r llynges o gychod bach i'w cludo i'r mannau glanio ar yr ynysoedd, ond cynhaliwyd y rhain ar lecyn mawr o dir ger pentre Marloes.

Ail-ffurfiodd Y Cyrff gyda nawdd gan Sanatogen Tonic Wine a llwyddodd Edward H. Dafis – ambell aelod nawr ymhell dros gant oed – i gofio geiriau eu caneuon mwyaf poblogaidd mewn cyngerdd mawreddog wedi ei noddi gan Stannah Stairlifts, neu Lifftrisiau Stannah, fel y bloeddiodd yr hysbysebion mawrion ar y ffordd i mewn i Sir Benfro. O, roedd hi'n Ŵyl a hanner, y math fyddai'n byw yn y cof tan i chi lithro bant o'r dwthwn hwn.

Daeth yr amser i'r Archdderwydd gwrdd â'r Trefnydd am eu cyfarfod blynyddol. Ond y tro hwn roedd mwy o bobl yno, ac yn eu plith Kevin yn croniclo.

Bu'r pennaeth marchnata'n brysur. *'We've arranged TV rights with Sky for the Chair and the Crown and people will be able to bet right up to the beginning of the adjudication,'* dywedodd y dyn o William Hill, sef dyn o'r enw William Hill – oedd yn medru drysu pobl.

'Odych chi wir yn meddwl bydd pobl yn betio ar ganlyniad cystadlaethau barddol?' gofynnodd yr Archdderwydd drwy gyfieithydd.

'Oh, people will bet on anything. We cleaned up at Crufts Dog Show, with one bet of two hundred thousand pounds on

whether a toy chihuaha would be placed fifth. People take these things very seriously.'

'Ond mae pob ymgeisydd yn y Steddfod yn ddi-enw. Mae'n rhaid i chi gael enw ffug, *nom de plume,* fel byddai'r Brenin Louis'n dweud.

Os taw Eisteddfod Genedlaethol Caerdydd a'r Cylch yn 2018 oedd y mwyaf llwyddianus yn hanes y Brifwyl, sdim dwywaith taw'r un ugain mlynedd yn ddiweddarch yn y brifddinas oedd yr gwaethaf, oherwydd y penderfyniad i gynnwys betio, yn ôl un o'i selogion mwyaf. Oherwydd, yn sgil y penderfyniad, daeth twyll a thrais …

Dyma beth oedd gan Kevin y croncilwr i'w ddweud am un digwyddiad annisgwyl iawn…

Eisteddai'r Prifardd Iestyn Tyne yn ei ystafell ffrynt llawn Cadeiriau Eisteddfod, set o ddwsin ohonynt, wedi'u trefnu o gwmpas hen fwrdd snwcer wedi'i addasu'n un celficyn sylweddol. Darllenai gyfrol gan Yeats, un o'i hoff feirdd yn yr iaith fain. Chwibanai'r gwynt drwy'r simnai a thrwy ffan y ffwrn ond tu allan roedd 'na sŵn estron, rhywbeth yn cwympo neu, yn wir, sŵn rhyw berson yn cwympo, ac yna ochenaid, cyn bod llais yn arllwys un llif o regfeydd. Ni allaf eu rhestru nhw yma, ond roedd ambell un yn ddychmygus ar y naw, gan gyfuno'r rhywiol a'r annuwiol yn un. Yna ffrwydrodd gwydr y drws cefn yn gawod o ddiemwntau bach cyn bod dau ddyn yn cerdded i mewn gan wisgo sanau dros eu hwynebau, fel giangstas o oes yr efeilliaid Kray.

'You Tyne?'

'I am.'

'The poet.'

'Tyne the poet, yes.'

'Then we need a word...' dywedodd y dyn gan hisian yn fygythiol drwy ei fwgwd neilon.

Pwrpas yr ymweliad oedd gwneud yn siŵr na fyddai'r bardd yn ennill ei drydedd Gadair yn olynol, gan esbonio y byddai'n rhaid iddo gynnwys gwallau a fyddai'n annerbyniol hyd yn oed i'r beirniad mwyaf graslon.

'And what if I don't?' meddai'r bardd yn heriol.

'Then people will be hurt. In fact poets – plural – will be hurt, so bear that it mind.'

Pan adawodd y ddau glown, cysylltodd Iestyn â'i frawd ar Skype i drafod y bygythiad, ond hefyd i chwilio am gyngor ynglŷn â beth i'w wneud.

Roedd ei frawd wedi edrych ar safle we'r bwcis yn barod ac wedi gweld bod yr ods yn erbyn ei frawd i ennill yn dal yr un peth, tra bo ambell fardd tipyn llai amlwg, megis Cynddeiriog Ifans, wedi symud o gant i un i dri chant i un, gan awgrymu bod 'na arian mawr i'w wneud petasai hwnnw'n ennill.

'Ma' gen i syniad bod ein hymwelwyr anghwrtais a bygythiol yn credu bod Mr Ifans yn mynd i ennill. Digon posib eu bod nhw wedi noblo pawb arall ar y rhestr.'

'Byddai hynny fel bygwth hanner aelodau Barddas. Sdim lot ohonom ni feirdd sy'n ddigon da i ennill.'

'Pwy sydd i ddweud nad yw safon y gystadleuaeth ar

fin gostwng yn sylweddol…?'

'Beth ti'n awgrymu, brawd?'

'Gwell i ti sgrifennu'r gerdd waethaf wyt ti erioed wedi'i sgrifennu. Jest i fod yn saff.

'Ond bydd pawb yn wherthin am fy mhen?'

'O leiaf byddi di'n medru clywed sŵn y chwerthin. Nid yw hynny'n bosib o oerfel y bedd.'

"Rili Gwil, oes angen bod mor felodramatig?'

'Mae arian mawr yn cyfnewid dwylo. Pobl yn betio ar y gadair mor bell â'r Phillipines, a sawl syndicet betio yn dysgu Cymraeg er mwyn deall beth yw beth a phwy yw pwy.'

'Ti'n jocan?'

Ond doedd e ddim.

Ffenomen anesboniadwy oedd yr hyn a ddigwyddodd pan ddaeth betio i mewn i gystadlaethau'r Ŵyl. Mewn cyfweliad ar gyfer *Russia Today* gofynnwyd i groniclwr yr Eisteddfod esbonio pam fod hawliau teledu i'r prif seremonïau wedi gwerthu am fwy na'r Superbowl y flwyddyn honno.

'Efallai bod pobl yn chwilio am rywbeth gwahanol,' atebodd Kevin. 'Un peth sydd wedi helpu yw'r ffaith nad yw Llywodraeth Cymru yn codi treth ar fetio, yn wahanol i bob gwlad arall yn y byd, oherwydd eu bod nhw wedi gweld bod creu nifer fawr iawn o swyddi yn y byd betio yn well i'w coffrau na chodi treth yn y ffordd gonfensiynol. Ond yn sicr, mae betio wedi cydio yn yr Eisteddfod. Mae 'da ni gyfnewidfa arian ein hunain ar y Maes ac mae pum llond awyren wedi cyrraedd maes awyr Caerdydd o'r Dwyrain Canol yn unig. Mae cwmni Emirates wedi trefnu bod awyren ychwanegol yn dod mewn i'r maes awyr bob dydd, gan gysylltu â Schiphol a Doha. Mae pob stafell westy yn ne a chanolbarth Cymru'n llawn. Glywais i am un boi yn Nhrelluest oedd yn codi mil y noson ar rywun er mwyn cysgu yn ei garej a hynny neb frecwast.'

'A dwi'n deall bod nifer fawr o'r ymwelwyr yma'n dysgu Cymraeg,' gofynnodd newyddiadurwraig *Russia Today* yn ei Chymraeg gorau, hithau'i hunan yn dystiolaeth bod rhywbeth mawr ar droed.

'Ac mae'r Athro Emeritws Dylan Foster Evans yn y Brifysgol yn trefnu gwersi trochi iaith i ugain mil ohonynt. Ugain mil! Es draw 'na ddoe a chlywais i ddeg gŵr busnes o Loughborough yn cynnal cystadleuaeth i adrodd cerddi gan Cynan ar gof.'

'Ac wrth gwrs, roedd 'na fetio ar hyn?'

'Mae pobl yn betio ar bopeth. Mae e fel 'se nhw'n caru dau beth – yr iaith Gymraeg a gamblo.'

'Ac r'ych chi'n hapus 'da hyn?'

'Os taw dyma beth sydd ei angen i achub yr iaith hyfrydaf yn y byd, wel…'

Roedd Iestyn Tyne wedi gorffen ei gerdd a'i hanfon yn electronig i'r swyddfa. Y dyddiau hyn gallech anfon eich gwaith hyd at wythnos cyn yr Ŵyl, oherwydd byddai cyfrifiadur yn tsieco'r gwaith i ddechrau cyn ei fod yn cyrraedd llaw'r beirniaid. Ond oherwydd y beto, ac i leihau'r siawns fod rhywun yn cael cyfle i noblo'r beirniad,

roedd enwau'r rhain yn anhysbys. Ond roedd Kevin yn
gwybod pwy oedd wrthi'n beirniadu eleni, a'r tri ohonynt
yn derbyn tri deg mil yr un am y gwaith. Meddyliodd
am arwyddocâd y symiau mawr hyn wrth iddo gerdded
ar draws y Maes, gan weld y baneri enfawr yn hedfan
fry uwchben yn bloeddio'r geiriau mawr 'Greggs the
Bakers Welsh Nash' tra bo awyren yn hedfan dros erwau
dŵr croyw Bae Caerdydd yn tynnu rhuban hysbysebu'r
gwasanaeth betio arlein newydd Bardd-bleidlais/Poet-vote.
Instant win £250,000. Chwarter miliwn o bunnoedd.
Mwy nag y gallai gamblwr cyffredin ennill ar y Derby,
Cwpan Aur Cheltenham a'r Grand National gyda'i gilydd.
Aeth pobl yn wallgo. Gamblo, gamblo, gamblo. Ar
dudalen flaen y *Racing Post* yr wythnos honno, gwelwyd
lluniau deg o feirdd amlycaf Cymru.

Gwawriodd dydd y Cadeirio gan ledaenu tensiwn drwy
galonnau nifer o'r rhai fyddai'n ymweld â'r Pafiliwn. Bu'r
bois drwg yn ymweld â beirdd ymhob cwr o Gymru, gan
fygwth hwn a'r llall. Aeth stori ar led bod nifer o brifeirdd
a beirdd da wedi dihuno i gwrdd â phâr o gorilas allan
o ffilm megis *Goodfellas*, tra bod rhai o'r clerwyr llai abl
wedi cael eu hysgogi i hala stwff i mewn hyd yn oed os
nad oedd y gwaith yn ddestlus, na heb ei gwblhau, hyd yn
oed. Cynhaliwyd cyfarfod brys ond cyfrin o Barddas yn
ogof Llywelyn ger afon Gwy yn Aberedw, a phawb mewn
cyfyng-gyngor, a rhai yn byw mewn ofn – ofn pur, y math
o ofn mae bardd yn teimlo pan mae'n gweld baril dryll yn
sgleinio yn y nos.

Gallai unrhyw un weld i ba gyfeiriad roedd pethau'n mynd pan roedd yr ods ar fardd cloff fel Stan Ishmael yn newid bron yn feunyddiol heb unrhyw arwydd fod ei grefft a'i ddawn wedi gwella. Hanner awr cyn y seremoni, pan roedd y betio'n cau'n swyddogol, gallech gael 2000-1 ar Stan, gyda'r holl sylwebyddion yn dweud na allai ef sgrifennu cwpled, heb sôn am awdl. Ond roedd arian mawr yn mynd ar Stan – nid miloedd ond miliynau.

Fel y gallech ddisgwyl, roedd Theatr Donald Gordon dan ei sang, a rhai pobl wedi prynu'r seddi drud ar gefn y llwyfan, gyda thocynnau i'r rhain yn cyfnewid dwylo am hyd at fil o bunnoedd yr un. Aeth ton o ryddhad drwy'r dorf o glywed fod 'na deilyngdod, a sŵn fel gollwng yr aer o deiars car wrth i bawb anadlu'n ddwfn. Diffoddwyd goleuadau'r theatr gan adael i'r llifoleuadau oleuo'r dorf fel dawns, sioe *son et lumiere* syml ac effeithiol.

"Ar sŵn yr utgyrn a wnaiff Iago Prytherch sefyll ar ei draed?' A dyma ddyn reit lawr yn y ffrynt yn sefyll ar ei draed a'r goleuadau'n chwilio amdano ar yr un pryd ag roedd y dorf yn ceisio chwilio amdano. Setlodd y llif-olau arno fe, ond erbyn hynny roedd rhywun arall ar ei draed rhyw bum rheng o seddi tu ôl iddo, a dyma feirdd eraill ar eu traed… yr holl feirdd o'r cyfarfod yn yr ogof gyfrin 'sha glannau Gwy – na, yn fwy na hynny, holl aelodaeth Barddas; na, mwy na hynny hyd yn oed. Bu'n rhaid i'r osgordd newid patrwm ac arwain y chwe deg, saith deg bardd yma i'r llwyfan fel arwain dawns conga araf ac urddasol.

Ac wrth iddyn nhw sefyll ar y llwyfan dyma'r

archdderwydd yn esbonio bod pob bardd wedi cyfrannu llinell yr un a bod hwn yn gywaith go iawn, ac er nad oedd y rheolau'n caniatáu hyn fel arfer, roedd Sanhedrin y Steddfod wedi creu rheol newydd. Felly nid un bardd, ond ciwed go iawn o feirdd wnaeth ennill, gan herio'r gangstars a'r syndicets gamblo a phawb oedd am droi'r gynghanedd yn ddim byd mwy na chyfres o ods.

Safodd y beirdd yn un llinell, eu pennau i fyny, ac yn llawn balchder ffit i fostio. Dyma fyddai pobl yn cofio am Eisteddfod eleni. Y beirdd, yn un rhes, unwaith eto'n herio'r drefn.

Y flwyddyn ganlynol stopiodd William Hill the Bookmakers noddi'r Ŵyl, ond llwyddwyd i gael swm bach teidi gan Fenter Iaith Los Angeles. A daeth gwahoddiad i'r Ŵyl fynd i dde Califfornia 'fyd. A bu trafodaeth frwd ar y pwnc, o do, dan arweinyddiaeth yr Archdderwydd newydd, gan fod yr hen un wedi mynd i Nursing Home, ac yntau ond yn ddeugain oed. Y straen, chi'n deall. Yr holl newidiadau a datblygiadau.

Ac yno byddai'n mwmblan rhywbeth am y beirdd i gyd wrth unrhyw un a fyddai'n gwrando, yr hen Arch yn eu cofio nhw'n sefyll yno wrth ei ymyl, dan yr holl oleuadau. Y beirdd, gwarchodwyr y gynghanedd, symffonïwyr sŵn a melodi geiriol. Cynheiliaid ein traddodiad hynotaf. Sara Borda Green. Aneirin Karadog. Miriam Elin Jones. Eirug Salisbury. Elan Grug Muse. Iestyn Tyne. Y bytholwyrdd Mererid Hopwood. Twm Morys. Hywel Griffiths. Morgan Owen. A'r un 'na gyda'r het wen am

ei ben. Yn un rhes, balchder yn eu glynu wrth ei gilydd.
Mewn undod mae nerth, meddyliodd y cyn-Archdderwydd,
wrth iddo lwyddo i gyrraedd darn clir ynghanol dryswch a
mieri gardd wyllt ei feddwl. Cofiodd hefyd y byddai nyrs
yma cyn hir, gyda bisgedi o Lidl. Gweddïai y byddai 'na
Fig Rolls, ei ffefryn ymhlith y ffefrynnau. Gallai ddarllen
y Cyfansoddiadau a Beirniadaethau wedyn. A'u dysgu
nhw, gair am air, gan fod ganddo'r amser.

*Mae Jon Gower wedi cyhoeddi sawl cyfrol o straeon byrion,
pentwr bach o nofelau ac amrywiaeth o lyfrau hanes ynghyd â
chyfrolau teithio a seico-ddaeryddiaeth. Mae ei nofel newydd
Y Düwch yn wahanol i'r rhain i gyd, gan ei bod yn dywyll
iawn, gyda seico go iawn ynddi.*

The Birthday Present

BARBARA VINE

PENGUIN BOOKS

PENGUIN BOOKS

Published by the Penguin Group
Penguin Books Ltd, 80 Strand, London WC2R 0RL, England
Penguin Group (USA) Inc., 375 Hudson Street, New York, New York 10014, USA
Penguin Group (Canada), 90 Eglinton Avenue East, Suite 700, Toronto, Ontario, Canada M4P 2Y3
(a division of Pearson Penguin Canada Inc.)
Penguin Ireland, 25 St Stephen's Green, Dublin 2, Ireland
(a division of Penguin Books Ltd)
Penguin Group (Australia), 250 Camberwell Road, Camberwell, Victoria 3124, Australia
(a division of Pearson Australia Group Pty Ltd)
Penguin Books India Pvt Ltd, 11 Community Centre, Panchsheel Park, New Delhi – 110 017, India
Penguin Group (NZ), 67 Apollo Drive, Rosedale, North Shore 0632, New Zealand
(a division of Pearson New Zealand Ltd)
Penguin Books (South Africa) (Pty) Ltd, 24 Sturdee Avenue, Rosebank, Johannesburg 2196, South Africa

Penguin Books Ltd, Registered Offices: 80 Strand, London WC2R 0RL, England

www.penguin.com

First published by Viking 2008
Published in Penguin Books 2009
001

Copyright © Kingsmarkham Enterprises Ltd, 2008

The moral right of the author has been asserted

Typeset by Rowland Phototypesetting Ltd, Bury St Edmunds, Suffolk
Printed in Great Britain by Clays Ltd, St Ives plc

A CIP catalogue record for this book is available from the British Library

ISBN: 978-0-241-97237-3

www.greenpenguin.co.uk

MIX
Paper from
responsible sources
FSC
www.fsc.org   FSC™ C018179

Penguin Books is committed to a sustainable
future for our business, our readers and our planet.
This book is made from Forest Stewardship
Council™ certified paper.

To Simon and Donna, Phillip and Graham

Acknowledgements

My gratitude is due to Alan Howarth for his invaluable help in gently setting so many parliamentary details right for me and to Richard Acton, as always, for his excellent copy-editing.

I

Thirty-three is the age we shall all be when we meet in heaven because Christ was thirty-three when he died. It's an interesting idea. One can't help thinking that the people who invent these things chose it because it's an ideal age, no longer one's first youth but not ageing either. It was Sandy Caxton who told me this when I sat next to him at Ivor's birthday dinner, his thirty-third of course, and Ivor said afterwards that he had a store of that sort of wisdom. My own opinion is that Sandy was just changing the subject because I'd asked him if he lived in London.

'I'm awfully sorry,' he said, 'but I can't tell you that.' And, noticing my mystified look, 'I used to be the Northern Ireland Secretary, you see, and we're not supposed to tell anyone where we live.'

I did see. I should have known. Ivor told me there was even a bodyguard somewhere at the party and wherever it was that Sandy lived the police with sniffer dogs searched the local church before he went to matins. Not that it did him any good in the end. They still got him at the time they chose. But more of that later. Iris had been sitting next to Ivor's friend Jack Munro, a favourite of hers, and it was rather reluctantly that she said goodbye to him as we had to leave before the others. We had a trustworthy babysitter but we wanted to get back to Nadine. She was our first child, the first of our four, and we were both so besotted that we fretted if we were away from her for long. Even to celebrate her uncle's heavenly birthday. Even when she was in the care of one of her grandmothers.

There was one person close to Ivor (in a manner of speaking) absent from the party.

'Ivor's girlfriend wasn't there,' I said as we were going up Fitz-john's Avenue.

'She wouldn't have been asked. You know Ivor. In some ways he's living in the distant past. One doesn't invite the mistress to meet one's friends.' Iris made the face she always used to make when her brother's peculiarities came up, her smile a little rueful. 'Besides, having to spend an evening out with her instead of in with her he'd think a waste of time.'

'It's like that, is it?'

'It's probably only like that,' she said.

Mention his name and most people will say, 'Who?' while the rest think for a bit and ask if he wasn't 'the one who got involved in all that sleaze back in whenever it was . . .'

Necessarily, because my brother-in-law was a politician through and through, I'll have to talk about politics. But increasingly I find how ignorant I am and how much the minutiae of politics bore me. I shall gloss over a great deal of this aspect of Ivor's life, only touching on what I hope are the interesting bits and, of course, because no one could speak of this period and leave them out, the departure of Margaret Thatcher, the coming of John Major and the general elections of 1992 and 1997.

I'm putting in Jane Atherton's diary. Not just some of it but the whole thing as it was sent to Juliet. Ivor's history and, come to that, Hebe Furnal's wouldn't be complete without it. The package arrived and then a letter under separate cover, as they say. Ivor never saw either. I don't suppose he even knew of the existence of the diary. Too much had happened to him for any more risk-taking and he was keeping his head buried in the sand. Jane was a friend of Hebe's and about as unlike her, it seems, as two female creatures belonging to the same species and living in the same time can be unlike each other. I suppose she was of use to Hebe. Whatever else she may have done for her, apart from filling a role as foil to her particular charms, she provided her with alibis. The chances are that if she hadn't agreed to provide a certain alibi, none of this would have happened.

I never met Hebe. I never even saw her. Like the rest of the world, I saw her picture in the papers after the accident, a pretty blonde, almost beautiful, with the looks of a model. And, also like the rest of the world, I confuse her with the other pretty blonde, the one the men thought they were taking when they took her, or the police or the press thought they were taking when they took her. The mystery of which girl was the intended victim was never publicly solved. How angry it made Ivor that anyone could mistake Hebe Furnal for Kelly Mason, though it seemed at first to his advantage that they did, as the assumption made by the police (or the press) moved the spotlight away from its search for him. And that's the way I see it, as if a torch was held in a hand which glanced probingly over dark corners, seeking for an instigator, its light once or twice nearly touching him before it shifted away.

Hebe Furnal, twenty-seven years old, a housewife with a degree in media something or other and a two-year-old son called Justin. Wife of Gerry Furnal and mistress of Ivor Tesham, MP. 'Mistress' is a bit of an archaism, but Iris used it and Ivor himself did when, a week or two after the thirty-third birthday, he asked me if I thought he should buy a flat for Hebe and visit her there. He would occasionally ask my advice, though of course he never took any notice of it. People don't, especially when they've asked for it. Anyway, Ivor had already made up his mind.

'In some ways,' he said, 'the idea appeals. You can imagine in what ways. But I don't think I will. It's too much like some eighteenth-century rake setting up his mistress in apartments in Shepherd Market.'

'You can't afford Shepherd Market,' I said.

'True. But I could afford Pimlico, say. Only I won't. It would lead to other complications.'

There was more of this but I'll come back to it. As to Kelly Mason, she was the 'Checkout Chick', the 'Supermarket Cinderella', who had married a television mogul and was famous for doing nothing but wearing blue satin with sequins and *not* being kidnapped. Where is she now? Rumour has it that she's in a private psychiatric hospital, but a more likely story has her and her carers in the isolated villa on the South Pacific island her husband bought for her. Whichever it is, it seems to be true that she is hidden away because she is too afraid to live in the world, and without Ivor's intervention in her life, unintentional though it was, she would be the happy occupant of a house in the Bishops Avenue and perhaps the mother of Damian Mason's children.

To introduce you to Ivor – you may not remember him from the days when he was a minister in John Major's government – I don't think I can do better than give you his entry in *Dod's*, the directory of Members of Parliament:

Ivor Hamilton Tesham, Born 12 January 1957. Son of John Hamilton Tesham and Louisa, née Winstanley; Educated Eton College, Windsor; Brasenose College, Oxford (MA law); Single; Called to the Bar 1980, Lincoln's Inn; Barrister specializing in Commercial Law. Contested Overbury 1987 general election; Member for Morningford since by-election 27 January 1988. Committees: Foreign Affairs, Defence; PPS in 1989 to John Teague: as Secretary of State for Defence; in 1990 Under-Secretary of State in the Department of Defence; in 1992 Minister of State for Air Power Overseas in the Department of Defence; Recreations: Theatre, music, reading; Address: House of Commons, London SW1.

I've known him since he was a small boy in Ramburgh and I was five years older. Though we moved away when I was eight, I was born in that village, as were Ivor and my wife. They look a lot alike, Ivor and Iris, and he is three years her senior. They are both tall and dark and slender. Sandy Caxton said Iris had the face of an Israelite princess, Rachel weeping for her children, though the only Jewish blood she and Ivor have came into the family in the early nineteenth century. I'm told Ivor was very good-looking, but I'm no judge of that. When he and I walked into a restaurant or a bar together I've seen women turn and look, and I'm pretty sure they weren't staring at me.

When all this happened he had been 'seeing' (as he put it) Hebe Furnal for about a year. Prior to that an actress called Nicola Ross had been his girlfriend and when the end came they parted amicably. I don't know why they did or why it was amicable, though Iris told me it had nothing to do with Hebe's coming on the scene. She seemed to think the Nicola Ross affair wasn't exciting enough for Ivor. They were both single and unattached. Some said they were made for each other. Nicola, who he always called Nixie, was a suitable woman for an MP to be going about with, a handsome blonde with an increasingly successful career, a year or two older than he. He had even taken her to Ramburgh House to meet his parents, but he had never quite reached the point of moving in with her or asking her to move in with him. That was his way, though. He had never lived with a woman. Then came the break-up and Hebe Furnal. When he asked if he could borrow our house (for a never fully explained purpose) he told me how they had met.

'It was at a reception in the Jubilee Room,' he said. 'I don't know if you've ever been in there. It's up a grim sort of flight of stairs at the far end of Westminster Hall. We were waiting for the seven o'clock vote and I'd nothing to do. Jack Munro said why not come along to this reception. It was being given in aid of a charity called HALT, the Heart and Lung Trust.'

'I heard someone make one of those appeals for them on the radio,' I said.

'Yes, well, Jack said I might as well come along and get a free drink, which means the gnat's piss which passes for Sauvignon in the Jubilee Room. Anyway, I went. The HALT fund-raiser's a man called Gerry Furnal, but I never met him. I met his wife instead.'

He smiled that little reminiscent smile of his.

'Go on,' I said.

'You know how these things sort of hit you. She's got the most amazing legs, as long as some women are high, if you see what I mean. And a lot of other things too. Her hair's a very pale blonde and it reaches to her waist. I didn't lose any time. I went up to her and said, "Ivor Tesham. How do you do?" and she said, "Hebe Furnal. I do very well, thanks, a lot better than I did five minutes ago." Here was a woman after my own heart, I thought, so I

5

pointed to the monitor up on the wall and I said, "You see that green screen up there? Well, in about five minutes a bell will come up on that, the word 'Division' will appear in white letters and I'll have to go and vote." "Then I'd better give you my phone number, hadn't I?" she said. "Have you got a good memory?" "Marvellous," I said, and just as she gave it to me the green bell appeared. I ran down the stairs and all the way across Westminster Hall, repeating that phone number over and over, with the division bell ringing, and I leapt up the stairs and along the corridor into the Members' Lobby. I was still saying that number in my head as I went to vote, but I picked up a bit of paper as I passed through and wrote it down.

'And that was the start of it. I phoned her next day. We manage to meet about once a fortnight and I'm going to have to do something about that, but meanwhile will you lend me your house for a Friday night somewhere around 17 May?'

'Sure,' I said. 'We always go to Norfolk on Fridays anyway.'

I hadn't hesitated. He wasn't just my brother-in-law but a great friend too. I didn't say to myself, this is a married woman living with her husband that you're encouraging Ivor to sleep with. By lending him your house you're facilitating an illicit love affair. Of course I didn't. I didn't say, you're helping to make an innocent husband unhappy and perhaps deprive a small child of his mother. One never does say things like that. I didn't even think them. Our house in Hampstead was very suitable for clandestine goings-on, ideal really.

He and Hebe Furnal usually met at his flat in Westminster. It was a long way for her to come from where she lived, somewhere up in West Hendon, the far side of the North Circular Road. The 'sticks', Ivor called it and sometimes the 'boondocks'. I never saw her house and nor, for that matter, did he. Before she left for their meetings she had to wait for the HALT fund-raiser to get home, because someone had to be with her little boy, Justin. Ivor told me on another occasion that he and Hebe had more phone sex than actual sex, every day in fact, and even this was sabotaged – his word, his PPS to a Defence Secretary's word – by interventions from two-year-old Justin shouting, 'Don't talk, Mummy, don't talk.'

I've said I didn't hesitate about lending him our house, but did I approve? Did Iris? She certainly didn't and she told him so. I tried not to be judgemental and what I felt wasn't any sort of moral condemnation but rather something that was near to physical distaste. It made me squeamish to think of this girl, this young mother – I don't know why her being a young mother should make it worse but somehow it did – going from Ivor home to her husband in a taxi paid for by Ivor and deceiving her husband with tales of the cinema she'd been to or the meal she'd had with a girlfriend. Going perhaps from Ivor's lovemaking to her husband's within the same few hours. And I simply didn't understand. I didn't understand why he'd want to do this or she would. I'd have understood even less if I'd known then the kind of things they did, she and Ivor, their games and dressing up and enactments. Iris, who did understand without sympathizing, explained to me, or tried to, how it was as if Ivor and she had found each other out of all the world, two people with exactly the same tastes, the same feverish desires, the same breathless greed. Love? I don't think so. I only know it was nothing like what Iris and I had and have.

For the best part of the nineteenth century a Tesham had represented Morningford in Parliament. Then there was a long period of Liberal members until Ivor's grandfather had the seat from 1959, when Ivor was two, until 1974. The man who succeeded him died while at the Conservative Party Conference in 1987, Ivor stood in the consequent by-election and won by a majority of just nine thousand. He was thirty-one, young to be in Parliament, exceptionally so, and very ambitious. A former president of the Oxford Union, he was something of an orator, made a memorable maiden speech and would have been on his feet at every available opportunity but for Sandy Caxton advising him not to speak too often. Members notice excessive eloquence and remark on it, not always favourably.

In 1989 he was made PPS to the Secretary of State for Defence.

In case you're like I was and don't know what that means, those letters stand for Parliamentary Private Secretary and set the holder of the office on the first rung of the ladder of political achievement. With luck and hard work, he would next be made a whip and then junior minister. Ivor played down his functions, as people in his position usually do, and said it meant dogsbody, someone who ran errands and kept himself *au fait* with his minister's diary, but you could see he was elated by the appointment.

The media weren't quite so intrusive or so savage as they are today but they were watchful, especially of young Conservative hopefuls. There had been scandals and sleaze. Margaret Thatcher had been prime minister a long time and, as always when long terms seem to be endlessly protracted, coups are talked of and plots and rebellions. But you'll remember all this and whatever I'm telling you, it's not a political assessment.

It's an account of a rise and a fall.

A couple of weeks after the birthday, Ivor asked me to dinner in the Churchill Room, a Commons dining room on the ground floor off the corridor which leads to the terrace. He said no one else would be invited; he wanted to talk to me about a matter which had nothing to do with politics or the Commons. It soon emerged that my advice was to be asked about the Hebe Furnal affair.

As I've said, he'd decided against buying her a flat and to continue in the unsatisfactory way they were carrying on their illicit meetings. He had already asked to borrow our house at some time in May, which was four months ahead, and when he mentioned it again I was a bit apprehensive. I thought he might be going to ask if he could use it on a regular basis. But I soon saw that this wasn't what he wanted. He had his own flat. The difficulty was not that they had nowhere to go – he could after all have used a hotel – but that for most of the time Hebe was Justin-bound.

'It's supposed to be the way to keep a relationship from flagging,' I said. 'I mean, making it hard to meet and the meetings few and far between.'

'I hate that word "relationship",' he said, looking peevish. 'Sorry, but the very sound of it puts a dampener on things. Think of meeting someone you're mad about, like I am about Hebe, and saying, "I want to have a relationship with you." Do you think people actually say that?'

That made me laugh. I said I didn't know, I wouldn't be surprised.

'Anyway, our affair isn't flagging. It doesn't get the chance to flag. I don't think it would if we met every day. Not that there's any prospect of that, the way things are.' He paused and gave me a sidelong look. 'I haven't asked her yet, but I'm thinking about it – I mean of asking her to leave Gerry Furnal.'

'And move in with you?' Remembering his time with Nicola Ross, I was surprised, but it turned out that this wasn't in his mind at all.

'Not exactly,' he said, looking at me and looking away. 'I've decided against buying, but I thought of renting a place for her.'

'You mean she's to leave her husband and not live with you but live in a rented love nest? And what about the little boy?'

I was very child-conscious at the time; still am, but in a more level-headed way. In the spring of 1990, when Nadine was six months old, my eyes were caught by every baby and infant I passed in the street. I couldn't read about child cruelty in the papers. I couldn't look at those pictures the NSPCC put out in their publicity. Someone took Iris and me to the opera, it was *Peter Grimes*, and I had to go outside when it got to that bit about Grimes being at his exercise and he's beating the boys. So my mind went at once to two-year-old Justin Furnal.

'She'd bring him with her, you know,' I said.

'Do you think she would?' he said. 'I hadn't thought of that. It would be a bit of a drawback.'

I'm very fond of Ivor but I wasn't then. As sometimes happened, I came near to disliking him for a moment or two. I'd be aware of his charm and that sort of dashing reckless quality he had and then he'd say something to turn it all round, almost shocking me.

'Even supposing she left her husband, and it doesn't seem to me

9

you've any reason to think she would, what happens next? Furnal and she would get divorced surely and she'd get custody of Justin.' I used his name because calling him 'the child' was distasteful.

'But would she, Rob? I mean, she'd have been the one committing adultery.'

I told him he was supposed to be a lawyer and hadn't he ever heard of no-fault divorce? Unless she was practically a criminal or a druggie she'd get custody, never mind how saintly Gerry Furnal might be.

'I hadn't thought of that,' he said. 'I couldn't stand having that child around. It's bad enough when we're talking on the phone.' He seemed not to notice my slight recoil. I took a deep swig of my wine. 'If Gerry divorced her I'd have to marry her, wouldn't I?'

'Ivor,' I said, 'for someone so advanced in your sexual tastes –' I remembered in time I'd better not admit to knowing what Iris had told me in confidence – 'you're surprisingly old-fashioned. A mistress in a love nest, a clandestine love affair, and now you think you'd have to save her honour. Of course you wouldn't have to marry her, but I think you'd have to share your home with her. You'd have to live with her.'

'I hate that word "home",' he said. 'In that context, I mean. Ghastly Americanism. Can't you just hear some fat woman talking about her lovely home? Oh, I'm sorry, I'm a bastard.'

I asked him tentatively if he'd given any thought to what the press might make of all this.

'At least you didn't say the "print media".' He laughed. 'I may be a new PPS,' he said, 'but I'm still a very small fish in a huge pond. My God, I've just realized, that's what "small fry" means, isn't it? Small fish. We live and learn. There's a pretty awful play by Barrie that Morningford Amateur Dramatic Society put on. It's called *Mary Rose* and of course I had to go and see it. Someone says, "We live and learn," and the reply is, "We live at any rate." It's the only good line in the play.' He smiled his small half-smile. 'The press aren't interested in me having a girlfriend. Prurient they may be when it suits them, but even they allow for a bit of sex in people's lives.'

'When the sex involves a girlfriend who's married and living with her husband?'

'They don't know that, do they? They don't watch her house or mine. If one of them happened to be passing on the relevant evening once a fortnight all they'd see is a beautiful blonde girl coming to my block. Might be visiting anyone. Might live there.'

'I don't know,' I said. 'I just think you ought to be careful.'

In the months to come I was to remember this conversation. It made me think about the unforeseen and how we walk all the time on that thin crust which covers terrible abysses. Things might so easily have been different from what they are if a word spoken or a word withheld hadn't changed them. If Ivor, for instance, had said 'no' instead of 'yes' when Jack Munro asked him to that reception in the Jubilee Room.

2

I get my surname, Delgado, from my grandfather, who came to this country from Badajoz in the 1930s, and I sometimes think it's a blessing I seem to have inherited a thin gene along with the name which is Spanish for 'slim'. It would be a liability for the overweight to be saddled with it. But I'm thin and tallish and otherwise inconspicuous, sallow and bespectacled – to please Iris I'm at last thinking of getting contact lenses – with an unexpectedly deep voice and, for some reason, an almost silent laugh. I laughed in my noiseless way when Iris said Ivor was borrowing our house because its raffish kitschy interior was appropriate for his purpose.

At that time we had a cottage in the country quite near Iris's family home in Ramburgh and another cottage or little house in one of the cobbled mewses of Hampstead. This was the place we were to lend Ivor. It had been a wedding present from Iris's parents, who had bought it for us with all the decor and furnishings fashionable in the 1930s, when the Hollywood Moderne style was in vogue, and unchanged by the previous owners. Coming in from the mews, it was quite a shock. The outside of the house was nineteenth-century brickwork hung with clematis and roses, green shutters at the windows and a lantern over the front door. Visitors walked in on chrome, black and silver, scuffed white leather furniture (soon to be stained by Nadine and her younger brother coating it with raspberry jam and Marmite), a great mural of the New York skyline at night and a wall-size black and yellow abstract framed in aluminium. Upstairs was worse, or the larger of the two bedrooms was. Our huge bed – was this what appealed to Ivor? – was very low, its mattress almost on the floor, which was covered in once-white shagpile. Someone before our time had spilt about a pint of coffee on it, or that was one view to take. Iris said it was more as if a former owner had given birth there. We meant to cover the stain with a rug, just as we meant to give the house a makeover when we could afford it. I insisted we keep the circular mirror which had light bulbs all round its frame and reminded me of an old film magazine photograph I'd once seen of Claudette Colbert's house in Beverly Hills.

I asked Iris what Ivor meant by 'appropriate for his purpose'.

'"The right atmosphere", was what he said. I didn't ask what sort of atmosphere he wanted.'

'I don't suppose we shall ever know,' I said.

We'd been invited to the theatre by Ivor that evening and we looked on it as a celebration for him. He had just been made a whip. The play was *Julius Caesar*, with a famous theatrical knight as Brutus and Nicola Ross playing Calpurnia. After it was over we all went round to Nicola's dressing room to have champagne and take her out to supper. It wasn't my business even to wish it, but I couldn't help reflecting how much better it would be if she and Ivor were still together and it was she he was thinking of living with. After a minute or two the young black actor playing Casca put his head round the door and Nicola called him in. She introduced him as Lloyd Freeman and we were soon all talking about black people taking parts which were intended for white actors. Was it a problem? If audiences could suspend their disbelief in middle-aged women playing Juliet and fat divas singing tubercular Mimi, why not accept a black Mark Antony? Lloyd said he was lucky to have the part he had, but he'd only got it because it was a very small one. Could we imagine him in a Pinero revival, for instance?

We talked about black and Indian characters in books all being comic or evil up to the Second World War and beyond, and Othello the only serious role for a black man, and I was starting to wonder how Lloyd made a living, when he said he also drove for a minicab company in which he was a partner with a friend. Ivor was interested – Iris and I agreed afterwards that he probably wanted to use one of these minicabs for taking Hebe home after their meetings – and Lloyd gave him a card. After that Lloyd went home and we went off to supper.

I never saw him again and I don't suppose I ever gave him a thought until the time of the accident. The papers had photographs of him too, though not so many as of Hebe. He was a good actor and whenever I see a play on the West End stage with black people in the cast I think of him. Because the impossible, which was the view he took, has happened. I saw a black Henry V last year and a black Henry VI last week and I thought how I might have seen Lloyd in *Julius Caesar* again, but playing Cassius this time. I never can because he's dead. It wasn't Ivor's fault that he died, but without Ivor he'd no doubt be alive today. He was thirty-two, so he'll have to age another year when he gets to heaven.

The other man, Dermot Lynch, I never met. I heard his voice once when I was in Ivor's flat. He had come round to collect Ivor's car and take it away for a service. 'I'll pop the keys through the door as per usual, guv,' I heard him say, and I wondered whether Ivor, who expected to be called 'sir', would object to being addressed like a police inspector in a sitcom. He can't have minded much, because Dermot Lynch was the other man he chose to carry out the birthday present.

I shall call it that now because it's as 'the birthday present' that Iris and I referred to it, rather than as 'the accident', whenever we spoke of it in the future. Back in the early part of 1990, of course, we had no idea what Ivor was planning, only that he wanted our house on the nearest Friday to 17 May and after a time we gathered this was Hebe's birthday. He bought her a present as well, a string of pearls, and, in an unusual display of openness, showed it to us.

'They're beautiful,' Iris said, 'but the trouble with pearls is that you have to be an expert to tell whether they're worth thousands or they came from a chain store.'

'That's not the trouble,' Ivor said. 'That's the point. She can wear them and Furnal won't know she didn't buy them herself.'

*

Ivor was a good constituency MP. Even after he got to be a minister he still went down to Ramburgh most weeks to hold his Morningford surgery on a Saturday morning. If the weekends he spent in London were usually free, the ones in Norfolk weren't. Especially in the summer, there would be an appearance to put in at some local festival or fête and often a dinner to attend and speak at in the evening. There was always a cause which needed his patronage or a concern one of his constituents wanted raised with the relevant minister. At the time of the birthday present or just before it was the proposal to close a local hospital, the kind of place they used to call a 'cottage hospital', he was opposing. He'd attended all the meetings of the Hands Off Our Hospital committee but he drew the line at taking part in the march through Morningford culminating in a mass demo in the town square. It was a Conservative government which supported the hospital closure and he was, after all, a Conservative whip. As he put it, he didn't want the wrong sort of limelight. He was very aware of this sort of thing, perhaps neurotically aware.

When he visited his constituency he stayed at Ramburgh House with his parents, a place considered by John and Louisa to be as much his as theirs. They had told him that when he married they would give it up to him and move into the lodge, quite an attractive but much smaller house at the eastern end of the estate. It seemed to me that they were safe for years as marriage was the last thing on Ivor's mind.

Ramburgh House was a biggish Queen Anne place, one of those manor houses which stand in the centre of the village, separated from its main street only by a narrow strip of grass and paving and approached through an arch in a high brick wall. All the land, the garden, the park and a couple of meadows and woodland were at the rear, and the lodge stood about half a mile away, at the end of what they called the East Avenue, a lane running between a double row of lime trees. It's a measure of Ivor's old-fashioned (and slightly absurd) sense of the dignity due to the landed gentry that he called the lodge 'the dower house'.

I don't suppose there is anything particularly remarkable about the grounds – the land is flat, its only distinguishing feature the little river running between rows of alders – and the house itself gets only a terse paragraph in Pevsner's *Buildings of Norfolk*. But Ivor was very fond of the place and, if his father behaved like a squire of old, he conducted himself a bit like the heir apparent, having the vicar and his wife to dinner and dropping in on the locals to hear their complaints about rents and repairs. Now, of course, most of the locals have died and the places they lived in have become weekend cottages for Londoners.

Our own cottage was ten miles away but well within Ivor's constituency. We voted in Hampstead and we had the right to vote in local elections, though not in parliamentary ones. It wasn't easy for us to attend any of those functions Ivor spoke at, but we did manage to get along to the Morningford Eel Feast, an annual thrash in the town hall whose origins were lost in antiquity. Traditionally, only local eels were consumed, but these had become scarce over the years and it was rumoured that half of those eaten at the April 1990 feast came from Thailand. I don't know if there are any eels in Thailand or if we import them if there are, but this was the story that went round the tables that year. Iris and I were able to go because the feast happens at lunchtime, so we could take Nadine with us.

Ivor made a speech, a very good speech I suppose it was, with the requisite eel jokes and stories about the glorious past of Morningford and its even more illustrious future, nothing about the hospital closure but rather a lot about the benefits the then government had brought to the town. Just the same, I wasn't sorry when Nadine started to grizzle and then to scream and we had to take her out. I heard afterwards that there had been one or two sticky questions put to Ivor, the most awkward being how long would Margaret Thatcher remain prime minister. Apparently, he got round it by heaping praise on her.

Very unusually for him, he had no engagement that evening and he came over to Monks Cravery to see us. Iris asked him how Hebe was and he said fine and he'd already told her about the pearls. This is a strange business, asking people how they are or someone close to them is. We all do it all the time, and now we're doing it even more than we did seventeen years ago. But the last thing we want is to hear about someone's state of health, and nothing is more boring than to be told in reply that they woke up feeling under the weather but they're a bit better now apart from a slight headache. No, what we expect is to hear news or details of some recent experience or escapade or even to be shocked by death and disaster. Iris wasn't anticipating anything like that, but nor was she content with Ivor's short response.

'Well, tell us, was she pleased?'

'Of course,' he said. 'Who wouldn't be? She'd been telling me for months how much she loved pearls. Of course she'd be pleased.'

I mention this because those pearls figured quite importantly in what was to come. Not for a long time, not until the quiet period when it seemed the birthday present (I mean the other one) was far in the past and Ivor had begun to think it was all over. Begun to think the terrible fear was gone for ever and nothing like it would ever come again, his sleepless nights and his dread of newspapers. Gerry Furnal was married to his second wife, Justin was growing up and was soon to have a half-sister. But through the years those pearls must have lain in their black leather velvet-lined case in a drawer somewhere in Gerry Furnal's house in his distant suburb or journeyed back and forth in Jane Atherton's handbag, their presence accepted by Furnal as he accepted Hebe's other jewellery, the stuff from Oxfam shops and Costa Brava market stalls. If they weren't worth a king's ransom (are kings ever held to ransom?) their value was probably the same as that of all the Furnal furniture and equipment put together.

Long afterwards, when it was confession time, advice time and desperate help-seeking time, Ivor told me about meeting Lloyd Freeman once more at a party given by Nicola Ross. Nicola was always giving parties; no reason such as an anniversary or Christmas was needed to excuse them. Iris and I were invited but couldn't find a babysitter.

Shy people get to parties early because if they're among the first they won't have to walk in on a room full of unknown guests. Ivor wasn't shy, far from it, and on this occasion he didn't arrive until the party had been going for about an hour. He intended, of course, to stay late. Nicola always invited too many people and the place was crowded. Ivor pushed his way through the throng, avoiding those he didn't want to talk to because they bored him, and came face to face with Lloyd. They talked for a minute or two, the usual how-are-you-what-have-you-been-doing stuff, Ivor said, and then he thought he might as well put his proposition to Lloyd there and then. By that time, he had already spoken to Dermot Lynch and Dermot had agreed.

A waiter hired for the occasion was going round refilling glasses and both of them had some more Merlot. In those days quite abstemious, Ivor always drank a lot at parties, though he never showed a sign of it as far as I could see. Lloyd, he said, gave him the impression of being one who stoked up on free wine when he got the chance. Ivor reminded him of what he'd told him in Nicola's dressing room about his minicab business. Would he do a driving job for him? He needed a posh sort of car (his words), maybe a black Mercedes with blacked-out windows in the rear. It was to pick up a girl and bring her to a house in Hampstead on a Friday evening in a few weeks' time. There'd be a second driver if need be.

'It sounds OK,' Lloyd said. 'How far would it be?'

'Five or six miles. No more. Five hundred pounds.'

Lloyd went quiet. 'What's the catch?'

'No catch,' said Ivor, 'but complications.'

'Look, why don't you call me? I've got to go. My girlfriend's looking for me.'

She came up to them, took Lloyd's arm and pulled him away. That was the first time Ivor saw her, a very pretty dark-haired woman, but white like a Spaniard or a Portuguese, with magnificent breasts shown off in a low-cut top. The ankles weren't mentioned at that time. Ivor noticed the breasts, as any man would, and the lovely face and full red lips, but she wasn't his type and he thought, he said, of Hebe's extravagant slenderness and delicate features and cascading fair hair. He asked himself too, in that moment, what the hell he was doing longing for a woman who ought to have been there at the party with him, a married woman who wanted the best of both worlds, a husband and a lover, and who couldn't escape more than once a fortnight. But longing and reproaching himself didn't stop him going on with the birthday present.

He phoned Lloyd the following week and arranged to meet him and Dermot Lynch in a pub in Victoria. He didn't know it and neither of them had ever been there before. That was the point, I suppose. Lloyd got there first and was businesslike about the 'complications', how he and Dermot were to buy balaclavas to wear, handcuffs and a gag for Hebe. Dermot, who was a great gesticulator, a man who talked with his hands, rolled his eyes at this, held up a thumb and winked when Ivor told them where they should go for these 'props' and handed them money to cover it and cover too the renting of the car. He repeated his offer of five hundred pounds to pick up a woman and drive her from a point north of the North Circular Road to Hampstead. Lloyd nodded and, though Ivor didn't ask him for any undertaking, said he wouldn't tell anyone.

Two hundred and fifty pounds each now, Ivor said, and the other two hundred and fifty in cash in an envelope on the hall table inside the front door of our house. Lloyd and Dermot wouldn't need a key as he would be there himself to put the door on the latch. They all had drinks, Dermot making his thumbs-up sign again and talking more than Ivor liked about the arrangements. He laughed a lot too.

'Where d'you get an idea like that from anyway?' He shook his head in wonderment at Ivor's powers of invention.

Lloyd was rather quiet. He had just split up with his girlfriend, though Ivor knew nothing about this at the time. The two men left together in Lloyd's car.

3

Another thing Sandy Caxton told me was that they used to believe the weight of the soul when it leaves the body at the point of death is twenty-one grams. Or it may have been twenty-one ounces, I can't remember. The Neoplatonists thought the soul was located in every part of the body. I hope Sandy's fled the moment the bomb was detonated, because he was blown to unidentifiable pieces. Perhaps it became a snow-white bird and nestles under God's throne until the last day. I'm told that some Muslims believe that.

I expect you remember what happened, though perhaps not the details. Sandy had spent the night at his home in Leicestershire with his wife and their two children. They slept in the house and his resident bodyguard and his dog were in the flat over the garage, which was a converted stables. Sandy was going out on the Saturday morning to play golf with another Tory MP, a backbencher, and his agent, who lived in the next village. The bodyguard performed his usual security check at seven, scrutinizing Sandy's car, a Rover, searching the garage, his German shepherd sniffing every corner. Because he knew his employer was going out, he fetched the car, closed the garage doors and left it on the paved area in front of the house.

Sandy got up at seven thirty, leaving his wife, Erica, and his boy and girl asleep. He made himself a cup of tea, ate a piece of bread and marmalade and left the house. The bodyguard had returned to his flat but he came downstairs again when he saw Sandy coming, said good morning to him and stood at a distance with his dog while Sandy got into the Rover. It wasn't when he turned on the ignition but when the engine started that the car blew up.

Flying metal and glass struck the bodyguard. Apparently, he didn't move but just stood there as if turned to stone. The dog, covered with blood and trembling, began to howl. The bodyguard stayed frozen there until Erica Caxton came running screaming out of the front door and then he ran to her, crying, 'Don't look, don't look,' but there was nothing to see if she had looked, only metal and glass and bits of clothing and blood, blood everywhere. The children, aged fourteen and sixteen, slept through it all.

It was the lead item in all the news programmes that day and the lead story in all the Sunday papers and Monday's papers. An hour after it happened the IRA announced in their usual way that they were responsible. Ivor was very upset. I could say disproportionately upset, but perhaps not. Sandy Caxton was fifteen years older than Erica and, though not quite his contemporary, had been a friend of John Tesham's since before Ivor and Iris were born. Ivor and his parents went to the funeral, but I stopped Iris going as she wasn't well and she was relieved that I had.

The funeral was a highly emotional affair, attended by most of the country's great and good. Among the coffin bearers were three Cabinet ministers and two university vice-chancellors. Though May, it was a bitterly cold day, a north wind driving the rain and the trees in the little village churchyard swaying and lashing their branches like angry arms, as Ivor put it. They played 'The Dead March' in *Saul*, this being Sandy's favourite piece of music, and it seems he was particularly fond of the story of Saul, Samuel and the Witch of Endor. There's no accounting for tastes. Why, incidentally, do we always talk about Handel arias and other music being 'in' *Saul* or *Theodora* or whatever it is, when they are 'from' if it's works by Mozart, say, or Beethoven? Nobody has ever been able to tell me.

Ivor came up to Hampstead after the funeral, accepted a stronger drink than usual, brandy with a splash of soda, and said in gloomy tones that he was so depressed by what had happened that he felt like postponing or even cancelling the birthday present. But he couldn't do that. He'd fixed it up with Hebe to see her on Friday the 18th and arranged things with Lloyd and Dermot.

Iris said surely he'd be better by that time, it was nearly two weeks off. And it was only his usual assignation with Hebe, wasn't it, apart from its taking place in our house and her being fetched by car?

'Not quite usual,' Ivor said, putting on his secretive look but not the little smile this time. 'There will be complications. But I'll tell you all about it when it's over.'

'Not *all* about it, I hope.'

'You know what I mean,' Ivor said, using a phrase I'd never heard from him before, his use of which I put down to his feeling low.

He didn't stay long but went off to Old Pye Street in a taxi, saying he had a lot of paperwork to get through before the following morning. After he'd gone Iris said, 'I do wonder about this Hebe, this mystery woman. What do you think she says to her husband when she goes off on these jaunts? Does she tell him she's going to the cinema? I should think she must do, because I can't think of anywhere else a *respectable* young woman with a husband and a child could go to on her own. I mean, could *say* she was going to on her own.'

I said I supposed she might say she was going somewhere with a friend. To have a meal, for instance, or even to a club.

'Then the friend must be an accomplice. The friend will have to be prepared with a story in case Hebe's husband meets her – it must be a her, mustn't it, or maybe a gay man – so that she can say how much they loved the film or the food. I can't imagine telling you I was going to the cinema when I was actually going to go to bed with another man. I don't think I could get the words out.'

'I hope you won't go to bed with another man,' I said.

'I'm sure I never shall, but if I did I'd tell you. Why does she stay with him? Because he keeps her? That's a bit low, isn't it?'

'The whole thing is low,' I said, 'and Ivor knows it. But he's fascinated by her. He doesn't love her but he wants to keep on with this. It may be that she stays with Gerry what's-his-name – Furnal – not because she loves him but because he loves her. For all we know, he may have some idea of all this but begs her not to leave him. Do what she likes but not leave him.'

Iris looked doubtful. She couldn't imagine it. 'But to have that between them,' she said. 'For her to know she lies to him and him to wonder if she does but be afraid to ask, what kind of marriage is that? I don't think you can be right, Rob.'

I was wrong, as it happened. It was true that Gerry Furnal loved Hebe, but perhaps without knowing the kind of woman he loved. He seems to have put her on a pedestal and worshipped what he'd created. It's quite a common way of going on, but it wouldn't suit realists like me. Anyway, I doubt if I'm capable of that amount of self-delusion. I'm not well endowed with imagination. The truth came out grimly and shockingly in the end in poor Jane's diaries, if it was the truth rather than only what she saw through the distorting lens of her self-pity. As to Jane, she was the friend who agreed to deceive Gerry Furnal by supplying him, if these became necessary, with ostensible reasons for Hebe's absences, and it wasn't to be long before we heard about her from Ivor. It was Iris who first used the word, calling this then unknown person 'the alibi lady'.

'We all use it,' I remember saying, 'but do we know what it means? I don't. Alibi – strange word, a sort of police word, but do the real police actually use it?'

'It sounds Arabic.'

I looked it up and found it was Latin for 'elsewhere'.

'Well, that figures,' Iris said. 'The alibi-ist will tell Gerry Furnal Hebe was with her when in fact she was elsewhere with Ivor. And there'll be lots of times when she won't have to, because I don't suppose she and Gerry meet that often. I wonder how she feels about it.'

'I imagine she tells herself her loyalty is to Hebe and not to Hebe's husband.'

'Do you know, Rob, I'm beginning to take an unhealthy interest in all this intriguing and I think I'd better stop.'

And stop she did. We had other things to think about. We told each other so and made a kind of pact, which we stuck to fairly well, not to speculate any more about Ivor and his clandestine affair. We would lend him our house as we'd promised and go away and leave him to it. I had given him the key the evening he came over after Sandy Caxton's funeral and he was to put it through the letter box after he left. That isn't to say we didn't involve ourselves much more closely when things developed. We had to. Otherwise he'd have been quite alone, bearing it alone – until, that is, Juliet Case came along.

That Friday was the first day something about poor Sandy wasn't on our daily newspaper's front page. Instead, the lead story was about the multi-millionaire Damian Mason's bid to buy some north of England football team, with a picture of him, a short heavy man with a little beard, and his wife, Kelly, in shorts and a tight T-shirt. Iris was beginning to get over her flu and I think that was the first morning she woke up feeling well. Nadine, on the other hand, was a bit fractious and cross but seemed well enough, so, after I'd made a couple of essential phone calls to clients, we set off for Monks Cravery. Before we left Iris changed the sheets on our huge low bed and, though I said not to bother, covered up the coffee or birthing stain with a rug from Nadine's room.

It was a lovely day, the first really fine day of spring.

4

I started writing this down because I had a premonition. It was when Hebe asked me to give her an alibi. She has been asking me to give her alibis for a long time and I always do, but this one was different. It was more important than any I had given her in the past. For one thing, I would have to provide it for longer than usual and the occasion was her birthday. I mean that where she was going and what she was doing were her birthday present.

When she said that I had a sense of foreboding. Things would go wrong. My premonition told me things would go disastrously wrong. I would have to be careful. That was when I decided to record events. I am not going to use a notebook but sheets of paper and clip them together as I go and put them in a shoebox, which I shall keep in the only real cupboard I have in this tiny flat. And if I move one day I shall take it with me. Shoeboxes are a nuisance and these days most shops ask you when you buy a pair of shoes if you want the box. Hardly anyone does want it, which makes one wonder what the shops do with all those hundreds, thousands, millions of boxes. The last pair of shoes I bought they made me take the box – I shan't go there again – and that's how I happen to have one to keep this record in.

Using this box is quite appropriate, because when I bought those shoes Hebe was with me and she bought a pair of boots. Maybe I should say I was with Hebe, because that's the way it always felt. The boots were black patent leather with very high heels and they laced all the way up the front to the knee.

'You won't be able to walk in them,' I said.

She laughed. 'I don't want to walk in them. I want to lie down in them.'

Remarks like that embarrass me. I don't know where to look.

We went to have a coffee and that was when she started telling me about the kinds of things she did with Ivor Tesham. Dressing up, acting out fantasies it was mostly, and that was all right, I suppose, but her descriptions of what after all amounted to S and M made me feel uncomfortable. Perhaps it was partly because it all seemed so distant from Gerry, who is a rather proper sort of person. Or so I thought then. I didn't really know. But nothing that's happened since has made me change my view. I asked her if she was in love with Ivor.

'I don't think so,' she said. 'But would I know if I was? I do fancy him like crazy. But as for love – I thought I was in love with Gerry when I married him and maybe I was, but it didn't last.'

I asked her why she stayed with him.

'I tell myself it wouldn't be right to take Justin away from his dad, but I don't know if that's really the reason. I've never had a job, you know. Well, of course you know. I married Gerry straight after finals and then Justin came along. What could I do?'

'Your degree's in media studies,' I said, another obvious remark.

'Like a million other people's. I wouldn't know how to get a job on a paper or in TV or whatever. I'm only good at one thing. I'd be a great whore, but I'd rather go on as I am.'

I reverted to the boots. Surely she wouldn't let Gerry see them? They had cost three times as much as my shoes.

'Oh, Ivor will pay for them,' she said. 'After all, they're for his pleasure,' and she drew out the soft sibilant of that sensual word, rolling it on her tongue. 'So would you be an angel and give me an alibi for 18 May?'

I said I would. 'But your birthday's the 17th.'

'I've got to go out with Gerry that night.' She made a face. 'You're babysitting – remember? It's a bore, but marriage is a bore. You have to face it.'

I had nothing to say to that. 'I've got a feeling that something bad is going to happen. Can't you make it another night?'

'Oh, Janey, you and your premonitions. Ivor wants to make it the 18th and I can't exactly tell him it won't suit *you*. Besides, I've already told Gerry you and I are going to the theatre.'

Without even asking me. I ought to be used to it, it's the way most people treat me. Starting with Mummy, they all know that if I am not with them I'm not likely to be going anywhere. It's a funny thing really. You read in the papers about young people going to raves and clubs, out every night, being promiscuous, drinking too much and taking drugs. Well, I'm young but I don't even know what a rave is. I could count on the fingers of one hand how many men have asked me out, and as for the number who have wanted to see me again – well, I won't go on. There's no point.

In actual fact, I have seldom had to give Hebe an alibi. I hardly ever saw Gerry, so I wasn't around for him to ask me if we'd had a good time at the Odeon or a nice dinner at the Café Rouge. He never actually checked. I mean he never rang up and asked if Hebe had really been with me. Probably he suspected nothing. Not then. It took a good deal to make him even mildly suspicious, for he had a trusting nature. Did my conscience trouble me? I used to have one, but maybe I don't any more. Spending so much of the time alone deadens things and one of the things it kills is conscience. It makes you simply not care any more.

I'd never done this sort of thing before and in fact I did very little of it for Hebe. Of course I promised various things, like not to answer the phone if it rang when she and I were supposed to be out somewhere but to put it on message, and to be aware of when and where Gerry thought we had gone so that if we did meet I could confirm our date. But that only happened twice, him asking what the film he thought we'd been to had been like and another time how Mummy was – she'd been in hospital – when I took Hebe to see her. I didn't even have to lie about that. I only had to say that my mother was getting on well.

So it wasn't too much of a strain and it only happened once every two or three weeks. I made myself take an interest in Hebe's love affair and I looked Ivor Tesham up in a directory called *Dod's*. I was working then in the Library of British History in Gower Street and it's full of directories and dictionaries, so there were plenty of places where I could find his name, but *Dod's* was the most comprehensive. He sounded rich and the photograph which accompanied the short biography made him look very handsome, unless the camera lied, which it sometimes does. He had one of those sardonic faces which women find attractive, very dark eyes and black hair. Looking at his picture, I wondered if he would ever get to be prime minister one day and that face would be famous. Hebe said he was very ambitious, though as far as I could tell she knew nothing about politics and cared less.

But I was talking about 18 May. The play Hebe had told Gerry she and I would be seeing was called *Life Threatening*. I never got to see it. I don't even know what it's about and I can't remember who wrote it, except that it was some new, very young playwright and was supposed to be very sexy and crude. But the name I can never forget and every time I hear or read that phrase – 'life-threatening' comes in newspapers quite often – it resonates with me, so that I see Hebe's face and hear her voice again and think of the way she died.

She had picked that play because it's very long – it ran for about three hours – so Gerry wouldn't wonder what was going on if she didn't come in till after midnight. I asked her what the scenario was for that evening with her and Ivor that she was going to be with him so much longer than usual and she said he was fixing up a birthday treat for her, her birthday present.

'I thought the pearls were your birthday present,' I said.

She'd told me about them, said he'd already given them to her and what a clever present this was because no one (meaning Gerry) would know whether they were valuable or if they came from some high-street jeweller's.

'I think I'll get them valued, though,' she said, 'and insure them, and then if they get pinched I'll get a lot of money.'

I asked her what they were going to do with the extra time on Friday night. She said she didn't know but she was to be picked up in a car as she was walking down the Watford Way. She had to be there at precisely seven. Hebe was famously unpunctual, so I couldn't help wondering what would happen if she turned up ten minutes late. I supposed Tesham or his driver would wait for her. It was all a million miles away from things that happen in my life. But I think that's one of the reasons why she liked me, because beside me she showed up as beautiful and popular.

'But what's the point?' I said.

She didn't know that either but she was going to wear her new boots and a long coat over a low-cut top and miniskirt. Or maybe the boots and a long coat over nothing at all. It wouldn't be the first time.

The evening Gerry was taking her out to dinner I was babysitting. I am not very fond of babies, I may as well say that, though I like them better than older children. At least they are not rude or rough. But I never told her or Gerry that as I don't suppose they would like it. Of course I am competent enough with them. I can bath babies and I know about reading them stories and not leaving them to cry or not for too long. I don't suppose I shall ever have one of my own and that may be just as well. Like I have said, I have very few friends and I don't get out much, but I wouldn't like only being able to go out when someone else could manage to stay and look after my baby. I wouldn't like not being able to go for a walk without having a baby with me in a buggy.

Hebe and Gerry lived in a little terraced house in a street more or less between West Hendon and Edgware. HALT (the Heart and Lung Trust) has its offices in Kennington, which meant he had a long journey to work every day on the worst of all London tube lines, the Northern. First he had to get a bus to Edgware station or walk to Hendon. And though he left work at five he seldom got home before six thirty. I wanted to see Hebe before he got there, so I drove myself up to Irving Road on the 17th by six fifteen, wished her a happy birthday, checked that everything was still all right for the Friday and found Justin in his high chair eating very small amounts of banana and yoghurt but flinging most of it about the room.

I set about cleaning it up and feeding the rest of it to him myself, something he seemed to quite like. At any rate, he didn't protest but swallowed the spoonfuls obediently. Hebe had gone upstairs to dress as soon as I got there and came down looking as impossibly glamorous as she always did in a short tight black dress and the pearls. She kissed the top of Justin's head from the back, keeping clear of the yoghurt and banana mixture.

'Oh, God, I'm so tired,' she said. 'Justin's been an absolute devil all day. I'd absolutely love to stay in but not a hope and it will be a dead bore. The trouble with marriage is that after a time you've nothing left to say to each other.'

Gerry came in soon after that, saw the pearls and asked where they came from.

'British Home Stores,' she said.

'They look lovely,' he said. 'I wish I could afford to buy you real ones.'

That made me feel very uncomfortable and I'm sure I blushed. If I did neither of them noticed. Gerry went upstairs to wash and put on a tie and change into a better jacket than the one he was wearing and Hebe stood in front of the living-room mirror, adjusting her hair and applying more lipstick. I must say she seemed to take as much trouble over her appearance when she went out with her husband as she did when visiting Ivor Tesham. She was the sort of woman who would redo her face if she was going to her own execution.

I cleaned Justin up a bit, took him on my knee and began to read to him, *Spot the Dog* being his current favourite. Hebe and Gerry tried to creep out without his noticing, but of course he did and began to wail on the lines of 'Justin wants Mummy,' a phrase I was to hear a lot of in the future. I got him on to the cat and dog game which I'd successfully tried before and it worked like a charm, with him being the dog and me the back-arching, hissing, mewing cat. We had a quiet bath-time session, then more *Spot the Dog* and Justin went to bed, falling asleep within five minutes.

At ten they came in. I didn't stay, for I had to be at work in the morning. Hebe said very pointedly in Gerry's hearing that she'd see me next day and I nearly asked what she meant but remembered just in time. They both came to the door with me and waved as I got into the car.

I felt the premonition very strongly as I drove home but if I am honest, and there is no point in keeping a diary if you are not honest, I didn't feel this would be the last time I ever saw her.

5

The article in a Sunday newspaper's supplement appeared only a year ago and the journalist claimed to be describing the latest craze among fashionistas. You may have seen it. Agencies were being set up to arrange these things for trendy young people, especially those whose 'relationships were getting tired'. I'd only read half a paragraph when I realized that this happening, adventure, exercise, whatever you like to call it, was exactly what Ivor had thought up for Hebe's birthday present all those years before. He'd even used that very phrase. It's called 'adventure sex'. An agency could charge up to thirty thousand pounds, the journalist said, depending on the accessories, additional characters, complications in the scenario, decorations and so on, to arrange an abduction of one's girlfriend. The pretend kidnappers would snatch her as she walked down a street – she would have previously been alerted as to what to expect – put her in a car with blacked-out windows, handcuff her and/or gag her, rope her ankles together and take her to an appointed venue. There they would carry her indoors and throw her on to a bed, ready for the instigator to walk into the room and find her waiting for him. Thirty thousand pounds. Ivor arranged his for one thousand, and half of it wasn't paid till a lot later.

It's not that I take some sort of moral stand about 'adventure sex' – how anxious we are these days never to appear moral – because I don't see how morality comes into it. I've nothing against it. Sadism and masochism seem all right to me if that's what everyone likes and no one minds hurting others or being hurt themselves. But, as I've said, I lack imagination. As an accountant and now a company doctor, I haven't much of it. I'm too ordinary. Dressing up and acting out fantasies I find grotesque, but to picture them doesn't shock or disturb me. It makes me laugh. Doctors and patients, tutors and schoolgirls, nuns and priests, mock rape – but I needn't go on. Though I don't suppose Ivor and Hebe did anything like that, their tastes ran along those lines and when I think about it my laughter is embarrassed. The truth probably is that if a couple of men threw a girl down on my bed to await my arrival – no, my weak imagination isn't equal to it.

The weekends we spent at Monks Cravery were the best times of our life in those early years. The countryside was pretty but not spectacular, and as for our cottage, there are thousands like it all over England: thatched roof, oak front door with jasmine if not roses round it, timbered ceilings, lattice windows, a crooked staircase, a kitchen you have to go through to get to the bathroom. But is there any house in the world more comfortable than the English country cottage? With a log fire burning and the curtains drawn, we were blissfully happy. We had nothing to do. During the week when we weren't there, Peggy came in to clean and her husband, Bob, did the garden. We shopped for food at a supermarket on the way down and on Saturday morning one of us drove over to Great Cravery for a newspaper. Usually we went for a long walk on Saturday afternoon, taking Nadine with us, of course, strapped in her sling to Iris's chest or mine – to mine now that she was getting heavy.

There are many kinds of mother but only two kinds of father, the besotted and the indifferent. Tolstoy might have begun a novel like that instead of with that dodgy stuff about happy and unhappy families. I'm one of the besotted kind and I've been lucky in that all my children have been born healthy and beautiful and are growing up strong. I sometimes wish I believed in God – and the soul weighed in grams and the age we meet in heaven – so that I could have someone to thank for that. But I don't, so I thank Iris's and my good genes, a gratitude which would please Richard Dawkins.

Those Saturday-afternoon walks were the best part of the weekend for me because I got to carry Nadine – if it doesn't sound too sentimental, even if it does – close to my heart. I used to feel that I could walk along like that for ever, along the green lanes where all the hedges were in blossom and primroses were on the banks, sometimes saying a word to Iris, breathing the fresh, clean air and feeling through the cloth and padding the warmth of Nadine's little body. Mostly she slept, but she'd stay awake too, gazing at everything we passed with round intelligent blue eyes and when I looked down at her she'd smile her enchanting smile. We'd reach our halfway point and I always turned back reluctantly. Iris teased me about it, laughing and saying that if I couldn't bear to be parted from my daughter she wouldn't stop me bathing her that evening and sitting by her cot till she went to sleep.

But that Saturday, though it was a fine day, we didn't go for a walk. I drove over to Great Cravery in the morning, rather later than usual because we'd had a lie-in, and bought one of the so-called quality papers. I glanced at it when I got back into the car and dropped it on the passenger seat. The headline across the front page was 'Crash Horror Ends Kidnap Bid' and the photograph underneath it was one of those vehicle-disaster pictures in which nothing is really recognizable, but when you look more closely you can spot something which might be a broken headlamp and perhaps a single tyre lying among ripped sheets of metal. I didn't look more closely. Not then. I drove back to the cottage and laid the paper down on the kitchen table in front of Iris, who was eating toast and marmalade with Nadine on her lap.

Some people flip through newspapers, reading only the items which interest them, and others take their time, lingering over every word. I belong in the first category, though I usually pay attention to the financial pages, but Iris is a lingerer. If it had been left to me I don't suppose I would ever have read that story about a kidnap and a crash; we'd have gone for our walk, had our neighbours round for drinks and driven home next day in contented ignorance. Iris read it. She got to the foot of the page, said, 'Here, you take her, Rob,' and, handing Nadine to me, turned over to pages two and three. Her expression had grown very serious, then aghast.

'What is it?' I said. 'What's the matter?'

She passed the paper over to me. It was open at page three and a glance showed me the photograph of a very pretty girl with long blonde hair.

'Ivor's girlfriend is called Hebe Furnal, isn't she?'

'Yes, of course. You know she is.'

'Then that's her. She's been killed. Read it yourself. Two men tried to abduct her but their car crashed and one of them was killed too. It's unbelievable but read it.'

When Ivor told us what had happened to him on Friday 18 May he was still in shock but he was fairly calm. The House of Commons seldom sits on a Friday; it hadn't that day. That was why he had arranged the birthday present to take place then. In the morning, as soon as he calculated that Gerry Furnal would have left for his long bus and train journey to work, he phoned Hebe and they had their requisite phone sex, with Justin complaining in the background. Lunch was at the Turkish Embassy, celebrating something or other, a treaty or a victory, and he got back to the flat by about half past three. He'd decided against driving up to Hampstead because even then it was difficult finding anywhere to park and, besides that, he knew he was likely to have a lot to drink, so he booked himself a taxi for six thirty. A black cab, not one of Lloyd Freeman's minicabs. Half an hour before the taxi was due he went out and bought a bottle of champagne and then, because it might not be enough, a second bottle. The five hundred pounds he'd drawn out of the bank in fifty-pound notes he divided into two and put two hundred and fifty pounds into envelopes. Then he wrote 'Dermot' on one and 'Lloyd' on the other.

It was just after seven when he let himself into our house. Seven was the time Hebe was supposed to be walking south along the Watford Way, where she would be picked up by Lloyd Freeman and Dermot Lynch, who would then bring her to our street, park the car and carry her upstairs. Ivor worked out that she should be there by seven forty-five at the latest, even allowing for Friday evening's heavy traffic. He put the champagne in the fridge. He laid the two envelopes on the hall table and went to check upstairs. Among the fairly horrible fittings in our bedroom was a very large wall clock, circular and of frosted glass with chrome hands. That clock told him it was ten past seven.

He told me all this to illustrate, I suppose, how suspenseful the waiting was and how much worse it got. Of course, at ten past seven, it hadn't really started getting suspenseful, but it did make him wonder why he'd bothered to get there so early. What was he supposed to do with himself? He started thinking about his scenario and about something he hadn't before considered. There was no doubt Hebe would arrive suitably dressed (which meant unsuitably dressed for any normal social occasion) but what of him? He went back upstairs, took his clothes off and put on a dressing gown he found in my clothes cupboard. It was mine, it had been given to me by a predecessor of Iris's, but I had never worn it and I'd only kept it because Iris liked it and said she'd a good mind to wear it herself, though she never had. It was black silk with a vaguely Chinese pattern in gold and a gold sash. Ivor said he looked like an actor playing David in *Hay Fever*. He passed another couple of minutes admiring himself in the mirror, but even then, according to the glass clock, it was only twenty-five past seven.

Because it was all over the papers, he had to tell me that it was on his instructions that Dermot and Lloyd handcuffed Hebe, roped her ankles and tied a scarf round her mouth. He showed no embarrassment in telling me but spoke of it as if this was normal behaviour. I didn't comment but I thought how extraordinary some people's tastes are, that this man, my own wife's brother, would get pleasure and no doubt excitement from something which would leave me cold.

By the time he was looking at himself in the glass, he went on, the two of them would have been on the Watford Way, a busy road at most times of the day, but residential too. The houses were set well back from the main highway and separated from it by their own front gardens, a service road and a strip of grass with trees.

Dermot, who was driving, would have pulled off the main highway on to this service road, where he could have remained parked while Hebe was trussed up. Ivor was taking it for granted she wouldn't have struggled much because, although she wasn't told what to expect, she knew to expect something which would ultimately be for her pleasure.

While this was going on, Ivor was waiting in our house. He never knew and probably no one apart from Dermot and Lloyd ever knew whether Hebe had been on time or late. There was one witness to the mock abduction. She was a woman called June Hemsley and she lived in one of the houses on the Watford Way behind the strip of grass, the service road and her own front garden. She had been standing in the window of her front room, watching for her son to return home from his violin lesson. He was due at seven and Mrs Hemsley had been standing in the window since that time. She told the police she had been there 'for ten minutes' (which means very little, it's what people say when they mean a short time) when she saw two men in balaclavas get out of a car which had been parked in the service road, say something to a girl who had been walking southwards and bundle her into the car. The girl didn't struggle much and the car didn't immediately move away but it had done so when Mrs Hemsley's son arrived after about five minutes. That worry off her mind, she debated with herself whether she should phone the police. She looked out of the window again but the car had gone and she hadn't taken its number. Still, she did phone the police at seven thirty-five.

This was the time when Ivor began to be restive. There was a phone in the car – *he* had a mobile, thick and heavy as a brick, and other people did, but to nothing like the extent they have now – and Dermot and Lloyd had our phone number and had been instructed to call him if there were problems. Ivor went out into the mews and looked up and down it, the way people do in these situations, though it doesn't bring the expected one any sooner. He grew afraid that the phone would ring while he was outside, so he went back indoors and as he came into the living room the phone did ring. It wasn't Dermot or Lloyd but one of our friends calling to tell us she couldn't come to a dinner party we were having. By then it was ten to eight.

Even if the traffic was very heavy, it was stretching things a bit to take fifty or even forty-five minutes, if Hebe had been late, from the Watford Way to the middle of Hampstead. Something had gone wrong. She hadn't come. Gerry Furnal had been late home or detained at work or the child had been suddenly ill. But if she hadn't come why hadn't Lloyd or Dermot phoned? At no time did Ivor suspect what had happened. He wasn't worried. He was angry. His anger grew and grew and at five to eight he poured himself a stiff gin with a drop of tonic. He wasn't going to touch the champagne just in case, by some miracle, she still turned up.

Was it possible Dermot and Lloyd had reneged on him, just hadn't gone to the pick-up place? He knew they had seen each other at least once after his encounter with them in the pub in Victoria. He had suggested that the two of them meet after a few days to arrange things, the renting of the car and the purchase of handcuffs, gag and balaclavas, and had seen them exchange phone numbers. Maybe they had simply decided to pocket the first two hundred and fifty pounds he had given each of them and do nothing. There was little he could do about it if they had.

He might have phoned the car but he didn't know the number. Besides, he was angry, not worried. He waited there till eight thirty, thought of going home but stayed on till nine. Then he changed back into his own clothes and left, taking the two envelopes with him but forgetting all about the champagne. At home he listened to no news bulletins, nor did he turn on the television. If he had he might have seen horrific pictures of the crash come up on the screen, though there was nothing that night about a kidnapping.

The story Iris and I read in the paper quoted the police as saying there had been a kidnap attempt and the victim was Hebe Furnal, 27, of West Hendon. Newspapers don't give precise addresses and often they don't give exact locations where events or accidents happen. They didn't in this case. They alluded vaguely to 'a Hendon junction' and a 'roads intersection in north London' and to this day I don't know exactly where the accident happened, though later on I did find out more details. The car had been 'in collision with' a forty-ton lorry the paper described, American-fashion, as a 'truck'. Hebe Furnal had been bound and gagged. The two men were wearing jackets with hoods. Lloyd Freeman was dead and Dermot Lynch, the driver of the car, was in hospital in a serious condition with brain damage and multiple injuries. The driver of the lorry, high up in his cab, I suppose, was unharmed.

There followed some biographical details about Hebe, substantially accurate except that her son was referred to as Jason, but no speculation as yet as to why anyone would kidnap her. That came later. Reporters must have been to Gerry Furnal's house to get the photograph they had used of Hebe. It was a nice photograph, not a studio portrait but a shot of her on a beach playing with her little boy.

I hadn't finished reading it before Iris was on the phone to Ivor. The phone rang half a dozen times and then it went on to message. She didn't leave a message – what could she have said? We kept trying to get hold of Ivor throughout the morning and at midday Iris said, 'I think we ought to go back.'

We went back and, without bothering about lunch, drove straight to Old Pye Street. Iris had just stopped breastfeeding Nadine, so we'd parked in a lay-by on the A12 to give her a bottle and some tinned stuff and she had slept contentedly ever since. (I know this should be about Ivor, not me, and that I say too much about my daughter. I shall watch it in future but can't promise anything.) So to Ivor. He was in. Yes, the phone had rung and rung, but he hadn't answered it because he was sure it was Hebe with excuses for why she hadn't turned up and he was still too angry to speak to her. At lunchtime he had gone out to buy a paper and he'd bought the one we had seen.

Ivor's flat was very elegant, full of good early Victorian furniture and quite valuable paintings. He had a private income – a great-aunt had left him a house to sell and a considerable sum of money when she died ten years before – and he had indulged himself. A compulsively tidy man (anal, said Iris, but fondly), he was in the habit of having a place for everything and he put everything back in its place. There wasn't even a cup or a glass about.

Iris threw her arms round him and held him close. 'I'm so sorry, I'm so sorry,' she kept saying.

I asked him when he knew.

'Not till about an hour ago. I don't bother much with bloody scandal sheets at the weekends, get too much of them all week. I read it in the paper shop. Christ, I had to go outside and sit down on a wall.'

It was then that he told us. It took a long time, but I think telling us did him good. Halfway through he wanted a drink, said he'd had a brandy when he got back to the flat after buying the paper, but Iris stopped him having another. She fetched him a glass of water and made him drink half of it. When he got to the end, to his coming back here and going to bed, still furiously angry, he looked up and said, 'God, poor little Hebe.'

Those weren't quite the only words I ever heard him utter which might be construed as expressing grief but they almost were. I asked him what he had done. Presumably, he had told the police.

He looked at me and there was a strange expression on his face. Secretive, certainly. Covert? Incredulous that I should have asked? Perhaps all those things.

'Well, no,' he said. 'I haven't.' His voice rose, was suddenly indignant, almost angry with me. 'How can I? For God's sake, how can you fucking ask?'

Iris had been kneeling down by Nadine's car seat. She had wiped Nadine's mouth with a tissue and given her a quick kiss on the forehead. She got up.

'Ivor,' she said, 'I'm not hearing this.'

'What aren't you hearing?' His face was very set and his voice was sharp.

'You must tell them. How can you, you say. How *can't* you?

Everyone thinks she was really abducted, the police, her husband – her *husband*, Ivor – do you ever think of him? You have to tell them it was you, you set it up.'

'Look,' he said, calming down, 'of course I've thought of the police. If it had been the accident only and nothing about their taking the pretend kidnap seriously, I'd have gone straight to them. I'd have told them and never mind the consequences. There's no doubt about that, I wouldn't have hesitated.'

'What do you mean, consequences?' Iris said.

'Gerry Furnal, for starters, and a snide little paragraph in the *Mirror* for another.'

I asked him what was different now.

'It wouldn't be a snide little paragraph,' Ivor said. 'It would be a front-page scandal story. MP stages kidnap of charity chief's wife. Besides, it's too late.' There was a clock on the mantelpiece and a watch on his wrist but still he asked me, 'What time is it?'

'Just gone four.'

'This has been news since – when? Last night probably. First thing this morning. All over the papers. On TV, I expect, only I haven't watched any. They're going to ask me, the first thing they're going to ask me, is why I've only just told them. I can't tell them, Rob. It's too late.'

We stayed with him. Well, I did. Iris went out and bought a loaf and some smoked salmon and made sandwiches for us. Ivor ate nothing. We turned on the early-evening news and of course it was the lead story, with more pictures of the crash and photographs of Hebe and a lot more about a kidnap attempt going wrong. They put Gerry Furnal on, a shattered man in tears, the tears actually streaming down his face, who said he didn't know why anyone would kidnap Hebe as they must have known he had no money for a ransom. There was speculation about someone they called a 'mastermind' behind the abduction. When he heard that bit, Ivor put his head in his hands and muttered, 'Turn the fucking thing off.'

A good deal later we took Nadine home. Iris was very tired but still we talked a lot that evening about Ivor's decision not to go to the police. I suppose neither of us could understand it. Iris said that if only he'd gone to them as soon as he'd read that newspaper at lunchtime everything wouldn't exactly have been all right, but a lot better than it was turning out to be. That news story we had seen on the TV would have been very different and there was a good chance his name wouldn't have been mentioned. Without the abduction element it wasn't much more than an ordinary road crash, the kind of thing that happened all too often and does even more now.

'You don't think some journalist would have found out he was behind it?' I said.

'Possibly, but even if someone had and had printed it, the only blame which could be attached to him was – well, having an affair with a married woman. He'd have had to give the newspaper an interview saying he deeply regretted what he'd done. The death of one of those men was a tragedy, et cetera, et cetera, he was broken-hearted over Hebe Furnal's death – he's not though, is he? – and he was very sorry for the whole business. The main thing would have been to establish that there was no abduction. It was a game, a set-up and a private matter. If he'd done that, don't you think it would have blown over in a couple of days?'

'It would have damaged his political career.'

'Not much, though. Not for long. His chief whip would be cross – I think. Would he, though? Men laugh about that sort of thing. I mean, it's no laughing matter now because two people are dead, but it would have been. Still, I don't think Ivor would have been blamed much. Gerry Furnal seems a meek sort of man, awfully wretched, poor thing. Those tears were dreadful, weren't they? He wouldn't want to fight Ivor. The worst he'd do is fix up a meeting with him and make a big scene. Couldn't Ivor have weathered all that?'

'Apparently not,' I said. 'I've never seen him so afraid. He was a different man.'

★

No one ever attempted to blackmail Ivor. Yet almost from the first he was blackmail material. Of the few people who knew about the birthday present, not one of them knew it all. Each of them knew some of it, from one aspect or another, but they could all have asked him for money, a large sum of money or a guaranteed income to keep silent, but none of them did. I'm sure this wasn't because of their loyalty to him or fondness for him which held them back, but it may have been fear. Or even a kind of diffidence. I wonder how many people there are who would try demanding money with menaces, as the legal definition has it, but for their reluctance to appear quite so base and low in their victim's eyes. Perhaps I'm being naïve. The fact remains that Ivor was an MP, a respectable man, a rich man on his way to getting richer, who had set in motion a train of reprehensible events which he very much wanted to keep secret. Still, an independent observer might have said that none of it was really his fault. Not at the beginning, at any rate.

6

We always think first of saving our own skin. I did when Gerry phoned. I was having a lie-in. Not that I had been out the night before. As usual. I'm tired at the end of the week and on Fridays I'm usually in bed by ten. Like an elderly person, as Mummy used to tell me before Callum came on the scene and she was scolding me for not finding a husband or even a boyfriend. I still like to lie in bed on Saturdays a bit later than my usual seven a.m. rising time. The phone rang at eight thirty and I thought it was Mummy, trying to catch me because I hadn't answered when she called the night before. I was still in bed. I reached for the receiver, picked it up and heard a man say, 'Jane? It's Gerry.' I didn't recognize his voice. It sounded like someone had tried to strangle him. 'You won't be surprised it's me. I should have called you before, I'm sorry.'

Caution, self-protection, whatever you like to call it, is a wonderful thing. I knew something was very wrong before he spoke again.

'You must have waited hours for her.'

How did I catch on so fast? I did, or partly. 'I did for a while,' I said, wondering what was coming next.

'She's dead,' he said. 'I ought to break it more gently. The police were gentle with me. But the very fact that they were police was enough, standing there on the doorstep. They didn't need to say anything. It was a car crash. God knows what she was doing, walking somewhere. She should have been in the tube going off to meet you. Still, it doesn't matter.' He drew a long, shuddering gasp. 'Nothing matters now.'

I don't know what made me say it. I don't offer to help people. No one helps me. 'Shall I come to you? I could do things.'

'It's very kind . . .' he began, then, 'Yes, please – would you?'

I got up and dressed, went round the corner and bought a paper,

44

staring at the headline. Gerry hadn't said anything about an attempt to kidnap Hebe. The paper said she was handcuffed and gagged, the two men were hooded and the car had tinted windows. It was a real drama I'd got myself into and it excited me. I don't get much excitement in my life. Ivor Tesham's name came into my head and I tried to remember what Hebe had told me about the plans for this birthday present. She was to walk along the Watford Way, where she'd be picked up by a car. Driven by Tesham or by his driver? She didn't say, perhaps she didn't know. A car *had* picked her up but it wasn't Tesham's. This was a real kidnap, a coincidence maybe, but nothing to do with him. He would have waited for her last night like I was supposed to have waited for her but she never came.

Driving up to West Hendon and Irving Road, I thought about the alibi I'd given, or been prepared to give, to keep Hebe from being found out. I had already lied to Gerry. The idea struck me like a splash of cold water that I might be questioned by the police and have to lie to them. Have to? Or was I to come out with the truth as to what Hebe had been up to? There wasn't much traffic about, there never was on a Saturday morning. I would be there in ten minutes. I knew I must make up my mind exactly what I was going to say when Gerry questioned me about the previous evening. It was then that I realized I didn't even know which theatre was showing *Life Threatening*. I pulled off the A5, parked and consulted the paper I had bought. The Duke of York's – where was that? St Martin's Lane, I guessed. I would have to say I hung about in St Martin's Lane until it was too late to go in. Why hadn't I phoned to find out where Hebe was? I would have to think of something to explain that. It was then, as I started the car once more, that it hit me. At last it hit me. Hebe was *dead*. We'd met at university and been friends ever since. I'd been her bridesmaid and was Justin's godmother, though God didn't come into it much. I'd never see her again. She was gone. She was dead. I stopped the car again and switched off the engine.

I ought to have been heartbroken but I wasn't. Of course I would pretend I was when I got to Gerry's. My best friend, we saw each other at least once a week, not to mention going to all those cinemas and out for meals together. That's where she was going, he would have told the police, off to the theatre with her best friend. How sweet and proper it sounded, chastely going to see a play with another girl. The paper hadn't said how she had been dressed when they found her body but maybe they didn't know, maybe the police wouldn't tell them, and I thought about how she said she might go off on her date wearing nothing under her big coat. I ought to have been sad – why wasn't I? Because, though she'd been my 'friend' all these years, I'd never liked her. We call people our friends without thinking how we really feel about them, that actually we fear them or envy them. How could I have liked a woman who had everything I've never had? Did she like me? Probably not, but she liked me being plain and dull and awkward while she was such a star.

I was the more intelligent one, that's all. She wouldn't have cared about that. She had had beauty and self-confidence, a husband, a child, a lover, and no worries. She had never had a job, so she didn't have the fear of losing one always hanging over her. She didn't know what it was like to be me, working for an outfit which was always threatened with closure or at any rate being severely cut in size. Her husband might not earn much but he did earn it and it would go on, he would keep her for the rest of her life and to avoid working herself all she had to do was keep having babies. I realized then that he wouldn't and she wouldn't, because she was dead. All the beauty and the charm and the unearned income were over for her for ever. I asked myself if I cared and I knew at once that I didn't. I was glad. I was *relieved*. I ought to feel happy, because all I had to worry about now was keeping the way I felt from Gerry, and keeping the truth from him too.

I drove the last mile or two and turned into Irving Road. It was one of those streets of terraces, about a hundred years old, I suppose, all the houses exactly the same, grey brickwork, slate roofs, a gable at the top and a bay window downstairs, nothing green, drearily

46

ugly. Once, about a year before, I was driving Mummy up there to see a friend in Edgware and I pointed out Hebe's road to her, deserted but for a van driver delivering something. The place looked a uniform grey in the drizzling rain. Mummy is so out of touch she thinks young married couples all live in lovely detached houses in leafy suburbs. 'He's not doing very well, is he?' she said. 'That's the sort of street your grandparents lived in when I was small. Of course, it didn't last long. We moved when I was seven.'

It wasn't deserted that Saturday morning. A crowd stood outside Gerry's house, filling the tiny front garden, spilling all over the pavement, people with cameras and a single policeman. It took me a moment before I understood. This was the press. As I parked at the kerb, as near to the house as I could get, reporters and cameramen swarmed up to the car and a flash went off in my face. I tried to push through the pack, their voices shouting at me, 'Who are you?' 'What are you doing here?' 'Are you Hebe's sister?'

The normal reaction is to cover one's face even if one has nothing to hide. I picked up the scarf that was on the seat beside the paper, held it up ineffectually to my mouth and nose and got out of the car. 'I'm only the babysitter,' I said.

'Would you call yourself a family friend?' someone asked.

'If you like,' I said, 'but I don't know anything.' I'd have loved to talk to them, tell them the truth about Hebe and Ivor Tesham, but I knew that would be just for the momentary pleasure of it. I had an interest in the long term and I needed to remember that. I elbowed my way through the crowd to Gerry's gate, shoving aside cameras they stuck in my face. 'Please let me get to the door.'

Gerry must have heard some of this, because he opened it just as I got there. The cameras homed in on him, their flashes blinding. He grabbed my hand and pulled me inside. The slamming door shook the house.

'Where's Justin?' I said with just the proper air of concern.

'My mother's been here and taken him home with her. I feel guilty about that. He ought to be with me. But he just walks up and down saying, "Justin wants Mummy," and it's unbearable.'

47

I thought he'd take me in his arms and hug me, it seemed the natural thing to do in the circumstances, but he didn't. He'd been crying and his eyes were swollen. I went into the kitchen and made us both tea. I carried it into the living room on a tray and drew the curtains to shut out the faces pressed against the glass. All the time I was telling myself, don't let it show that you're enjoying yourself, don't let him see you're excited.

'There's a police officer out there,' Gerry said, 'but he says he can't do anything unless any of them breach the peace, whatever that means, or do criminal damage.'

The noise they made, a kind of threatening hum, punctuated by shouts, reminded me of the sound of distant battle I'd heard in war programmes on television.

'Was it really an abduction?' I asked him.

'The police say so. It must have been. She was *handcuffed*, Jane. She had a scarf tied round her face. I don't really know much more, only that one of the men is dead and the other is in a very bad way in intensive care. He's unconscious and has been since it happened.'

'The lorry driver?'

'It seems not to have been his fault. He's uninjured apart from cuts and bruises. I mean, the lorry was so big and the car so comparatively small. They haven't said, of course they haven't, but the general idea seems to be that it was the fault of this man Dermot Lynch. He was the driver of the car.' He thought he was changing the subject. Maybe he thought the idea was to spare me atrocious details. 'How long did you wait for her at the theatre?'

'Only till it was too late to go in,' I said. 'Only about a quarter of an hour.'

'You didn't phone me?'

Impossible to get out of that one without a lie. I lied. 'I did try. There was no answer.'

'Odd,' he said. 'I was here. What time would that have been?'

'About twenty to eight. I had to find a call box. The phone rang. Perhaps I'd got a wrong number. You know how it is – you misplace one digit.'

48

'That's what it must have been,' he said. 'Were you worried?'

'Not really,' I said, ad-libbing. 'I thought there must have been some crisis at home and I didn't want to bother you. I was going to phone this morning.'

'Yes,' he said. 'Yes, of course.'

It was soon after that that he began to cry. He put his hands on the arm of the chair, put his head in his hands and sobbed. I didn't know what to do so I did nothing. Probably the best thing I could have done was join him and cry myself, but I couldn't. Only actresses can make themselves cry. I remember once seeing Nicola Ross with real tears pouring down her face in some play. But I am no good at acting. I just sat there and listened to the battle hum from outside and the racking sobs inside and after a while I made more tea. When I came back with it, his crying was over and he was sitting very upright, red-eyed and hollow-cheeked.

In a voice made hoarse by all those tears, he said, 'I don't understand why anyone would want to kidnap her. What for? Not for a ransom surely. I haven't got any money. Would I live here if I had?'

'I don't know,' I said.

'I asked the police if they could have mistaken her for someone else but they said no.'

That evening, of course, they were saying yes.

I did his washing. I made a casserole for his supper and Justin's and put it in the oven. The kitchen wasn't an advertisement of Hebe's housekeeping skills but I couldn't see why I should clean it up. He wouldn't notice. At midday I battled my way through the reporters and photographers – I found controlling myself and not talking to them the hardest part – drove to a supermarket at Brent Cross and shopped for him, Justin and myself. Mrs Furnal, a bright talkative woman, very unlike her son, brought Justin back at five, struggled through the mob, shouting to them to go away, to leave her son alone, to have some compassion and think of the child's feelings. I would have known better than to say any of that nonsense. She almost fell into the house when I opened the front door.

Justin ran ahead, calling, 'Justin wants Mummy.'

Quickly recovered, Mrs Furnal sniffed my casserole, pronounced it delicious, almost in the same breath telling me I could go home now as she meant to stay for the evening.

'Please let me know if you want me again,' I said to Gerry.

We'd been in the kitchen and hadn't noticed a lull in the pandemonium outside. It was half past six. When I opened the front door all the reporters had gone. There was just one cameraman remaining and he was about to leave, loading his equipment into the boot of his car. I was rather disappointed, because I kept wondering if one of them would eventually force his way into the house or climb up to the half-open bedroom window. But it wasn't to be, as Mummy would say. The phone rang and Gerry went to answer it. It was the police to tell him there had been a new development and they would call on him 'shortly', but I didn't know that at the time. I said to his mother to say goodbye to him for me. I tried to kiss Justin but he jerked his cheek away and then I left. Halfway to Kilburn, where I live, I decided I was going to phone Ivor Tesham. I'd find his number somehow and I'd call him. Why? I don't know really, but I felt that I needed to speak to him. I could feel the adrenalin racing through my veins, or whatever it does, something that seldom happens to me.

Oddly perhaps, I didn't think much about why the press had removed themselves from outside Gerry's house. I was naïve, I suppose, I didn't know much about that sort of thing, and I thought they'd given up because it was getting late, it was Saturday night and they weren't finding out anything new. When I got into my flat the first thing I did was turn on the TV and I caught the tail end of the news and about two minutes devoted to the crash, the abduction and the serious condition of Dermot Lynch. They had a shot of Gerry at his front door with a tearful Justin in his arms and one of me running with a scarf held up to my face.

The phone rang twice in ten minutes. I didn't answer it but I guessed it was Mummy. Like the way I have premonitions, I can always guess when it's Mummy who phoned. She didn't leave a message and I knew why. She wanted to get hold of me herself and talk for hours about the kidnap, something she knew she could only do when she was paying for the call. When I'd poured myself a glass of wine and drunk about a third of it, I got the phone book and looked up Ivor Tesham. I didn't expect him to be there, I thought he'd be ex-directory, but there he was: I. H. Tesham, 140b Old Pye Street, SW1. Finding him had been quick. Bracing myself to dial that number took longer. The adrenalin had gone back to wherever it came from, so I drank some more wine, took a deep breath and dialled the number. Of course I was fairly confident he wouldn't be there, not on Saturday night, and I preferred to think of him getting the message I'd leave and feeling he'd perhaps have to phone me. He answered.

Not with his number or his name, not with 'Hello' but a simple cool, 'Yes?'

I took a deep breath. 'Mr Tesham,' I said, 'my name is Jane Atherton. Hebe was my friend. I have been with her husband all day and now I'm at home I thought you might want to talk to me. I mean, I know you arranged for Hebe to be picked up last night. I thought there might be things you wanted to know.'

Silence. It endured so long that I thought for one moment that she might have made it up. She was a fantasist. Maybe she had some other lover, some *ordinary* man, but to make me envious had told me it was this glamorous MP. The pearls were fake, she'd bought them herself at some cheap place.

'Mr Tesham?'

At last he spoke. 'I think you must have been her alibi.'

'Yes.'

'A rare occurrence for me, but I am at a loss for words.'

'I don't mean to upset you,' I said, remembering what Mrs Furnal had advised about compassion. It doesn't come naturally to me.

He laughed. It was a laugh without amusement. 'What are you going to do?'

'I don't understand,' I said.

'Really? Let me be more explicit. Do you have information you want to pass on to the – er, the authorities? Mr Furnal? Perhaps you'd be good enough to tell me.'

I didn't know what he meant. Did he think I was threatening him? My excitement died and the tears I couldn't shed when Gerry was crying pricked my eyelids now. A cold drop ran down my cheek. I could cry for myself.

'I'm not going to tell anyone,' I said. 'I don't know anything to tell anyone. All I know is that you sent a car that was meant to pick Hebe up last night.'

'Ah,' he said. 'I think you've confused things, Miss Atherton. *A* car picked Hebe up last night, but it had nothing to do with me. The two men inside it intended to abduct her. Does that clear things up for you?'

It was he who confused me. He made me feel the way good-looking sophisticated men always do, even when I can only hear them. I said, 'Yes, thank you,' and to that I added, 'I'm sorry.'

I really cried then. Great tearing sobs. I'd made a fool of myself. On a high all day, I had dropped down into the depths in the space of the three minutes the call lasted. Why I should have remembered at this point how Hebe had humiliated me, I don't know. Unless it was because he had done the same. Back into my mind came her kindly suggestions that such and such a boring man, some colleague of Gerry's, their next-door neighbour who lived with his mother, the elderly widower who was my boss at the library, might be persuaded to fancy me. That was what led to me inventing Callum. I started wondering if she had liked going about with me because seeing us together pointed up her beauty by contrast to me. So I cried and drank some more wine and went to bed, only to get up again when the phone rang.

Mummy, of course. Was it my friend all that stuff on the news was about? The girl who lived in that rather squalid house in the middle of nowhere?

'That's a bit rich from someone who lives in Ongar,' I said.

'Please don't start by being rude to me, Jane. I've been ringing and ringing you all day. The least you can do is tell me if this thing on the television is true.'

So I told her what my day had been like, with special reference to how upset I was at losing my best friend.

'Well, really, Jane, I would have thought I was your best friend. I'm sure no one does more for you than I do.'

That I ignored and went on a bit about Gerry being devastated, a word she uses a lot herself, and poor little Justin. I'd done the shopping for them, I said, and cooked and now I was exhausted, so if she wouldn't mind I'd ring off. The phone rang again almost immediately and of course I thought it was her, wanting to reprove me for being offhand. It wasn't, it was Gerry.

The police had been and had told him they had reason to believe that Hebe had been abducted by mistake for someone else, a far more likely victim, the wife of a multi-millionaire. That was why the press had gone. This news would be in the newspapers next day and on the television.

If I could spare the time, would I come up to Irving Road again tomorrow? I hesitated and then I said of course I would. There wouldn't be the excitement there had been today. The media people would now be outside the multi-millionaire's place, wherever that was.

I said I had come down from my high and dropped into the depths, but now I sank even lower. I suppose that unconsciously I'd been thinking, certainly hoping, that Ivor Tesham might have been in some way responsible, but now I knew he couldn't be. It was a real kidnap and the woman they meant to abduct was someone else, someone who maybe looked like Hebe but that was all.

Why had I said I'd go up to Irving Road again? What was in it for me? The fact was I had nothing else to do and that is true for me on most Sundays. As I lay down in bed again I had another premonition, a very powerful one this time. 'Premonition' means something bad to come, though, doesn't it? This wouldn't be bad but maybe a real future for me. Like I often do, I saw it in pictures

– one single picture really. I was in the house in Irving Road, in the living room, and Gerry was there sitting in the other armchair. All the photographs he keeps of Hebe about the place had gone and I had a wedding ring on my finger.

7

Ivor was relieved in an entirely unreasonable way. It was as if the crash and the abduction had nothing to do with him but were only something which he, like almost every newspaper reader in the country, had read about. Press attention had shifted to Kelly Mason, to her husband and his millions, to his purchase of a football team; police attention had shifted away from Irving Road, West Hendon, to the Bishops Avenue, Hampstead Garden Suburb. He knew this theory must be false, he knew what had really happened, but it seemed to him only like a heaven-sent reprieve which carried with it a free pardon.

'I'm off the hook.' He punched the air exultantly. 'The worst is over.'

'Hebe is still dead,' Iris said.

'I'm well aware of that, thank you.'

'What exactly were you afraid of, Ivor?'

'Afraid is a strong word,' he said. 'I was starting to feel increasingly uncomfortable about the possibility of my little adventure coming to light. In some gossip column, for instance.' He gets pompous and talks like a politician when he is excited. 'In some diary piece. If I'd gone to the police, as you helpfully suggested, that's what would have happened. Now, you see, anything like that would have been quite unnecessary. It wasn't Hebe they meant to abduct. It was this Kelly Mason.'

He placed the scathing stress on 'Kelly' up-and-coming Tory notables always do put on names they perceive as working class. Iris looked at him sadly. She was more affected by all this than I was, but then she loved him a whole lot more than I did. She shook her head.

'But you know that isn't true. They did abduct Hebe. It may

55

have been a mock abduction but it was aimed at Hebe, not Kelly Mason. Don't you have to get that clear, whatever the police and the media may think?'

Ivor had turned up without warning halfway through Sunday morning, his arms full of Sunday papers. Our reception of the news hadn't been the wholehearted congratulations on his escape he had expected.

'Whatever,' he said dismissively. 'Have you seen a paper yet? Have you seen the news on television? It's extraordinary. This chap Damian Mason has been getting anonymous letters threatening to kill his wife if he doesn't give up buying whatever-it-is United football team. He even had one threatening to abduct her. I imagine he told the police it wasn't Hebe but his wife poor old Dermot and Lloyd were after. I feel like going up there and shaking his hand.'

'I wouldn't,' said Iris.

'Of course I won't.'

I had picked up the *Sunday Times* and was looking at the photograph of Kelly Mason, a pretty blonde not all that unlike Hebe.

'You can see the resemblance,' I said.

'To Hebe? Oh, please. You jest.' He had an irritating habit of saying this, like some minor character in Shakespeare, instead of 'you must be joking'. I don't think I'd ever disliked my brother-in-law so much, though I knew my antipathy wouldn't last. 'Hebe was beautiful,' he said. 'She had a delicate, ethereal sort of beauty. Actually, I can't bear to think of that damaged, spoilt. That really distresses me.'

It was at this point that Nadine, who had been asleep upstairs, let out a disgruntled cry. I went up to her, glad of the chance to get away. When I came back with her in my arms, Iris was asking what Kelly Mason would have been doing walking down the Watford Way at seven in the evening or any other time. Wouldn't she more likely have been in her Lamborghini in Hampstead Garden Suburb?

'It's actually a Porsche she has,' Ivor said, laughing. He could laugh. His bouncing from frightened gloom into adrenalin-fuelled ebullience was almost manic. 'Apparently, her mother lives in one of those roads off the Watford Way. She'd been there on Friday – in the Porsche of course – and was safe at home when they thought they were abducting her.'

Iris corrected him. 'When the police *think* they thought they were abducting her, you mean.'

'You know, if I wasn't convinced of your sisterly devotion, I'd begin to think you rather resented my escape from disgrace. That's what the press call people in my position who've come to grief, you know, "the disgraced MP". Is that what you'd like?'

I'd had enough of this, so I took Nadine into the kitchen, where I laid her down on a counter and performed that task which, in the eyes of women's magazine journalists and nannies, is supposed to be the test of good fatherhood: I changed her nappy. She kicked and smiled and laughed, and as always I was lost in adoration. She is almost eighteen now, gratifying me with her splendid A-level results, four passes at A grade, and it says something for her good sense that if she heard this, my talking about her as a baby would provoke no more from her than an amused, 'Oh, Dad.'

Though richer and neither more nor less beautiful, Kelly Mason hasn't enjoyed such good fortune, such love or happy family life. She knew nothing beforehand about the anonymous letters – her husband had kept them from her – but she knew when she read those Sunday papers. They called her a 'Checkout Chick' and a 'Supermarket Cinderella' because she worked for Tesco when Damian Mason first saw her. He was in there buying a packet of crisps and two hundred cigarettes. It was his first ever visit to a supermarket and probably his last and he fell in love with her. Everyone said she was lucky. He took her to some South Pacific island on their honeymoon and bought her a big house (the papers called it a mansion) in Hampstead Garden Suburb.

She had always been nervous, a shy diffident sort of girl. The journalists who interviewed her after the attempted abduction mocked her cruelly for having no O levels (GCSEs were called O levels when she was at school), for wearing high heels with white jeans, for enjoying television sitcoms. The photographs they used of her were the ones in which she was standing awkwardly, her mouth open or her eyes shut. The press that assembled outside her house terrified her. She was afraid even to go near a window. After four days of it she had a miscarriage.

Kelly Mason passionately wanted children. She never had any. She had several what were then called mental breakdowns instead. Psychiatric wards in private hospitals became places with which she grew very familiar. She spent six months in one of them and long periods in others. Most of this found its way into the papers as Damian Mason's riches increased and his fortune passed the five hundred million mark. You can probably remember all this. When it seemed unlikely that Kelly would ever emerge from her incarceration in some expensive hydro for the incurably insane, Mason divorced her. He married again last year and his new wife has just had a baby. I'd be the first to say that all this wasn't Ivor's fault, but without his idea of a birthday present for Hebe Furnal it would very likely never have happened.

I went back into the living room and found them both still sitting where they had been before but Iris drinking a glass of water and Ivor with his usual gin and tonic. That reminded me.

'Thanks for the champagne,' I said.

He laughed. 'You thought I'd put it in your fridge to thank you for lending me your house. No doubt I should have done, but I didn't. I forgot it. Still, you're welcome.'

I put Nadine on a blanket on the floor and we watched her kick and roll about and laugh.

'Isn't she lovely?' Iris said.

'Very lovely.' I think he meant it. 'I'm proud to be her uncle.'

'Would it do you any real harm if all this got into the papers? It wasn't your fault. If it was anyone's, it looks as if it was Dermot Lynch's.'

I don't know if it was her mention of the press or Dermot Lynch's name, but a shadow seemed to cross his face. The young, carefree look he'd had from the moment he came into the house an hour before had gone.

'It depends on what you mean by real harm. The Lady –' Ivor always referred to Margaret Thatcher as 'the Lady' – 'wouldn't like it. If I'm in line for promotion I wouldn't get it or not yet. If they used stuff about the handcuffs and the gag they'd make me look like some sort of pervert.' He tried to sound confident but didn't quite succeed. 'You see, there'd be the little difficulty of me not going to the police when the media made it look like a real abduction and perhaps rather a larger difficulty when I didn't after they thought this Kelly Mason was the victim. But I really think that's all over now. I mean, with the interest moving to the Masons – even if Dermot comes round and talks, a pretty unlikely eventuality, would anyone believe him?'

I'd decided not to join in this conversation.

Iris said, 'They'd want to see you, though, wouldn't they? They'd ask you if there was any connection between you and the Masons and maybe between you and Hebe.'

He had thought of that, but being reminded of it brought that sullen look back to his face. 'Well, perhaps, but no one knows about me and Hebe except you.'

'Are you sure of that?'

One person knew or half knew, the woman friend of Hebe's who had provided her alibi. She had phoned him the night before but he didn't tell us that then. He wanted to get off the subject, that was clear. He had said he was off the hook and now it was starting to look as if he was still hung up on it. Ivor's is one of those natures that will put the best construction on a situation if possible, take the brightest view, be optimistic. It's a useful trait in a politician. After all, they never get up in Parliament and say the war was a mistake, the economy is in dire straits and only darkness lies ahead, do they? Ivor sat up straight in his chair, asked for another gin and said he had a feeling everything was going to be all right. It would blow over.

'Let me take you out to lunch.'

We didn't like going to restaurants with Nadine in her buggy. Disapproving glares from other diners made me cross and Iris nervous because I was cross. We assembled various leftovers, along with a cold chicken, for lunch and after that we all went for a walk on the Heath. It was sunny and getting warm, a beautiful time of the year, and we talked about other things.

That was the last we saw of Ivor for a while. Iris told me at the beginning of June that she was pregnant and I of course was overjoyed. But even though we were preoccupied, Ivor wasn't absent from our minds and we thought about him a lot. We both felt he ought to have been in touch with the police from the moment he knew about the accident and this, up to a point, estranged us from him. Iris kept saying not going to the police was unlike him, she wouldn't have believed it of him. As for me, I thought it behaviour characteristic of politicians, who become different people once they have a little power and can see the possibility of more power to come.

We read the papers every day, more papers than we usually did. We watched more news on television and listened to more on radio. Most of the anonymous letters Damian Mason had received appeared, photographs of them or printed facsimiles. Tabloids daily carried pictures of Kelly Mason running out to her car or her frightened face at a window. One of her sisters, stupidly but in innocence, gave them a photograph of her in a bikini. No paper paid much attention to the inquests and only one of them, a broadsheet, mentioned them. Hebe Furnal must have had a funeral but no reporters or cameramen appeared to have attended it. Lloyd Freeman's, on the other hand, was a much-photographed big affair, his coffin half hidden by extravagant wreaths and crosses. There were nearly as many photographs of him as of Kelly Mason, including one taken at that party of Nicola Ross's, his arm round a woman who was probably his girlfriend.

The most significant new information to appear was the police release that among the objects found in the crash car and strewn about the street where the accident had taken place was a gun. A nine-millimetre pistol, the Bond gun. When we read it Iris and I assumed this was part of the 'props', the paraphernalia Ivor had got

60

Dermot to buy, but in this country, then and now, you can't go into a shop and buy a gun as you can handcuffs and gags. And this was a real one, though it seemed no ammunition was found with it.

During that first week reference was made just once, as far as I saw, to Dermot Lynch. This was in a small paragraph at the foot of an inside page. It said that he still lay unconscious in hospital, but not which hospital, and that he had been visited only by his mother, Mrs Philomena Lynch, and his brother Sean. Hebe had passed entirely away from media interest. A mistake had been made, they seemed to believe, and the best way to exonerate themselves from reproof was to avoid all mention of error. Hebe had been in the crash car, Hebe had been seen by a witness being forced into that car and Hebe was dead, but all that was unimportant, was in the past and best forgotten. Whether the police also thought that way I doubt. Probably they were looking at both possibilities, that either Hebe or Kelly Mason might have been the intended victim, but if they were the press was uninterested.

Ivor had tried, with some success at first, to make us believe his worries were over. Dermot Lynch would never recover, would never speak rationally and coherently about what had happened. But he didn't really think this way. Very badly injured people do recover consciousness, sometimes after months of coma, and they especially do so now (and seventeen years ago) that medical science has made such advances. Ivor knew this as well as I did and worried about it. In the weeks following the accident he apparently made several attempts to find out where Dermot was and what condition he was in. He told us this later on, but only when he wanted help in finding the hospital Dermot had been taken to.

He had the Lynchs' address in Rowley Place, Paddington, a Westminster City Council complex of blocks of flats where Dermot had lived with his mother and brother. He had their phone number. Of course he also had the phone number of the garage in Vauxhall where Dermot had worked. But he was afraid to phone either number, though 'afraid' wasn't the word he used. All the time, while this business was troubling him, he was hoping Dermot would never 'come to', as he put it, preferably would die, and because of his upbringing and education and social life, and hangovers from a religious teenage he still retained, was aware too that this desire of his was monstrous and shocking.

He had thought and thought often that he could phone Mrs Lynch, say he was a friend of Dermot's and ask after him, but there were objections to this. One of these was his voice. His was the accent of the upper class – and their accent is quite different from that of an educated middle-class person, as I expect you've noticed – and he had no gift for disguising it. He might be Dermot's employer (which indeed he briefly had been) or a client of the garage (which he was) but Dermot's mother would never believe he was Dermot's friend. There was the question too of how much about the birthday present Dermot had told his mother. Very little probably, because she would most likely have disapproved. But he might well have told his brother and told him the name of the man who employed him. Ivor decided this was unlikely, as Sean Lynch would surely have come forward if he had information for the police, but still he disliked the idea of calling Sean Lynch in case he put ideas into the man's head which might not have been there before.

Attempting to discover Dermot's whereabouts was a better way forward. Ivor told us, or told Iris, that he had never before phoned a hospital to find out the condition of a patient but he assumed the switchboard would put him through to the appropriate ward. This didn't happen. He was asked if he was a relative and, when he said he was just a friend, was told they could give out no information except to close relatives. His enquiry as to whether Dermot was in there met with a frostier response. They couldn't tell him that either. And so it went on. At last a hospital in north-west London admitted that Dermot was among its patients but it could tell him nothing more because he wasn't a relative. Ivor considered posing as a relative but soon dismissed this idea. He couldn't bring himself to do it, for he thought he would be worse off afterwards, ashamed, full of self-disgust and maybe even more vulnerable. It would be his first admission to the outside world of his involvement in the abduction and the accident. Almost superstitiously, he thought he would be exposing himself to discovery and could expect those things he had so far avoided, visits from the police, phone calls from the press, dreadful paragraphs in diary pieces.

The kidnap story disappeared from the front pages, went inside, vanished altogether from television, until one day it was gone. It had blown over. Everywhere but in Ivor's mind, that is, and also one supposes in Kelly and Damian Mason's. To Ivor, contrary to what he had expected, the absence of the story was worse than its presence. Its departure left him to imagine silent workings under the untroubled surface and his imagination was very active. It presented to him awful scenarios. Unknown to him or to almost anyone, except perhaps Gerry Furnal and Damian Mason, along with the police, wheels were turning, schemes were being concocted and plans laid. Dermot had regained consciousness and, in his fuddled and confused state, muttered a hitherto unconsidered name, hinted at a game, a joke. His mother was even now talking to the police about terribly damaging revelations. Then, also, there was that unknown quantity, Lloyd Freeman's girlfriend. At the tail end of the story, one of the last images on television had been Lloyd's funeral and the wreaths and crosses of spring flowers. There had been a woman at that funeral, young as far as could be seen, a veil of black gauze covering her head and face, making her unrecognizable. The same picture was in the papers and Ivor got it into his head that this was Lloyd's girlfriend, a woman to whom Lloyd might have told everything before he went off that evening on his last drive.

All these imagined happenings he passed on to Iris when he called her one morning to ask for her help. I was away in Manchester for a couple of days, sorting out the problems faced by a firm of insurers based in that city. If I'd been there I don't think she would have done what he asked. Certainly I'd have tried to dissuade her. But she did it. She phoned Philomena Lynch, said she was from a local newspaper and was enquiring about her son Dermot, who, she understood, was still in hospital.

She told me about it when I got home. It was bad enough doing it, she said, but it would have been worse to keep it from me.

'He was in such a state, Rob. He'd worked himself up into absolute terror. He's been imagining police coming into the House of Commons after him.'

'What did she say, this Mrs Lynch?'

'Well, she said Dermot was still unconscious but the hospital had told her not to give up hope. They'd known worse cases where the person had come through and been all right.'

'Satisfy my curiosity,' I said. 'Which newspaper did you say you worked for?'

'The *Paddington Express*. I made it up. I thought it was quite clever.'

'It sounds like a train,' I said, and she laughed, but it was an uneasy laugh.

In fact, there was a local paper called the *Paddington Express*, but I don't know if they ever found out about Iris's impersonation. Ivor was somewhat comforted by the results of this phone call. At least it showed him that his worst fears were groundless, all that paranoid stuff about wheels grinding and turning under the surface and the police silently planning when to strike. Iris was rather ashamed of herself. Not long after she'd made the phone call she said she put herself in Philomena's shoes and wondered how she'd feel if Nadine were in hospital and some impostor called to find out how she was.

About three weeks after this, towards the end of June, Ivor was alone in his flat in Old Pye Street. It was coming up to nine in the evening and the phone rang. He was still in the stage of never answering the phone without being apprehensive that it might be Jane Atherton or Gerry Furnal or the police (not to mention Lloyd Freeman's girlfriend or a member of the Lynch family) and he kept to his new habit of replying with a single brusque, 'Yes?'

It wasn't any of those people but one of the Prime Minister's aides at Number Ten. The Prime Minister would like to see him at eight thirty on the following morning. Ivor wasn't so far gone in paranoia that he thought Mrs Thatcher wanted to cast him into outer darkness because she'd found out about the birthday present. He knew what the phone call meant. A mini-reshuffle was expected and this was promotion. Elevation. By eight forty-five next day he would be an Under-Secretary of State in a government department, the next rung on the ascending ladder to power.

8

Hebe tried to change her accent to what is called received pronunci-
ation, but the Newcastle came through in unguarded moments.
Still, I hadn't realized that her parents were quite such Geordies,
the sort of people who would call their daughter Hilda before she
renamed herself. She had more or less cut herself off from them for
years. They came down for the funeral, as they put it, though
Mummy always says that wherever you live you come *up* to
London, and they brought an aunt of Hebe's with them, a woman
who looked like someone's cleaner. A lot of friends of Hebe's were
there, girls I had never seen before, not all of them dressed as I
think one should be. You don't wear skirts inches above the knees
for a funeral and you don't wear bright red. Gerry's mother came,
of course, chatting away to everyone. She only managed to shut
up while the vicar was conducting the service.

The least I could do was offer to go up to Irving Road on the
following Monday, but when I got there I found a strange woman
in the kitchen, drinking coffee and giving Justin his breakfast. She
wasn't really a strange woman but the one in the red miniskirt I'd
seen at Hebe's funeral. Gerry was there too, of course, about to go
to work. He introduced me, said this is Grania and didn't I get the
message he left on my answering machine? I didn't. I get so few I
mostly don't bother. He said he had had so many offers of help he
has got someone coming in every day this week and next. I thought
how awful this would be for Justin, one strange woman after
another, but I didn't say anything. I went up to Justin to kiss him,
but he turned his face sharply away and leaned as far away from
me out of his high chair as he could without falling.

I'd taken a week of my holiday which was owing me but I didn't
say that either. When I had spoken to him at the funeral Gerry had

asked me if I'd do him a tremendous favour and get rid of Hebe's clothes for him. Sort them out and take them to the Oxfam shop or something. Perhaps I'd also dispose of her jewellery. She'd been buried with her wedding ring but he would like to keep her engagement ring and one or two other things he had given her, a locket with a picture of Justin in it and a gold bangle. I said I would do that, but I didn't much like the way I was being treated, considering I was putting myself out for him.

'I can't do it today,' I said. 'It will have to wait.' Hebe always used to say that if you want to get hold of or keep a man you should play hard to get. Why not begin as I meant to go on? 'I'll come back on Thursday. I'll be free then.'

This was Grania's cue. She handed me a cup of coffee and said she could do it, it would give her something to do while she was there. I was about to tell her she would have enough to do in that house without sorting through clothes – I suspect she likes clothes a lot, even if they're someone else's – but Gerry got in first and said she'd have her hands full with Justin. Jane will do it, he said, and then he went off to work.

When she was sure he was out of the house and heard the front door bang, Grania said, 'I'm glad to have a chance to talk to you.'

I said nothing but drank my coffee. Justin put up his arms to be lifted out of the chair but he put them up to her, not to me. She lifted him out and told him to go and play.

I said, 'What do you want to talk about?' and she said, 'Did you know Hebe was having an affair?'

So I wasn't the only one she had confided in. I said nothing, just kept very still.

She looked at me with her head a bit on one side. She is a tall, thin woman, about thirty, with long, dark hair. Her jeans were very tight and her heels were very high and it looked as if bending over to pick Justin up might have been a problem.

'I phoned once or twice in the evenings and she wasn't in. Gerry said she was out with you. It must have been three times I phoned and that's what he said. I thought it a bit strange Hebe going out with a woman in the evening. She could have seen you in the daytime or the weekends, couldn't she?'

'What do you want me to say, Grania?'

'I don't know what you mean by that,' she said, looking offended. 'I asked her. She said he was a VIP and something in the government and it was bound to come out into the open some time but to keep it dark for now.'

I said I knew nothing about it and then I went to find Justin. But it proved one thing to me, that I was no more important to Hebe than she was. Justin was in the living room, sitting on the floor, surrounded by the contents of his toy box, saying, 'Mummy, Mummy, Mummy,' in a singsong but not obviously unhappy voice. When he saw me he rolled over on to his front and stuffed his fists into his eyes.

By the time I went back on Thursday Gerry had left for work and this time the woman-in-residence, the Justin-carer, was Lucy Compton, who was one of Hebe's bridesmaids. I was the other one. We must have looked ludicrous in our pale blue satin and wreaths of cornflowers, for Lucy is five feet ten and I am five feet two. But she was a welcome change from Grania. I didn't mind her. On Monday I had thought I was Hebe's best friend, her closest woman friend, but now I was beginning to doubt it. Justin behaved with her as if he was used to her being in the house: let her pick him up and cuddle him; as soon as she sat down, went to her and climbed on her knee.

It makes me feel like Hebe deceived me, the way she deceived everyone, letting me think I was really important to her. I may as well be honest and not pretend. I feel rejected, jealous of her because of Hebe as well as Justin. The past is being destroyed, made to mean something different from what I'd thought, and I wonder if Hebe just made a convenience of me, if I wasn't important to her at all. I was useful because I agreed to provide an alibi for her whereas perhaps these others didn't. Maybe she had asked Lucy but Lucy wouldn't. I waited for her to ask me if I knew Hebe was having an affair but she didn't, she just said a lot of very conventional things about how terrible it is to die young and what a tragedy for Gerry and Justin.

When I could escape from these platitudes I went upstairs to begin my task of clearing out Hebe's clothes, but first I went to the drawer where I know she kept her jewels. There was a lot of junk in there, necklaces mostly, which I wouldn't dignify with the name of costume jewellery, and a small plastic box containing the engagement ring, the locket and the bracelet. I'd brought three large plastic bin bags with me and a carrier. The junk went into the carrier and I felt in the back of the drawer and brought out the flat black leather case in which the pearls were lying on a bed of pink velvet.

They were beautiful but could I say they were more beautiful than any you see in a chain store? I couldn't and I know Gerry couldn't. She'd told him they came from the British Home Stores and he took her word for it without question. I wondered what Ivor Tesham paid for them. A thousand pounds? Five? More? I sat down on the bed, which Gerry said he hadn't slept in since she died, and I began thinking a lot of thoughts which are bad and base, not to say criminal. Do other people think like this when temptation comes in their way? Do they consider possibilities which would land them in court, in prison? Or do such things never cross their minds because they are honest, they are *good* people who, if these possibilities were suggested to them, would simply shake their heads and smile? Well, I expect I'd be good and all smiles if I'd had their luck and their chances, but life hasn't been very fair to me, to say the least.

Who would know if I took these pearls to a jeweller and asked him to value them? And when he had valued them said to him, will you buy them from me? Gerry believes what Hebe told him about where they came from. As far as he knows or cares, they are worth no more than the string of red glass beads I had just dropped into the carrier. He will expect them to disappear along with the beads and the carved-wood bracelet and the plastic lapel pin. My parents gave me the deposit on the studio flat I live in but I have a mortgage and I am poor. The library pays me a wage – it calls it a salary –

not much more than half the national average and my (late) father called it disgraceful for a woman with an upper second from a good university. My car once belonged to my parents, who gave it to me when they bought a new and better one. The furniture in the flat is their cast-offs.

I would like a new car and a new carpet and a decent big TV. I'd like some clothes and not the sort that come from Dorothy Perkins. I didn't have to decide then and there, I could think about it, but there was no reason why I shouldn't take the pearls home with me. After all, if I left them behind, one of these friends of Hebe's, whoever was on duty next day, some other greedy gossip, might go rooting about in this room and find them and take them home with her.

I'd brought my handbag upstairs with me and I put the pearls in their case inside it. I didn't have to decide. I didn't even have to think about it, but I did think about it. I couldn't help myself. I'm still thinking about it now. A jeweller might refuse to buy them from me unless I could prove they're mine and I have a right to them. I've heard that's what happens. I took the case out of the bag again and read on the underside of it that the pearls were bought from Asprey's. I know where Asprey's is, it's in Bond Street. Suppose I were to be very bold and tell the jeweller they were given to me by Ivor Tesham and if he wanted to check Mr Tesham would confirm it? Would he confirm it? I think so. He would if he was afraid I'd tell Gerry he was Hebe's lover.

I read two significant items in my paper this morning. One was that Tesham has been made a junior minister in the Department of Defence and the other is that the police had found a gun in the wreckage of the crash car. I am wondering now if those men in the car *really* made a mistake when they took Hebe. She was going to Tesham, she told me so; she was going to be taken there in a car and given her birthday present. It looks like he paid them to fetch her but he can't have done. He wouldn't have had a gun, not an MP – would he?

I started going through her clothes. I took them off their hangers in the clothes cupboard and laid them on the bed: light summer dresses, miniskirts, T-shirts, tops, jeans, a couple of coats, no rain-coat. Women like Hebe don't have raincoats, they totter on high heels holding up small umbrellas and getting wet, squealing because the rain is spoiling their hair. Did Gerry never look in this cupboard? I suppose not. At the back, behind the shoes, mostly strappy things with high heels, was a small case standing on the bottom of the cupboard. I opened it and I was shocked. But not only shocked. I thought, I have found the excitement I thought I had lost.

A dog collar of black leather with spikes is the first thing I see. There are thigh boots – not the lace-up ones, she was wearing them – and crotchless knickers and platform bras, fishnet stockings, a black lace corselette. A black leather miniskirt, very brief, a corset with suspenders, the kind of things you see in Ann Summers's windows if you look, only I don't look for more than half a minute. Why would I? They aren't for women like me. I give them a quick glance and then look away. Because all this stuff gives me a strange feeling that I don't want. I hate it, I disapprove of it, but it excites me. And not in a way that I like. If I feel desire, I mean sexual desire, I want to feel it for someone, not like this, a kind of intense but undirected longing – for what? For myself? To be touched by *anyone*? It wouldn't matter who.

I didn't take the things out of the case. There was more under-neath I didn't even look at. I could feel a pulse beating in my chest. I was breathless and if Lucy had come in I don't think I could have spoken. I closed the lid and fastened it and put the case inside one of the plastic bin bags. What I'm going to do with it and its contents I didn't know. I still don't know. Temporarily, the pearls had gone out of my head.

The bin bags and the carrier and my handbag I took downstairs and put them in the boot of my car. Lucy had gone out with Justin. I walked about downstairs a bit, thinking how Gerry had wanted me with him and would have gone on wanting me if those other girls hadn't interfered. I thought then that I'd probably seen him for the last time. As for Justin, he used to like me, we always got on all right. I suppose the truth is his father has turned him against me or Grania and Lucy have. But this sort of thing is always happening to me. I ought to be used to it by now. I wrote a note for Lucy, saying I'd taken all the clothes and to tell Gerry I'd dispose of them, and I left without a backward glance.

At home in the evening with nothing to do and nowhere to go as usual, I looked at the pearls again, at the creamy pallor of them, the delicate bloom which is on all pearls, real or cultured or fake. But I wasn't really thinking about them, I was thinking about Ivor Tesham. He would have left the House of Commons by this time and be at home in his flat in Old Pye Street, Westminster. Unless he had gone out. I pictured him leading an exciting life, dizzy and expensive, in clubs and at premières, very unlike my own – the sort I don't know much about apart from what I read in the papers. A new girl would be with him, for I don't suppose he was being faithful to Hebe's memory. He and his life are so different from me and mine that we might belong not just to different sexes but to different species. Unlike me and Gerry. We are the same sort of people. I'm much more his sort of woman than Hebe was. She was like Tesham or would have got like him if she had lived a bit longer. I suddenly see them together in a luxurious bedroom, she in that corselette and that dog collar and he gazing at her, a picture I squeeze my eyes shut to escape. That man frightens me and makes me shiver, but I knew then that I couldn't let him get away from me and disappear from my life.

It was several evenings later, and my holiday that was no holiday from the library was over, when I phoned him. I'd put the pearls away in a drawer but I got them out and looked at them every day, and they seemed to me not just beautiful but a weapon of power. When I was a child and afraid of someone, Mummy used to say to me, 'They can't eat you.' Ivor Tesham couldn't eat me. I'd forgotten his number but it was in the phone book. This time when I'd looked it up I wrote it down on the pad I keep by the phone.

When I'd spoken to him before he'd made me feel naïve. I'm not naïve now, I've changed and grown older. I'd started crying too and now that seems ridiculous. I picked up the phone and dialled the number on the pad, but before anyone answered I put the receiver back and tried to think a bit more about what I was doing and what I was going to say when I spoke to him. If I did. Should I just trust to the inspiration of the moment? I poured myself a glass of wine and sat by the phone, thinking. I was conscious of a new feeling, something I'd never felt before. It was a sense of power and it came to me through the pearls. I fetched them in their case, opened it and touched them. I can have power over Ivor Tesham, over a Minister of the Crown, a law-maker. And not quite knowing what it is he had in mind when he got those two men to pick up Hebe in the street, that didn't matter. He won't know that I don't precisely know, only that I know he is involved, a major actor in the play.

I remembered his voice and his suave tones, his photograph in *Dod's*, his biographical details (Eton and Brasenose, called to the Bar), where he was and where I was. For he is rich and good-looking, a Member of Parliament, some kind of minister, increasingly powerful, while I belong to an invisible group, the ignored women that most people don't know exist in the 1990s. In the 1890s, yes, they'd say, but not now. Not sixty years after all women got the vote, after the success of the feminist movement, after no profession is closed to them and equal pay is coming. But we are there and in our thousands. We go to bed alone and get up alone, go to work on a bus or a tube, eat a sandwich for lunch alone or with another similarly placed woman, go home by bus or tube to a tiny flat or a room in a shared flat. The highlight of the week is a film we see with the flat-sharer. There are few or no men in our lives because we never meet any. The men at work are married or engaged or living with someone. We have all, of course, had at least one affair or a two- or three-night stand, with a married man whose guilt or fear soon deprived us of his company. Weekends that mean so much to the attached, the ones with lovers or husbands and families, are our worst days and afternoons our worst time. None of us is much to look at, of course, none of us has charm or that vitality men like. As we approach thirty and pass it we know there are no unmarried men left for us and there will be no children except the sort that come out of a bottle. I don't suppose Ivor Tesham has given a thought to a single one of us, the faceless tribe, except, as in my case, to whether we can provide alibis for his married girlfriend when she comes to prance about his bedroom in lace-up boots and frilly camisoles.

I was just going to dial that number when the phone rang. I hoped it might be Gerry but, of course, it was Mummy. How had the funeral gone?

'It went,' I said. 'What do you expect?'

There was no need for me to speak like that, she said, she was only making a simple enquiry. It wouldn't be right if she didn't take an interest. 'How is he taking it?'

I said he was all right. It hadn't been a very happy marriage.

'You've never said anything like that before, Jane,' she said.

'Maybe not, but she wasn't dead before, was she?'

Responding to that was beneath her notice, I suppose. She said she'd paid 'a certain sum' into my bank account in advance of my birthday next month. 'A certain sum' with her is always fifty pounds, so of course I said thank you very much, though I don't have a very high opinion of people who think they can buy your affection with money. But, for some reason, talking to her gave me confidence and when she had rung off I took a deep breath and dialled Ivor Tesham's number. It started to ring. They have red boxes to take home, these ministers, don't they? Boxes full of papers, I imagine, though of what kind I don't know. After the tenth ring he picked up the phone (looking up from those papers, I suppose) and again said, 'Yes?' in that supercilious tone I don't think he would use if he expected the Prime Minister on the line.

'This is Jane Atherton.'

A pause. He's great on pauses. Then he said, 'Ah, the alibi lady.'

That voice had its effect on me. Not enough to make me cry and put the receiver down, as it did before, but sufficient to sap my energy and make me feel like abandoning whatever I'd intended to say to him. But what had I intended to say?

'I think we should meet,' I said. 'We have things to talk about.'

I don't know what I meant by that or what I would have to say if we did meet. The words just came into my head and I uttered them. I waited for him to be patronizing or insulting. He was neither and so I knew he was afraid.

'Very well,' he said, using a phrase I've read but never heard anyone say before. 'When and where?'

He'd refuse if I suggested we meet in Westminster at his place, so I suggested it and he did. How do I, who have never before done anything like this, know how to do it? I said, come to my place instead, and I gave him my address. 'Tomorrow evening, seven thirty?'

He agreed to that and said, 'Till then,' in a pleasanter way, and 'Goodbye,' in a friendly tone.

I understood why. He had high hopes of me because I'd invited him to my home in the evening. That, in his book, meant I'm willing to sleep with him. He was hoping I'd turn out to be another Hebe, as beautiful and – dare I say it? – as easy.

Next day was Wednesday and I went shopping. If Ivor Tesham was coming to my flat I would have to entertain him. At least get something for him to drink. Whisky, gin, vodka, these were the names that ran through my head, but what if he only drank brandy or Burgundy or beer? It was useless and very wasteful to buy anything. I can't afford it. I drank the last of that bottle of wine after I'd talked to him and I shall make him a cup of tea.

Just as I had cold feet about the available drink, I now had second thoughts about my flat. I doubt if he has ever been anywhere like my flat. It consists of a bed-sitting room, which becomes a kitchen at one end, and the only door apart from the front door leads into the bathroom. There is a table which belonged to my grandmother but was in her sheltered housing living room and isn't the kind of grandmother's table which might be in Ivor Tesham's family, made by Chippendale of course – or did he only make chairs? I have chairs too, the fireside kind with sagging brown seats and wooden arms, and a rug worked by my mother as therapy when she was on medication for depression. My bed can become a sofa, but only does so when someone is visiting because working the mechanism which needs to be set in motion for the conversion to take place is a back-breaking exercise. I used to do it when Hebe visited but haven't since she died. As he was to have tea in lieu of spirits, should I also have let him confront the unmade bed? That he would probably have construed as a further invitation, so I manipulated its hinges and creaking shafts and turned it into a sofa, scattered it tastefully with cushions and massaged my back.

I'd decided by then what I'd say to him. It amused me a bit to think that Hebe's jewellery, the tat as well as the pearls he gave her, were in the kitchen, inside a drawer where I keep the brochures that tell me how to use my minute fridge, baby oven and mini electric kettle. Perhaps I should ask him if he will confirm that he gave me the pearls when a jeweller rings him up to ask him.

But I knew I wouldn't, because I was quite suddenly overcome with shyness – no, not shyness but fear, real fear. There were three-quarters of an hour to go before he was due and though I'd resolved to do nothing to my appearance and nothing more to the flat – I'd done quite enough – I went into the bathroom and had a shower, washed my hair and blew it dry with great care, sprayed myself with the last of my perfume and put on my only dress, tights and the highest-heeled shoes I have, which aren't very high. On an impulse I fastened the pearls round my neck, but quickly took them off again. Hebe was always trying to teach me make-up techniques but I didn't pay much attention and now, when I try to do ambitious things to my eyes, it all goes wrong and I have to wipe it off. I ended up with a sprinkling of powder and some carefully applied lipstick.

He was almost due and I knew he would be on time. His job and the kind of life he leads make sure of that. And just as the green digits on the microwave clock changed from 19.29 to 19.30 the doorbell rang. I pressed the key to let him in and heard it buzz downstairs. A great calm had descended on me and a feeling that nothing mattered any more.

The photograph in *Dod's* is a good one. The camera hasn't lied. He is very handsome, if you like that kind of chiselled regularity, the thin mouth, the aquiline nose. I couldn't read his expression, what he thought of me, if he thought anything. He said, 'Good evening,' and called me Miss Atherton, which made me wonder if I know anyone else who does that. He is a graceful man and elegant in the dark suit and white shirt I suppose he wore in the House of Commons today. Of course he didn't look me up and down with scorn or amusement, and now I wonder how I could have imagined such behaviour. Writers sometimes talk about thoughts coming to you 'unbidden' and the thought that came to me then I certainly hadn't looked for. I wondered what it must be like to be the sort of woman who was squired about wherever she went by a man who looked like him and spoke like him.

I asked him to sit down in one of the 'fireside' chairs and offered him tea. I was wrong too to think he'd look round my flat incredulously or with contempt. He took it in his stride and the chairs and the tea – only he didn't take the tea. 'That's very kind of you but no, thank you,' he said.

What to say to him, how to use this time, maybe half an hour, came to me quite suddenly. I sat down opposite him and said, 'You will have been wondering why I asked you here.' Here I made myself pause. 'Don't look so worried,' I said, though he didn't. 'It's only that I thought you might like something of Hebe's as a keepsake – well, to remember her by.'

He slightly inclined his head. It wasn't quite a nod, more like someone doing what I think is called a court bow. What had he expected me to say? Something about the car and the crash and the gun, I expect. I looked for some sign of relief from him but saw nothing. His colour, which is a pale olive, didn't change. I wonder if I am the only person in the world who knows he and Hebe were lovers.

'Hebe's husband asked me to take her jewellery and do what I liked with it. I've been getting rid of her clothes to charity shops. Would you like to see some of the things?'

This time he did speak. 'Thank you, I would.'

He has a beautiful voice, measured, civilized, very public school. And now relief was in his tone. I guessed this was because he understood that I'd asked him here not to harangue him or threaten him but simply to make that very ordinary and usual gesture of offering a memento of the dead to the bereaved.

There was nowhere in this flat where I could be out of sight of a visitor but the bathroom. I couldn't pretend Hebe's things were anywhere but where they are, in the kitchen drawer. However, he didn't watch me. He sat in his fireside chair, looking out of the window beside him at the uninspiring landscape of Kilburn–Brondesbury borders, the terrace of red-brick villas climbing the hillside, the squat Nonconformist church. I took all the jewellery but the pearls out of the drawer, put them on a tray, a plastic thing with a selection of British birds on it, and carried it over to him, putting it down on my mail-order flat-pack coffee table.

He expects to see the pearls, of course, and sees instead the string of red glass beads, the silver-gilt chain off which the gilt is peeling, a red and a green plastic bangle, something which I think is an anklet, a white metal ring with a large pink stone which is probably glass, half a dozen pairs of earrings, trashy sparkly things, and a pink porcelain brooch in the shape of a rose.

'She had some good things too,' I said, and I know he thought I was going to mention the pearls. 'Her engagement ring, a locket and a gold bracelet. Gerry wants to keep those, as you can imagine.'

'Quite,' he said, because he had to say something.

The last thing I had expected was happening to me. I was enjoying myself. I felt something I've never known before. It's power I feel and it's heady. Was he going to ask about the pearls? He wasn't. He couldn't quite bring himself to do it. He couldn't say, I gave her a valuable necklace because I thought I would be her lover and she would be mine for years. I didn't give it to her husband. But no, he couldn't. He would rather lose five thousand pounds or whatever the pearls are worth than expose himself to me as mean and greedy. Probably, he was brought up to think talking about money was vulgar. I should be so lucky.

'Is there anything you would like?' I said, so full of power that I had to stop myself laughing out loud.

'Perhaps this little brooch?' He picked up the china rose.

I smiled and said, 'It's quite pretty, isn't it? I'll find a box to put it in.'

The box I found contained the red beads. I put the china rose inside it and, as I did so, I laid my hand for a moment on the black leather case where the pearls lie in their pink velvet bed.

Ivor Tesham thanked me too profusely. It's all terribly kind of me. He added that he knows I was a good friend to Hebe. Then power got the better of me and I said, 'Because I lied for her and deceived her husband?' I laughed loudly to take the sting out of that and, after a stunned moment, he laughed too. He hadn't shaken hands with me when he arrived but he did then. I listened to his footsteps going fast, too fast, down the stairs and the front door being closed too sharply.

Did he wonder what Hebe, who was so beautiful and sexy, saw in me? Did he wonder why she called me her friend? He doesn't know how much she enjoyed having someone to patronize and show herself off against, the sparrow that no one notices when the golden oriole perches next to it.

Gerry phoned me and I couldn't help feeling he had only got in touch with me when he had exhausted all other possibilities. He had no one to look after Justin on Friday, so could I come? There are some people, especially men, who think others don't have to work. But considering I had been thinking I might never see him again, this was good news, so I said I would take the day off work and come. This time Justin didn't turn his back on me. He didn't tell me to go away but let me kiss him when I arrived and put his arms round my neck. And Gerry seemed pleased to see me, telling me how grateful he was for all I'd done. He could rely on me the way he couldn't on anyone else. He wished I lived nearer.

I went out into the hallway with him when he was leaving for work. Saying, 'Oh, Jane, I miss her so,' he put his arms round me and hugged me. It was the first time anyone had held me like that for years. I could feel his warmth through my clothes and his heart beating. Back in the kitchen after he'd gone, I lifted Justin out of his high chair and danced about with him in my arms, singing, 'Here we go gathering nuts in May, nuts in May, nuts in May . . .' until he shrieked with laughter.

Gerry would marry again. Why shouldn't he marry me? I was much more suited to him than Hebe had ever been. I wouldn't be unfaithful to him. Justin would soon love me as much as he'd loved her. Gerry wouldn't have hugged me like that if I hadn't begun to mean something to him. Was he beginning to see that Hebe had never been much of a wife to him, never really loved him?

As I put Justin into his buggy and prepared to walk him down to the Welsh Harp and the fields of Kingsbury Green, I realized I didn't know how to catch and keep a man. I didn't know how to begin except by being there, someone he relied on more than anyone else.

9

The trouble with being a minister, Jack Munro once said to me, is that you're an MP as well. You don't stop representing your constituents in Parliament just because you've been made an Under-Secretary of State at the Home Office, or, as in Ivor's case, Under-Secretary of State in the Department of Defence. In the two years he'd been in Parliament Ivor had been a good constituency MP, holding his surgeries at fairly regular weekly intervals, accepting as many engagements in Morningford as was possible for anyone who couldn't be in two places at once, giving a sympathetic ear to the concerns of constituents. And once he became a minister he kept it up. He was ambitious; he wanted to be good and be seen to be good. But it was hard. No one pretends it isn't hard. Only the indispensable mass, the people who put you there, the electorate, haven't the faintest idea.

Ivor acquitted himself well. He sat on the government frontbench when there was room for the lowlier ministers; he spoke well and at not too great length. He attended the innumerable meetings which are a minister's lot and in July, a week before the House rose for the summer recess, flew off for two days to the Balkans to give support and comfort to our Air Power Overseas. And when the House had adjourned on a Thursday and he could leave, he drove down to Ramburgh, all prepared for his Saturday-morning surgery, for opening the flower show or the harvest festival, for speaking in the evening at the Conservatives' annual dinner or·the Chamber of Commerce High Street Traders' Supper.

On 2 August Iraq invaded and overran Kuwait. US forces, supported by troops from various European, Arab and Asian countries, were sent to Saudi in an attempt to shield the kingdom from Iraqi assault. Although the Commons wasn't sitting, all this kept Ivor even busier than usual. The crisis deepened and made more work for him when Iraq announced on 28 August that Kuwait had become the nineteenth Iraqi governorate and extended the borders of Basra south into Kuwait, thus creating a new province. This situation, in which Ivor was closely involved, might have been thought so much bigger and more momentous than his personal problem as to make it seem petty, perhaps even to distract him from it. But we human beings aren't like that. Those things which are close to home, matters which affect our individual pride and reputation and the way we are viewed by others, those come first.

Whatever decisions he made, no matter how often and how far he travelled, he still carried his burden of stress. He was never free of worry. Dermot Lynch was always in the forefront of his mind. Those weekends when he was in Morningford and not in West-minster or the Middle East he would always find an hour to come over to us at Monks Cravery. He came to talk, to unburden his soul, I suppose. We were the only people he could talk to, for although others knew some of it – Nicola Ross, for instance, knew he had had a girlfriend he never talked about and that he had known Lloyd Freeman; Hebe's nameless friend, the 'alibi lady', knew a little more than that – we alone knew the whole thing from start to finish. The whole sorry mess, as he put it.

Nothing more had been heard of Dermot. I might say that nothing ever was heard of him; the newspapers had only mentioned him during the first couple of weeks after the accident. It wouldn't have been much of a story for them, I could see that, especially if he recovered fully and was liable to be up in court on a charge of causing death by dangerous driving. They would have to be very discreet about anything like that in the offing.

All the time Ivor knew that the thing he was worried about wasn't the thing he ought to be worried about. Hebe's death was what should have concerned him, hers and Lloyd Freeman's, but he hardly thought about their deaths. And he cared very little about Dermot's guilt or innocence in the matter of who caused the crash. He was solely troubled about the man's regaining consciousness and talking to the police. Or the press or anyone at all, come to that. And, of course, he imagined him saying, 'It wasn't a real abduction. This MP called Mr Ivor Tesham set it up as a kind of joke. Hebe Furnal was his girlfriend and he wanted her kidnapped and handcuffed and gagged and brought to his house. For her birthday. Like a game.'

Something else which constantly bothered Ivor was the gun. The handcuffs he knew about, they were part of his planned scenario, and the balaclavas and the gag and the blacked-out windows in the car, but not the gun. One of them, Dermot or Lloyd, must have brought that gun along as a bit of additional colour, a surely indispensable adjunct in their Hollywood-driven ideas of what an abduction should be. The gun was a serious business; that it had been in the car at all was serious. The chance of its being connected to him made Ivor physically shiver. I saw a shiver actually run through him when he talked about it, sitting in our cottage by the log fire, for it was autumn by then and turning cold.

'I'm obsessed with Dermot Lynch,' he said. 'I dream about him. I dream about him in bed in that hospital, just moving his hand and opening his eyes. Then he opens his mouth and he speaks my name. His mother's there and she says she can't hear him and to say it again. It's his mother to the life in her overall and her slippers. She sits there holding his hand and he moves his hand and she's so happy.'

I tell him he needs a drink and I'll get him one, but he says no, he's driving, and he reminds me that though he now has a government car, using it and the driver who comes with it for constituency work is forbidden. He's got to be back in Morningford by seven. All he needs now is to compound his villainy by being done for driving over the limit.

Iris says, 'How do you know his mother wears an overall and slippers? You haven't ever seen her, have you?'

There was silence and then he told us. This man was in his thoughts all the time until he couldn't stand it any longer without doing something. He'd gone on the tube up to Paddington, but found when he got there that Warwick Avenue would have been the nearer station to William Cross Court in Rowley Place. He walked, aided by the London A–Z, over Brunel's bridge, through an underpass under the Westway and up into the genteel streets of Little Venice and Maida Vale. William Cross Court, built in the 1970s, had been sandwiched in between gracious stucco villas. It was a sprawling block of mustard-coloured council flats with washing hung out to dry and bicycles on the balconies. Ivor might have been to Eton and Brasenose but he was an MP who'd done his canvassing along council-flat walkways. It wasn't new to him. He wasn't surprised that the hallways were covered in graffiti and the lift was out of order. He walked up to flat 23, not knowing what he was going to do when he got there.

As he came to the top of the third flight the door of number 23 opened and a woman came out. She was about sixty but startlingly like Dermot, or he was like her. That was when he saw the overall and the slippers. A parcel had been left on the step outside her front door and she had come out to pick it up. Ivor walked on past, up the fourth flight, and she didn't see him. Or she took no notice of him if she did.

'You didn't speak to her?' Iris asked.

'Of course I didn't. Of course not.'

'What was the point of going there?'

'I don't know,' Ivor said. 'I know Dermot used to live there but I didn't know if his mother was living there alone or the brother lived there with her. I suppose I went there because I feel I can't go on like this. I can't but I have to, I've no choice. Since then I've found out everything I can about the family, but it doesn't exactly help. I mean, the brother's called Sean and he's some sort of builder. He's not married or anything.'

I asked what 'or anything' meant.

'Cohabiting, as we politicians say,' said Ivor.

'And Dermot wasn't?'

'It appears not. They're first-generation English. Both parents came over from Ireland in the 1960s and lived first in Kilburn.'

'What's the point of knowing all this?' Iris said.

'I don't know.' Poor Ivor gave what Iris tells me 1920s novelists used to call a mirthless laugh. 'There wasn't any point. I tell myself I'm interested because I ought to do something for the Lynchs. Because it was my fault, if you see what I mean. Of course you see what I mean. But Lloyd Freeman's dying was just as much my fault, you could say, and I haven't done anything about him. But he had a girlfriend he'd been cohabiting with.'

'Well, don't do anything about him,' Iris said. 'You've got enough on your plate with Dermot Lynch.'

'I want him not to recover. If I spell it out frankly, I want him to die. Isn't that the most appalling thing you've ever heard? Doesn't it make you want to turn me out of your house? He's done me no harm, yet I want him to die. I must be an utter shit.

'I know which hospital he's in. I know the name of the ward. I think I could bluff my way in to see him. I imagine that happening. I dream about it. I see myself sitting by his bed, waiting for him to wake up. And then I'm talking to a doctor, a consultant, and he's telling me he'll never wake up, and I'm so happy I start laughing and everyone stands around me and stares.'

So it went on. He came back next day. He'd done his red boxes, which were sent to his constituency, and he was on his way home to London.

'I meant to go over to Leicestershire,' he said, 'and see Erica Caxton, but I haven't had a moment. I try to see her and the children as often as I can.' Ivor never said 'kids', though both young Caxtons were well into their teens. 'I'll go next weekend.'

We had tea and he told us what it meant to be a minister. His Private Secretary was a woman called Emma, in charge of organizing his life, keeping her eye on him and keeping him on the straight and narrow path. Iris asked him what he called her and he said 'Emma' but, according to protocol, she called him 'Minister'. It was the same for all his officials. However, so decreed the tribal custom, he and his Permanent Secretary exchanged Christian names. Ivor liked all this, as one does enjoy the arcane rules of a club one belongs to, rules that are incomprehensible to those outside Whitehall and the pale which is the walls of the Palace of Westminster.

But I had the impression all the time he was talking that he valued it more than he might have done previously because he saw it as being under threat now. A word to the media about what had happened that evening in May and what hadn't happened – his going to the police, his admitting to them his part in it – would bring down all this dignity and responsibility and power. Not at once, of course. It would begin with a snide diary paragraph, be taken up next day perhaps as a few lines in an article on government sleaze. And then, after three or four days of this, would come the single-column story, the interview with him, the police comment, the few words from a 'friend' in Parliament or his constituency. By the end of the week it would be on the front page, in the tabloids the lead, as the kidnap, the gun and the two deaths reappeared in print. By then his resignation would have been asked for or he would have voluntarily resigned.

None of this was said that afternoon. We had said it all before. After he'd gone Iris asked me if I didn't think Ivor was 'seeing rather a lot of Erica Caxton'.

'I don't know,' I said. 'He's not seeing her at all today. He hasn't got time.'

'I'm not finding fault. I quite like the idea. Isn't it time he got married?'

I said she was years older than he and her husband had only been dead a few months.

'Only four years older,' Iris said. 'I'm not saying anything would happen straight away, I said I like the idea. You know Mother and Dad will give up Ramburgh House to him and move into the lodge. I wouldn't mind Erica for a sister-in-law.'

That was never to happen. I mention it only because of the events which followed, or, rather, one event.

Back in May, the kidnap story had driven Sandy Caxton's murder from the front pages. But the inside pages kept it in the public mind.

Questions were asked in the House (and repeatedly in the papers) as to the guarding of former Secretaries of State for Northern Ireland. Wasn't it taken for granted that such people were protected not merely during the time they held that office but for the rest of their lives?

Since Sandy's death a series of IRA attacks had been carried out in mainland Britain and West Germany. Hooded men shot dead a young soldier and wounded his two companions as they waited for a train on Lichfield station. A bomb on the roof of the Honourable Artillery Company in London exploded, injuring seventeen civilians, most of them students at a twenty-first birthday party. Another, planted a few feet inside the doorway of the Carlton Club, haunt of Tory grandees, seriously injured a porter and wounded two others. And there were many more, including the murder of a nun in County Armagh and an explosion at the London Stock Exchange.

At the end of July, in an assassination which seemed an echo of Sandy Caxton's murder, Ian Gow, the member for Eastbourne and at one time PPS to Margaret Thatcher and a Minister of State at the Treasury, was killed when an IRA bomb exploded under his car in the village of Hatcham, near Eastbourne, where he lived. In a statement issued next day, the IRA said Gow had been killed because he had been central to the formulation of British policy in Northern Ireland, including that during the hunger strikes of the early 1980s and the shoot-to-kill operations of 1982. Like Sandy's, Gow's name had been found on an IRA death list discovered in a south London flat in 1988.

There was nothing in the papers or on the television as to police investigations or attempts to find Sandy Caxton's killers until a small paragraph appeared in the *Evening Standard* a week after Ivor's visit to us in Cravery. All it said was that a London man was helping the police in their enquiries into Sandy's murder. I read it but took no more notice of it than would any other member of the public, indignant at the outrage. Next morning things were different. This was headline news. The man the police had been holding for thirty-six hours was Sean Brendan Lynch, 29, of Paddington, west London.

I was pretty sure Ivor would be aware of it. He read at least two papers a day from front page to back, every word. But I thought I ought to see him. I wondered if he understood the seriousness of this and I phoned him and asked if I could come into the Commons for a drink at six that evening.

He said, 'You've seen it, then?'

When we met he told me he had read it in his office. All the papers were placed on a table there every morning, of course, and the *Standard* appeared around lunchtime. Mostly, he had no time to go anywhere for lunch. The days of lunching out at a leisurely pace were gone. His lunch was brought to him, two sandwiches and a bottle of sparkling water, and he made the mistake of offering one of the sandwiches to Emma. 'Oh, no, thank you, Minister,' she said in shocked tones.

The *Standard* had been brought in. He took a bite out of one of the sandwiches, got up to read the lead story, something about the Prime Minister and Geoffrey Howe, then an account of a rape trial. Underneath, at the foot of the front page, was a paragraph headed 'London Man in Caxton Killing Probe'. He said he gripped the edge of the table where the papers lay, afraid he might fall. For the first time in his life he knew that sensation of the room going round and he hardly knew how he kept himself from crying out. Fear of Emma coming rushing in, no doubt, or the Assistant Secretary or the Deputy Secretary.

'I told myself to read it again,' he said. 'I knew I must read it, however much I longed to chuck the whole thing into the waste-paper basket. I read it but got no more out of it. A man called Sean Brendan Lynch was at a police station, answering questions, being interrogated. Because, obviously, he was suspected of being a member of the IRA, very likely *was* a member of the IRA, and must have done something or been concerned in something to make him a suspect in Sandy's assassination.'

'This man is Dermot Lynch's brother?'

'The very same. Things would be bad enough if it came out that I'd employed Dermot and Lloyd Freeman to snatch Hebe, but that's nothing compared to my being connected with the brother of a known member of the IRA and Sandy's assassin.'

He reminded me that the Conservative Party loathed the IRA and had done so ever since the horrors of the Brighton bombing. It was impossible to over-estimate the disastrous results of anyone connecting him with Sean Lynch.

'Or any of the Lynch family,' I said.

'I know.'

'See you do know, Ivor. Last week you were telling us about going to the flats where the Lynchs live and about your dreams.'

He took a deep draught of his Merlot, which is probably something else ministers aren't supposed to do when they may be going to speak. 'They were dreams. That's all they were. I won't go near the Lynchs again. I'll bear it in silence.'

He gave a wild sort of laugh. People turned round and someone, a woman, smiled and raised her eyebrows.

Soon after that the division bell rang. He finished his drink and said, 'It's a funny thing but I'll always remember it, the division bell ringing when I first met Hebe and repeating her phone number over and over and going to vote and writing the number down.' He gave a sort of sigh, half despair, half exasperation. 'I won't do anything silly, Rob,' he said, and was gone.

There was a lot he didn't tell me that night. He had in fact already been back to William Cross Court and plunged himself even more deeply into what he'd called the sorry mess. But it was not until weeks later that I learned this.

He had promised not to go near the Lynchs again. Perhaps by that he had meant only that he wouldn't speak to Sean Lynch, something he could hardly have done while Sean was in custody. But I don't know. Anyway, he broke his promise.

You have to understand that to go there at all was almost impossibly difficult for him when the Commons was sitting. A minister, even a junior minister, is expected to be attending all those meetings, chatting to his coterie of fans, picking up gossip or, in the latter part of the day, in the division lobby to vote. His job isn't like that of some other professional who can easily take two hours off here or there once he has reached a certain status. But that autumn there was a conference he attended in Brighton – not the Conservative Party conference, that had taken place a month before in Bournemouth, but something to do with aircraft production and technology. He was taking part in a brains trust and next day speaking to a group about the vital importance of a certain kind of bomb being used by Air Power (or some such thing). Once that was done he came back briefly to London. He had been taken to Brighton in his government car but he couldn't use that for this clandestine visit. A train took him to Victoria and from there he got the tube up to Warwick Avenue.

It's hard to say why he went, what he hoped to accomplish. When the time came for him to tell me, he said he didn't know. I expect a psychologist would say that someone with an obsession needs to keep its object within his sight as much as he can. He needs it not just in his mind but as concrete visible substance. In his case the concrete, in more ways than one, was William Cross Court.

He had thought about this a great deal. I might say that he thought about little else. The same fears and hopes and speculations went round and round in his head before he spoke at the conference and when he'd finished speaking, when he was having a drink at the hotel bar, when he was having dinner and, most of all, incessantly, horribly repetitively, while he was alone in his bedroom at night. He knew it had to stop. If he wasn't to have some sort of breakdown he had to put an end to it. In spite of all objections and all warnings, in spite of her son Sean still being questioned down the road at Paddington Green police station, the only way was to speak to Philomena Lynch.

He had decided to introduce himself and tell her that Dermot had serviced his car and he had been increasingly concerned about him. He would say he knew he should have come before but his unwillingness to intrude on family troubles had held him back. Now, because he happened to be in the neighbourhood, he had remembered her address and had come on an impulse to enquire after Dermot.

This sounds so transparently false – what was wrong with the phone? – that one wonders why a man of Ivor's intelligence could have considered it. It looks too such a foolhardy act, so near to career suicide after what he had promised, that when he did tell me I found it almost beyond belief. But he came up with an explanation I could very nearly understand. He said it was like some game where you cast a dice and the whole of your fortune and your future hangs on your throwing a six. In fact, the odds in his case were much lower. If he threw a six Philomena Lynch would talk to him and tell him her son would never regain consciousness and she was considering switching off the life support. He would be off the hook, all would be well, the agony of the last months would be over. Other outcomes of his throw would be that she refused to talk to him, that she talked and told him Dermot was getting better; and, worst of all, that as he improved Dermot had told her he had something he wanted to talk to the police about.

It was worth risking one of those three possibilities for the prospect of getting a six. I suppose this is the way all gamblers think. The six is such a glorious result, the ultimate peace of mind. If I'd ever experienced months of unbroken anxiety, Ivor said, I'd know what he was talking about. But while he was thinking like this, climbing the stairs at William Cross Court, between the graffiti-daubed walls, he was also castigating himself for the enormity of his mindset, that he was hoping and longing for another man's death.

In the event, he never went into the flat. He never asked Philomena Lynch about Dermot or even talked to her. Because, as he reached the third flight, he heard footsteps behind him. They were the footfalls of a woman wearing high-heeled shoes. Unlikely that this was Mrs Lynch but he didn't want to chance it, for he was still, after all these hours and days of heart-searching, uncertain how to begin what he had to say to her. So he went on up the fourth flight, as he had done before, and again, as he had done before, paused at the top and looked down. The woman who came to the top of the third flight, crossed the landing and rang the Lynch doorbell was Lloyd Freeman's ex-girlfriend.

He had seen her only once before and that had been at Nicola Ross's party, when she and Lloyd were still together. But he knew her at once. She was a beautiful woman, generously made but not at all fat, with nearly perfect features and a mass of thick, dark, curly hair. Somewhere in her late twenties or early thirties. The long skirt she wore, red with a pattern of black swirls, just skimmed very fine, delicate ankles. You could see, Ivor said, irrepressible womanizer that he was, what the Victorians meant when they got excited by a glimpse of ankle. Lloyd Freeman's girlfriend glanced up and saw him just as the front door opened, but plainly she didn't recognize him.

It was a fine day for mid-November, sunny but rather cold. Ivor went downstairs and somewhere in the gardens of William Cross Court found a seat beside a bed of straggly geraniums. He sat down to wait for the woman to come out.

When half an hour had passed and she hadn't come out Ivor began an internal argument with himself. What was he going to say to her when she did appear? Introduce himself? She might know the whole story of the birthday present or part or none of it. What he must not do was assume, as he had begun to do, that she and Mrs Lynch were conferring up there as to how to expose him or even get some sort of compensation out of him. The chances were that this woman – had Lloyd ever called her by her name in his hearing? – had got to know Mrs Lynch because she sympathized with her. They were, after all, more or less in the same boat. Lloyd had been killed and Dermot terribly injured in the same car accident. Nothing could be more natural than that the tall dark woman with the perfect ankles had befriended Dermot's unfortunate mother.

But there was no point in his waiting for her, was there? He couldn't go up to her and ask how Dermot was, for he was sure now that this was what they must be talking about up there in flat 23. He didn't know her and she didn't know him. She might be hours. Wouldn't it be best to leave now, return to the conference or just go home? And continue to suffer agonies each time he opened a newspaper or a journalist spoke to him? This was all very well, but it's my opinion that at least part of his reason for waiting was that the woman was attractive. She was far more attractive, she was more beautiful, than he remembered from that previous sighting. And however fraught with anxiety he might have been, Ivor was Ivor.

As it happened, he had no longer to wait. After she had been in there three-quarters of an hour she came out of the entrance to the flats. She came out quite briskly and, not looking in his direction, walked into the street and off towards Warwick Avenue tube station. He got up from his seat and followed her.

Ivor told me that if she had looked back and seen him or had noticed him as they went down into the station and approached the escalators, he'd have given up the idea of following her. But she didn't look back. She must have had a return ticket. He hadn't. He bought one at the ticket window, the most expensive on offer, because he had no idea how far she would go. At the foot of the escalator he turned first to the platform where trains are southbound, but she wasn't there. He spotted her at the far right-hand end of the northbound platform.

The areas this part of the Bakerloo Line reached were unknown territory, Queen's Park, Kilburn Park, Willesden Junction. Nowhere near West Hendon, as far as he knew. This was the sort of thing he was proud of not knowing. For someone like Gerry Furnal not to know where Jermyn Street was or the Carlton Club betrayed him as a dowdy provincial, while Ivor's ignorance of the whereabouts of Willesden Junction station only showed his urbanity. Well, the train came in and he got into the carriage next to the one Freeman's ex-girlfriend was in. He began to be conscious then of the unreality of what he was doing, a Minister of the Crown, a Member of Parliament, tailing someone like a disreputable private eye. And he was constantly aware that the whole thing was undignified, base, he should stop, give up; but he didn't. He stayed in the train until at Queen's Park he saw her walk past his window. Quickly he got out and followed her on to the street. Still she didn't look back.

He tried to remember the area code of the phone number Lloyd had given him but he had never used it and he knew only that it was one preceded by the digits 081. Had Lloyd and she lived together or been lovers with separate homes? He castigated himself now for not finding out her name when he had seen her at that party. But why would he have? He had no idea then what the future held. If anyone had told him then that he'd be desperate to talk to this woman he wouldn't have believed them.

For the first time, she looked round and saw him behind her, a long way behind. Did she recognize him? If so, she gave no sign. She was leading him towards what he supposed must have been Queen's Park itself, or rather to a street running along one side of it, a place of small semi-detached houses, neat, quite attractive. At number 34 she turned in at the gate, put her key in the front door lock, let herself in and closed the door behind her.

There were two bells on the left-hand side of that front door: the lower one was marked J. Case, the upper John Dean-Upwood. As he turned away, he paused inside the gate and looked back at what must be her window. She was standing between the half-drawn curtains, watching him. He almost ran. He had to tell himself that she would only think he had been delivering something or even had come to the wrong house, and controlling himself, he walked quite slowly away.

Back in the flat in Old Pye Street, he looked up J. Case in the phone book and saw that the number he had for Lloyd was the same. So they had lived there together. It was five in the afternoon. He poured himself a generous gin and tonic, drank it and went back on the train to the conference.

In London again, he set about getting in touch with Freeman's former girlfriend. First of all he made enquiries of Nicola Ross, taking her out to dinner and picking her brains.

'What does the J stand for?'

'Juliet. A tad fanciful, don't you think, darling? She used to be married to Aaron Hunter.' Of course Ivor knew the name. He had seen Hunter on the stage, as we all had, but notably when he and Nicola appeared opposite one another in a revival of *Private Lives*. 'She's an actor.' Nicola never said 'actress'. 'But she doesn't get much work. God knows what she lives on. She and Lloyd had been together two or three years but they'd split up a while before he was killed.' Then she said rather sharply, 'Why do you want to know? Have you met her somewhere?'

Ivor hadn't got as far as thinking up a plausible reason for making these enquiries. He said lamely, 'I saw her at your party. When Lloyd was killed I thought about her. I wondered if there was anything I could do for her.'

I've sometimes thought that Ivor and Nicola Ross ended their affair because Nicola was too astute to suit him in the long term. She would have seen through him. Ivor was quite ruthless enough, when embarking on what he intended to be a permanent relationship, to foresee a time when he might want to start an affair with someone else. From the first, Nicola would have been on to him. His apparently artless speculation as to how he could help Juliet Case didn't deceive her.

'I've never seen you as a philanthropist, darling. I suppose you fancy her. Are you talking about giving her money? Compensation for losing Lloyd, would it be?'

He must have winced a bit at her directness. 'Well, I don't suppose anyone else thinks of her.'

'You can't know that. Anyway, I told you. He'd scarpered weeks before. What are you planning to do? Schlep over to Queen's Park with a cheque for a thousand quid?' She fixed on him her penetrating stare. 'It's not as if you had anything to do with the crash, darling, or did you? I've always found it hard to – well, equate abduction with what I knew of Lloyd.'

'Of course I had nothing to do with it.'

'Only joking, darling. Don't be cross.'

She had seriously frightened him. But no more was said about Lloyd and they talked of other things. Still undecided as to how to get to speak to Juliet Case, Ivor was due to go on television next morning – the day, as it happened, of Margaret Thatcher's departure – and talk about the worsening crisis in Kuwait. These TV studios provide a waiting room for people appearing on their programmes, a kind of small lounge with chairs round a table where coffee, tea or water is brought to them until it's their turn to go on and they're called. There's a TV screen on which they can watch the programme they will be on. Ivor had done his stint, answered the questions put to him and gone back into the waiting room to pick up the briefcase he'd left there. Aaron Hunter was sitting in one of the chairs, reading the *Guardian*. Ivor recognized him at once, the rather rubbery blank face which could become handsome or hideous at the actor's will, the full lips, the ultra-short hair the colour of ageing thatch. He only spoke to him because he had to in order to retrieve the case which was on the floor beside Hunter's left leg.

'Excuse me, would you? That's my briefcase.'

Hunter looked up from his paper and Ivor saw his flat light blue eyes, steady and expressionless. 'You're Ivor Tesham. Aaron Hunter. You were good.'

'Thank you.'

'Of course I can't agree with the politics.'

'No? Fortunately for me, many do.'

A shrug of the shoulders from Hunter. He seemed about to say more but he was called at that moment. Ivor picked up his case and left, wondering what the actor was going to be interviewed about. The play he was currently in, he supposed. Two days before, when closely examining *The Times* for more possible news of Sean Lynch, he had come upon a photograph of Hunter on a page devoted to theatre and opera notices. It was one of those pictures, usually of an actor and actress in a scene from the play, grappling with each other or in a passionate clinch, which newspapers insert into reviews. This was a fight, the two of them struggling on a marble floor. The man was Hunter but the woman was no one Ivor had ever heard of.

But the interview wasn't about the play, though it was mentioned in passing. I watched the programme myself and what Aaron Hunter talked about was sleaze. Specifically, political scandal, politicians who were unfaithful to their wives or stayed in hotels paid for by sheikhs or accepted expensive presents and lied to Parliament afterwards. He blamed, somewhat obscurely, the party machine and put forward the view that proportional representation and more independent members (there were none at the time) would provide an antidote. The interviewer suggested that perhaps Hunter himself should stand at the next election, which would be in 1992. Hunter said he might at that – who knew?

About this, at the time, Ivor knew nothing. He was on his way in a taxi to St Margaret's, Westminster, where at ten that morning the memorial service for Sandy Caxton was to be held. While a distinguished baritone sang 'Birth and Fortune I Despise' (not exactly Ivor's own sentiments) from Sandy's favourite *Saul*, he sat in the row behind Erica Caxton and her children, thinking of Sean Lynch. His own name might one day be associated with Sean Lynch's and the IRA and then his presence, pious and caring, at this service to bid farewell to a murdered Northern Ireland Secretary, would be remembered.

The same day Sean Lynch appeared in court and was immediately released without any case to answer. No explanation was given, of course, but it must have been that there was insufficient evidence to warrant taking matters further. Ivor was still terribly afraid of Dermot's regaining consciousness and telling what he knew, but he no longer felt that he was under threat of being labelled some sort of IRA informer or spy. For a while, apparently, he had even been afraid of going to prison. Now the lack of evidence against Sean Lynch lifted a load from his mind. He could concentrate on the pleasant task of getting to know Juliet Case.

II

Last week I got the sack. They didn't use that term, naturally they didn't, but a worse one I thought was a joke that only came up in TV comedy. The Librarian, who's now called the Director, called me in and said – he actually said and he wasn't smiling – they were going to have to let me go.

It wasn't a total surprise. The Library of British History had been in a bad way for quite a time. We rely on private funding and though we've applied for government grants we're always turned down. I'm going to start saying 'they' now, 'we' being inappropriate, so it was 'they' who had to sell one of our collections last year and it fetched a lot of money, but not enough. The Director told me they had decided to close a whole floor down and of course it was my floor where the histories of the late medieval period are kept. The collection wouldn't be sold, he said with a kindly smile, as if to comfort me, and actually said that if I ever wanted to look at anything among all that sixteenth-century stuff, there would be no difficulty about 'granting me access'.

I was on a month's notice, that month charmingly coming to an end a week before Christmas. They would pay me for the month but prefer me to go at the end of the week. Once I'd got over the shock, my big anxiety was how I was going to pay the mortgage. I'd have to find another job but I didn't know where to start. Companies or local authorities who run libraries aren't exactly going down on their knees, begging the unemployed to come and work for them. But I made a start the evening of my last day at the library, noting down every possibility I found in five sets of situations-vacant columns and applying for ten of them – eight of these extremely unlikely.

Mummy phoned. The only solution she could come up with

when I told her was to give up the flat and come and live with her in Ongar. In case you don't know – and why should you? – Ongar is a pretty village-cum-outer suburb served by volunteer-run trains you have to catch in Epping. Needless to say, there are no jobs in Ongar, no buses going anywhere one might want to go to and nothing to do in the evenings. When my father died two years ago he left everything to my mother, house, apartment on the Costa del Sol, a lot of money – well, three hundred thousand, which is a lot to me. I got nothing. I'd have been amazed, knowing my own luck or lack of it, if I had. No doubt he thought I was doing all right. I was young, I had a job and a home of my own. But I've sometimes thought that it wouldn't have hurt Mummy to give me, say, fifty thousand. Still, she didn't. I don't think it would have crossed her mind.

In all the misery of being sacked I had forgotten about the pearls. I only found them because I couldn't remember how to reset the clock on the microwave and the instructions were in that drawer. When I fixed the clock I opened the case the pearls were in, looked at them and wondered how much they were worth. If it was only five thousand pounds it would be a godsend to me now, but if they were worth four times that they'd pay off my mortgage. Why shouldn't I take them to Asprey's and ask them? I could mention Ivor Tesham's name, give them his phone number, tell them to call him and enquire. But I knew I couldn't rely on him agreeing that he'd given them to me. Perhaps he would if he thought I knew too much about what happened the night of the birthday present, when Hebe and that other man died and the driver was injured. But I didn't. I suspected him but I couldn't see how he might have been involved and, as far as I knew, he was innocent.

It was a month since I'd been to Irving Road. I'd called Gerry's number three times. The first time a girl who wasn't Grania or Lucy answered. I don't know who she was, she didn't say. I took care to make my second call fairly late in the evening so that Gerry was bound to answer. He sounded tired and he said Justin was being very difficult, he'd stopped talking, just maintained silence, and though he slept in bed with him most nights, he was wakeful and restless and of course kept Gerry awake. He was going to have to have a nanny, though it would be a strain to afford it. He'd interviewed two women who answered his advertisement for a nanny, but both were so unsuitable it was a joke. The girl who had answered the phone to me was called Emily and was a friend of Grania's, but she was only temporary and had had to leave when her university term started. I asked him if I could do anything but he said, quite coldly I thought, that he was already overwhelmed with offers. It wasn't a shortage of help that was the trouble but the constant change of helpers. I offered again the next time I phoned and he started the conversation by saying he couldn't stop. He'd been on the point of leaving the house – his mother was babysitting – and he had a taxi waiting. No, he didn't need me, thanks very much. His mother was being wonderful.

Naturally, I wondered where he was going in a taxi. I was surprised he could afford taxis, but perhaps he'd got the promotion and consequent salary rise Hebe had said he'd been promised. And I thought a bit about the unfairness of life. I who had no friends and virtually no money had got the sack, while Gerry Furnal, who had Justin and a house and was surrounded by women friends and supporters, was getting a step up the ladder and more money. And now, it appeared, was going out at eight in the evening in a taxi to meet someone – a girl? Was it possible he had found himself a girlfriend when Hebe had been dead for less than a year? He should have been meeting me. I was the suitable one, the woman he had known for years, his dead wife's friend.

Didn't he care about Justin losing the power of speech? Because that's what it was. I'd heard of it happening to children as the result of some trauma, loss of a parent or a sibling, for instance. Gerry had passed over it lightly as if it wasn't important and he went on letting his little boy be looked after by one empty-headed female after another, the sort that thinks only about their appearance and men and sex.

★

The clothes I'd brought back with me from Irving Road, I mean the kinky weird stuff, were still in the case behind my sofa-bed. I hadn't looked inside it again but I did that evening. Again I imagined Hebe wearing the boots and the corset and nothing else, spread out on a bed with Ivor Tesham standing over her, his eyes on her, and again I got that excited feeling. I suppose I was putting myself in her place and I thought of taking these things back and showing them to Gerry. Why not? The truth was that I should have shown them to him when he first asked me to clear out Hebe's wardrobe. If I showed them to him and showed him the pearls too, if I told him the pearls didn't come from the British Home Stores but were a very valuable gift from someone, he'd know what Hebe was really like. He'd know he was well rid of her.

Christmas came and as usual everything stopped. Letters weren't delivered, except the ones that were Christmas cards, so there was no chance of getting replies to my job applications. I went to Ongar to have what Mummy calls 'festivities' with her. When she suggested it, I asked why we couldn't go to her place in Spain instead. At least there would be some sunshine there. She said she had put the house on the market, she couldn't afford the upkeep, and she's had an offer, so to forget it. Christmas in Ongar is normally grim, but this time it was worse, with her saying what was to become of me every few minutes and coming up as often with her own answer: live with her in that bit of the house she'll have converted for me. The present she gave me was a twinset, a garment or, rather, two garments I thought had gone out of fashion for good about thirty years ago. It was lilac and it seemed to me about the biggest antithesis of that kinky stuff Hebe had that you could think of. I came home next day, bringing with me about five pounds of meat from the largest turkey two people ever sat down to eat together. Still, it was food I didn't have to spend money on.

Seven replies finally came to the ten job applications I'd sent, six to say the vacancy had been filled and one offering me an interview. This wasn't really a librarian's job at all but PA to the director of a small museum in the City 'with the chance of outstanding work leading to an assistant curator's post'. I've never been much good at interviews. If I'm asked personal questions, and I'm bound to be, I get flustered and defensive – or so I've been told. The interview was for the Thursday in the following week and when Mummy phoned that evening I told her about it.

'If you get it,' she said, 'it would be quite convenient for you living here. I mean, being in the City. Where did you say in the City?'

I hadn't said. 'Bishopsgate.'

'Excellent,' she said. 'You come and live here with me and you could take the Central Line from Epping to Liverpool Street. It takes just about an hour.'

Not to mention the half-hour spent waiting for the train first.

'If I get the job,' I said, 'I wouldn't need to live in Ongar. I can go on living here. Or I might move in with Callum.'

That was met with disapproval, as I knew it would be. 'Once you do that,' she said, 'you can give up all hope of marrying him.'

An acrimonious discussion followed, with me saying every married couple I knew had lived together before they were married and her replying that all she could say was that I must know some very unprincipled people. While she reverted to the 'lovely home' she was offering me, I couldn't help asking myself if I was mad. Was I really getting angry and shouting at her over a man who didn't exist?

'You could have the whole top floor, you know,' she said. 'I've told you again and again, I don't mind spending money on having it converted.'

But you'd mind handing it over to me instead, I thought. That night I was very near to deciding to take the pearls to a jeweller's next day. But I didn't. After sleepless hours, worrying about being alone – suppose I died, who would ever find me? – lack of money, the mortgage and how I'd get on at the interview, I fell asleep at four, only to wake up wondering if the jeweller might call not Asprey's but the police. I seemed to recall reading somewhere that this is what jewellers do if they suspect they're being offered stolen goods. Well, they were, that's what they would be offered. I dared not do it.

I didn't get the job. The interviewer was a woman. She didn't look a bit like Hebe, but it was Hebe I thought of when first I walked into the room and saw her. The skirt she wore just covered her knees and she had high-heeled boots and a low-necked cleavage-showing top. Her dark hair was long, coming halfway down her back. Naturally, she wanted to know why I'd left my job at the Library of British History and when I told the truth and said I'd got the sack, she made a note on the sheet of paper she had in front of her. I couldn't tell her I was interested in eighteenth- and nineteenth-century children's costumes, because I know nothing about them, but I said as enthusiastically as I could that I was a quick learner. She seemed doubtful.

She looked me up and down then. I'd meant to wash my hair but hadn't had time and I'd thought it better to go without tights rather than wear a pair with ladders across the instep. I had hoped the hems of my brown trousers would hide my bare skin, but they didn't quite. She didn't comment but she didn't need to. All she said, after I'd had to tell her I'd never used a computer but again I could learn, was thank you for coming and she would let me know. She did, two days later, in a letter full of false regrets and excuses.

I'm sure it was my less than perfect appearance which lost me the job, but surely we should be honest in our daily lives and stick to our principles? It really annoys me the way people's looks, especially women's looks, seem to be getting more and more important as we move towards the twenty-first century. I just wonder if I would have been successful if I'd gone to that interview with bleached hair and lipstick and wearing some of Hebe's kinky stuff – anyway, the boots. That woman wouldn't have cared about my lack of computer skills or my not knowing when children wore pantaloons.

That afternoon I took some of the stuff out and tried the boots on. They fitted perfectly, making me inches taller. I made myself walk up the road wearing them to the paper shop and a man on a building site actually whistled at me. Back at home I fastened the dog collar round my neck and imagined Callum coming in while I was wearing the boots and had my skirt pulled up above my knees, but I had to stop and switch off. The feelings it brought on made me too uncomfortable. My whole body was throbbing.

I made myself turn to reality. The *Evening Standard* was carrying a few ads for vacancies in the kind of thing I could do and I forced myself to apply for two of them. The pearls in the drawer were starting to trouble me, almost to haunt me. They were worth so much – but not to me. And if it might look to someone else (i.e. the jeweller) as if I'd stolen them, wouldn't it look to everyone as if I had? Didn't I really know I had? Gerry had asked me to dispose of Hebe's jewels but to leave behind the valuable things. He hadn't known the pearls were valuable but he would have included them with the engagement ring and the locket and the bangle if he had known. Then I had an idea.

Suppose I were to take them back and ask him if I could keep them? Maybe he'd offered those other women, Grania and Lucy and Emily, to help themselves to a keepsake but he hadn't asked me. I could say that to him and ask for the pearls. Then it wouldn't matter if Asprey's or some small jeweller called the police, because Gerry could say he'd given them to me. He would say it too, I knew he would, even if he was told how valuable they were.

Phoning him again wasn't on. I dreaded hearing disappointment in his voice when he realized who it was. Of course I'm used to hearing that, and not only from him, but it still hurts. I would drive up there and see him.

Driving the car for the first time since Christmas, I wondered how long I could afford to keep it. The way cars depreciate and so quickly is very unfair. If I sold my flat I would get far more than I paid for it five years ago, but if I sold my car I would get a sum in hundreds rather than thousands. It wasn't worth selling it.

The evening was wet and miserable, and it's a grim drive anyway up to West Hendon. I was halfway there when I began thinking that maybe Gerry would be out, would have gone off somewhere in a taxi to meet whoever it was and in charge of Justin would be Grania – or Emily if it was Grania he had gone out with. If that happened I would just come back and try not to calculate the cost of the petrol I had wasted. But he was in. He opened the door to me.

'This is a surprise,' he said in the sort of voice you'd use to tell someone you're sorry their dog's been run over. He asked me in but I had a feeling he'd have preferred not to. It was long past Justin's bedtime but he was still up. He was in the living room watching television or he was sitting on the sofa staring vacantly into the air above the television screen. I sat down beside him but he didn't look at me and of course he didn't speak. Gerry had lost weight and was by then painfully thin. I had taken the pearls out of the case which said Asprey's on it and put them in a box which had once contained the nasty cheap perfume my mother had given me for my birthday. Gerry barely glanced at them.

'Perhaps you'd put them away with the locket and her ring,' he said.

I should have made my request then but I didn't. He went on talking about all his problems, how worried he was about Justin, how he'd taken him to a child psychologist who'd only said to give him time, his voice would come back eventually, and about his new responsibilities at work – I should be so lucky – and the longer hours this entailed and how sometimes he was at his wits' end. While he was speaking I had turned to Justin and just touched him on the shoulder. I thought he might throw my hand off but he didn't. It was as if a miracle had happened. He turned to me and held up his arms for me to take hold of him. I put my arms around him and lifted him on to my knee, where he sat and leaned his face against my chest. Gerry stared. He was silenced. And then an idea came to me. I'd really have liked more time in which to think about it, but I didn't have more time. The pearls had been my excuse for coming and once they were gone I would have no reason ever to see him – or Justin – again. It was now or never.

'Would you like to take me on as Justin's nanny?'

He didn't hear me the first time, or pretended he hadn't. 'What?'

'Would you like me to be Justin's nanny? As a job, I mean.'

'You?' he said. 'You wouldn't want to, would you? What about your own work?'

'I've lost my job,' I said, seeing no reason not to be honest.

'But you've had no training.'

'The ones you interviewed had and much good it did them.'

He smiled a little at that. He got up and turned the television off. Justin helped things by snuggling up closer to me and closing his eyes.

'If I agreed to it, how would we arrange things? You'd come here every morning at eight, say, and go home again when I got home?'

Charming. He couldn't have made it clearer how he felt about me. 'That wouldn't work at all well,' I said. 'I'd have to live here. I'll have no other home, because I'd have to let my flat. Think how useful it would be, having a nanny with a car. I'd have my own room. I wouldn't get in your way.'

'Oh, Jane, I didn't mean –'

Yes, you did. 'Think about it,' I said, 'but don't think too long. I'll take Justin up to bed now.'

I went upstairs with him in my arms and laid him in his father's bed, not bothering to undress him. Then I put the pearls back where Hebe's other jewellery was. I wasn't losing them, after all, they'd still be near me, because I'd be working here. At the bottom of the drawer, at the back, was something I hadn't noticed before. It was a cutting from a newspaper inside a clear plastic envelope, a photograph of Ivor Tesham after he won his Morningford seat in 1988. I put it in my jacket pocket. Before I went downstairs I kissed Justin, rehearsing, I suppose, for my role as his nanny.

Gerry said when I came in, 'I'm very grateful. Thank you. Of course it would be on a trial basis.'

'A one-week trial,' I said. 'I need to know for sure. I shall need to let my flat. And now we'd better talk about money.'

12

When I began writing this I said I'd avoid politics as far as I could, but some political matters have to be mentioned. The by-election to fill the seat vacated by a Conservative MP's death was one of them and Ivor went up to his Suffolk constituency the weekend before to support the candidate. It wasn't he but someone else whose name I've forgotten who lost the seat by declaring that voting for anyone but the Tory candidate would be a triumph for IRA terrorism. The result of that was a victory for the Liberal Democrats. The electorate are wayward and capricious and don't care for being bullied. That much politics I do know.

There was much wailing and gnashing of teeth (as Bible-orientated Sandy might have said) among the Tories, who were beginning to see the increasing likelihood of the Labour Party getting in at the next general election, which was not much more than a year away. Even Ivor was worried about it, temporarily distracted from his personal concerns. He hadn't yet got in touch with Juliet Case, though he did so in the week following the by-election. Iris and I knew nothing about this. We had never heard of Juliet Case at this time and were beginning to think that he was settling down to some sort of acceptance of the status quo. No one but, presumably, Mrs Lynch and her son Sean and perhaps a few relatives knew what condition Dermot Lynch was in, but we supposed that if he was still in a coma after eight months the chances were that he would never come out of it. In fact, Dermot was by this time at home in Paddington with his mother and brother. He had come out of the hospital two days after Ivor saw Juliet leave William Cross Court and followed her home.

Although he knew nothing about it at the time, this marked a turnaround in Ivor's fortunes. And when he did know, and knew the condition Dermot Lynch was in, things began to go better for him. He had aged in the preceding months and got very thin. One day in January, when I was having a drink with him in the Commons and he'd gone off to vote, a Lib Dem I knew slightly came up to me and asked me if my brother-in-law had cancer. He didn't put it quite like that but that was what he meant. From the moment (from the day, rather) Ivor found out about Dermot, his health and appearance improved and this in spite of his working harder at this point than he'd ever worked in his life.

What had happened was that he'd phoned Juliet Case, told her he'd met Lloyd a few times but only learned of her existence very recently. He owed Lloyd a sum of money he had believed he would never now be able to repay but thought it right that she should have it. How much screwing up of his courage this took, he didn't say. For some reason he expected a sharp rejoinder but she was, to use his own word, 'charming'. She had a beautiful voice and he wasn't surprised to know she had been to RADA. She invited him to her home but, being reluctant to make his way up to 'darkest Queen's Park' again, as he put it, he asked her to have dinner with him. Iris says that this was always Ivor's answer to any problem with a woman. He asked her out to dinner.

Now, of course, I don't know exactly what they said to each other in that restaurant. I only know what Ivor told me, what he necessarily précised for me. So I have constructed their conversation from what he said and my knowledge of him (and later on of Juliet), but I think it's accurate enough. I did know Ivor very well and this is pretty much how it would have been.

By this time, apparently, he had forgotten that she had seen him before. When he had come away from her front door after checking the doorbells, he had seen her looking at him out of her front window. But, as I say, he'd forgotten, and he was surprised when she recognized him immediately. He had only just come into the restaurant himself and was giving his name to the girl who kept the bookings list when Juliet came up to him, held out her hand and said, 'Juliet Case.'

Then he did remember but he said nothing about their previous encounter. He was, he said, admiring her. He wondered how he could ever in his own mind have labelled her 'big'. She had a perfect figure, an hourglass figure. The plain black dress, decorously calf-length but startlingly low-cut, he said, was just right. The ankles which he'd remarked on while he was following her half across London looked even finer and more delicate this evening. He could easily make a fetish of those ankles, he said, and knowing enough about Ivor and fetishes, I had no doubt of it. Her thick black curls were piled high on her head but she was very lightly made-up, her fine dark eyes as nature formed them, and she wore no jewellery but pearl earrings.

Those earrings reminded him of the pearls he had given Hebe, an act of generosity he now regretted. She asked for a dry martini and Ivor had one too, though he was well known for never drinking the stuff except when he was in New York and could have it in the Oak Room at the no longer extant Plaza Hotel. He had come to hand over a cheque for a thousand pounds, which, now he was sitting opposite her and admiring her attractions, he was finding rather difficult to do. They had been talking of Aaron Hunter, the subject of her ex-husband having been raised by Juliet, who asked Ivor if they had met while appearing on the same television programme. She had seen it and was now struck by the coincidence. Had Ivor seen him in his new play, a revival of O'Neill's *Anna Christie*? Ivor hadn't, and he apparently had to restrain himself from asking her if she'd come and see it with him. But that would have been premature. He had to get this business of the money over first and get over as well the delicate business of asking her about Dermot Lynch. That, after all, was the purpose of their being there. She was so friendly, so charming and – well, *sweet*, that he wondered if he was going to be able to do it at all. But he was getting used to doing difficult awkward things, as a minister has to be. He took the cheque in its envelope out of his pocket and handed it to her.

'I want you to have this. It's what I owed Lloyd.'

He had rather hoped she wouldn't open it then and there but she did. She looked at the cheque, lifted her eyes to him and said quite slowly, 'But you only owed him a quarter of this.'

Those words told him she knew Lloyd had been employed by him on the night of the crash. Two hundred and fifty pounds was the remaining sum to be paid on completion of the mock kidnap. When she said that, Ivor had a quick and vivid picture of himself scooping up the two envelopes from our hall table when Hebe hadn't come. For a moment he said nothing. He was thinking that if she knew about the payment, what else must she know? Everything, surely. And then, quietly and with a small smile, she confirmed his fears.

'Lloyd told me what you were paying him to do. It looked easy. It would have been but for Dermot's driving. I think I ought to tell you that Lloyd and I were still on – well, friendly terms, but we'd split up, we'd not much feeling for each other any more. I'm not saying I hadn't loved him once or I wasn't sad when he died, but I couldn't say it devastated me.'

Ivor was only interested in how this affected him. That was natural. 'You know all about that night? About how they were supposed to bring her – Hebe – to me?'

'Yes,' she said.

'And you knew how they were meant to pick up Hebe Furnal and not Kelly Mason?'

'Yes. You're going to ask why I didn't go to the police.'

'You could ask me that,' Ivor said.

'If it had been Lloyd who was injured and Dermot who was dead I would have, I'd have wanted to – well, clear him of blame. But Lloyd was dead. And Dermot was unconscious and couldn't speak. I thought that if I said it was a sort of game they wouldn't believe me and, you see . . .' Here she hesitated, then said quickly, 'Lloyd never told me your name.'

Ivor felt as if he'd been struck a heavy blow. It rocked him. '*What?*'

'Please don't be cross. It's true. He never told me your name and I never asked.'

'Oh, God,' Ivor said and then, 'I won't be cross.'

'Lloyd came over in the morning that Friday to pick up some of his stuff he'd left in my house. He was renting a flat somewhere. He owed me some money – just the amount you owed *him*. He gave it to me and said this MP Nicola Ross had introduced him to was paying him to pick up a girl, put handcuffs and a gag on her and take her to a house in Hampstead. The girl would know, it was just a game, and he was going to get five hundred pounds for it. I could have asked what MP but I didn't. I wasn't really interested. I just thought it was good money for doing very little, and then Lloyd and I talked about other things.'

'So you'd never have known who I was if I hadn't told you on the phone.'

She smiled. 'That's right.'

He knew he had betrayed himself. 'What are you going to do?' It was the same question he had asked Jane Atherton and he got much the same answer.

'Do? I don't understand.'

I don't know if there was a long silence after that but it was long enough for Ivor to consider his position, as employers are supposed to say when they're about to give someone the sack. Next day he was due to speak in the Commons on a new aircraft which had just been perfected with a view to its use in the Middle East, should war come. He imagined the police arriving – would they be permitted to enter the department and find him in his office? – and he still being obliged to make the speech, knowing he would be arrested when he left the chamber.

'I made up my mind in those few moments that I'd kill myself,' he said when he told me.

'Don't be ridiculous,' I said.

'No, really. Not possessing a handgun like all those bloody Americans do, I thought I'd hang myself. At home, of course, not in the department.' He gave one of his wild laughs, laid a hand on my arm. 'Don't look like that, Rob. It never had to happen.'

He wanted to ask her if she was going to blackmail him or try to blackmail him, but he couldn't bring himself to say the words. A waiter came to their table. Juliet gave him her order and Ivor, though he felt he couldn't eat a thing, said he'd have the same. Drinking wasn't beyond him, though, and he ordered a bottle of wine without asking her what she'd like. When the waiter had gone he looked at her in despair, his head full of suicide plans. When she had told him her intentions, he thought, he would pay the bill, perhaps empty his pockets and simply put all the money he had on the table, get up and leave. He'd go home, drink half a bottle of whisky and do the deed, trying not to think about it too much beforehand.

'He's such a drama queen,' Iris said when I told her. 'What's the masculine for *diva*?'

'It didn't come to that, anyway,' I said. 'Of course it didn't. She just said she wasn't going to do anything. It wasn't her business. It was in the past and telling the police or the media wouldn't serve any useful purpose.'

'I imagine he could hardly believe his ears. The trouble with Ivor is he always – well, nearly always – believes the worst of people even when he doesn't know them. Juliet sounds rather nice.'

'She was very nice to Ivor.'

He found he could eat his dinner after all. The wine he had ordered to drown his sorrows or help him on his way to his death now became a celebration drink. Everything was going to be all right. A small setback came while they were eating their main course. It was a case of the good news and the bad news, only neither of them put it like that. The bad news, Ivor said, was that she told him Dermot Lynch had come home, the good that he had no memory of the crash or what had led up to it. Lloyd had told her Dermot was to drive the pick-up car and the two of them had met a couple of times after the Victoria pub meeting and before the birthday present evening. A few weeks after the crash she, Juliet, had gone to see Mrs Lynch, solely, it appeared, because she felt sorry for her, and since then had visited her every so often but had never told her about the MP and the kidnap set-up. What would have been the point?

'You mean, you went to see her just out of the kindness of your heart?'

'It was no big deal,' she said. 'Three stops on the tube. She's a very gentle, simple sort of woman. She's had a lot to put up with. Sean being questioned like that about Sandy Caxton's murder and now Dermot. He'll never be quite right, you know.'

Ivor asked her what that meant.

'He had a lot of brain damage. He can move around and talk a bit and so on, I've seen him, but he'll never work again. Look, it wasn't your fault. It was his. It was he who drove through a red light, not the lorry driver. And he took the gun along. Sean told me. Sean brought the gun back from a package tour to Poland before the Soviets went. Someone sold it to him for a few dollars.'

It was that simple. Sean Lynch hadn't had access to some secret IRA store of firearms. His brother had 'borrowed' a souvenir of a foreign trip to give appropriate colour to a mock hijack. Ivor imagined them laughing about it together. He had a heady feeling of everything at last going his way. It was over, he thought, forgetting he had felt that way before. Of course there still remained things for him to do. One must be to compensate the Lynch family. He must find a way of paying some sort of pension to Philomena Lynch or perhaps to her son who would never work again. It would be tricky but it could be done. And there was no longer any need for him to obey my injunction not to go near the Lynch family, for both he and Sean Lynch were innocent of any wrongdoing. I think Ivor genuinely believed by this time that he had done nothing wrong as he basked in the sweet smiles of Juliet Case, contemplated her cleavage and thought about those ankles, at that time invisible under the table, with no wider a span, he said poetically, than the silver ring his napkin had come in.

Surely with extreme exaggeration, he said she was the only woman he had ever taken out to dinner who thanked him. Perhaps he had forgotten that Hebe hadn't had the chance to thank him as they had never had a meal together. He took Juliet home in a taxi and she invited him in for a drink. A character in Shakespeare says,

'Our courteous Antony, whom ne'er the word of "No" woman heard speak.' That was Ivor. At any rate, no woman as attractive as Juliet Case had ever heard him say no. It was already eleven, he had a heavy day ahead of him with an important speech to make, but he didn't hesitate. The inevitable happened – inevitable with Ivor, that is, I don't know about her. He didn't stay the night, though, but left at two and was lucky enough to find a taxi at Queen's Park station.

He told us this very discreetly but there was no doubt what he meant. Juliet Case, who had been Lloyd Freeman's girlfriend, had slept with him the first time they met.

'But there you are,' he said airily. 'My luck's come back.'

Next morning he sent her two dozen red roses with the always irresistible message that carries an undercurrent of breathless urgency: *When can I see you again?*

What answer she made I don't know but he did see her again and again and again. Soon Ivor was in the middle of a full-blown affair with Juliet Case. We nearly quarrelled, he and I, when he said he wished, instead of parting with them to Hebe, who hadn't lived to enjoy them, he'd held on to those pearls and given them to Juliet. I told him he was a callous shit, but he was too pleased with himself and her to care.

13

'After all your education,' my mother said. 'A sixteen-year-old with no O levels could do that.'

I asked her if it wasn't better for a child to be looked after by an educated woman than by someone who was ignorant of everything but pop music and clothes, but all she said was, a frequent rejoinder, 'Oh, you know what I mean.'

It was plain that Gerry didn't want me. He especially didn't want me living in his house. But he needed a nanny for Justin, and Justin, who hadn't liked Grania or Lucy or Emily or the nameless one – whose name, I discovered, was Wendy – seemed now to like me. Second only to Gerry himself, he liked me. This was a mark in my favour in more ways than one. If you were getting married, wouldn't you prefer someone your child liked?

Letting my flat was fairly easy. I found a tenant within days of advertising, a woman of about my own age called Pandora Flint. She was the fourth prospective tenant I'd seen. There had been objections on my side or theirs to the other three – two found the place too small for the rent I was asking and the third wanted me to take out my furniture and let her bring hers in – but Pandora seemed all right. She loved the flat and didn't hesitate when I asked her for a deposit and two months' rent in advance. It was a year's lease with an option for renewal she was taking on and that suited both of us. If any problem existed it was that I disliked her on sight.

To look at, she was very much like Hebe. I suppose Hebe's isn't an uncommon type, tall, slim, blonde with regular features and long legs. You see them all over the place, two-a-penny, as my mother would say. Hebe had been my friend, so it would have been logical for me to be predisposed to Pandora, but things don't work that way. Hebe had been warm and effusive and demonstrative, a touchy-feely woman; Pandora was cool and distant, with one of those remote whispery voices which sound as if its possessor is just coming out of a trance. None of this mattered to me if she turned out to be a good tenant, as she did. Unfortunately, she was less than perfect in other ways.

I don't know what it was like in other parts of the country but in the district of London where I lived and the district where Gerry lived there were scarcely any waste bins to be found on the streets. Fear of IRA bomb attacks was so great that street bins in which explosives could be placed had all been taken away and so had left-luggage lockers at stations. If I wanted to dispose of Hebe's fetishistic stuff before I moved into Irving Road, I had to do it at once. Unthinkable to take them with me to my new home. I would have to put them into the bag in my own kitchen bin and take the bag down to one of the dustbins which permanently stood outside the front door common to all six flats. The idea of this troubled me a lot. At the beginning of January, the man called Michael in one of the ground-floor flats had rung my bell and, when I answered, held up the small plastic carrier I had put in one of the dustbins ten minutes before. I recognized it at once and was perfectly aware of its contents before he told me.

'I was sure you didn't mean to throw away a Christmas pudding in a basin,' he said, 'and a dozen mince pies and a present which hasn't been opened.'

'On the contrary,' I said, 'I intended to throw them away and I did. Perhaps you'd be kind enough to put them back where they came from.'

Considering the indignation I felt, not to say anger, I think I'd been very moderate in what I said. Later on I checked the dustbins and neither the carrier nor its contents were there. No doubt, he'd eaten my mother's Christmas pudding and mince pies and given whatever was in the package that my aunt had sent me to his girlfriend. But I dared not risk anything like that happening again, not when you consider what would be in the bag this time. Spiked dog collars and lace-up boots and corselettes aren't the kinds of thing you can take to the Oxfam shop. Eventually, the day before I left for Irving Road and when all my stuff was packed in the car ready to go, I went to the luggage shop in Kilburn High Road and bought a sturdy suitcase which locked.

When I got back to the flat the window cleaner had come. He always turns up without warning and needs to go inside the first-floor flats and the two on this floor. Mummy says they used to climb up ladders to reach the windows and, if the inside wanted doing, people cleaned their own. Those days are gone, I tell her, it's a question of health and safety. This window cleaner is called Stu, short for Stuart, I suppose. If he's got a surname I've never heard it. He's coarse and rude and intrusive and once he asked me why I didn't grow my hair. I would look a lot better with long hair, he said in his charming way.

He took an incredibly long time cleaning my three windows and while he was doing it he stared at me a lot. I couldn't start on transferring Hebe's things into my new suitcase while he was there, because he'd see all her kinky stuff and comment on it. I can imagine the kind of thing he'd say, though I'd rather not. So I had to sit about and pretend to read a book. His charges go up every time and we haggled about the cost but he won. He always does.

'I won't be here next time you come,' I said. 'There'll be a new lady living here.'

'Lady, is it? Be ten quid to speak to her. Where are you off to, then, Grosvenor Square?'

I didn't answer but said he needn't think he'd seen the last of me. I was just letting the flat as a temporary measure.

'Flat, you call it? I hope the *lady* knows that what she's getting is a room.'

I hoped he would hand out the same sort of treatment to Pandora. I wouldn't put up with him for a moment if it wasn't that the managing agents of this house employ him, not me. Once he'd gone I drank all the wine left in a bottle I'd started on and dressed myself in some of Hebe's things, the corsets and the fishnet stockings and a see-through top, and looked at myself in the mirror. It would be the last time and, my body throbbing and moist, and not just with sweat, I thought it was just as well I'd be leaving this stuff behind. I turned my back on the mirror, stripped the things off and put them into the case. I laid a blue woolly dressing gown (suitable for a septuagenarian) Mummy had once given me on the top. I locked it, put the key in my bag with my house keys and the case in the only built-in cupboard in the flat. It's between the kitchen cabinets and the bathroom door and it's got four shelves inside it. I laid the case flat on the floor under the bottom shelf and put a roll of carpet cut-off in front of it. Anyone opening the cupboard door wouldn't have known it was there.

I am living in Irving Road now. As a nanny, I have one day off a week and I take it, but naturally I have to come back here in the evening. I have nowhere else to go. When I go out I tell Gerry I'm meeting Callum. My Sundays are supposed to be free too but I've nowhere to go and anyway I don't want all this time off. I want to be with Justin as much as possible so as to make him like me, or make sure he goes on liking me.

On his third birthday, in March, he got his voice back. 'Justin is three,' were the first words he spoke after being silent so long. Then he said, 'Jane.'

Though he used not to be interested in me, Gerry has asked me about Callum. What does he do for a living? Are we engaged? I've told him he's a businessman, is thirty-two years old and has his own flat near Sloane Square. No, we're not engaged, not yet. I think Gerry may be jealous. If he is he will probably be the only man I've ever known who has been. I am going to work on it, tell him things to show it's possible for a man to want me. He has moved back into the bedroom he used to share with Hebe. I, of course, have the smallest bedroom, the boxroom, as Mummy would call it if she ever saw it, which she won't. Any other nanny would expect an en suite bathroom and television. I am not unreasonable, I know Gerry can't put in another bathroom specially for me, but I don't think it would have hurt him or Justin, come to that, to have given me Justin's room and put him in mine. A child of three doesn't need a large bedroom.

When I first came Gerry made it plain without actually saying so that he expected me to spend the evenings in that little cell after Justin had gone to bed. Or perhaps in the kitchen like a maid. Hebe had had a small black and white television in there and it was still there, up on a high shelf. He looked surprised that first day when I came into the living room with the book I was reading and sat down quietly in the armchair opposite to him. 'Oh, hello,' he said, as if I was the last person likely to walk in.

It wasn't a good beginning but I persevere. He usually puts on the television once the evening meal has been eaten and stares at it in silence. If Justin calls out he tells me to stay where I am and he goes up to him himself. My intention was not to perform any household tasks, but I now see that I must if I want to make myself indispensable. The idea originally was that Justin and I would eat at five and Gerry would get his own supper, make himself a sand-wich or scrambled eggs on toast. Now, for the past week, I have been giving Justin his tea and then I cook a meal for Gerry and me. 'That's nice,' he said the first time I did it, and after that he took it for granted.

He is unhappy, I can see that, but still his gloom and misery make me impatient. I can't help it. After all, I know what Hebe was really like. I know how misplaced all this *posthumous* devotion is. He was no more to her than a meal ticket and not a very superior one at that. Once she had found a better she would have been off. She would have left him a 'Dear Gerry' note, taken Justin, the pearls and her clothes and gone off to a more promising future. If she had lived, would that superior provider have been Ivor Tesham? I think about him a lot. I think about that evening, ten months ago now, when he sent a car to pick her up on the Watford Way. If he ever sent a car, if the car that crashed was the car he sent. 'What are you going to do?' he asked me. Well, I'm not going to do anything. Why would I? But it was strange that he asked.

I mentioned the pearls just now. They are upstairs in Gerry's bedroom in their box, side by side with the bangle, the engagement ring and the locket with Justin's picture in it. Gerry hasn't asked. It's plain he doesn't care. After he has left for work in the mornings and Justin is in the living room playing with his toy cars – he has about a hundred of them and each new one is a cause of excitement. Well, he's a child, so it's only to be expected – I go upstairs, open the drawer, take the lid off the box and look at the pearls. Something strange has happened. I look at them in a different way from the way I did when I had them in my flat. I was greedy for them then, calculating how I could sell them, what the risks were, what would happen if I dared to try it. Now I see them as a kind of nest egg or insurance policy. It's because I know Gerry isn't interested in them. Gerry doesn't care. He wouldn't know if they were there or not. So I think of them as my *savings*, my pension if you like, something to fall back on when all else fails. Then I shall dare try it. The worst that can happen is that the jeweller will get in touch with Gerry, not Ivor Tesham, and tell Gerry what they are worth, and then he will know what his beloved wife was.

He has begun to talk about her. The evening silence has been broken and he opens his heart to me. This, he says, is because he knows that I too miss her, I too loved her. He has lost his wife, the only woman he ever loved, but I have lost my best friend, someone, incidentally, that I had known for longer than he had.

People in love don't know the object of their love at all. It has taken being here and listening to Gerry's maunderings to show me that. Not having any personal experience of the condition, I had never noticed it before. Gerry has created a Hebe who isn't the Hebe I or anyone else knew and certainly not the Hebe Ivor Tesham knew. It isn't the woman who told me she talked sex-talk on the phone to her lover half an hour after her husband had left for work or the woman who got on a bus to meet her lover dressed only in boots and a long topcoat and fixed up plausible alibis with a compliant friend. This woman is a wonderful wife and devoted mother who never looked at another man – his actual words – in spite of men's attention and her beauty. She desperately wanted another child but agreed with him at once when he said they couldn't afford it. But for having no one to look after Justin, she would have gone out to work. It was he who stopped her, told her not even to think about it.

I listen, I nod, I say, 'Really?' I say, 'You're right, I know.' That's all he wants, agreement, acceptance, sympathy, and he gets it from me. Once or twice he cries, putting his head in his hands and sobbing over this woman who couldn't have cared less if he had lived or died. Well, except that she might have had to work if he had died and Ivor Tesham hadn't been there to rescue her.

Last evening Gerry said, 'I didn't like the idea of you living in, Jane. I couldn't face having another woman living here.' He looked at me, not rudely or particularly critically, but as if I'd be anyone's last resort, the best of a bad job as Mummy would say. 'But it's been a good idea. I can say honestly I don't know what I'd do without you.'

'Thank you,' I said.

'If you were more like Hebe it would be difficult, but no two women could be more different.' This after he had just been telling me how beautiful she was, how clever, how witty, funny and such good company. Then he said, 'I know I shouldn't be selfish but you won't leave me and get married to Callum, will you?'

'Maybe one day,' I said, 'but that's a way off.'

Far from Gerry's idealized notion of her, Hebe wasn't a good mother. I now know, though I didn't at the time, that all the Granias and Lucys and the rest of them, not to mention Gerry's mother, were roped in as often as possible to mind him when she went clothes shopping or took herself to the cinema or the hairdresser. She put him to bed as early as she could and left him to cry if he was in bed and she alone with him in the house. I was determined to be an exemplary mother-substitute and I think I am succeeding. It is rather painful for me to remember the spontaneous expressions of affection from him to her, the many times I had seen him go to her, climb on her knee and hug her, sometimes cover her face with his kisses. And it's a mystery to me why a little boy of his age will show so much love to someone who is, let's face it, absolutely unworthy. Hebe didn't deserve Justin's love. I shall deserve it. My hope is that gradually, as time passes, as more and more weeks and months lie between her death and the present, he will forget her and come to think of me as the only mother he has had.

It hasn't started to happen yet but it will. If I am steadfast it will. He still asks for her, especially when he is tired, and it's no longer 'Justin wants Mummy' but 'I want my mummy' or simply, plaintively, 'Where's my mummy?' He is leaving babyhood and becoming a little boy. I hug him when he calls for Hebe, but he becomes petulant and pushes me away. Hebe was a completely insensitive person, totally unaware of other people's feelings, and I am hoping Justin hasn't inherited this trait from her, but it's more than possible he has. Can there be a gene of selfishness? Perhaps. Or it may be that Gerry was right when he said he was selfish and didn't want me to leave him and get married.

Things are going rather well, though, and that's something I don't often say.

14

To understand Ivor you have first to accept him as the quintessential English gentleman. That sounds like a paradox when you know how he behaved over the crash and its aftermath, but really that behaviour was quite in character. The English gentleman is brave to the point of foolhardiness, courteous to women of his own class, a good soldier, arrogant, proud, generous and bold. He has an old-fashioned sense of honour. Extraordinary as it must appear to a great many people, he is still in that mindset which was the stuff of adventure fiction in the early part of the twentieth century. Carruthers (or Frobisher or Carew) will be blackballed in the morning, so the night before his best friend sends him into the library, where he will find a gun in the third drawer of a certain desk. You will know what to do, the friend says, and Carruthers does. He prefers death to dishonour and he doesn't hesitate.

But he has a weakness. He is very afraid of ridicule. On that Saturday morning, when he first read about the crash, Ivor didn't tell the police about his part in it because he feared the ferocity of the popular press. No one would have blamed him for the accident. No charges would have been brought against him. Only his evident adultery could have been construed by puritans as dishonourable, but English gentlemen don't care for puritans and they commit adultery all the time. After all, the puritans are Roundheads and they are Cavaliers. It wasn't the law but the tabloid newspapers he feared. He feared the destructiveness they would have meted out to him in respect of the sado-masochistic aspect of the thing, the handcuffs, the gag, the hooded kidnappers and the blacked-out windows of the car. All this would, of course, have been contrasted with their pseudo-sympathy for the Lynch family, for the 'loved ones' of Lloyd Freeman and, above all, for the cuckolded husband of Hebe Furnal. Destructiveness it would have been and it would have gone on and on. Every time he made a speech in the Commons it would have been resurrected.

Later on, it was a different matter. With the Kelly Mason complications, the discovery of the gun and the questioning of Sean Lynch, all possibilities of going to the police were ruled out. It was too late. It was too late to do anything but lie low, but wait and hope.

And so Ivor had suffered many months of acute anxiety. But his fortunes recovered in the spring, coinciding apparently with the affair he had embarked on with Juliet Case. They had become what was being called an 'item'. There had even been a photograph of them together in the *Evening Standard*. That was just after the Gulf War and the air offensive against Iraq began. Ivor had made a statement to the Commons and three days later got himself into the papers again when he spoke with patriotic indignation (as an English gentleman would speak) about the captured allied pilots Iraq had paraded on TV. He abhorred Iraq's action, he fulminated against such 'vile exploitation', but he liked the publicity for himself. That was the kind of press attention he enjoyed.

His reaction to the mortar attack on 10 Downing Street in early February must have been a mix of outrage and the jitters. It was described as the most audacious IRA operation on the UK mainland since the Brighton bombing. All the windows were blown out in the room where the Cabinet was meeting at the time. Ivor was shocked and angry, but I suspect those feelings were subservient to the nervousness he always felt when anything to do with the IRA came up. He would inevitably think of the Sean Lynch connection.

But Iris and I had other things on our minds. Our son had been born on 20 February after a frightening drive to St Mary's Hospital. A few hundred yards away a bomb had exploded at Paddington Station two days before. Hoax bomb-warning calls led to station closures, closed-off streets and traffic hold-ups. Because of this we nearly didn't make it and Iris feared she might give birth in the car, but all was just about well and it was a midwife's hands, not mine, which delivered him. He was a big boy, four kilos (or eight and a half pounds, as we fuddy-duddies say) and within the hour we had named him Adam James.

Ivor came to see the baby but was too busy in the then busiest of government departments to stay long. And after that our troubles began at home. Nadine, who had been the sweetest child, the most loving and, in the best possible way, the most precocious, reverted to crawling and refusing food. It was rather uncanny to hear her new manner of crying, not the strong ear-splitting crying of an eighteen-month-old but the soft mewling of an infant. We didn't need a child psychologist to tell us she was jealous of her new brother. Pathetically, this was her way of trying to win us back, by emulating his behaviour, which she must have assumed pleased us more than her more mature ways.

'Maybe we shouldn't have had another child,' Iris said, worn out as she was by two yelling, demanding infants.

'Too late now,' I said, attempting robustness. 'It'll be all right. It'll work out, because if it doesn't everyone would be an only child.'

It did, but it took several months before Nadine accepted her brother and a couple more before she grew to love him with a fierce protectiveness. During that time, though I went to work, of course I did, we stayed at home, afraid to leave the children with a babysitter, afraid to leave them even with my mother. And we made it clear we wanted no visitors. All our attention was needed by Nadine and Adam. So our only contact with Ivor was the occasional phone call and, of course, what we read about him in the newspaper. And throughout that year we met seldom. He told us that he hardly went out. His evenings as well as his days were occupied with the Gulf War and the continuing efforts of the IRA. He tried to maintain his friendship with Erica Caxton and any other free time he got he spent with Juliet Case.

In the following year he knew he would have an election to fight. As you know, we've a system in this country which other nations find curious, that of not announcing the date of a general election until twenty-one days before it takes place. Everyone knows this election is going to happen and approximately when it will happen, but the date is only disclosed three weeks beforehand. That year, 1992, the Labour Party expected to defeat the government and the existing administration feared they were right. But they were wrong and in April John Major's Conservatives were returned with a rather dodgy majority of twenty-one. Ivor got back in in Morningford, his own majority slightly reduced. He had worked hard to get himself returned, faced as he had been with the almost superhuman task of fighting a strong Labour candidate in his own constituency while attending to his departmental work in Westminster. Up in a Midlands constituency Aaron Hunter, standing as an Independent on an anti-sleaze ticket, failed to unseat the Tory member.

'Not surprising, since no Independent has sat in the Commons for almost fifty years,' said Ivor.

It was a long time before we met Juliet, but it happened at last. As Iris said to me, being called Juliet must confer on its bearer the obligation to be sweet and romantic and is therefore something of a liability. But this Juliet can have had no worries on that score. Sweet she was and beautiful in unexpected ways. I say unexpected, because I believed Ivor had a type, the tall slender blonde, into which category Nicola Ross came and Hebe Furnal, of course, had come. Juliet Case I have already described. I have quoted Ivor's accolade. But even Ivor failed to convey her warmth, her sweetness, and that rare quality, the mastery of keeping silent. She was kind too. I never heard her say an unpleasant thing about anyone. To look at her, voluptuous, dark, with the velvety white skin of the Iberian type, the ready smile, the deep brown eyes which seemed always to be seeing happy visions, you would have expected her to be talkative, loquacious, readily laughing. But she was a mistress of tranquillity. When she had nothing to say she said nothing. I once heard Ivor address her as 'my gracious silence', which, Iris tells me, is what Coriolanus calls his wife. Listener as she was, you respected all the more her utterances when she did speak.

We had all met at our house before going out to dinner, leaving my mother with the children. We went to a restaurant in Hampstead, in Heath Street, because Iris was nervous about going too far away, though Adam was fifteen months old by then and Nadine getting on for three. Iris and I had noticed that, although it wasn't the precise anniversary, this was the week, two years ago, of the crash in which Hebe had died. We had noticed but there was no sign that either of the others had. Perhaps they had and it was only discretion that stopped them mentioning it. Hebe wasn't, after all, the only one who had died. Juliet's ex-boyfriend Lloyd Freeman had also been killed. And I wondered a lot about that. I had talked to Iris about it and found she had wondered too. Wasn't it rather strange of Juliet to be going about with Ivor when she *knew* he was responsible for, if not causing the accident, organizing the set-up which led to it?

'He seems to have been her ex-boyfriend by that time,' Iris said. 'Perhaps she hadn't much feeling left for him.'

I said I found that rather hard to swallow. When you think about that sort of thing you have to put yourself in the other person's shoes, as far as you can, and imagine how you would feel. I put myself into the shoes of a male version of Juliet and pictured hearing about the death in an accident of the girl I'd been going about with just before Iris and I met, and I thought, notwithstanding falling in love with Iris at first sight, how upset I'd have been, how shocked, how determined to have nothing to do with the man – but no, it didn't work. Sophie couldn't drive, wouldn't have taken part in a mock kidnap; the whole thing fell to the ground, as my fantasies usually do. But in spite of my failure to imagine Juliet's feelings, I was left with the conviction that her behaviour was odd, that perhaps she had some ulterior purpose in going about with Ivor. I'm afraid too – and I'm not proud of this – that I rather flinched from a woman who would sleep with a man the first time she went out with him.

At that dinner we talked about his election success. Juliet mentioned her former husband Aaron Hunter's defeat by an MP Ivor knew quite well called Martin Reed. That was when Ivor made that remark about no Independent having sat in Parliament for nearly half a century. We talked about that, Juliet exhibiting as much calm indifference to the fate of Hunter as she seemed to be doing to that of Lloyd Freeman. She smiled, she maintained quietness. When she spoke she was witty and amusing, and this had something to do with the contrast between this and her silences. Iris asked her if she was acting at present and she said she wasn't, she said she hadn't had a part in anything for several years.

'Luckily I've got a little money of my own to live on,' she said.

Later on we asked each other if that 'little money' came from Ivor. We both watched her with great interest and we watched the way she looked at Ivor and he at her. She was dressed in black, short-skirted to show off the legs – the feet in stilt heels – low-necked to display the fine bosom. A thin red stole, embroidered in black, rested on her shoulders. His glances at her were almost wolfish, while she sat in calm repose. One day, I said to Iris on the way home, she will be vastly fat and she won't care.

'She ate an awful lot,' Iris said. 'You don't often see women eating like that. I don't mean she hasn't got perfectly good table manners, I don't mean that at all, but she eats with a kind of concentration. She shovels it in almost delicately but she does shovel it.'

I laughed. We let ourselves into the house. My mother said with proud satisfaction that both children had enjoyed unbroken sleep all the time we were out.

Ivor had never lived with a woman. There had been times he seemed to be on the point of doing so, such as when he was having his affair with Deborah Liston and he spoke to us of her 'thinking of moving in'. Almost immediately after that he met Nicola Ross and that was the end of Deborah and her move. Nicola, apparently, suggested he come and live with her. She had no intention of leaving her house by the river at Hammersmith, but Ivor wouldn't do it. I believe he thought there was something diminishing of his manhood in sharing a woman's home. Or perhaps he just didn't care for her enough to set up house with her. As for Hebe, he and I had, of course, once been into the possibility of his buying her a Pimlico flat, but the point of that was to avoid his having to live with her while being free to visit her whenever he chose.

Would he break his rule, if rule it was, for Juliet? It didn't look like it, yet he seemed to spend every free moment he had with her. He had driven her down to Ramburgh to meet his parents and their enthusiasm seemed, if anything, to increase his feelings for her. Was that love, passion or sex alone? I don't know. That is, I didn't know then. Ivor and she went to a fellow MP's wedding in York and got their picture in the papers along with the bride and groom, Juliet in a black lace cartwheel hat and a white linen dress. The local daily, the *Morningford Gazette*, carried a photograph of them at the Norfolk Show just after Ivor went up another rung of the ladder and was made a Minister of State. Iris and I asked each other if her parents had said any more about moving out of Ramburgh House when Ivor got married.

'If he is going to get married,' Iris said, 'I'd rather it had been Erica Caxton.'

I said I thought she liked Juliet.

'Well, I do. But that doesn't mean I want her for a sister-in-law. I don't know why, but I think she'd be unfaithful.'

'That would make two of them,' I said, for I couldn't imagine Ivor being with one woman, wife or not, for long.

On the face of it, so many things had been forgotten. On the rare occasions when we saw Ivor alone he would sometimes refer to the accident, even mention Hebe in a rueful sort of way. Poor dead Lloyd also received a little of his attention, as once, for instance, he spoke of the first time he had seen Juliet, at Nicola Ross's party. He even said he regretted asking Lloyd to take part in his kidnap scenario. Lloyd had been a promising actor, he thought, and so young. It had been such a waste of talent and of life itself. But of Gerry Furnal and Hebe's child he never spoke. They might not have existed as far as he was concerned. The alibi lady he also seemed to have expunged from his memory. As for the Lynchs, the absolute dread he had once had of them, his horror of Sean Lynch and not even hidden wish for Dermot to die, all that had gone, might never have been. The possibility of compensating them for Dermot's injuries also seemed forgotten. Or so it appeared that summer and autumn.

Iris and I had at last decided we must move. The Hampstead mews house, which had been her parents' wedding present to us, was too small for a couple with two children of opposite sexes. It would really have been too small for a couple with children of the same sex. The second bedroom was very small. There was room in it for Nadine's narrow bed and Adam's cot and that was all – no clothes cupboard, no chest of drawers. We had put it on the market in the summer. In September, on the day which came to be known as Black Wednesday, the government – Ivor's government – was forced to withdraw the pound from the European Exchange Rate Mechanism. Among other currency disasters, the housing market crashed. How we came to sell our house at all I don't know, but we did, and were lucky to sell it a month later. But I received less for it than my father-in-law had paid six years before.

Ivor had visited us in that house many times and had brought Juliet there more than once. I used to expect him to show some sign that he recalled, surely unpleasantly if not painfully, the evening he had spent there, waiting for Hebe to come. An involuntary wince perhaps, a hesitation before he crossed our threshold, even a silent glance around our living room as he thought of that wait and of his ignorance at the time as to what was really taking place. But none of that happened. It may be that he was determined it should not and so he exercised an iron control over his features and his eyes. He was good at iron control was Ivor.

So we moved out in November and into the new house we had bought on a bigger mortgage than I had hoped for in the far north of London, on the Hertfordshire border. With his elitist ideas and English gentleman's notions of the only place to live as being in something two centuries old in the country or the heart of town,

Ivor looked tolerantly at our 1960s red brick, our double garage and our half-acre of garden. 'Just the thing,' he said, 'if you have children.' He reminded me of a story told me by a banker I know. This man, whose name was Jonathan, bought a house in South Kensington and took his father to see it. While approving up to a point, the old man said to Jonathan, 'Very nice, my boy. And where will you have your town house?'

Ivor was taking Juliet to Nice for a few days. It would be the first real holiday he had had for nearly three years. Before he went he drove up to Leicestershire one Sunday to see Erica and her children and on his way home he called on us. Although she knew all about it, and I knew she did, I never liked to mention anything about the crash in Juliet's presence. For one thing, I wouldn't have cared to speak of Lloyd in front of her and it would have been difficult to avoid speaking of him. But now we had Ivor to ourselves and he had got on to the subject of Erica, how she seemed at last to be recovering from the loss of Sandy, digressing only a little to talk about the latest IRA atrocity, I asked him if he ever had any news of the Lynch family, particularly of Dermot Lynch.

'Why would I?' he said. 'You always went on and on about how I ought to be careful never to go near any of them.'

15

I have been keeping this scrapbook since the time when Hebe died. It is a companion book to the diary which isn't a book at all. When I came to Irving Road I brought both with me. Ivor Tesham is its subject and that includes a lot of peripheral stuff, pictures of the accident, for instance, photographs of all the people involved. After all, I have to do something more than look after Justin and cook evening meals for Gerry. I have to have a hobby and keeping cuttings about a really famous celebrity wouldn't be all that interesting. There would be too many of them. I'd reach a point of having to pick and choose, of selecting which to keep and which to discard. The choice I've made is perfect. Ivor Tesham is well enough known to get his name in the newspapers perhaps once every two or three weeks but no more and his photograph far less often. I confine my searches to the *Guardian*, which is delivered here every day, and to the *Evening Standard*, which Gerry brings home with him and which I carry away upstairs to my room when he has finished with it.

No one else knows about the scrapbook. But when you come to think of it, who is there who could know? I don't really know anyone except Gerry and my mother and the girls. Grania, I mean, and Lucy and Wendy. And of course I know Gerry's mother and my tenant, Pandora Flint. That's quite a respectable list of friends, isn't it? Except that none of them are my friends. I thought Gerry would be. I hoped Gerry and I would grow closer as time went on, but we haven't really. We did for a while, when he talked to me about Hebe, how he missed her and how wonderful she was, and I listened and said yes and no and of course. But that didn't go on for long. It went on for months and then it stopped. Instead of talking about something else he just stopped talking. This was partly because Justin started staying up later. He wouldn't go to sleep at six – he got into the way of wanting someone to sit with him – so Gerry let him stay up till eight. I don't agree with it. I think children need their sleep and grown-ups certainly need a bit of peace. Gerry says he never gets a chance to talk to his son unless he lets him stay up later and, of course, he is the boss, he makes the rules. As for me, I talk about Callum less than I did. Maybe Gerry doesn't believe in him any more. A real boyfriend would phone, wouldn't he? He'd call for me. And there's another difficulty. If you have an imaginary friend – because, let's face it, that's what Callum is – you always know he's imaginary unless you're mad, and you lose interest in him, you forget to talk about him, and worse, you forget what you said about him before. Gerry looked suspicious when I said Callum was thirty-one and I realized I'd taken a year off the age he was a year ago. He asked me if I was sure of that when I said he lived in Kensington.

But to get back to the scrapbook and Ivor Tesham. Or, rather, to get back to Ivor Tesham. The scrapbook can look after itself, it's locked in a safe-deposit box in my tiny cell, and it's not even very interesting, just a man's political life in journalese and illustrations. But it's his private life as well. There are several photographs of him with his new love, his bosomy girlfriend who rejoices in the unlikely name of Juliet Case and calls herself an actress, though what she has *acted* in is a mystery to me and, I suspect, to everyone else. Tesham didn't wait long. He wasn't faithful to Hebe's memory for more than a few months. I sometimes wonder – no, I often wonder – what Gerry would think if he knew there was a man out there in the world, a man also in London, though in a rather different part of it from this dump, a man who was Hebe's lover but who forgot her once she was dead.

Juliet Case is also a bit different. From Hebe, I mean. At any rate, whatever else she may have been, Hebe was beautiful, ethereal-looking, delicate, fair as a lily (as Gerry often says), while this woman looks as if she ought to be at a bullfight with a rose between her teeth. Carmen, no less. I wonder too how much she knows about that Friday evening, about the crash, if she knows anything.

I have thought about it to the point of exhaustion. The cuttings which half fill the scrapbook have given me some help. I have read and re-read the pieces which describe the crash and looked again and again at the photographs. A few days after it happened and when the police thought Kelly Mason was the intended victim, they were looking for the man who was behind it all, the man who organized it and set it up. Then we heard no more about it till last week, when an article appeared which resurrected the whole thing and said the police were still looking for this *mastermind*. It is over two years in the past but they are still looking.

The article didn't name this man. It named Lloyd Freeman and Dermot Lynch and it said Lynch was a motor mechanic who serviced MPs' cars. Ivor Tesham doesn't just have a government car; he has one of his own, a big BMW. One of the photographs in the scrapbook shows him getting into this car outside his flat in Westminster. Suppose Dermot Lynch used to service this car? It's very likely. The conclusion I drew from working this out made me feel very excited. It could mean that the only person in the world who knew both Lloyd Freeman and Dermot Lynch was Ivor Tesham. He was the mastermind.

Of course I can't be sure of this, but isn't it the only possible answer? Ivor Tesham didn't intend to drive the BMW to pick up Hebe or send another driver in the BMW to pick her up, but paid Dermot and Lloyd to do it in a rented car, so that she could be *delivered* to him like a sexy parcel from a mail order company, dressed in absurd gear, flung down, I suppose, on his bed to await him. That's how it has to be. That's why he asked me that question: 'What are you going to do?' I can see the fear in his face now, I can smell it, but what he was afraid of I don't exactly know. A story in the papers? Can anyone be so conscious of his reputation that he's afraid of a few lines on a diary page making him look faintly ridiculous? Apparently, he can.

No one seems to know what has happened to Dermot Lynch. It's said that the police never give up on a case like that. None of it gets in the media because quiet persistent work behind the scenes, searching, sifting, considering, isn't the hot news the press likes. Sometimes when I look through the scrapbook at the picture of Ivor Tesham and Carmen at his friend's wedding or the picture of him grinning, one fist raised, when he retained his seat at the general election, I imagine myself walking into the nearest police station and telling them about that single meeting I had with him. And how he asked me what I was going to do.

One picture I shan't be putting in the scrapbook and that's the one I found in the back of Hebe's jewellery drawer.

We depend on the television in this household. I don't particularly care for it, I never have, but Justin loves it, as all children do, and Gerry watches it compulsively. I used to think he was an intelligent man but I've had to revise my opinion. He and Justin sit on the sofa – I sit in an armchair – and watch programme after programme with no discrimination whatsoever. Well, I shall correct that. If anything very horrible comes on, battles and corpses – they don't seem to mind showing dead bodies any more – he doesn't turn it off, he changes channels. There used to be a phrase current when I was a child: 'Glued to the glowing cathode.' I think that was quite clever, it was so apt. Gerry will change to anything Justin may want to watch, the most banal cartoons or pop music rubbish, but if I dare to ask for something *marginally* more intellectual, he always says Justin wouldn't like it or it wouldn't be suitable for Justin. I have actually said in reply that in that case I'll go and watch it on the set in the kitchen and, outrageous as it seems, he hasn't said a word to stop me. Usually it ends in my going upstairs to work on the scrapbook, writing captions to some of the pictures and putting names to the people with Tesham and Carmen in some classy venue.

So when the television broke down a couple of weeks ago I was rather pleased than otherwise. At least it would mean we might have a proper conversation in the evenings, Gerry talking to his son, which he was supposed to want to do when he started letting him stay up late. Or we could even listen to the radio. But things happened differently. The man who came to repair the set said he would have to take it away and it might be gone for at least a week. You would have thought the end of the world had come. The black and white set in the kitchen would have to be brought into the living room, Gerry said. Never mind that my daytime viewing would be at an end or my alternative viewing in the evening.

I don't know what made me say what I did. Or, rather, I do know, I know only too well. It's the way I am, the way I act. Bluntly, brutally, I want them to love me – well, to like me, for that's all I can expect. It hasn't been allowed to happen. How could it when Gerry is always telling Justin how wonderful his mother was, showing him her picture, telling him in a soppy outdated way that his mother is in heaven, loving him and watching over him? I'd hoped Gerry would – well, perhaps not love me, I gave up on that long ago, but at least grow fond of me, tell me again that I was indispensable. But there are no signs he feels any different towards me than he did when first I came. None at all. So to make them like me, fool that I am, I offered them my television set.

It was at home in my flat, of course, but put away in that same big cupboard where the case full of Hebe's stuff is. Pandora had bought a new one, something special, I don't know what, but the latest thing. I'd seen it on the only occasion I'd been back, when I went there to fetch a book I wanted to re-read. Anyway, I don't think I'd ever had such a response from Gerry to any offer I'd made. His smile, the warmth in his face, this was what I'd wanted to evoke from him all the time I'd known him, not just since I've been here. We were standing up at the time. We were in the living room, looking at the defunct set and waiting for the man to come. Gerry actually took my hands, he took both my hands in his, saying how grateful he'd be, what an act of kindness.

The next thing was that I'd have to go and fetch it. I said he'd have to help me carry it in from the back seat of the car but first I'd phone Pandora and let her know I'd be coming for it. She's hardly ever in on the rare occasions I phone her and I have to leave messages, but this time she was.

'Don't you worry,' she said in that distant whispery voice of hers. 'I'll bring it myself. I'm coming up your way. Irving Road, isn't it? I've got a friend in Herbert Road and I'm coming to see her. Michael will help me get it in the car.'

Michael was the man on the floor below, the one who had told me off for throwing away that Christmas food. I'd never spoken to him since and I didn't want him here. Come to that, I didn't much want her here either. In my experience when people call, even if it's only on an errand like this one, they always expect a drink or a cup of tea or even food. Grania and Lucy are like that. They 'look in', as they put it, on their way home from work or on a Saturday afternoon, and always they say, 'I'm parched' or 'I'm dying for a drink', and I'm the one who has to get it. Still, that Saturday it was pouring with rain and I was glad I didn't have to schlep (as Hebe would have said) all the way down to Kilburn and get wet in the process of carrying that heavy set to the car.

Just before Pandora was due, Wendy turned up. I don't know why those girls come. I don't know what they get out of it. They bring nothing, they do nothing and their conversation isn't worth listening to. Well, I do know why they come, of course I do. They're all after Gerry. He's young, he's quite good-looking, he's free and though he's mean with his money he earns quite a lot. Those girls think that one of them will get him. I don't think myself they've much of a chance. I had more chance than they had, but that's over now. Like the fool he is, he'll stay faithful to Hebe's memory for the next twenty years. They really ought to know that with all their cuddling up to Justin and bringing him presents, they are just wasting their time.

Wendy was wearing a dress like a school gym tunic, with her hair in pigtails, and she's a good ten years too old for that. 'I didn't have time for lunch,' she said. 'I'm starving.'

Gerry gave her a plateful of leftovers from our own lunch and asked me if I'd 'be kind enough' to make her a cup of tea. While she was drinking it, sitting at the kitchen table, Pandora arrived. I've mentioned before that she belonged to the same type as Hebe, tall, slim and with long blonde hair, but there, I'd thought, the resemblance ended. She had this peculiar husky voice, as if she'd got a throat infection, whereas Hebe's had been strong and clear. But when she walked into the hallway something strange happened. It was a dull day and no one had yet turned lights on. Justin came out of the kitchen, where he'd been drinking juice at the table with Wendy, came to fetch some toy he wanted to show her, and when he saw Pandora he stopped and he stared at her. His lips parted as he looked up at her and then disappointment seemed to spread across his face, a desolation that changed him, briefly, from a boy of four into a little old man. It was quite interesting to see. He turned and ran into the living room, where Gerry was, and I heard the sounds of his sobbing.

'What's wrong?' Pandora said. 'What did I do?'

'Nothing. I don't know.'

I wasn't going to tell her that, just for a moment, for an instant, the child had thought she was his mother come back. For that, I'm sure, was what it was. I switched the light on. I took Pandora into the living room and introduced her to Gerry. He was sitting with the still-weeping Justin in his arms, held tightly against him, so he couldn't get up and couldn't shake hands, but he said hello and thanked her for bringing the television. I'd half expected him to react in the same way as Justin had, but he showed no sign of seeing any resemblance. He couldn't leave Justin, so Pandora and I went out to fetch the set, joined after a moment or two by Wendy, who was more hindrance than help.

More tea had to be made once we'd got the television up and running, and Wendy found a cake in a tin I was saving for next day, when Gerry's mother was coming. But there was no use saying anything. She always behaves as if she has a right to the run of the place when she 'looks in'. Justin calmed down and began to behave with Pandora as he would with any ordinary stranger, a bit shyly, answering her warily when she spoke to him and once or twice running to his father to hide his face against Gerry's knees. Gerry and Pandora were getting on famously, their conversation being all about his terrible loss of Hebe. As far as I know, Pandora had never previously heard of her. Still, she made all the right sympathetic noises, which I could see annoyed Wendy.

After they'd both gone he asked me why I'd never said what a nice friend I'd got.

'She's not my friend,' I said. 'She's my tenant.'

He went on talking about her and how kind she was, as if the television she'd brought was hers, not mine. 'She reminded me just a little of Hebe,' he said.

'Really?' I said. 'I can't see it myself.'

By that time I had more or less given up hoping for any return from Justin of the love I had offered him. I am afraid he is naturally sullen, as Hebe was when she couldn't get her own way. But nothing had prepared me for the outburst of rage, a real sustained tantrum, he indulged himself in that evening. It wasn't just sobs this time but full-blown screaming as he flung himself about on his bed. What he needed was a good smack. That's what Mummy would have given him, but I knew what the result would be if I did. I could imagine the reproaches, the sulks, Gerry threatening me with the loss of my job, as if he could get anyone else to do what I did. So I shut Justin up in his bedroom, listened for a while outside the door to the sounds of hysteria and, to tell the truth, wondered how I had ever fancied I was getting fond of him.

Gerry was out. After all that nonsense about needing a television, about how it was the only thing to distract him from his memories, he had abandoned it the first day it arrived and gone off to make a speech at some charity do. It was quite pleasant to have the place to myself for a change. No television for me, of course. I was glad to do without it. I fetched the scrapbook down and quite enjoyed going through it, from the first picture of Tesham at Sandy Caxton's funeral to the most recent, Our Hero (as I call him to myself) presenting some award or medal to a flight lieutenant.

Justin must have fallen asleep, for there was no more noise from upstairs. I tried to imagine Tesham paying those men, *explaining* to them what he wanted, waiting for Hebe to come and cursing when she didn't. When he had been thwarted. None of this was at all hard for me to picture. I wondered too, if she had all that gear, did he have *sex toys*? I don't really know what sex toys are, I've heard the term, that's all. Dildoes, perhaps, and furry objects. Did they play with them? Thinking of him, his suave manner and his austere looks, I couldn't imagine it and I stopped then, because you can only get excited up to a point, after which you start to feel sick.

16

For all Ivor might say about suburban houses and double garages, he seemed to like visiting us, with or without Juliet. He was fond of our children, which rather surprised me, I don't know why, and he had found a young adorer in Nadine. His car, which he parked in the street in Westminster, kept taking knocks from passing drivers, once quite a serious dent in the offside, and he asked us if he could keep it in our second garage 'just until he moved', whatever that meant.

When he came up to fetch it for the drive out to his constituency, he would arrive early and those talks we had used to have about the situation he found himself in two and a half years before resumed. Up to a point, that is. Now what he said was more a reflection on the things that had happened, even a kind of wonder that he had been almost mad with anxiety, with terror of what the following morning would bring, unable to sleep and always on the verge of a panic which must at all costs be concealed.

'I used to feel,' he said, 'like that character in Shakespeare who says he'd like to read the book of fate, so that I could have some idea of what would happen next week, even next day.'

I said he wouldn't like it if he could. We only want access to the book of fate when we can read something favourable to us in it. What if it had told him Dermot Lynch would come round next Thursday in full possession of his faculties and memory? He laughed. He actually laughed.

'On the subject of Dermot Lynch,' Iris said, 'I take it you've kept to what you said and haven't been near that family?'

'I suppose I may as well tell you,' he said.

Nadine came into the room then and climbed on to Ivor's knee. Half an hour later he'd fetched the car and gone to pick up Juliet for their weekend in Morningford. It must have been about a fortnight later that I was in Maida Vale, visiting a client who lived in one of those big Italianate houses that front on to the canal in Blomfield Road. As well as being wheelchair-bound, my very wealthy client never answered letters and nor did his wife, so I had no choice but to go to him, taking with me a number of forms which needed signing for the Inland Revenue. It was almost Christmas, a day or two before Christmas Eve. Christmas trees were glittering with lights in the windows, holly wreaths hung on front doors and there were strings of lights along the canal. After I left my client I lingered a while, leaning over the railing to look along the shining stretch of water up to the lights in the café on the bridge.

I began to walk down towards the underground station, not to get into the tube – no one in his senses would try to travel by tube from Maida Vale to where we lived – but to hail one of the taxis which head up Warwick Avenue from Clifton Gardens. I was about halfway down, looking in vain for taxis coming that way and from the opposite direction, when I noticed the couple who had walked over the bridge and were waiting to cross Blomfield Road. It was dark but a clear evening and I couldn't have been mistaken. The two people, arm in arm, now halfway across, were Ivor and Juliet Case. I started to hail them, lifting my right arm, but the taxi driver, coming at last, took this for a summons to him and stopped for me. I got in; I wanted to get home. Whether or not Ivor had seen me I didn't then know.

'Where do you think they'd been?' Iris asked when I told her.

I said I didn't know. How would I know? Paddington Station?

'Why would Ivor go to Paddington Station or come from Paddington Station? On foot? He wouldn't. I'll tell you where they'd been. To William Cross Court.'

I'd forgotten the name. I'd forgotten who lived there. I had to ask her.

'The Lynchs, of course. Mrs Lynch and her sons live in William Cross Court. It's in Rowley Place and Rowley Place runs from St Mary's Gardens to Warwick Avenue. Don't look at me like that,

Rob, I do *know*. I looked the place up in the *A–Z* when I was phoning her for Ivor.'

'He wouldn't go there,' I said. 'He might have done once but not now. Why would he?'

'I'm going to ask him.'

And she did. Christmas happened first, of course. Both children were by then of an age to be in paroxysms of excitement anticipating the day. Wearing a white beard and dressed in Iris's hooded red dressing gown with cotton wool stitched on to it in appropriate places, I sat on the stairs for hours without number, my sack of stocking gifts beside me, waiting for them to go to sleep. I don't think Nadine ever did sleep that night. I unloaded my presents into her stocking at five in the morning while she gazed at me enraptured, having no notion then that I might be only her father in disguise. I could go on and on about that Christmas, joy and glory for Iris and me as much as for our children, but I won't. I'll proceed to Ivor, who came alone on Boxing Day, bearing gifts.

I may as well tell you, he had said a few weeks ago. Then Nadine's interruption had put it out of our heads. 'It's absolutely all right,' was how he began now, and varying it, 'Absolutely OK. Juliet's been visiting them since before Dermot came out of hospital. She and Philomena are friends.'

'*Philomena?* You mean you're on those sorts of terms?'

'I don't know what you mean by "those sorts of terms", Iris. It's usual these days for people to call each other by their Christian names or hadn't you noticed? Juliet suggested I go there with her one day and I did. They wanted to see me. It was all perfectly pleasant and friendly, and a great relief, I can tell you.'

He did tell us and it took quite a long time. At first, when Juliet suggested he go and visit Philomena Lynch and see Dermot, he was adamant. Absolutely not, he had said, it's out of the question. But they don't bear you any ill will, she said. He asked her how much they knew.

'Dermot told Sean about it when you first asked him,' she said.

'I don't think Philomena knows. They wouldn't have said anything to her for fear she'd have been shocked, as she would have been, Ivor. She's an old-fashioned, deeply religious woman. She's a staunch Catholic. But Sean knew from the start. He says he and Dermot had a laugh about it.'

All this had happened in the previous summer, when Ivor was still sufficiently alive to the danger he was in to shudder at those words. Sean had to know, Juliet went on, because Dermot wanted to borrow his gun. It was true that Sean bought the gun from a man in Warsaw who was trying to get American dollars or British sterling together to escape the country, but his motive in buying it wasn't as naïve and innocent as she had first told him. Sean had a criminal record, which was why the police had questioned him over Sandy Caxton's murder. At this point in Ivor's narrative Iris let out a cry of horror.

'I think you must be mad!'

Ivor shrugged. 'Wait till you hear the rest of it.'

'It can't get any worse, that's for sure.'

Juliet said to him that Dermot was living on some government allowance which is now called Invalidity Benefit but had a different name then. He would never work again. His mother went out cleaning. Sean was a builder's labourer but the work wasn't regular, it was sporadic, and often there was none at all. It was this which changed Ivor's mind for him. Or so he said. Well, he was an English gentleman and English gentlemen are good to the poor. They perform charitable acts to the lower orders and hand out eleemosynary alms.

'I suppose I ought to do something for them,' he said.

Juliet thought he ought. 'I hoped you would say that,' she said.

Next day, she phoned Mrs Lynch and the two of them went over to William Cross Court. Ivor must have noted the contrast between this visit and his last. Then he had skulked about on the stairs, hiding from observers; now he went as a prospective honoured guest. It was the end of July and the beginning of the parliamentary summer recess. William Cross Court, which he had in his mind labelled a dump, looked rather nice in the sunshine, flowers on some of the balconies and more in Westminster Council's neat flowerbeds. The lawns were bright green, with not a weed showing.

'I suppose you thought,' Iris said, 'that made it all respectable.'

'As a matter of fact that's exactly what I did think.'

It was at this point that I wondered what would have happened if I hadn't seen him and Juliet walking along Warwick Avenue that evening. If, for instance, I hadn't spent two minutes leaning on that railing and admiring the canal and the lights. Would he ever have told us? Would he have changed his mind about having something 'I may as well tell you', said nothing of this visit and subsequent visits to the Lynchs until disaster came – if disaster was to come? I think so. But I had lingered and I had seen him and now it was all coming out.

Sean Lynch opened the front door. Ivor said he couldn't believe his eyes when this man – this bricklayer or whatever he was, this one-time criminal, this suspect in his friend's murder – put his hand on Juliet's shoulder and kissed her on the cheek.

'It took a bit of getting used to, that,' he said, and then, oddly, 'Of course, things are different now. I somehow thought he'd call her "Miss Case". I thought they'd all be tremendously respectful.'

'When are you going to start living in the real world, Ivor?' Iris was furious. 'These people are probably planning just how they're going to blackmail you.'

'No,' he said in a vague, dreamy sort of way. 'No, they're not. It's not like that. Philomena was rather awestruck. I suppose you'd call that respectful. She kept saying she couldn't believe I was actually in her flat. An MP, she kept saying, a Minister of the Crown.'

'Oh, my God,' Iris said. 'I don't believe it. I'll wake up in a minute.'

'It was horrible,' he said, 'seeing Dermot. I remember him as a very lively, jolly sort of chap, the sort of man who'd be dumb if he lost the use of his hands. He was always gesticulating, holding his hands up, clapping, flicking his fingers. He never moves them now.

He can walk – shuffle, rather. His speech is like – well, you know what a Dalek sounds like. Or a zombie. Juliet told me afterwards that whole areas of his brain are gone, just lost.'

Mrs Lynch had given them tea that first time and a cake she said was 'Mr Kipling'. She talked a lot about Mr Kipling cakes and how good they were, though not a patch on something called Kunzle cakes, which were in vogue when she was a girl. Sean kept telling her to give it a rest, no one was interested, and what would Mr Tesham think of her. They were still calling him Mr Tesham then, though that changed on his next visit. Dermot had a towel tied round his neck to protect his clothes while he ate his cake. He got chocolate icing all over his face and Philomena had to fetch a wet flannel to clean him up. He appeared not to recognize Ivor, which was something of a relief. On the way there Ivor had worried about that, imagining him jumping up, the scales falling from his eyes, and presumably too his mind, as he denounced the author of all his sufferings. Eating his cake and drinking his cup of mahogany-coloured tea, Ivor saw – with very real pity and horror, I believe – that Dermot was beyond all that; Dermot was in a different world, a place of shadows and incomprehension and oblivion.

As for Sean, Ivor confessed that he had never before come across anyone like him. It was unusual for him to be frank about his own lack of experience in any aspect of life. There was no question from the start, he said, of taking him for other than what he was, for he exuded menace, he radiated ruthlessness, he would be a good person to have on one's side if one were in trouble.

'And you think he's on yours,' I said.

'Some of the things he said made me believe so.'

Iris made that sound that is usually written 'Huh'. 'What about the other things? The menace, for instance?'

'That wasn't directed at me. I'd arranged with Juliet that I wouldn't mention money that first time. All I said was that I'd like to do something for them and that I'd come back and we'd talk about it.'

He went back two days later but without Juliet this time. The arrangement he'd made was for six in the evening and he took a bottle of champagne with him. While Iris was asking him why and where did he get his crazy ideas from, I was thinking of the champagne he'd left in our fridge on the night of the birthday present. Ivor was a great one for champagne. Once I heard him refer to it as 'the drink that is never wrong' or TDTINW. I think he saw it as the panacea for all ills, the smoother-out of all difficulties, the breaker of all possible kinds of ice. And, of course, the bringer of desire and stimulus to the libido.

Again it was Sean who opened the door. 'Mr Tesham' was dropped and he greeted him as 'Ivor'. 'How are you doing, Ivor?' were his words. But instead of according the champagne as enthusiastic a welcome, he said in a repressive tone that he didn't drink. Never had, didn't like the taste. Anything alcoholic was out of the question for Dermot, but Ivor opened the champagne (elegantly, I expect, as he always did, without spilling a drop) and he and Philomena Lynch settled down to drink it. Out of pottery mugs. There were no glasses in the place, not even the water kind. No one ever drank water or, come to that, fruit juice, or anything but tea.

The room they sat in was crowded with shabby chairs, an ancient sagging sofa and a table big enough for somewhere twice the size. But you barely noticed that. What you noticed was the religious bric-à-brac, the crucifixes and icons – Ivor called them icons – the Sacred Heart of Jesus bleeding in Mary's hands, the face distorted with agony underneath the crown of thorns, the figurine of the Virgin holding the blessed child. There was a superfluity of them and they oppressed Ivor. He hadn't noticed them so much on his previous visit and he didn't on subsequent visits, but that particular time he needed the champagne to offset them, to escape their accusation. This may in part have been due also to the presence of Dermot shuffling about the room, his lustreless eyes wandering from statuette to crucifix, until they came to rest on a framed picture of a pallid-faced woman with a veil covering her hair. He stood in front of this picture, staring, his mouth working, possibly in prayer.

'Talking to St Rita,' Philomena said in an admiring tone. 'Dermot has a real devotion to St Rita.'

Sean cast up his eyes and, behind his mother's back, mimed the playing of a dirge on a violin. Ivor poured more champagne and got on with what he had come about. When he got home, or probably when he next went into the Commons library, he looked up St Rita and found she was the patron saint of lost causes. She had suffered all her life from a chronic illness and was known in Spain, where she came from, as *la abogada de imposibles,* the saint of desperate cases. It seemed appropriate.

If the true reason for the offer he was about to make was to ward off blackmail, Ivor had no intention of even hinting at that. And perhaps that wasn't the reason. It really was from friendship – and pity. He didn't mention that either. Instead he said Dermot had serviced his car over such a long period (actually it was three years and how many times do you have a car serviced in three years when you only use it at weekends?) and had been so thorough and efficient, so pleasant and so insistent on always returning the car himself, that he felt they had become friends. It must have cost him something to say that, in that place and in that company, with big rough Sean, red-faced like the drinker he wasn't, wearing a dirty white singlet and khaki shorts, his greasy yellow hair down on his shoulders, making faces behind his mother's back. But he did say it. He said he felt he had a duty to that friendship to make Dermot and his family's life easier. Therefore he hoped they'd accept an allowance of ten thousand a year.

17

There was no argument. Ivor had supposed there would be some polite demur, some disclaimer. 'Oh, we couldn't possibly take it,' or 'That's far too generous.' Something like that. The trouble was he didn't know his audience. He didn't know people like the Lynchs, people from their social stratum, their background, their financial condition. He might be an MP and a minister but he had no idea that men and women existed whose whole life, for some of them from early childhood and certainly to the grave, was a struggle for subsistence, a struggle to get money, to live with some dignity. Not a lot of money, not even enough money, but sufficient to possess some of the things he took absolutely for granted: warmth in winter, an occasional holiday, a television set; not a new car, not that, but an old banger or a motorbike. He ought to have known. He was involved in public life, he had canvassed for election, he had talked to teenage mothers with babies in their arms, to pensioners in slippers, to the unemployed on benefit. But he had done so on doorsteps for two minutes at a time.

So he was surprised and perhaps a little piqued (though he didn't say so) that the only rejoinder he got was a nod from Sean and a 'Right,' and from Philomena, 'That would be a help,' though she looked, not at him, but at one of her figurines, as if a plaster saint – truly, a saint made from plaster – was responsible for this largesse. He was disappointed. Like my daughter Nadine, bestowing the first Christmas present she had ever given, he expected extravagant gratitude, repeated thanks. She was three and a half and she got it, but all he got was an apparently indifferent acceptance.

He asked Philomena for her bank details. Oh, Ivor, Ivor, did you? Did you really do that? She didn't know what he meant. She had never had a bank account. Nor had Sean. However, she had a Post

Office savings account and it was into this that he arranged to pay the ten thousand each year on 1 September.

'Yet you go on seeing them,' Iris said. 'Is that necessary?'

'I don't want them to think I'm paying them off. It's a bit awkward, isn't it? Sean knows, you see. I've told you that. He knows I set the whole thing up. It wouldn't do to make him think I was paying him because he constituted a threat to me.'

'Well, aren't you?'

'Absolutely not, Iris. They think it's done out of friendship and they're right. As a matter of fact, Sean regards me as a friend now. His girlfriend was there when Juliet and I went round the night you saw us and Sean introduced me as his friend. "This is my friend Ivor," he said.'

'Right. You're his friend. You meet him for a drink, do you? You have him in the Commons for lunch? You and Juliet and *Sean* and his girlfriend have dinner together? I don't think so.' Iris was looking at him the way I've never seen her look at him before, with an exasperation which wasn't at all amused. 'I said I think you've gone mad and I do. This man's got a criminal record. Do you know what for? You say he's some sort of labourer, but does he ever work? Or is his work petty crime?' They were near to quarrelling and, though they sparred, they never quarrelled. She changed tack a little. 'Can you afford ten thousand a year?'

'Yes,' he said. 'I promised, so I have to.'

Whether he really could at that time I don't know. Ten thousand was a lot more in 1992 than it is now. But he certainly could afford it by the spring of 1993. His and Iris's father died. John Tesham and I had never seen eye to eye on a lot of things, but I liked him in spite of our differences and I specially liked his manner with our children, his sweetness to them and his patience. He had gone out for a walk with his dogs, no doubt along those lanes, or lanes like them, where I had so much enjoyed walking and carrying my daughter, on a fine day in late April when the trees were in new leaf. The dogs came back without him and led his wife and a neighbour to a spot in the churchyard where he lay dead among the cowslips.

Ivor made a stirring speech at his funeral, praising him for all sorts of things I never knew he had, devotion to the Church of England, a love of the poetry of Thomas Hardy and a tenderness towards animals, among others. That last surprised me, as I remembered the hecatombs of pheasants and partridges he shot every winter. Ivor called him 'one of the last of the English squires' and even referred to him as the lord of the manor. There was a reading of the will afterwards, something which I, though I'm an accountant, didn't know still happened. John Tesham left Ramburgh House to his wife in trust for her lifetime and a considerable income, fifty thousand to his daughter, Iris, and twice that in trust till they were twenty-one to each of his grandchildren. Everything else went to Ivor and it was such a large sum that even I, who am used to dealing with large sums (mostly other people's), was surprised.

Ten thousand a year would be peanuts to him in the future. He was too much of the English gentleman to give a sign that this fortune which had come to him – huge even after inheritance tax – was any consolation for his loss. We had all driven up to Norfolk together and he talked most of the way back about his father's virtues and his own sorrow. It was at least a month and the third anniversary of Hebe's death was past, before he mentioned, almost in passing, that 'now I can afford it' he meant to buy a house in London. The move he had earlier envisaged when he parked his car in our garage would be to another, larger flat, but now a house in Westminster was a possibility.

Juliet was still living in her flat, her half a house, in Park Road, Queen's Park. She spent her weekends at Ivor's in Old Pye Street, though as far as I know, he never spent his in Park Road. He would never have said so, but I think he would have considered it infra dig to have been seen to be staying in that part of London, he a Minister of the Crown (as Philomena Lynch repeatedly referred to him with pride), he an MP who was also becoming a television personality. He had been interviewed by David Frost and had held his own. Presenters of political panel programmes sought him out. His was a recognizable face and not, in his view, permitted to be recognized by the denizens of Kensal Green borders when nipping down to Salusbury Road to pick up a taxi.

Yet there was no sign of Juliet moving in with him. His flat was on the market and one of those professional house-hunters was – well, hunting for a house for him. Such people take 3 per cent of the purchase price and Ivor expected to enrich this man by forty thousand pounds.

'I haven't the time to mess about with estate agents and orders to view,' he said.

What did Juliet live on? She never worked. Today, with the cult of the celebrity at its height, some of the glamour that was beginning to attach to him would have rubbed off on her and she might have been one of those good-looking women who become famous for doing nothing. For just being and for being a well-known man's girlfriend. But society hadn't then reached that stage. Her going about with Ivor certainly wouldn't have helped her get parts in the theatre – if she was even trying to get parts. She dressed very well. Gone were the patchwork skirts and the ethnic bangles. She had grown her hair long and always, when we saw her, wore it up and done in such a smooth yet intricate way as to make me, and more significantly Iris, think she must be at the hairdresser's three times a week. Ivor, we decided, must be giving her some sort of allowance, and we were old-fashioned enough, though Iris was only two years her senior, to feel there was something distasteful about a man supporting a woman who was not his wife, was not even what was just beginning to be called his partner.

But we didn't know. We couldn't ask and wouldn't. It wasn't our business and we both liked Juliet, her apparent frank openness, her obvious affection for Ivor, her charm, so necessary to a woman with her name. But our puzzlement at her behaviour was still there: how could she have so readily taken up with Ivor when, however you looked at it, it was he who had caused her former boyfriend's death? Or to put it slightly more accurately, without Ivor's birthday present scenario, her ex-boyfriend – and how ex had he been? – would still be alive.

She knew all about it, every detail, from the request and offer to Lloyd and Dermot to the crash, through the kidnap, the police and press misapprehension, Dermot's terrible injuries and, possibly though not certainly, the questioning by the police of Sean Lynch over Sandy Caxton's death.

A strange and rather unwelcome thought came to me one night, in the small hours. I had got up to see to Adam, who was crying. A bad dream had wakened him. What kind of nightmare does a happy two-year-old have that wakes him screaming, calling in desperate fear for his mother and father? He couldn't tell me, so I sat with him, his hand in mine, until he went to sleep, and when I made my way back to our bedroom I thought suddenly, she knows but she tells no one, she never will. Does he pay her to keep silent?

In the morning I talked about it with Iris. 'There's a kind of blackmail,' I said, 'where no threat need ever be made, where you might say the *reverse* of a threat is made, so that she says to him, "You know I'll never say a word." But the knowledge is there. He knows that she knows even if she never mentions it again. So he puts her under an obligation to him by giving her – what? Twice what he's giving the Lynchs? She'll never say a word because she won't want to lose this generous allowance, though nothing has ever been said between them about why he gives it to her.'

'Even more to the point,' said Iris, 'nothing has ever been said about why she's happy to receive it. But can it be, Rob? He's in love with her, isn't he? She's in love with him. Can those two things exist side by side, love and – what? An unspoken threat?'

I said I didn't think they were mutually exclusive. Besides, we didn't really know, did we? Juliet might have some other source of income, something perhaps from her ex-husband, Aaron Hunter.

'I hope so,' Iris said. 'I don't like to think of my brother paying out two lots of blackmail, both to people who threaten him only in his head. What must be going on in his head if he sees these threats coming from more and more people? Because they could, they could.'

'Could they? Who, for instance?'

'Jane Atherton?'

Not just after it happened but a couple of years later, when he seemed to be on safe ground, Ivor had told us about his meeting with Jane Atherton, at her flat, when she asked him to choose a keepsake from Hebe's jewellery. He had been terrified, he said, for he had never forgotten the words he had used to her on the phone when he'd asked her what she was going to do. That was something he regretted almost daily. Leaving the Commons and taking a taxi up to her flat, he thought about her manner of inviting him, her words: we have things to talk about. That could mean only one thing, that she had decided what she was going to do. Climbing the stairs, he felt a tightness in his chest he thought might be the onset of a heart attack. His relief when she asked him to pick a memento was enormous, but it wasn't all-overpowering. He could still wonder if she was going to show him the pearls. She didn't and he couldn't ask.

He had never heard from her again but she still existed, no doubt. She still knew what she knew.

I mentioned Aaron Hunter. Having failed to win the seat he had contested in the general election, he had gone back to the stage, where there had apparently been widespread regret at his ever leaving it. All four of us, Iris and I, Ivor and Juliet, went to see him in *Lear*. Not playing the king, of course, he was still rather too young for that, but a critic-acclaimed Edgar. I'm too squeamish for *Lear*. The putting out of Gloucester's eyes is too much for me and with every production I see, the director, or whoever is responsible for these things, makes it more hideous, more gruesome. As the poor man's eyes are pulled out I have to shut mine and hang my head and Iris is similarly affected. The other two seemed to watch it unmoved – as far as I know, I couldn't see – but I sensed their coolness, their civilized acceptance. We went round afterwards to congratulate Aaron Hunter, he and Juliet being on perfectly good terms. (I had the impression Juliet would be on good terms with everyone from her past, and come to that her present, but I may have been wrong.) Ivor had met him before and, instead of the theatre, the two of them talked politics, on which they had to agree to differ, their views being diametrically opposed. We asked him to have a late supper with us but he refused. He was tired; he was performing again next day.

The restaurant we went to was in Westminster, very near Ivor's flat, halfway in fact between his flat, currently 'under offer', as the estate agents say, and his new house in Glanvill Street. Because the house-hunter had found somewhere for him, an elegant Georgian three-storey place with five steps up to the front door and lacework railings on the balconies. After supper we went round to look at it, lit up by the old-fashioned lamps in the square.

'And Juliet is coming to live there with me,' Ivor said, putting his arm lightly round her shoulders. 'I think she likes the idea of being the only woman I have ever lived with.'

An invitation came to Ivor's house-warming. Having a party to celebrate his move wasn't the kind of thing he did. It must be Juliet's idea, we decided, for Juliet was gaining a hold over him as no woman had done before. Recalling Iris's taunt when Ivor had called Sean Lynch a friend of his, I asked her what the betting was that this man wouldn't be at the party, and I thought she'd say that went without saying. Of course he wouldn't be there.

'We shall see,' she said, 'but I'm going to take you on. Ten pounds he's there.'

'You can't be serious.'

'I am, perfectly serious. Sean Lynch will be at that party and we'll be introduced to him.'

Ivor's house was very nice inside, but it was exactly what anyone who knows the Georgian houses of London which have undergone a makeover would have expected. The previous owners had converted the ground floor into a kind of open plan but segmented into a number of alcoves and areas divided by arches or a series of columns. It was furnished – by a design company or by Juliet? – with perfect correctness for its period. Little groups of chairs and low tables stood about, portraits hung on the walls and, in the main open areas, political cartoons of the Gillray era. The curtains at windows both at the front and at the back hung sheer to the floor, heavy satin drapes in a deep bronze. A spinet and a gilded jardinière each supported large flower arrangements.

We had been there perhaps five minutes, already noticing that there were far more guests than either of us had expected, when Ivor came up to us with a stocky man in a too tight suit in tow. Jack Munro and his wife, who had been on their way to us, turned abruptly in the opposite direction and headed instead for Erica Caxton. It seemed to me that Ivor greeted us with more effusiveness than usual. He introduced us to his companion, a stocky red-faced man.

'Iris, Robin, I want you to meet my friend Sean Lynch.'

If we had been at a table Iris would have kicked me under it. Her broad smile and readily extended hand were a metaphorical kick. I too shook hands, while Ivor made some of the most flagrant small talk I have ever heard. What did we think of his table lamps? They had been made for him by a marvellous woman in West Halkin Street. The eighteenth-century French clock we would recognize as coming from Ramburgh. Living here was very convenient, it being not only near the Circle Line at St James's Park but no more than ten minutes' walk from Pimlico tube station. I thought of Hebe, who might, had she lived, have had her home even nearer that station.

Having done his duty, Ivor passed on, first to encounter Nicola Ross in draped black and white satin and then Aaron Hunter in jeans and leather jacket. Reluctantly I turned my attention to this man I'd been sure wouldn't be there and didn't much want to know. There is a certain cast of face I think of as essentially Irish. It is full and rather fleshy but with fine features, the nose aquiline, the eyes dark and full of fire, the mouth thin-lipped but sensitive, turned up at its corners in the precursor of a smile. Sean Lynch was exactly like that, a broad powerful-looking man, not very tall, but instead of dark hair, his was a curious brownish-yellow and curly, long enough to reach his shoulders. He also looked a brute. I half expected him to talk with an Irish lilt, but when he spoke it was with the accent of Paddington Green.

I had barely heard what he'd been saying to Iris and she to him as he stood there cockily with a glass of orange juice in his hand. I remembered then that Ivor had told us he didn't drink. He had refused Ivor's champagne when they talked about the money he and his mother were offered. I didn't know what to say to him. The only thing I came up with, which I hope wasn't loaded or sly or probing, was, 'How long have you known my brother-in-law?'

I need not have worried. He took over the conversation. 'Not long,' he said. 'Not long at all.' And there I heard the note of Irishism, something he must have picked up from a parent. If I couldn't think of much to say to him he wasn't similarly inhibited with me and soon he was in full flow. 'Long enough to know him for a true gentleman. What a wonderful man he is. It's not often you find a man of his class who's got no side, not a scrap of side in his make-up. And generous too, the soul of generosity. I'll tell you something, I reckon I'm the only *working* man here, but does he let that make any difference? No, he does not. He does not. He's introduced me to some of the most famous people in the land since I've been here. In the land . . .'

And so he went on. We had his disabled brother, his saintly mother on her hands and knees to earn a bare subsistence, his own inability to find work due to various injustices in his past – he didn't elaborate on this – his girlfriend's adoration and awe of the great man, so intense as to make him, Sean, quite jealous. Here he laughed throatily, shaking his head so that his curls bounced from side to side. He'd do anything for Ivor, he said, anything. Anything. Say the word and he was on. He looked like a hit-man and the implications of what he said didn't bear thinking about.

We were rescued at last by Juliet, who had come to take him away and drag him round the half-rooms and between the pillars to meet various minor celebrities of right-wing persuasion. It was

Iris, not I, who said she looked stunningly beautiful in a simple white dress, her hair piled up but with tendrils escaping the golden combs, like one of those Jane Austen heroines on film, an Emma or a Marianne Dashwood.

We had no intention of staying long. Iris was expecting our third child and, though very well, got tired easily, but such parties are not always straightforward to escape from. We were on the point of leaving, Iris whispering to me that she wanted her tenner now, on the nail, when Ivor was back at our side, introducing a QC who lived next door. His name was Martin Trenant, John Major would give him a peerage in his resignation honours, and I mention him because he played a small but significant part in what was to come. It wouldn't be an exaggeration to say that he saved Ivor's life. Just by being there, by being at home and having a key.

I knew none of that at the time, of course. We talked – about what? The neighbourhood, I suppose, and Trenant's wife being away in Marrakesh and the sudden cold snap. Then Nicola Ross came up to us, warm and effusive as ever, her arms spread to hug us, her talk punctuated with 'darlings'. Martin Trenant melted away and Nicola began talking about Juliet, that she was lovely enough for the most discerning but still she, Nicola, would never have imagined her and Ivor as an item, never in a thousand years.

In the taxi home Iris and I talked about Sean Lynch, his obvious admiration and fondness for Ivor. It was hero-worship, but Iris was sure it was sincere. The way he'd talked, she said, and the way he looked, made her see him as Ivor's bodyguard, though why he should need a bodyguard she couldn't tell.

We weren't so far wrong except in one respect. Ivor wasn't afraid of these people. He had no fear of Juliet and none of Sean. He seemed to have cast out fear once he'd made that offer to the Lynchs and I saw him as becoming more and more like the Ivor of his first years in Parliament, the Ivor who had picked up Hebe Furnal in two short sentences and several appreciative glances, and had leapt up flights of stairs, summoned by the division bell.

Well, we were wrong in another way too. If we hadn't understood the Lynchs' motives, we hadn't understood Juliet at all. Perhaps we weren't naïve but cynical.

At Ramburgh my mother-in-law remained in the house and Ivor seemed happy with this arrangement. He took Juliet down there every time he visited his constituency and his visits to his constituency were frequent. Remembering our own creepings about passages in the dark during our engagement, Iris asked him what 'Ma' thought of their sharing a room while they stayed there.

'I know you're only trying to wind me up,' he said in rather a lofty way, 'but don't be quite so silly. I'm thirty-six years old.'

This wasn't an answer but she didn't pursue it. Ivor, we knew, though he had never been explicit on the subject, was looking towards a secretaryship of state and with it a seat in the Cabinet. There was talk of it. One 'quality' daily had gone so far as to suggest him as a suitable Home Secretary, young for the post but not perhaps too young. There appeared to be only one serious unlikelihood of this ever happening: the Conservatives had been in power for nearly fifteen years, a long time for any administration, and the electorate were beginning to think they might prefer the Labour Party. The *Sun* newspaper helped by taking every opportunity to slam the Tories, quite open about wanting to get rid of them. A general election, in the normal course of things, would still be more than three years off, but it could come soon if dissatisfaction with the Tories continued to grow. Ivor must have felt acutely the passing of time while his status remained unchanged. There was a lot of talk in the papers about women's biological clocks running down as, successful in their careers but unmarried and childless, they moved nearer the menopause. Ivor's was his political clock and it was ticking away towards his party's climacteric.

In those days of sleaze, with one Tory after another finding himself in trouble, his name sullied by sexual misbehaviour, perjury or other offences, Ivor retained his pure image. He was clean and manifestly seen to be clean. The only cloud on his horizon, and it was a very small wisp of a cloud, no bigger than a man's hand, was that he was living with a woman he wasn't married to. Of course times had changed. Very few people saw anything wrong in cohabitation. Ivor wasn't divorced, he had never been married, he had jilted no one, left no woman to bring up his child as a single mother. But he lived with a woman he wasn't married to. She was, apparently, a nice, good and undeniably beautiful woman. It was true she had been divorced and all the newspapers knew who she'd been married to. But this was rather liked; it had a touch of glamour about it. There had even been a photograph in one paper of Juliet chatting to Aaron Hunter with Ivor standing beside her. No newspaper had ever revealed her association with Lloyd Freeman, but why should it be revealed? Lloyd's acting career had hardly been distinguished. No one had ever heard of him and certainly no one but Nicola Ross had ever connected him with Ivor.

Their relationship was all perfectly proper by 1990s standards, but there were mutterings. Some ancient Tories in the Lords turned up their old noses and clicked their old tongues. In Morningford the old soldier who was Ivor's agent told him it would be a good idea for him to get married.

'Before the election, you know, my boy. It would look well.'

My mother-in-law passed this on to Iris. I don't know how she got hold of it, but she knew James Maynard, the ex-colonel, very well, so perhaps he told her himself. Louisa Tesham was keen for Ivor to marry and if it had to be Juliet, it had to be. Much as she liked Juliet, she would have preferred the Sloaney daughter of one of her Norfolk neighbours, someone whose grandparents Ivor's grandparents had known, but, she said, it wasn't up to her.

'It sounds like heresy,' she said, 'but sometimes I think there is a great deal to be said for these arranged marriages that go on in some parts of the world. After all, we *are* wiser than your generation, you know, just as you'll be wiser than Nadine's.'

Ivor was beginning to see that remaining unmarried wasn't the wisest course he could take. He was well endowed with imagination and he could picture Juliet in Tory's wife wild silk dress and coat, her lovely face half shaded by a wide-brimmed hat, standing at his side while he presented awards or sitting two places from him on the top table at some Chamber of Commerce dinner. But he was no longer quite young. He knew quite a lot about life and he knew himself. Could he be content with one woman for the next, say, forty years?

If he married and a long career at the top of the political tree lay ahead of him, he would have to remain with that woman and be faithful to her. Or be secretly unfaithful to her in a way which would take a lot of energy and planning. 'Deceit' was not a word he mentioned. The Pimlico flat would become a reality or else too dangerous to consider.

'Whenever I think about it,' he said, 'I tell myself, you'll only fuck one woman for the rest of your life, and when I say that, Rob, I get cold feet. I get the shivers. I mean, Iris is my sister and I adore her, as you know, but I don't know how you manage.'

I smiled and then gave my noiseless laugh, but said nothing.

18

He has put away all her photographs except one. This is the one where she's windblown and laughing with Justin on the beach, which the newspapers used. The rest have disappeared. Once he'd gone to work I found them in Hebe's dressing table, in the drawer below the one where she'd kept the picture of Ivor Tesham and where I put her engagement ring, the gold bangle, the locket and, of course, the pearls. They are all still in their frames.

It's a sign that he is getting over her. At last. He's taken his time about it. Alone with me in this room in the evenings, he no longer talks about her. To my relief, I don't think I shall ever hear that misplaced praise again. He has begun going out in the evenings, and not exclusively to fund-raising functions, for he has left the job he took soon after Hebe's death, or 'moved on', as he puts it, and is now the chief executive, no less, of a charity dedicated to improving the lot of people suffering from something called Marfan syndrome. He's getting a lot more money, I'm sure, and why he doesn't move us all out of this dump to somewhere a bit more 'leafy' and up-market I don't know.

He goes out alone, he says, maybe to the cinema, maybe to eat, but I think he takes one of the girls, Grania or Winsome Wendy. Lucy (surprise, surprise) has got married. Who would marry her I can't imagine, but you only have to look at some of the married women going shopping round here not to ask that question ever again. Once I would have been jealous of Gerry going out with women, but now I don't care at all. I was set on falling in love with him when I first came here but he killed my love, there's no doubt about that. He killed it with his coldness, his obsession with Hebe and the way he took me for granted. Now he has started saying he will never marry again – well, he has said it once or twice – and I am glad of that, because although this job isn't what I had in mind when I first went to university, it's *a* job and with what he pays me and the quite high rent I get from Pandora, I don't do badly. I'm saving up for a new car. I don't want second-hand this time.

I rather like all these evenings on my own. I can relax, which I can't do nearly as well when he is there commenting on TV programmes and changing channels without asking me. Last night I saw Ivor Tesham in a programme called *The Question of the Hour* along with Nicola Ross (whom I once saw crying real tears on the stage), a Labour MP, Lib Dem peer and a film director. He was quite good, full of confidence, not a bit put out by the Labour man attacking him over schools and the poll tax and unemployment. Justin came down in the middle of it, which is something I don't encourage. He wanted his father. I don't know why, but he has just started school and is being difficult.

'Daddy goes out quite a lot in the evenings now,' I said. 'He can't stay in with you all the time. You'll have to get used to it.'

I admit this wasn't doing Gerry any favours, but I resent the fact that after all I have done for him and after all Gerry *hasn't* done, Justin is still obsessed with his father and doesn't treat me as his new mother, as I hoped would happen. I don't know why not and going to this primary school hasn't improved matters. He cries when he gets there and cries when he sees me waiting for him at the school gates, but I can't tell him that's not logical behaviour, because he doesn't understand. He doesn't even *try* to understand.

I took him back to bed, telling him it was no good sitting up for Gerry as he wouldn't be home for hours. He wasn't. In fact, I had gone to bed, though I was still awake, lying there in the dark. When I checked the time I saw it was after two. Where can you go in West Hendon till two o'clock in the morning? It beats me. When I used to tell him I was out with Callum I could never think of a place we might have been.

Ivor Tesham has moved house. There was nothing about this in the papers – of course there wasn't, it's hardly news – but I saw about it in one of those colour supplements, the property section.

It's a beautiful house, somewhere in Westminster, the kind of place only the very rich can afford, and it makes me wonder where he gets his money from. His father died a few months ago, I saw the death notice, and a bit about him leaving a son and a daughter, Ivor and Iris, so I expect Ivor got the lion's share of the money. In the magazine photograph he's standing in front of the house on the steps leading up to the front door and Carmen is with him in a black suit that's a wee bit too tight for her and on her feet she's got what Hebe once told me were called 'fuck me' shoes. That's the sort of thing he'd like. It's all of a piece with the mask and the dog collar and the sex toys.

The picture I cut out and gummed into the scrapbook. I wonder why I keep it and why I keep on adding to it. I suppose I think it will come in useful one day. Mummy once said to me that keeping a scrapbook is a sign of mental disturbance in an adult.

All the time I've been in Irving Road I haven't had a holiday. I could have – I will say for Gerry that he's not a slave driver – but I didn't know where to go, let alone who to go *with*. When I worked at the library I had a few people who could just about be called friends and one of them would probably have come with me, but once I left they drifted away. The truth is that none of them bothered to keep up with me. No doubt they have found more amusing company. Well, if it isn't a holiday, the time has come when I have had to take two weeks off. Mummy is ill – well, not really ill. She's had a hysterectomy and she had to have someone with her when she came out of hospital. Gerry didn't make a murmur. He said that now Justin was at school the two of them would be fine. One of the girls, Grania or Wendy, would be happy to come in. He is such an ungracious man, he seemed glad to see the back of me.

I got to my mother's house a day ahead of her discharge and I must say I quite enjoyed my day and night alone there. It was quite different without her, quiet and restful. While she was always bustling about and handing out gratuitous advice, I had never much liked the place, but appreciating my solitude in the kind of attractive surroundings I am not used to, I started thinking how happy I could be there if she never came home. If it was mine, if I had inherited it. But of course she did come home. I fetched her next morning.

She made the most appalling fuss about herself. A very nice and highly efficient nurse had assured me she wouldn't be in any pain, just very tired. I mustn't let her lift anything heavy. Well, there was no problem with that. Mummy didn't try to lift anything, barely even a teacup. She sat down all day with her feet up and complained that she had backache and a headache and said she felt as if all her insides had been scooped out, her words, not mine. All my pleasure in being in that house was destroyed and I actually began to look forward to the return to Irving Road.

I had left Gerry her phone number but he didn't call, not once. I was determined not to bicker with Mummy and I kept to that, just smiling and saying nothing when she began saying provocative things, but after I'd been there ten days, exercising an iron control, I could stand it no longer, I shouted back and we had a terrible row.

It started with her asking about my job and she prefaced that by saying she hadn't mentioned it before, she thought it would be more tactful to wait a few days, but she couldn't restrain herself any longer. She was worried about me. If I really wanted to be a nanny, wouldn't it be best to do a proper training course? There was something called a Norland nanny. Did that mean you went to a place called Norland? If they charged she would pay. I was furious. Wasn't I old enough to make my own decisions in life? If she wanted to spend money on me she could give me a lump sum out of what my father had left.

'After three years at a good university,' she said, 'you shouldn't be in a position to have to ask for money from an elderly woman who has barely enough to live on.'

I can't stand that kind of irrational argument. She had barely enough to live on but she had got eighty thousand pounds for that flat in Spain and said she could afford to pay nanny-training fees for me. I reminded her that I had given up my holiday to come and look after her. She said she hadn't asked me, only told me about her hysterectomy; her friend next door would have been happy to come in twice a day. This developed into a slanging match, she was totally unreasonable, and it ended with my saying I was leaving. I had been there ten days anyway. Doing my best to behave in a civilized manner, I went next door and told the neighbour (an enormously fat woman with a perpetual grin) that I was going next day and would she be kind enough to look in and attend to Mummy's wants.

No one was there to answer the phone when I called Gerry. I left a message to say I would be back next morning. At four in the afternoon the house was empty. One of the girls or Gerry's mother would have fetched Justin from school. Or so I thought. It was half past seven when they came home, long past Justin's bedtime, or what his bedtime would be if I had any say in the matter. I had shopped on the way home, which was just as well, as there was almost no food in the place, so I was able to manage a meal for both of them.

Before they came I had been all over the house, fearing I would find a mess, Gerry being hopeless at housework and even at basic tidying up. But everywhere was quite neat and clean. Bathrooms are always a giveaway but our sink had been wiped over after the last person washed his hands in it and the bath had been rinsed. The towels didn't look too dirty, the way they were when I first came and Grania (or Lucy or Wendy) had been in charge. I went into Gerry's bedroom and was very surprised to see the bed had been made. Men seldom make beds. They don't see the point, unless some woman is there to nag them into it.

I opened the drawer where Hebe's remaining jewellery was. I was almost sure that when I last looked in there – I often did so to check on the pearls – the locket, engagement ring and bangle had been in their silver-coloured cardboard box on top and the old perfume box with the pearls in it underneath. 'Almost.' I couldn't be absolutely sure and what if it was? Gerry had been giving that stuff the once-over. It was his, he had that right. Maybe he'd sat up here in the evenings, mooning over the woman who had worn it.

His clothes seemed more tidily arranged than they used to be. But that was nearly three years ago and he might have pulled himself together. My room was just as I had left it, neat and tidy, of course, though covered in dust. Well, I don't expect miracles and for Gerry to have dusted the place would have been a miracle. Justin's was the last room I went into. I was beginning to doubt that sensation I had had on coming into the house that someone else, and not one of the girls, had been in there in my absence. I had to rethink that once again. Justin's room was as neat as when I left it. I always made him tidy up everything before he went to bed, but he made a tremendous fuss about it and time after time Gerry countermanded my orders and told him he could leave it. Neither of them had done this, I was sure of it. And Justin had a new toy. It was a model of a farm with cows and sheep and pigs, a couple of carthorses, about a hundred chickens, a duck pond and a haystack. A farm, I may add, the like of which no one had seen for half a century. The farmer with his pitchfork and his wife with her milking pail looked like an Amish couple. Still, I suppose he liked it. Someone, probably his grandmother or one of the girls, must have given it to him – no, someone who didn't know him very well if they thought they were consoling him for my absence.

Though the relative positions of the silver box and the pearls box made me speculate a bit, I wasn't much troubled. I had wished for a minute or two that I had laid a hair on top of the pearls box as then I'd have been able to be sure it had been moved. But I hadn't and it hardly seemed to matter. I made pasta for our supper, with salad and some good wholegrain bread. Justin turned his nose up at this last, as he always does, and said he liked white sliced bread like they had had somewhere or other. I thought they must have been eating out quite a lot and that was all I did think then.

Gerry was very nice to me, nicer than he'd been for months, years probably. He asked about Mummy and said I must take time off whenever I liked to go and see her. Stay over a couple of nights if necessary. I said it was only in Ongar, no more than twenty-five miles away. I can't say either of them seemed to have missed me. We settled down to our usual evening television viewing, though I insisted on Justin going to bed first as it was already nearly half past eight. Gerry's niceness went on and on. He actually asked me if I had a preference as to which programme we watched.

I dusted my room before going to bed and shook the duster out of the window like Mummy used to do when I was little.

This next bit I am writing two days later. I am doing it because I don't know what else to do, because I am still in a state of shock. It's Saturday and Gerry took Justin out to buy him a pair of shoes. Their feet grow so fast at his age that they go through three pairs a year. They would have their tea out somewhere, he said, and wouldn't be back till late.

'Not after seven, I hope,' I said. 'He was late last night and he shouldn't get into bad habits.'

It wasn't a nice day. Intermittent rain had been falling since midday. I decided not to go out, though really I should have gone to the library as I'd nothing to read. Instead I looked through Gerry's meagre collection of books, two shelves of them, that's all. Hebe, of course, read at most a couple of trashy novels a year and Gerry devotes all his time to the television, an absurd amount of time for an educated man. However, I found Charlotte Brontë's *Villette* – an O-level set book for one of them, I imagine – which I soon discovered was a depressing book if ever there was one. I am under no illusions about my condition and position in this world and I couldn't help seeing the parallels in *Villette* and my own case. The heroine might have been modelled on me if I had been alive at the time. Lucy Snowe, *c'est moi*. But Brontë makes the woman's neglect and loneliness a bit strong even for me, so I gave up and tidied the kitchen cupboards instead.

They came in at twenty to eight and they weren't alone. Pandora was with them and Justin was holding her hand. That was the first time I had seen her since she brought my TV set but I didn't guess,

I suspected nothing, though there was no sign of the new shoes. She took off her jacket, looked in the mirror in the hallway, smiled radiantly at me. I thought they had met her by chance somewhere and she had come back with them to talk about the flat, about something being wrong with the flat. Better talk about it face to face than on the phone. I nearly asked her.

'I'll have to get Justin straight to bed,' I said.

'Not for a moment, Jane,' Gerry said. In an unexpected departure from the norm he had poured glasses of wine, which he was handing to us.

I sat down. 'Apart from our parents, Jane, we want you to be the first to congratulate us. Pandora and I are engaged. We're going to get married in November.'

19

After Gerry made that announcement I struck out with my right hand – I don't know why, perhaps to push him away – and I knocked over the glass of wine. The glass broke and the wine went everywhere. I shut my eyes, turned away and ran to the stairs, ran up the stairs. In my room I threw myself down on the bed, hearing his words like a hammer beating against the inside of my head.

'Pandora and I are engaged. We're getting married in November.'

How long had it been going on? Since she brought my TV set here, it must have been, since she walked in here and *insinuated* herself by being nice to Justin. The way to a father's heart. And it was my own fault. I felt that from the start as I lay on my bed. It was my own fault and typical of my luck. In trying to be kind, to be thoughtful, I had offered Gerry Furnal my TV to replace his broken set. I might as well have told him I had found him a wife and I might as well have invited her to seduce him.

She came upstairs after me. I had known she would – but no, I hadn't *known* it, I had still expected more consideration, more tact. We go on hoping to find the best in people, however jaundiced we are. She came up and knocked at the door. I said, 'Go away,' but she didn't. She came in, her face all false concern and fake sympathy.

'I'm sorry you're so upset, Jane,' she said. 'There's no need. We want you to stay. We shall need you if I go on working, as I mean to.'

I said to her to get out.

'Gerry shouldn't have told you like that,' she said. 'It must have been a shock. But you'll see how little difference it will make. I know there's not much room in this house but we shall buy a bigger house and we'll see if we can give you your own living room. Jane, we can be *friends*.'

That was when I struck out at her. I jumped up and hit her with my fists. She tried to seize hold of my wrists but gave up with a cry when I clawed at her face with my nails. *He* came up then, because she was screaming, and he took hold of me and said he would get the police. Of course he didn't, he wouldn't want the neighbours seeing something like that. I struck him hard across the face and then I stopped. I don't know why but the fight went out of me and I lay on my bed, sobbing. Even then they didn't leave me. There was barely room for them in the room, but they stayed, she sitting on the end of my bed and he in the one chair, and they talked all forgivingly and sweetly about how they knew I hadn't meant to attack them. I was ill, they knew I was.

'You need counselling, Jane,' she said, 'and we're going to see you get it. We owe you that.' Isn't it amazing the way a man and woman only have to know each other for five minutes before they're talking about 'we'?

'There was never any intention on my part,' Gerry said in his pompous way, 'of asking you to *leave*.' He put his hand up to his cheek, where I had hit him. It was bright red. 'We'll forget all this,' he said. 'It'll be as if it had never happened. Now do stop crying.'

'I'll go down and make you a cup of tea,' she said.

I said that if she did I would throw it at her. That sent them away, but the house was so small and the walls so thin I could hear them conferring in the room next door. I could hear him saying to leave me alone, I would be better in the morning, and her saying she would stay with him, she wouldn't leave him alone to 'cope with it all'. I knew then that it was she who had been in the house in my absence in Ongar, she who had given Justin the farm and had moved the jewellery boxes. I shouted something but they didn't hear me or pretended they didn't. She must have looked at the pearls and planned on wearing them when she is installed here.

The strange thing was that I slept after that. Those two had worn me out. I lay there, thinking I would have to get up and go to the bathroom, I would have to do it without them seeing me go across the landing, but the next thing I knew was it was deep darkness, the street lamp that always lit this miserable cell of mine had gone out, and when I looked at my digital clock I saw it was four in the morning. Fully clothed still, I crept out to the bathroom. He had left his bedroom door open. My eyes getting used to the dark, I could see the two of them in his bed, Hebe's bed, his head on one of the pillows, hers on his shoulder. I didn't expect to sleep but I did and didn't wake again until eight.

'I don't think you need counselling,' he said to me next day when I told him I'd rather die than stay there. 'You need a psychiatrist.'

I quote that to show the kind of insults they levelled at me. She told me in her patronizing way that she knew our agreement said she would have to carry on paying me rent for my flat. That was all right, she'd be happy to do that. I could see the scratches on her face I had made with my nails. I wonder how she explained them to other people. If you want to get another nanny's job, he said, I'll give you a good reference. After telling me I needed psychiatric help? I laughed at him. He went on as if I hadn't laughed and said they would forget all about last night. 'Why not stay till our wedding?' he said.

I didn't reply to any of this. The previous evening I had tried answering, I had seen where that got me, and now I could see the only thing was to be silent. Send the two of them to Coventry. I looked at them in what I hope was dignified silence and shook my head ever so slightly. I couldn't quite bring myself to treat Justin the same way. He was an innocent child – well, he was a child. But he needed some explanation of the noise and fuss those two had made the previous night.

'I shan't be seeing you any more, Justin,' I said. 'Daddy and Pandora have been very unkind to me so I have to go. Do you understand?'

He stared at me in that disconcerting way he has. 'I don't know,' he said.

That day she fetched all her stuff from my flat and I put mine into my car. We didn't speak. In silence she put the envelope with a cheque for my rent in it into my hand. He had gone to work without giving me the promised reference. There was no way I would dream of working as anyone else's nanny ever again but he wasn't to know that. He forgot; he didn't bother. She had unpacked her car and I had packed mine and I was putting the front door key he'd given me two and a half years before on the hall table, when she broke her silence.

'Jane,' she said, 'you need help, you really do.'

Could anything be more insulting? I didn't answer her. I got into my car and drove away, back to Kilburn. As soon as I was inside I went all round the place, looking for damage she might have done to it. And sure enough (as Mummy says) there was a burn mark from a hot dish on the draining board, a chip out of one of the bathroom tiles and one of the window blinds was badly torn. I didn't hesitate. I took my writing materials out of the drawer below the one where I had kept the pearls and wrote Pandora a formal letter, citing the damage and telling her that, in view of it, I wouldn't be returning the deposit she had paid me.

I was in the middle of doing this when Stu, the window cleaner, let himself in. No warning, of course. He didn't even ring the bell. He told me I had turned up like a bad penny and that the woman who had just left was a 'smashing-looking bird'. The first thing I had meant to do when I had finished the letter was check that Hebe's things in the case at the bottom of the cupboard were all right, but I had to postpone that for an hour until Stu had gone. I unlocked the case, lifted out the blue woolly dressing gown and found everything underneath just as I had packed it. I will say for Pandora that the flat was quite clean and tidy too. Apparently, if she is nothing else, she is quite houseproud.

Help I don't need but I do sometimes wonder what I have done to deserve all this. Things were really going quite well for me (as well as they ever get, that is). I was getting on all right with Gerry and Justin, I was saving money, I was planning on replacing my car. Then came this bombshell to shatter everything. I just wish I knew *why*. I had some money in the bank, more than two thousand pounds, plus I had got her cheque and no deposit to return, but no more than that. Three-quarters of the rent she had paid me had gone on my mortgage. When I'd used up what money I'd got, how was I going to pay the building society?

I would have to get a job, of course I would, and soon. Not a nanny's job – I meant what I had said, never never again. That meant another library, didn't it? The one I'd worked in, the Library of British History, had closed, had disappeared altogether. You can look down lists of appointments every day for weeks before you will see one for a librarian. I had to tell Mummy and she was full of helpful suggestions. Shops and cafés in Ongar High Street were always advertising for staff, she said, having forgotten the comments she'd made on the kind of job someone with a degree merited. When I told her I hadn't yet descended to working in a shop, she suggested doing a teacher training course. If I couldn't get a grant she would pay.

'I hate children,' I said, and that was the end of that.

I went to the Job Centre. It was the most humiliating thing I had ever done but I went there. They weren't very interested when I told them I had left my last job of my own accord. But they put me on their list, telling me I was over-qualified for most of the work I was likely to get. I went home and got down to answering advertisements for PAs and secretaries. Twenty letters I wrote that first week and thirty the next. Out of all that lot I got an interview for one job. It was receptionist/secretary to three solicitors working in partnership. I didn't like the look of the place, a converted shop next door to one selling old clothes. The interview was for twelve noon. They kept me waiting ten minutes and when I said I hadn't any computer skills the woman who was interviewing me looked down her nose. There was nothing about computing skills in your ad, I said, and she said it was taken for granted, it shouldn't need to be stated.

I had been back in my flat for six weeks and I'd applied for getting on for a hundred jobs when, looking through what the classifieds in the *Standard* had to offer, I came upon, under Marriages, the announcement of Gerry Furnal's to Pandora Anne Flint. I'd heard the phrase 'reopening old wounds' but I had never really felt it applied to myself till then. I felt those wounds opening on my arms and legs and Gerry Furnal rubbing salt into them. Had he ever thought for one moment what he was doing to me, forcing me to leave, driving me to give up my job? I had sacrificed everything for him, abandoned an *intellectual* post in a distinguished library, looked after his child, cooked his meals and done his housework, not to mention removing the disgusting perverted clothes his precious wife had worn to titillate her lover. And had I breathed a word to him about the stuff I had found? Had I told him what she was really like? No, I had not. Had I mentioned her lover or even hinted she had one? Again, no, no, I had not. Rather, I had listened to him going on and on about how wonderful she was, how good, what a marvellous mother, and handed out so much sympathy that it made me sick to think of it.

What a hypocrite he is. The moaning about Hebe I had to listen to went on evening after evening for *months*, how he could never think of another woman, but three years later – a mere three years later – he had taken up with my tenant. How shallow must he be to have fallen for a woman who looks superficially, for that's all it is, like his late wife? I wondered what Hebe would think of him if she knew. Maybe she does know. There may be an afterlife – who am I to say? Gerry used to tell Justin she was in heaven, watching over him from up in the sky. Perhaps she is watching us all – Gerry Furnal, poor little Justin, me and even her lover, Ivor Tesham – and drawing her own conclusions.

Life is unfair. That's the first thing I ever remember Mummy saying to me. I must have been about four. 'Life is unfair, Jane,' she said. 'You have to get used to that.' I think of it now when I contrast the lives of Ivor Tesham and me. I don't suppose for a moment he knows what it is to apply for job after job and get either one of two possible results: no reply at all or a reply saying the position has been filled. Of course he hasn't. Rich, powerful relatives got him jobs. Influential people gave him a helping hand into Parliament.

Private incomes came along so that when bribery and corruption were the only possible ways for him to get advancement, he had the means to bribe and to corrupt. I always read the Births, Marriages and Deaths in the paper. That's how I knew about Gerry Furnal's marriage. That's how I knew Ivor Tesham's father had died: *John Hamilton Tesham, suddenly at home, beloved husband of Louisa and dear father of Ivor and Iris* . . . I suppose he left his son a fortune. No one has ever left me anything. My mother's house in Ongar must be worth half a million. What's the betting, when she dies, someone will get planning permission to build an estate on her doorstep and halve the selling price?

I am sitting down now in my bedsitter – for Stu was right, what else is it? – looking through the scrapbook. I've gone right back to the beginning and the newspaper cuttings of the accident in which Hebe died. There are four of them, the same scene of carnage and destruction shot from different angles. I can see torn and twisted metal, ripped tyres, shattered glass and glass splinters and great shards of glass, but no bodies or body parts, no spatterings or splashes or lakes of blood. The only thing to give any sign that human beings were in that car, that human beings died in that car, is part of a coat or jacket draped over the back of a ruined seat. Had they taken the bodies away by the time those pictures were taken? Had they cut the driver out of the wreckage and removed him, broken and bleeding, to some emergency room? I don't know and I don't suppose anyone can tell me.

I've written my own captions to these photographs. One of them says: *The remains of the black Mercedes driven by Dermot Lynch, of Paddington, west London.* I had forgotten his name. No wonder, really, after all I have been through. I have had other things to think about, to say the least. Now, though, I have nothing to think about except getting a job, getting money, to stay alive. No, that's an exaggeration. I shan't die. All that will happen to me is that I shall give up this place, the building society will foreclose and I'll go and live with my mother. It's not an exaggeration to say that would be a fate worse than death.

If I dwell too much on that I won't have the strength and the energy to write any more job applications. I won't make it to the interview I've got tomorrow, receptionist in the front office of a firm making breeze blocks in Craven Park, wherever that is. So I turn the pages of the scrapbook, past the photograph the *Daily Express* used of the gun they found in the car, until I come to the first photo of Ivor Tesham. Of course there is nothing, there never was anything, to connect him with the crash.

I wonder what has happened to Dermot Lynch of Paddington, west London. He was very seriously injured. Perhaps he died. I find the west London phone book, the residential section. Paddington is W2. There are a great many Lynchs, a lot of them with the initial D., but none in W2. In fact, among all the Lynchs, only one is in W2 and that is a P. H. Lynch at 23 William Cross Court, Rowley Place. P. H. could be his wife or his father or brother.

I would like to know if Dermot Lynch is still alive.

20

I didn't get the job with the breeze-block manufacturers. On my way back from Craven Park the car broke down. I was stuck in the Harrow Road, unable to get the car to start and very much aware, once again, that this was only going to be a problem because it was going to cost me. For one thing, I had let my membership of the RAC lapse and for another I had given up using my mobile phone. I'd only had it to use in the car and practically the only time I needed it . . . Well, I had to leave the car where it was and walk to a garage half a mile away that a local shopkeeper said might help me. They did. They agreed to tow the car, look it over and assess what needed doing, but when I got back to it in their truck, I had got a parking ticket.

Getting home by public transport would have taken hours. The only bus available was a number 18, which went nowhere near where I wanted to be. I got a taxi, though I couldn't afford it. The driver took me along the Harrow Road into Warwick Avenue and, because the road ahead was up, turned into Rowley Place. And there, on the right-hand side, a little way along, was William Cross Court. Was this a piece of luck? If it was, it was the first I'd had for years. Luck doesn't come my way, so I suspect it when it does. I can't help wondering if maybe it isn't luck at all or if it has a sting in the tail.

What was the use of it, after all? I already knew a Lynch lived in William Cross Court if he lived anywhere. I could have found the place for myself without the intervention of an expensive taxi and a taxi driver. He turned into a road called Park Place Villas and up Maida Avenue to the Edgware Road. Of course he was going the longest and therefore most expensive way possible.

*

My car is going to cost eight hundred pounds to put right, new crankshaft, new fan, four new tyres, a lot of new parts for the engine and, of course, a new battery. And even then, the man says, it won't be as good as new. Frankly, he says, it should go to the scrap heap. I've started asking myself if I need a car, if it wouldn't be better to leave it where it is and ask Mr Know-all to dispose of it.

By bus and on foot I have called at six employment agencies and while I wait for something to come from them – from *one* of them – I scan the Situations Vacant in the newspapers. I stare at most of them in bewilderment. I don't know what they are. What is a people coordinator? What's a regeneration officer, an economic policy manager, a democratic services team leader? It's no good applying for them if I don't even know what the job description means.

I have to be more positive. I have to think of my advantages, such as they are: my good English degree, my library experience, my two and a half years as a child's nanny. Surely that ought to help me get something in the health sector or, preferably, something in the health books sector, if there is such a thing. I start writing an application to a London authority – I can't go to Lancashire or Glasgow – for a job as a child care and family support officer, when the typewriter ribbon comes unravelled. It's worn out anyway. When Hebe saw it she said I must be the last person in London still using a typewriter and didn't believe me when I said I couldn't afford a computer. I suppose I can get a new ribbon tomorrow – if you can still buy them.

I wouldn't have got the job anyway, I expect they want a social worker. The other letters I write by hand, one for a reviewing officer to a campaign called Child Alert and the other for a junior health economist, a post which trains you 'to allow career progression towards a health economist position'. I won't get it. I know that. I won't be junior enough.

Mummy phones. She hasn't heard from me for two weeks, she says. Is something wrong?

'I don't know what put it into my head, Jane, but I got the idea you and Callum had parted. He hasn't left you, has he?'

Not 'you haven't left him', I noted. I tell her Callum is dead. He died in a car crash when his car collided with a forty-ton lorry on the M1. I don't know why I do that, unless I was thinking of the crash in which Hebe died. It just comes into my head to put an end to him. Kill him, the way writers kill off characters they have invented.

She gives a gasp and a little scream. There is no doubt she believes me. 'You poor darling,' she says. 'I'm so terribly sorry. Tell me what happened.'

I say I would rather not talk about it. I tell her about the car and the typewriter. You have to have a car, she says. How are you going to get here without a car? That kind of selfishness almost makes me smile, it's so transparent. Never mind my needs, my feelings. All that matters is that I should be able to come to her. Sometimes she reminds me of Hebe and Justin, just as they reminded me of her.

'Oh, I can walk half a mile to Kilburn Park station,' I say, 'take the Bakerloo Line to Oxford Circus, half an hour *at least* for a Central Line train going to Epping and then spend a fortune on a taxi to Ongar. Easy, no problem.'

'There's no need to be sarcastic,' she says.

I say that there is, there is need, sarcasm is my last resort, and she says she will pay for the repairs to the car. Meanwhile she will pay for me to rent a car. I ask her why she's doing all this. Has she turned over a new leaf? That makes her start crying. She has done her best for me always, she says between sobs, and now all she is asking is that I should let her pay for a rented car that will bring me to her. I'm tempted to put the receiver down but I don't. I realize something. I realize that she is all I've got, she is all I have got left. She's my only friend. I've no job, no money, no prospects. I soon won't have a home. Callum doesn't exist and never did, and my only friend is my mother. Of course I will let her pay for the repairs and the rental of a car. I've no choice.

'I'm sorry, Mummy,' I say, my teeth gritted, and then I spin a long story about my last meeting with Callum, how dreadful it was getting the news of his death and how I feel I shall never recover from it. This was quite enjoyable and made me think I must do something like it more often. I could live in that fantasy world and invent a whole new personality and lifestyle and experience for myself, escape from the real dreary me. I could become a different person. I agree to go down and see Mummy at the weekend – not that weekends have any significance for me – and I shall stay a few days. Her voice sounds full of tears. Well, too bad.

I went to Ongar and stayed longer than I meant to, but it was quite pleasant to have someone to look after me for a change, instead of me looking after them, and while I was there I did my best to put my worries out of my mind. Mummy said she'd pay my mortgage for me until I got a job, that is she'd pay it for six months. I'd surely find something in that time. It all goes to show she must have far more money than she lets on.

She kept talking about Callum, saying I must be in mourning for him. We had been together so long he was practically my husband. She likes going on in this way and I am sure she tells her friends about it. They are mostly widows and now as a sort of semi-widow I am of their company. When I start thinking Callum really existed, I shall know I am going mad. Mummy used to say, and probably still does say, that one of the things which distinguishes the mad from the sane is that mad people don't know they are insane. But I read somewhere lately that schizophrenics have flashes of insight into their condition as it is taking a hold on them. I wonder if that is what is happening to me. I wonder why seeing the madness of inventing Callum and then killing him didn't stop me doing it, why I didn't say to Mummy that it was all nonsense. The answer must be because I am no longer quite sane and if things go on being bad for me I shall sink further into madness.

That was gloomy enough, even by my standards. Back here, three letters were waiting for me, two turning me down for the people

183

coordinator and team leader jobs, no surprise there, and one from, of all people, Pandora Furnal, as I suppose I must now call her. As *she* calls herself. It was only two days old.

I expected more abuse but there wasn't any and nothing about wanting her deposit back. But that, I was sure, was because she was holding her fire. She wanted something, but she took the whole side of the page and half the other side before she got there. I may as well set down her letter in full.

35 Fortune Vale
London NW11

Dear Jane

It is a long time since I have been in touch. As you can see from the address on this letter, we have moved. We are now living in Golders Green, an area I like because it is quite near to Hampstead Heath. I much prefer the school Justin goes to over the one in Hendon. Our house has four bedrooms, which is essential as, guess what, I am expecting a baby. It is due in August and, as you can imagine, we are both very excited about it. Gerry is over the moon. He is such a marvellous father.

I enclose a cutting from a newspaper I found in your room when we moved. I know it must be yours as your writing is on the back. It had fallen down the side of the bed. I don't know if it is important but I thought it best to send it to you. I am sorry it has taken so long but we have been up to our eyes in it with the move.

There is something else I want to run past you. Nothing personal or relating to what happened before you left. This simply concerns Gerry and me. Could we meet up some time? I could come to your place or we could liaise somewhere. I would really appreciate it.

With best wishes,
Pandora (Furnal)

As if I'm likely to know a dozen Pandoras. So she is pregnant. She didn't waste any time. A four-bedroomed house, indeed. He must be doing well. (These were some of my thoughts at the time.

I soon left them behind to concentrate on what she was sending me and what she was asking.) 'Run past' me, indeed; 'liaise'.

The cutting she enclosed was the picture of Ivor Tesham still in its plastic folder I had found in that drawer in Hebe's bedroom which I must have left somewhere in the house. As a matter of fact, I'd forgotten all about it. No wonder after the way they had treated me. I had a closer look at it than I ever had before. He was standing by a microphone, punching the air. A newspaper had used it when he was standing for Morningford in the by-election of 1988. I had never even turned it over but I did now and there along the top margin, not in my handwriting but in Hebe's, were the words, *Must ask him for a real photo next time.*

My instinct was not to answer the letter or else write and tell her what I thought of her. The new typewriter ribbon works all right, though I don't suppose it'll be long before the machine lets me down again. But to reply or not to reply? I was curious. I wanted to know what she could 'run past' me. Something to do with Hebe's writing on the back of that picture? But she thought it was *my* writing. If Gerry had seen it and seen the writing, he would know whose writing it was. If he had, it was clear he hadn't told her and clear too that he didn't know about this letter. No, she thought the writing was mine and the picture had belonged to me. She had said it was nothing personal and nothing to do with their throwing me out. Should I phone? I couldn't. She gave no phone number and they wouldn't yet be in the book. I wrote instead, fixing a date and asking her to tea. The day I chose was 14 May, just before the fourth anniversary of Hebe's death. It had to be tea and not a drink; it had to be when Gerry and Justin weren't home. I sensed Gerry knew nothing about this meeting and I was right.

She had three months to go but she was huge. I think women should wear loose clothes when they're pregnant, but Pandora's blouse or tunic or whatever it's called fitted tightly over that great mound. You could see her navel protruding. I provided tea and biscuits. She ate them voraciously.

'I'm always hungry,' she said. 'I'm eating for two.'

I smiled politely.

'I hope I haven't made you take a day off work,' she said. 'I thought you might have insisted on the weekend and that would have been a bit awkward.'

I know myself. I'm not proud. 'I have no work,' I said. 'I don't have a job. I haven't had one since your husband got rid of me. If it wasn't for my mother helping me I'd be homeless.'

'Oh dear,' she said, embarrassed. 'I'm sure you'll get a job soon. You're so clever.'

I let the silence prolong itself. Then I said, 'What did you want to see me about?'

'Well,' she said, relaxing a bit, 'it's rather strange. When we were moving I went around the house, checking on what stuff we'd keep and stuff we'd throw out, and – well, in our bedroom I found something rather weird.'

Something I'd missed, I thought. It wasn't only Tesham's picture I'd left behind. A sequined mask, maybe, or a black lace corset. But no.

'There was a string of pearls in a box. I'd seen them before when I was tidying the place up but I hadn't taken much notice of them. I took notice of them this time. Gerry had told me they were there, but he'd said they were Hebe's and they came from Woolworths or Marks or somewhere, she'd bought them herself. But, Jane, she can't have. They can't have come from a chain store. They're enormously valuable.'

I nearly laughed. But I didn't. I asked her how she would know.

'I used to work for a company that marketed pearls.'

'I thought you were in PR,' I said.

'I was. I was with this pearl firm a while ago, when I was in my early twenties. I was never a grader, never any sort of expert, but I *do* know. I know a string that comes from Marks from one from Bond Street. These pearls are large and perfect. Most people don't know it, but large pearls are worth more than small ones. It could be worth six or seven thousand pounds. Don't you think it's odd?'

I used, with some relish, the clichéd phrase from a hundred bad books and plays: 'I expect there's a perfectly simply explanation.'

'There can't be. Hebe couldn't have bought them. She hadn't any money. She never even worked. Someone must have given them to her.'

'What does Gerry say?'

'He doesn't know. I haven't told him.'

I asked her why not.

'Isn't it obvious? He – well, he cherishes her memory. I don't mind that. I understand how he worshipped her. It means he's a good husband, doesn't it? Someone gave her those pearls and – well, come on, he didn't give them to her because he'd admired her from afar.'

'I don't know,' I said, and I asked her what she was going to do.

'Perhaps nothing. Can I tell him and destroy his illusions? And yet – look, Jane, we could do with the money. It was very expensive, moving. And we've got this baby coming. We could sell those pearls for six thousand, maybe more. It frightens me sometimes to think we've got them in the house.'

She went on like this for a long time, torn between keeping her precious Gerry in ignorance, to preserve his unsullied love, and longing for the money. She wanted to know if I had known about it.

'You were a close friend of Hebe's,' she said. 'Didn't she tell you she'd a lover? Didn't she say anything about the pearls?'

I said that what Hebe had confided in me was a sacred trust. Pandora liked that. It's the sort of high-flown stuff she indulges in herself. But it made her more suspicious, as I knew it would. As she was leaving, I said, 'Oh, by the way, that photo you sent, it's not mine. The writing on the back is Hebe's.'

'Hebe's? Are you sure?'

I looked sad, said, 'She was my best friend, Pandora.'

'I don't like to ask, but do you know who the man is?'

Shaking my head, I said, 'That's easily found. The paper looks like *The Times* to me.'

She left after that, still uncertain what to do. I think her love of money will overcome her scruples eventually. And it won't only be her love of money. Whatever she says, she'd prefer Gerry to be disillusioned about Hebe, she'd rather his memories of his first wife were spoilt, because then he'd be bound to love her more.

If I look facts squarely in the face, I don't think I'm ever going to get a job. Well, I could go out cleaning, I could be someone's gardener, but even if I could bring myself to do such a job, I wouldn't earn enough to pay the mortgage. Mummy is still paying it, just as she's paid for the car repairs and, come to that, pays for me. Now I've got nothing in the bank I'm thinking of going on benefit and then the Department of Social Security would pay the interest on my mortgage. Does that mean I stay on it for the rest of my life? At any rate, till I'm sixty? Thirty years of living on the dole?

Gerry Furnal has brought me to this. No, that's not quite right. I have to go back further than that. Ivor Tesham has brought me to it. He was the one who arranged the mock kidnap in which Hebe died. It's because Hebe was dead I went to work for Gerry Furnal and be Justin's nanny. If she had lived I would still have lost my job at the Library of British History but I would have got another. It was those years out of the job market, years doing a menial task out of the goodness of my heart, that wrecked my chances. Someone was behind it, but was it Ivor Tesham or just those two men in the car? He or they started the chain reaction, he set the ball in motion, gathering snow as it rolled down the hill. And now he is successful, rich and happy, living with his lover in a beautiful house, tipped in the newspapers for high office and a seat in the Cabinet, while I am poor and jobless and forgotten. Friendless too and dependent on my mother.

I sit here alone in the evenings thinking about it and wishing I knew a little more. I don't know enough about these things. I don't know if the police tell the newspapers about something like that. If they do he may have been afraid it would get into the papers. Is that what he meant when he asked what was I going to do? It must have been. The police soon thought it was Kelly Mason they meant to kidnap and by then maybe it was too late for him to tell.

There was a gun in it somewhere, but I don't know whose or where it came from. He can't have meant to shoot anyone. Perhaps it was there to frighten Hebe. But why would he want to frighten her? Apart from Ivor Tesham, one person only knows what he meant to do with the gun. And there is just this one person who can tell me, if he's still alive, if he can tell anyone anything.

Why do I want to know? I have to have money. There are more ways of getting it than by having a job or living on benefit or being helped out by one's relations. Once the idea of asking for money in order to keep quiet about a secret would have been something I had read about in books or seen someone doing in a sitcom. I wouldn't have seen it as applying to me.

But I have tried to get a job and I feel sick when I have to ask Mummy or take it without asking. I haven't come down to going on benefit yet, but I will if it's a choice between that and starving. The one thing that remains no longer looks unreal. It looks like an option worth serious consideration. He has a secret, and probably by now more secrets piled on top of it, that he wants kept and he has a lot of money. I know the secret and won't tell a newspaper what it is if he pays me money. It's a simple exchange, a business transaction.

I can't sleep. I haven't been able to sleep since I dreamed Callum came into this room, in the night, in the dark, with a big dog on a lead. I knew it was Callum, though I have never pictured him, not even when I first invented him for Mummy. He looks a bit like Ivor Tesham and a bit like Gerry Furnal. He let the dog go and it jumped on to my bed with a low groan. I woke up screaming.

21

The Bosnian crisis and a lot of IRA activity had kept Ivor busy throughout much of 1993. He was always on his feet in the chamber, constantly the subject of media political comment, and a broadsheet newspaper had carried a full-page profile of him in March with a lot of personal stuff about his 'beautiful home' and his 'attractive companion, Juliet Case'. He battled with John Humphrys on the *Today* programme and if he didn't win, he wasn't ignominiously vanquished either. In April, on that late-night programme *The Question of the Hour*, he boasted about John Major's recent assertion that the country was beginning to see economic recovery, though this wasn't his area of expertise, and said that 'things were getting quite sharply better', citing the fall in unemployment figures.

Next day he had just got out of his government car in the City when an IRA bomb exploded fifty yards from him. It was half past ten in the morning and he was about to go into a meeting. The bomb knocked him flat but he was otherwise unharmed. Others weren't so fortunate. One person was killed, forty were injured and damage was estimated at a thousand million pounds. Ivor got his picture in all the papers this time and quotes from him about his own luck and his distress at the loss of life. He was becoming quite famous.

His picture was in the papers again when he was among the NATO defence ministers meeting in Brussels to discuss the Vance–Owen peace plan, aimed at finding a lasting solution to the situation in the Balkans. They got a shot of his elegant figure mounting the steps into the aircraft at Heathrow, apparently preferring a photograph of him to one of the Secretary of State. He was certainly better-looking. Three days before this John Major had carried out a large-scale reorganization of government, replacing Norman

Lamont as Chancellor of the Exchequer with Kenneth Clarke, who had been Home Secretary. Michael Howard was the new Home Secretary and John Gummer took his job at Environment. There were other steps upwards, but nothing for Ivor. Optimistic as always, he refused to be downhearted. He was young yet, the government was more popular in his opinion than it had been for a long time, they would get back in at the next election. So the months had passed without promotion, without change.

It was probably all these pictures of him in the papers which led to Beryl Palmer ringing his front doorbell and asking for his autograph.

'But that must have been rather nice, wasn't it?' Iris said when he told us.

'Yes and no,' he said. 'I'm not exactly a celebrity. It was something of a novelty. I don't believe I've ever been asked for my autograph before. She wanted it for her granddaughter, had the child's album with her.'

I asked him who she was.

He was reluctant to tell us yet he had to tell us once he'd started. That, after all, was the point of his starting. But I knew that look of his and Iris knew it. It presaged the revealing of something of which he wasn't proud, if not exactly ashamed.

'It worried me rather. I mean, it was quite flattering and all that. It was really *who* she was.'

'All right. Who was she?'

'She used to clean the flat next to mine in Old Pye Street – well, she cleaned several flats in the building. She was walking along here one day and she saw me come out of my house and recognized me.'

'Ivor,' said Iris, 'who is she?'

'She's Hebe's aunt.'

Iris said she didn't understand. How did he know she was Hebe's aunt? Did she tell him? And that meant . . .

'Precisely. I must say, you're uncommonly slow on the up-take today. Hebe's mother is her sister, though apparently she doesn't have much to do with the family, though she did –' he

191

hesitated – 'go to Hebe's funeral. She told me she was coming out of the flat on my floor about four years ago and Hebe got out of the lift.'

'Surely Hebe didn't tell her where she was going?'

'I don't quite see what else she could have done, do you?'

'Does it matter, Ivor?'

He hesitated. 'I don't know. Of course I'd rather a woman like that – never mind. It probably doesn't matter.'

His look of distaste, I'm sure, was caused more than anything else by his former girlfriend's aunt being a cleaner. Yet, however out of touch Beryl Palmer was with her family, she must know of Hebe's death and the circumstances of that death. He thought he detected something in the woman's expression he didn't quite like as she told him about the meeting with Hebe outside his flat, a knowing look, a sidelong glance that spoke more than words could of a naughty secret.

'You signed her grandchild's book?'

'Yes. I kept thinking this child must be Hebe's cousin. She didn't say anything about Hebe's death and I thought very little of it at the time, but afterwards it seemed rather strange. No, it seemed very strange. It was the obvious thing to mention, yet she didn't. And, well, I didn't. Perhaps I should have.'

'I suppose you invited her in,' I said.

'Of course. I more or less had to. She said she'd been in the Commons once or twice to hear me speak.'

'But I thought she only recognized you when she saw you come out of this house.'

'I know. It was all a bit odd.'

Candidates are often selected a considerable time before an expected general election. The deadline for the next one was May 1997 and Ivor, the sitting member, almost without question, was the Conservatives' choice for Morningford. No surprise there and no surprise perhaps that Aaron Hunter was standing again and once more with that bound-to-lose label, Independent. The difference this time was that he was standing for the constituency of Imberwell, an industrial town and port on the coast of Lincolnshire. In an interview he gave to the *Guardian*, he said that his grandfather had come from Imberwell and his cousin was the leader of Imberwell Borough Council. He had strong family ties to the place.

He also said in the interview that he stood for uprightness and decency in public life and against sleaze, of which there had recently been in the government an unacceptable amount. This sort of thing is always a challenge to certain areas of the press and one scurrilous right-wing newspaper tried to dig dirt out of his past, but without much success. Aaron Hunter was a respectable husband and father of three children; all they could find prior to his marriage was that he had once been married to Juliet Case and divorced eight years before. Juliet Case, the newspaper added, was now the 'companion' of Defence Minister Ivor Tesham.

This made Ivor furiously angry, though without much cause, as far as I could see. What did it amount to, after all? No one had said a word against him. 'Hunter must have told them about Juliet,' he said. 'How would they otherwise know? Anyway, he hasn't a hope in hell of getting in. The Imberwell electorate aren't going to vote for him just because his cousin's on the council. We've never had a member for Imberwell, though of course we've got a very sound candidate. The present Labour man's standing down, he's nearly seventy, but there's a very strong young Labour candidate and the Lib Dem'll put up a good fight. You'll see.'

'Ivor couldn't care less about Labour and Lib Dem candidates,' Iris said after he'd gone. 'What's bothering him is calling Juliet his "companion". He knows it's not doing him any good living with a woman he's not married to, and the closer we come to the election the worse it'll get.'

He had paid us a flying visit – all his visits were flying now, he was always on the move – to see his new nephew. He described him as a 'handsome bruiser'.

'He'd better be,' he'd said. 'He's bound to be a gangster with a name like Joe Delgado.'

Iris asked him if he didn't sometimes think he'd like 'one like that' of his own.

'Women may think along those lines,' was all he said. 'Men don't.'

'Robin does.'

'I read an article about Evelyn Waugh in which he was quoted as mentioning each new child he fathered as "my wife's baby". I expect I shall be like that.'

'Really. And when will that be?'

'Oh, in about twenty years' time.'

Once he had begun paying the ten thousand a year to the Lynch family, I believe Ivor had more or less ceased to worry about the events of May 1990 ever coming out. It wasn't blackmail. It was no more blackmail than Juliet's living with him and, presumably, being entirely supported by him were blackmail. Her love for him was undoubted. She showed it in every glance, in every touch, in every hand laid lightly on his sleeve, every word spoken to him. If he liked sprightly tongued women with a provocative turn of phrase like Hebe Furnal or prettily affected actressy women like Nicola Ross, he hadn't found one in Juliet. She was warm and sweet and she loved him. She loved looking after him, refusing help in the house except when they gave a big party. If he hadn't paid much attention to our children – affairs of state keeping him at a distance – she often came to see them and was particularly keen on bathing Nadine and Adam. With Joe in her arms, she looked like some Spanish painter's Madonna. No, her presence in Ivor's life had nothing to do with blackmail. And nor, apparently, had Sean Lynch's.

I had to admit, though only to Iris, that I had been wrong when I warned Ivor, and warned him very forcefully, to have nothing to do with the Lynch family. If it wasn't directly his fault, it isn't too dramatic to say that his action had led to the ruin of Dermot Lynch's life. But for him, Dermot would have been happily servicing cars and repairing engines and making his funny gestures. It was right for him to pay recompense to him and Philomena and Sean, especially because he could easily afford it. He could pay it and would always be able to pay it, without really noticing the loss.

But I said 'more or less'. There was still the alibi lady. He never heard from her and more than three years had passed since his visit to her flat, when he had hoped she was going to hand over the pearls. I don't know if he ever thought about her. Perhaps he believed she had married and gone to live in some distant place. Beryl Palmer had worried him more. He sometimes reverted to her visit, even saying in a fretful way that he couldn't understand why Hebe hadn't told him she had met her outside his flat.

'I can understand it all right,' Iris said. 'She knew what a fearful snob my brother is. She wasn't going to say she'd met Auntie Beryl with her bucket and mop.'

My noiseless laugh came into play.

The general election was still over three years away. I wouldn't say the Tories were doomed to lose that election or fated or anything like that, though that sort of language was being used. Most people could see it coming. Eighteen years is a long time for any government to be in power and it would be eighteen years by the time the election came round.

Ivor would never have made a statement like that. He never did make it. Whatever he privately thought, he always talked as if his party was invincible, would go from strength to strength, and nothing said in the media or by a muttering electorate made the least difference. What he never said either was how he hoped for a Cabinet post. Secretary of State for Defence was what he wanted and of course he wanted it well in advance of the election – the election which he couldn't for a moment consider losing.

He was never to get it. As time went on he must from day to day have waited for the summons to Number Ten. When the corridors of the Palace of Westminster throbbed and shivered with predictions of a reshuffle, he must have told himself, alternately, that he was bound to get that call and at the same time that it would never come. But he was an optimist, always had been. He looked on the bright side. How fortunate his life had been! How good luck had followed him! Not that he hadn't worked to make that luck happen, worked like a political slave, done all the right things, been a good party man, a good minister and the best of constituency MPs. Ever-faithful he was, dogged yet brilliant, industrious yet calm and laid-back, popular and with a throng of keen supporters. Why didn't that summons come? How long must he wait? His political clock was ticking away and so, perhaps, was Juliet's reproductive clock.

22

I keep thinking of what Mummy said about people you are frightened of not being able to eat you. As if anyone ever thought they would. As if being the victim of cannibalism was a usual sort of fate for an eight-year-old. Saying that to me never made me feel any better, though I suppose she meant a kind of metaphorical eating. That's what I am afraid of.

I've been contemplating going to the Lynchs for a long time now. A slight shift in my circumstances has helped postpone it too. I'm drawing benefit. I've had to put myself down as looking for a job, but until they find me one they'll pay the interest on my mortgage repayments and give me enough for a bare living. I don't think I could take a regular job now, I'm not fit for it. This is partly because I don't sleep and when I do I dream I'm walking with Callum and his dog across a vast open space, a kind of heath or desert. It's dark or half dark and I know that when we reach a certain point in the walk, a place that's marked by an obelisk pointing up into the night sky, he is going to kill me.

Mummy doesn't understand about being on benefit – how could she, the sheltered life she's led, with all found for her? – and she goes on sending me a monthly cheque. So for quite a while I'd been able to put off the Lynch encounter. But now I've got to face it. I've got to find out if Ivor Tesham paid Dermot Lynch and Lloyd Freeman to drive a car and pick up Hebe on the evening of 18 May 1990 and if that was the car which did pick her up. It's the link I need to know about. So far as I am aware, Dermot Lynch is the only person alive, if he is alive, who knows the answer – apart from Tesham, of course. I have to go to William Cross Court and see Dermot Lynch or, if he's dead, anyone else he may have told. The papers said he had a mother and a brother but no paper I saw ever said if he recovered from the crash.

Remembering that helped me manage some of the self-confidence Mummy tried to instil in me with her 'they can't eat you' talk. The Lynchs weren't cannibals, they couldn't eat me, so I dialled the number in the phone book for 23 William Cross Court. A man answered.

'Is that you, Dermot?' I said.

'He can't talk now,' the man said. 'Who wants him?'

I put the phone down, my heart pounding. So he was alive and he lived there. Maybe the man who answered *was* him but didn't want to admit it. I have to go there. I know that now.

First I went up to the newspaper library in Colindale. My car's been done, so at least I was able to drive. I asked to see newspapers from 18 to 28 May 1990, the more sensational ones. I didn't bother with *The Times* or the *Telegraph*. Pictures of the two men were what I wanted to see and there they were, plenty of them. None after the accident, of course, all these must have been given to the reporters by the Lynchs and perhaps, in Lloyd Freeman's case, by a theatrical agent.

He'd been a good-looking man, tall with curly black hair and the sort of Caucasian features whites admire in black people. They don't care about what a *black* person might find attractive. One picture the newspaper may have had on file. It was of Lloyd wearing a toga when he was Casca in a production of *Julius Caesar* and it came from a review of the play. But the one that really interested me was the sort of photograph that's taken by professional photographers at functions. Or so I suppose. I've never been in such a shot myself – I was never invited to anything so grand – but I remember Gerry Furnal showing me photographs taken at some reception he organized for HALT and he was in one of them, standing next to a minor royal. The one Lloyd was in wasn't very good of him, as there were too many other people trying to get in shot, but the woman next to him, her arm through his, I recognized at once. It was Carmen a.k.a. Juliet Case.

I just stopped myself giving a shout of triumph. They wouldn't like that in the newspaper library. I suddenly felt sane again, in control, my own woman.

I have been there and I wish I hadn't. Ever since I was there the name of that play Hebe and I were supposed to be going to see keeps running round in my head: *Life Threatening, Life Threatening.* I'm very frightened. All the way home I was shaking and trembling like an old person with Parkinson's disease. I sat in the tube with my right leg jumping up and down and my hands vibrating. A woman stared at me. I shut my eyes and tried taking deep breaths. I thought a walk might do me good, so I tried walking from the nearest tube station instead of getting the bus, but I shook and shivered so much that I had to sit down in a bus shelter. Only for a moment, though. A man was in there with a dog like Callum's. I walked on and when I looked back there was no one there.

What happened at 23 William Cross Court I don't want to have to think about, but I must if I am to do the thing I went there for in the first place. If Sean Lynch frightens me so, how am I going to confront Ivor Tesham? Of course there is a difference between them. Sean Lynch is a thug and Tesham – well, he's what Mummy would call a gentleman. I had better set down my experience there and get it over. Maybe it will get it out of my mind, lay it to rest.

An old woman answered the door. She was wearing tracksuit bottoms in bright purple with a flowered blouse and brown cardigan. I asked her if she was Mrs Lynch and she nodded. She never said her own name.

'Westminster Social Services,' I said.

She shook her head, then nodded.

'All right if I come in?'

She didn't like it, but by then I was in, walking ahead of her into a living room. The first thing anyone would notice about the place was the religious icons, the statuettes, the pictures. Above the mantelpiece was a crucifix with spilt red paint bleeding from Christ's side. The room was crowded with furniture, far too much for the size of it, and in one of the chairs, hemmed in by two other chairs and a wicker table, sat a man. Somewhere in the depths of his fat face, under the lardy layers, behind his dull eyes, you could see the remains of Dermot Lynch. He wore loose corduroy trousers and a check shirt under a sleeveless pullover, his big red hands lying slack against his big protuberant belly. He was perfectly still and silent.

'I've come about fitting some aids for the disabled in your home,' I said. 'We provide a service along those lines.'

I was beginning to feel the confidence Mummy couldn't teach me. The two of them, he the epitome of apathy and incomprehension, his head hanging, she ignorant and fearful, gave an impression of utter humility, and this inspired me. I felt strong. I felt in control. It would be easy.

'This is your son, Dermot?'

She nodded. 'That's right.'

I looked at some printed sheets I'd brought with me. 'We don't seem to have any record of the accident which caused Dermot's injuries,' I said, pretending to read. 'Exactly what was that and when did it occur?'

He spoke. It was a robotic voice, toneless, all on one note, as if generated by an electronic device. 'Car crash,' he said, and again, 'Car crash. Bad,' he said, 'bad, bad.'

I turned to his mother. 'Was he driving the car?'

Again she nodded. The two of them were like a pair of mechanical dolls, programmed to nod and shake their heads and utter mono-syllables. I referred once more to my printed sheets, running my forefinger down the lines, as if looking for a particular word or name.

'Mr Tesham's car that would be?'

I expected, I really did, uncomprehending stares. This time it was he who nodded. The robot lifted its head and made it vibrate, up and down, up and down. It was his mother who spoke and more volubly than she had done up till then, a slight flush of animation appearing on her cheeks.

'Mr Tesham's been very good. He looks after us.'

It was the link. It was what I wanted. I got up. People with more nous, people who had a basic idea of what the social services did, might have expected me to request a tour of the place and check on where handrails might be needed or ramps installed. They knew nothing of that.

Mrs Lynch said, 'Is that all, then?'

As she spoke there was a sound of a key turning in the front door lock, the door slammed and a man came in. He was rather good-looking in a heavy-set, thuggish way, his yellow-brown hair in long greasy curls, falling on to the shoulders of a black leather jacket. There was a lot of leather about him, the glossy, quilted sort, his jeans stuffed into thick black boots with multiple straps. What is this stuff with leather? Is it the smell or the feel or the shininess or all of that?

'Sean Lynch,' he said to me and, 'Who's this?' to his mother.

'A lady from the council.'

Apart from giving me his name, I might not have been present for all the words he addressed to me. 'What's she want?'

Dermot said, 'Mr Tesham.' The nodding began again, up and down, up and down.

Suspicion oozed out of Sean like sweat. At last he spoke to me. 'You got any ID, have you?'

'I'm afraid not,' I said.

'You'd best be afraid. What's this, then?' He snatched the printed sheets out of my hand. It was my gas bill and two pages of the kind of literature no one ever reads that had come with it. He threw it on the floor, said, 'What's Mr Tesham to you?'

I heard my own voice, thin and hoarse as my throat dried. 'Nothing. Your brother said he drove Mr Tesham's car.'

He took hold of me by the shoulders and shook me. Not much and not for long, but I heard my teeth click together. I tried to cry,

'Stop it,' and, 'Don't,' but only a strangled whisper came out. He flung me away.

'You fucking spy,' he said. 'You interfering bitch.' His mother made a sound of protest but only a sound, a tiny yelp. Dermot had once more hung his head. 'You should be bloody ashamed, coming here after my brother. Scaring my mother. Look at them. You've scared them stupid.'

'I'm going,' I managed to say. 'I'm leaving,' and, 'Let me pass.'

He filled the doorway. As well as being all those other things, leather, especially black leather, which is only after all the hide of a harmless animal, is horribly intimidating. A man in black leather, any man, is more frightening than a man in black cloth. Why did Ivor Tesham want Hebe in black leather when black silk and lace are feminine and pretty and make their wearer desirable? I don't know. Sean had a belt round his waist of thick black leather, studded with brass bosses and spikes. It reminded me of the dog collar I found among Hebe's things.

I made a sort of whimper. I said, 'Please let me go.'

Mrs Lynch had turned her back. She moved towards Dermot and laid a hand on his slack shoulder. Sean said, 'You're not *going*. I'm going to put you out.'

He turned me round, joined my hands together behind my back as if he was going to handcuff me and propelled me towards the front door. My back was pressed against the front of him, straps and buckles digging into my flesh. His breath was hot against the back of my head, moving my hair. This was somehow the worst sensation until at the closed front door he pushed me forward, banging my forehead against a wooden panel. I cried out then. He pulled me back, shaking me hard, flung the door open and pushed me out with a great shove in the middle of my back. I stumbled and fell, spread-eagled on the concrete floor.

I heard the door slam behind me.

That was three days ago.

Nothing was broken but I'm badly bruised. There's a lump on

my forehead where he pushed me against the door. My knees and the palms of my hands are scraped like children's are when they fall over. But the shock of it is past, the shaking and trembling are over. And I have got what I wanted, the link, the connection between the Lynchs and Ivor Tesham. I need never go near Sean Lynch and Dermot and their mother again. We will never meet again. I don't think any of them would want to come near me either. They don't know who I am or where I live.

Sleep is impossible, though. Worse than it was before. I don't get Callum and the dog keeping me awake, I get a picture, still but in full colour, of that man banging my head against the door. I can see the green paint of the door and the picture of the suffering Christ next to it. But when I fall asleep the action starts, the movement and sensation, the hot breath on the back of my head, the buckles and studs stabbing into my back, and feeling these things is sharper and more painful in the dream than it was in reality. I wake up crying real tears, my heart beating irregularly, sweat soaking the front of my nightdress. *Life Threatening*.

Lying there in the dark, shivering from the sweat, I tell myself I am too frightened to confront Tesham. I know that if he sets Sean Lynch on me I shall cave in. I shall fall on my knees and cry and beg for mercy. And it may be worse than that. My heart may fail; I could have a heart attack. But these are the fantasies of the night, when law-abiding people become gangsters and extravagant behaviour calls for wild responses. In the morning I feel differently. We always do feel differently in the morning. Knowing that, why can't we use this knowledge to help ourselves in the dreadful dreams of night? I don't know. No one knows.

I must confront Tesham. I haven't come so far and been through so much to give up now. I used to think we only went mad at night, that we were strangers to ourselves at night, but now it's in the daytime too. Will it get better when I have money? When Tesham gives me money, will I be free?

I never used to notice dogs, but now I see them all the time. Callum didn't have a dog while he was with me. He's got one since we split up, a mastiff I think it is, and it wears a black leather collar with spikes. Someone else walks it now, takes it past this house on the way to the High Road.

Because Callum is dead, isn't he?

23

In early 1994, Ivor was kept busy at the Defence Department. There were more IRA bombs, though none actually exploded. An army helicopter was hit by an IRA mortar bomb in Crossmaglen, injuring an officer of the Royal Ulster Constabulary, though its pilot managed to land without injury to the crew.

Ivor's party was doing badly. In local elections held in early May Conservative representation in contested seats fell by 429 to 888 and the Tory majority was lost in eighteen of the thirty-three councils where it had had control before. On 12 May John Smith, leader of the Labour Party, dropped dead of a heart attack. This was a terrible blow, but when the party rallied Tony Blair began to be regarded as a contender for the leadership.

Whether Ivor noticed that 18 May was the fourth anniversary of Hebe's death I have no idea. We went to dinner with him and Juliet in Glanvill Street a day or two later, when the other guests were Jack Munro and his wife and Erica Caxton with the new husband she had married in February. The talk was all of Ivor and Juliet's forthcoming engagement.

Engagements are not what they used to be, essential precursors to marriage. In some ways they have become like the civil partnerships for heterosexual couples we didn't have then and still don't have now but are talked about a lot. The girl wears a ring that might as well be a wedding ring except that it usually has a diamond in it; the couple refer to each other as 'my fiancé(e)' instead of 'my husband' and 'my wife'. They have no tax concessions but otherwise they might as well be married. The chances are, of course, that they never will be.

Ivor and Juliet got engaged at the end of May. The occasion was another excuse for a party in Glanvill Street but this time we didn't go, for the simple reason that we couldn't find a babysitter. It's harder when you've three children, especially when one of them is only months old. My mother was in Mallorca, Iris's mother herself at the party. We had to be content with the pictures a tabloid used, one of celebrity guests arriving and another of Juliet holding Ivor's arm and showing off her diamond and sapphire trophy. I wondered if all those photographs would spark off another visit from Beryl Palmer, but if it did Ivor said nothing about it.

If he heard nothing from her, a disquieting piece of news came to him from Sean Lynch. Ivor had more or less discontinued his visits to the Lynchs, but he apparently made up for this by inviting Sean to any functions he could attend and yet be lost in the crowd. When I pointed this out to him he denied it angrily. His attitude to Sean was no different, he insisted, from that he had for any of his friends, for Jack, for instance, or Erica Caxton or the Trenants. I could have commented that he met all these people in tête-à-tête situations with Juliet, but I didn't. He wanted to tell me what Sean had to say about a visitor to the Lynchs' flat.

Ivor's engagement party wasn't the ideal occasion for imparting unwelcome news but I suppose Sean had no choice. He took Ivor aside and told him he had come home and found a woman there questioning Dermot and his mother about the crash in which Dermot was injured. She said she was from Westminster Council but Sean didn't believe this. Ivor asked him her name and, when he said he didn't know, to describe her.

'A dog,' Sean said in his brutal way. 'Short, skinny, frizzy hair.'

Ivor said he felt Sean was keeping something back. He was genuinely angry, Ivor could tell that, but disclosing only as much as he thought Ivor needed to know. He almost confirmed this by saying, 'You don't want to worry, Ivor. You've got enough on your plate without that. I can handle her, the cow. I just reckoned it wouldn't be right to keep it from you.'

Sean's description wasn't conclusive. Ivor had to ask. 'You don't know who she was?'

'Not a social worker from the council. Let's leave it there, shall we?'

'It was Jane Atherton,' Ivor said to me. 'Sean wouldn't say but I'm sure.'

He was made nervous. Perhaps the good time, the quiet months, years really, were past. Things were starting to happen, small things, of little importance, but they added up. Maybe the next one wouldn't be so small. But time went by and he heard nothing more from Sean and nothing from Jane Atherton or Beryl Palmer. He began to think that freak storm was dying down. But something much bigger was looming.

The function to which he and Juliet had been invited was in Carlton Gardens, a fund-raising reception for the Marfan Syndrome Society. Ivor knew very little about Marfan and wasn't particularly interested in it, but Juliet was. Her father, now dead, had suffered from it and so did her brother. Once she was in her teens and it was clear that she didn't have it, she had learned it was genetic and could be inherited. Marfan, apparently, is one of those hereditary conditions which, if you have it, you have a fifty-fifty chance of passing it on to your children, hence the brother showing its symptoms. Juliet knew by then that, since she didn't have it, it had so to speak died with her and she could never pass it on. As Iris and I had noticed, she wanted children and was anxious too, of course, that when they came (if they ever came, if Ivor would permit it) they should be healthy. She retained her interest and with it a hope of helping sufferers, so she accepted the invitation and they both went to the reception.

Through the years that had passed since Hebe's death, Ivor told me he had carefully avoided being present at anything connected with the Heart and Lung Trust, of which Gerry Furnal had been chief fund-raiser. He avoided all charity functions unless going to them was politically expedient except for those taking place in his constituency and these he attended for that reason. How much of this came from a fear of encountering Gerry Furnal I don't know but certainly Furnal was unlikely to be promoting the interests of

HALT in Morningford. It's possible that Ivor would have put aside caution and gone to a HALT reception if it had taken place there, but it's more probable he would have pleaded government business kept him away.

It seems that he'd assumed Hebe's husband was still in the job he had at the time of her death, though he could easily have found out whether he was or not. Perhaps he thought that the process of finding out, even if done in privacy, would make him look cowardly to himself. And how he looked to himself was very important to him. He and Juliet arrived about half an hour after the Marfan party started, Ivor hoping not to have to stay long as they had a dinner engagement. There were rather too many people for the size of the room and moving about was difficult. Someone he didn't know mounted the podium, introduced himself as the chairman of the association and announced their principal speaker. It was Gerry Furnal.

Ivor had noticed Furnal bustling around, fiddling with the microphone and shifting it about on the podium, but hadn't recognized him. Of course he had seen him before. He must have seen him at that HALT gathering in the Jubilee Room when he first met Hebe, but he had hardly noticed him. In Carlton Gardens, if he hadn't been introduced by what he called 'some other do-gooding luminary', Ivor wouldn't have known him. When the man's name was announced, he whispered to Juliet, 'You know who that is?'

She didn't. I think she'd forgotten Hebe's surname. She shook her head.

'Hebe's husband,' he said.

'Oh dear, does it embarrass you?'

Ivor doesn't care for it to be thought by anyone that he could be embarrassed. English gentlemen aren't. It implies a weakness, I suppose, just as being asked if you're shy does or if you dislike speaking in public. He wanted people to believe him far too sophisticated to be embarrassed, while at the same time disapproving of the word 'sophisticated' as applied to himself or to anyone else, approving of it only as a qualifier of concepts. So, 'Not at all,' he told Juliet, 'but I shall avoid him as I dare say he'll avoid me.'

Gerry Furnal spoke quite eloquently (Ivor said) on the subjects of research into the treatment of Marfan and of possible future gene therapy. He named sums in millions which were needed to further these advances and spoke of an appeal which the society was shortly to launch. There was applause, amid which he stepped down and was immediately surrounded. As Ivor had told Juliet he would, he set about avoiding him. This wasn't a difficult task as for the first ten minutes after making his speech, large numbers of people wanted to speak to Furnal and hemmed him in. Ivor and Juliet circulated, losing sight of each other after a while, taking glasses of wine from proffered trays. Juliet stopped in her progress to talk to the society's president, whom she knew.

Ivor was temporarily alone, making his way towards a Tory peer he had spotted on the far side of the room, the only person he felt like talking to, when Gerry Furnal came up to him. Ivor said he wasn't fazed. He was probably the most important guest there and it was only to be expected that MSS's chief fund-raising officer would wish to speak to him. Smiling, he held out his hand.

Furnal didn't take it. Ivor said he was absolutely cool and quiet, for which (being the sort of man he was) he rather admired him.

'There was no exchange of pleasantries,' Ivor told us, 'none of that how-are-you-good-of-you-to-come stuff. Well, there wouldn't be in the circumstances. He put his hand in his pocket and pulled out a pearl necklace. It wasn't in a case or anything, it wasn't even in a bag. I didn't recognize it. The fact is I'd forgotten all about the bloody thing. He said, "I believe you gave this to my late wife. Perhaps you'll take it back, as I have no use for it."'

'My God, Ivor,' Iris said. 'It must have been a hell of a shock. Did you blush?'

'Don't be silly. I don't blush. I said I didn't want it, he'd much better keep it, and he said very pompously something about its being dirty and he no longer wished to be soiled by it. A lot of people had gone by then, so there was a bit more space, and a couple of women were staring. I didn't have a choice really. I put the pearls in my pocket and walked off, found Juliet and we went.'

I asked him if that was all Furnal had said.

'That was all.'

'How did he know?' Iris asked. 'How did he know it was you who gave her the pearls?'

'I couldn't exactly ask, could I? I'm sure Hebe never told him. It's possible he remembered seeing me speak to Hebe when I first met her in the Jubilee Room. I wouldn't think that was enough. I mean, that's putting two and two together and making about fifty-seven, isn't it?'

I asked him when this MSS reception was and he said two days before. 'Has anything happened since?'

'If you mean have I heard from him, no, there's been nothing. I doubt if anything will happen. He's had his moment of triumph and he'll probably dine out on it for the rest of his life. If he dines out, that is.'

'I don't think he'll dine out on it,' Iris said quietly.

'Yes, well, please don't tell me I've ruined his life or anything like that. Men get cuckolded, end of story.'

He had brought the pearls with him in a Boots plastic bag. 'God knows what he's done with the case,' he said, and he tipped them out on to the table. Nadine and Adam had joined us by this time and my little girl was, of course, entranced by what she called 'the big beads'. To Ivor's amusement, she picked them up and ran them through her fingers. 'I offered them to Juliet, but she said, "I don't do pearls." I said she was wearing pearls in her ears when I first met her but to no avail. She was a bit cross.' He put his head on one side and a hand on Nadine's shoulder. 'You can have them, sweetheart – would you like to?'

Iris was furious. She snatched the pearls out of Nadine's hand, stuffed them back into the bag and shouted at Ivor, 'No, she can't. Never dare say that again! She doesn't want your ladyfriend's leftovers and nor do I.'

Nadine began to cry. More than cry, she screamed and shouted, frightened by an anger she had never heard from her mother before, and Adam gave fraternal support by joining in. It took a long time for all of them to calm down, Iris taking Nadine on her knee and promising her 'a lovely pearl necklace' of her own. We all had drinks after that, gin for the grown-ups and orange juice for the children, while Ivor told us in a much more sensible and rational way that he thought the worst was over, the worst had been at the MSS reception, and there would be no more. Gerry Furnal wasn't going to talk to the newspapers.

When a couple more days had gone by and nothing else had happened, things began to look hopeful. With luck, I was thinking, we should hear no more of Gerry Furnal, when Iris read an entry in the Births column of the newspaper which had carried the birth announcements of our daughter and our two sons. Since Nadine was born, she had regularly read them and, of course, often come upon babies born to friends of ours, as happens when you're the sort of age we were then.

'"Furnal,"' she read aloud to me, '"On 1 September, in the Royal Free Hospital, Hampstead, to Pandora and Gerald, Ruby Anne, a half-sister for Justin." It must be him, mustn't it?'

'I'm glad he's married again,' I said. 'I hope he's happy. I always felt he'd had a raw deal.'

'So did I,' she said.

Judging by my own experiences at a time like this, Gerry Furnal would have his hands too full and his emotions too much engaged to take any more vengeful steps against Ivor. Once again he had got away with it. Knowing Ivor had given Hebe an expensive present virtually proved she had been his mistress but not that he had arranged the abduction. It was likely, anyway, that, as most people, Furnal still believed Hebe had been abducted by mistake for Kelly Mason. He would need more information than he apparently had to link it with Ivor. He wasn't a threat. But thinking like this troubled me, as I know it troubled Iris. I didn't like the situation we seemed to be living in, where we had to tick off the names of people who no longer threatened her brother and grade those remaining in order of danger quotient: Jane Atherton, the second Mrs Furnal (?), the Lynchs, Beryl Palmer and even Juliet herself.

24

Stu the window cleaner was here when Pandora phoned and told me about the baby. I don't know why she phoned. It's not as if I was dying to know. I wonder if they've realized they've given it a name rather like Hebe. Hebe, Ruby, both just four letters long, both two syllables and both ending in a 'be' sound. Must be a sort of unconscious way of commemorating her on his part. I wouldn't like it if I were Pandora.

Ostensibly polishing the windows, Stu hung about listening to our conversation. When I'd put the receiver down he asked if that was a pal of mine who'd had a baby. I said that was right and it was the woman who'd lived here.

'Time you had one yourself,' he said with a sort of leer.

I didn't answer that. I said that, on the contrary, it was time he got on with his work.

'I've finished.' He put the polishing cloth in his pocket. 'You want to come out for a drink?'

I couldn't believe what I was hearing. I stared at him, then shook my head. 'No, thanks,' I managed to say.

'Suit yourself.' He slammed the door behind him.

What a nerve! How dared he? I looked in the mirror and saw I'd blushed quite deeply and the remains of the blush were still there. The funny thing was that I wasn't all that angry and when Mummy arrived here I told her about it, altering things round a bit, of course.

'His name's Stuart,' I said. 'I hardly know him but he asked me out. Of course I'm not going.'

'I should think not,' she said, 'with Callum not long dead.' She didn't want me going out with him but – typical of her – she wanted to know what Stuart did for a living.

'Something to do with glass,' I said. 'His father's got a company that manufactures windows.'

'You young ones,' she said. 'Have you forgotten people have surnames? You never told me Callum's surname.'

'He didn't have one,' I said. 'He had a dog.' She gave me a strange look, the kind you give to people who talk to themselves or laugh without a reason for laughing. Before she could ask me what I meant, I invented, 'Stuart's called Chumley-Burns.'

But I've other things to think about now, the principal one being how to get access to Ivor Tesham. Calling him and inviting him here worked last time but that was four years ago. Nothing has happened to damage him in those years and he has gone on climbing up the ladder or, as Mummy would say, gone from strength to strength. Her presence here is another reason for not inviting him. With her in the flat I can't have him here – he wouldn't come, anyway – and I don't stand a chance of getting into his place. So I have a choice, I can phone him or write to him, and to be perfectly honest (again as Mummy would say) I'm afraid to phone him. I'm afraid of that voice, that accent, on the phone, even supposing he ever answers a phone himself. Even supposing I could get hold of his home number. I have to find out his address somehow and write to him.

But I am altogether afraid of him. Handsome, sophisticated men frighten me. I realize now that they always have and Tesham is the handsomest, most sophisticated man I've ever met. It's humiliating to remember how I had a shower and washed my hair and got dressed up when he came here, though I was determined not to. I started to enjoy it when I could see he was expecting to get the pearls, but that enjoyment was short-lived. Hebe would have said the feelings I have about him are sexual and perhaps they are, but does that mean I'd like to go to bed with him? Suppose I'd had my hair done and I was beautifully made-up as well as witty and sophisticated myself? Suppose I were sitting in a restaurant with him, his fingertips just touching mine across the table? I won't write any more about this in case I start imagining what I'd feel if

I was with him in a bedroom wearing Hebe's dog collar and black leather boots and a black leather corset.

Mummy came here two days ago. She was desperately worried about me, she said. I wasn't answering her letters and I left my phone on message. The only way she knew I was alive was that I was cashing the cheques she sent me. All this I got from a message she left, of course. And when I tried to phone her and tell her not to come, please not to come, she left her phone on message – thus, as she said, hoisting me with my own petard.

On her previous visits, not long after my dad died, she'd wanted to 'see the sights'. London is where she has always lived, yet she's never lived there. You can't call Ongar and Theydon Bois and Havering London, but what else are they? No man's land, outer suburbs, sticks. She's always lived in one or other of them and her London has been 'coming up to town' and shopping in Oxford Street. Until I took her, she hadn't been to the Tower or the National Gallery or Hyde Park. Visiting places by car was all right six or seven years ago – well, it was never really all right for me – but now the traffic is making it impossible. She still wants to, though. Or she says she does. I think trailing about by bus and tube is intended as therapy for me, to bring me 'out of myself', to do what people mean you should when they say you need to get out more.

She's come up here to take me in hand. I'm living like an old retired person, she says, an older and more retired person than even she is. Not that she ever did anything to retire from. She means to stay at least a week, she says. Every evening she takes me out for a meal to some local Italian or Chinese restaurant. This is to save me money and 'give us a chance to talk over a glass of wine'. We have to share a bed, there's no choice about it. Fortunately, it's a wide bed and she sleeps deeply while I lie awake or dream of Sean Lynch coming into the bedroom in his black leather with his German shepherd dog. Mummy doesn't snore or fidget, but she always has to get up at least once in the night to go to the bathroom

– normal, I suppose, in a woman her age. The annoying thing is that she thinks I'm not aware of her creeping about on tiptoe and when I say I am she tells me that I was 'dead to the world'.

When we talk, which is too often to my mind, it's always about my situation and what's to be done. The best plan (her words) is for me to come to Ongar 'on a permanent basis', live with her until part of the house can be converted into a self-contained flat for me and get 'a nice little job' locally.

'I've always believed you have to cut your garment according to your cloth, Jane,' she says. 'It's no good having all these high-flown ideas. It used to upset me thinking of you taking these menial jobs after your education, but I've come down to earth now. There's nothing wrong with working in a shop, it's honourable toil.'

I don't want to scream at her so I say nothing.

'Anything is better than living on the assistance.' She doesn't know it's years since that expression was in use. 'When I was young people would rather starve than be supported by the government.' I wonder where she thinks the government gets the money. Doesn't she know what happens to taxes?

She talks as if she's a hundred and workhouses still exist, instead of only a bit over sixty. But when she says that about the government I smile to myself, because that's just what I mean to do, be supported by at any rate one member of the government. While she drones on about working in a shop in Ongar High Street or being a mother's help ('Goodness knows, you've had the experience, Jane') or a traffic warden, I think about the letter I'm going to write to Ivor Tesham, a very discreet and subtle letter, hinting at connections and links, just mentioning Lloyd Freeman and slipping in Hebe's name. I'll suggest we meet to talk about old times, but first I'll drop the name of a famous journalist who specializes in digging dirt about well-known people and say I know him. I don't, but I easily may do in the future. I have now forced myself to think only about the actions I shall take, not about my feelings and my fears.

Mummy talks about the flat she's planning. I am to have a bedroom, a living room, a kitchen and a bathroom. The house has three floors, the top one being smaller than the lower two, and it's 'absolutely perfect' for conversion. The short landing will become my hallway and all that has to be done is put the front door in at the top of the stairs.

'Are you listening, Jane?'

I tell her that of course I am, though more than half my mind has been on how I'm going to find which house Tesham lives at in Glanvill Street. Perhaps I can take Mummy to see the Houses of Parliament and Big Ben and after I've told her I'm not queuing up to go inside, we could take a little walk along the streets behind Millbank. Maybe go and look at that church they call Queen Anne's Footstool. There's bound to be something on the house or outside the house to show he lives there – but is there? I've seen his car, but that was four years ago and he may have a different one or it may be in a garage. Perhaps either he or Carmen will show themselves at a window. I hope it's not a very long street or we'll be all day about it. And when I say 'we' I have to remember that Mummy knows nothing about this and mustn't know.

'You haven't heard a word from this Stuart,' she says. 'Hasn't he got a phone?'

I have seen Sean Lynch again.

It doesn't really matter because I'm sure he didn't see me. It happened like this. Mummy and I went to Westminster and when we'd been in the Abbey I suggested having a look at St John's Church, Smith Square. Then we went along Great Smith Street and turned down Glanvill Street. It's grand, like everywhere else around there, sombre and ancient and somehow *political*. I wonder how Carmen likes it. Well, I expect I'd like it if living there cost me nothing and I had all found for me. She's not afraid of him. But then she's what men call beautiful and I suppose beautiful women aren't afraid of handsome men. They are theirs by right, only what they deserve. Stu is what I deserve, I suppose.

But we couldn't find Tesham's house. I say 'we', though of course Mummy didn't know what I was looking for. No one looked out of any windows; no one came out of any of the houses. The place was still and quiet and empty but for a ginger cat sitting on top of a pillar and it was as still as everything else in the street, its eyes shut. We went home on a series of buses. Mummy enjoyed it, gazing out of the window at government buildings and shops and theatres and pubs and dirty back streets. Bored by the snail's-pace progress, I pondered ways of getting Tesham's address, ignoring Mummy's proddings and suggestions that I should look at some particular architectural monstrosity or exotic shop-window display. Of course I had already looked for Tesham in the phone book, while knowing he wouldn't yet be there. He wasn't. I'd even thought he might have his phone in Carmen's name, but Case wasn't there either. Wasn't there something called the electoral register? I wondered where such a thing was kept and if the public were allowed to look at it.

The second bus we got on was a mistake. I soon realized it was taking us too far west. I tried to tell Mummy we'd have to get off in a minute and find one going in the Camden Town direction, but she was too absorbed in looking at the Lebanese restaurants in the Edgware Road to take any notice. It was then that, at last obeying her command to 'just look at that one and that woman in a veil', I leaned across her and brought my face to the window. Walking towards the Edgware Road from a side street was Sean Lynch.

I shouldn't have been surprised. He lived just round the corner. Perhaps it was more shock than surprise, as I'd often in the past weeks congratulated myself on the likelihood that I'd never have to set eyes on him again. He was in his black leather gear, just as he'd been when he'd thrown me out of the flat in William Cross Court. Perhaps he always dressed like that, changing only the T-shirt and the jeans. I withdrew my head, sat back, feeling beads of sweat sting my upper lip.

'What's the matter with you, Jane?' At last my mother had taken her eyes off the outside and was peering at me in a concerned and very intrusive way. 'Your hands are shaking. I really wonder sometimes if you're quite well. When did you last see your GP?'

I hadn't a GP. I hadn't registered with one since I left Irving Road. But there was no need to tell her. She'd have gone on about the wonderful medical practice she went to in Ongar and the breathtakingly clever woman doctor who would be 'happy to look after you, Jane' when I came home with her 'in a week or two's time'.

We got off the bus and on to another one. Mummy lost interest in external panoramas and returned to her plans for my future. The wisest thing I could do, she said, was put my flat on the market immediately. If it didn't look like selling in the next fortnight, say, I could leave the keys with the estate agent and move out. She was sure I'd agree with her that I had very little furniture worth worrying about. Why not have one of those firms that clear flats come in and dispose of the lot? With an eye to my consenting to these arrangements, as she'd known I must, she'd set aside a sum of money for furnishing the new flat, just as she'd already spoken to her 'tame builder' about the conversion.

'Are you listening to me, Jane?'

I said I was. It was as if a bit of my mind that dealt with dull and boring things that would never happen anyway had split off from the main part and was replying to her automatically. The rest was making decisions about Ivor Tesham and how I was going to find out about the electoral register – wasn't it also called the voters' list? – and how I could make phone calls without Mummy being there and listening. But that part was preoccupied too with a kind of irrational fear of Sean Lynch. It was some time since I'd been to his flat and been subjected to that horrible treatment but, I told myself, it was a one-off. I'd never go there again. I'd never go near the place. I'd never even use Warwick Avenue tube station. There was nothing to worry about. It was surely just that his manhandling me in that way was something that never happens to people in our society. No one did that sort of thing to a person who had just called at his home and been perfectly polite. That must be why I was so – well, frightened, when I saw him out of the window of that bus. So frightened that my hands had started shaking, the way they had when I went home after that awful encounter. They way they did regularly in my dreams.

It's over, I kept saying to myself, it's over and can never happen again. He doesn't know where you live, there's no way he can know. You never even told his mother your name. He has forgotten all about you. Even if he had looked up and seen you on that bus he wouldn't have recognized you. He doesn't have dreams. Thick, stupid people don't.

Mummy never goes out without me. She says she'd get lost. So I've bought her a small paperback copy of the London A–Z street guide. I'm desperate to get her out of here so that I can make a couple of phone calls. Phoning Westminster Council will be a start, or more than a start, maybe the answer to my problem. But I can't make that call with Mummy there, curious to know why I do everything that I do. She spent last evening reading the A–Z, commenting every few seconds on London districts she'd never heard of or curious street names. Did I think all the Alexandra Roads were named for Princess Alexandra or the late Queen Alexandra? Did I know there was a Fifth Avenue in Kensal Rise, just as there was in New York?

'You'd better get out there and explore,' I said. 'You could go and have a look at this Fifth Avenue – see if it's grand or just ordinary.'

'I'd be nervous, Jane. It's not like Ongar. There's so much crime on the streets.'

Next day it was bright and sunny and I had to pull down the blinds at one of the windows, the light that came flooding in was so glaring. Mummy was up and in the bathroom. I put the coffee on and went downstairs to pick up the post and the paper. *The Times* was there, on the hall table with my name on it, and there was an envelope for me – fairly unusual this. It was from the people who supply me with gas and when I opened it I saw it was a red final notice. I hadn't paid my gas bill.

This is something that never happens to me. However skint I

am, I always pay my services bills, go without decent food and drink if I have to, and I couldn't imagine I'd failed to pay this one. Upstairs again, I went straight to the drawer under the kitchen counter where I put bills and receipts. (Incidentally, it's underneath the one where I keep instructions for using equipment and where I'd put Hebe's pearls – long gone now, of course.) The original gas bill wasn't there. Perhaps they'd never sent it to me. If they had I'd have put it in this drawer. Where else? The flat's so small it hasn't numerous drawers and cubbyholes to store stuff in. I took out the equipment instructions from the top drawer one by one in case I'd put the gas bill in there by mistake.

Mummy came out of the bathroom in her dressing gown while I was hunting for it. Inquisitive as usual, she wanted to know at once what I was looking for. To keep her quiet, I showed her the final notice, but of course it didn't keep her quiet. The advice, the suggestions, the reproofs streamed out of her as she poured coffee and made toast. She always paid her bills on the nail, by return of post actually, but then it was most unwise to put bills away in a drawer. That way they were soon overlooked. It was unimportant now to find the mislaid gas bill. The 'gas people' wouldn't have made a mistake, they didn't in her experience. All I must do was pay the bill now, this morning. Surely I wouldn't have any difficulty in doing so, seeing I had received my 'welfare' the day before, not to mention the cheque she had given me.

'Don't mention it then,' I said, goaded.

'Thank you for that, Jane. I'm well aware gratitude is something you don't begin to understand.'

I'd seriously offended her. It's a funny thing but you can snub people like her, you can ignore them or put them down, but fail to treat them *reverently* in money matters and they're really upset.

'I think I will go out,' she said. 'On my own, I mean. Please don't offer to come with me. I don't want your company just at present, thank you.'

'What about all that crime on the streets?'

'I shall just have to risk it, shan't I?'

For some reason she tied a scarf round her head and, saying like the man who went with Scott of the Antarctic that she might be some time, borrowed one of my umbrellas. There wasn't a cloud in the sky but she took an umbrella. The A–Z was in her bag, as if it was a guide to some foreign city and she a tourist.

Once she'd gone it came to me quite quickly what must have happened to my gas bill. Stu had taken it. He must have opened the drawer while I was on the phone with my back to him. There didn't seem any reason for him to take it except to cause trouble and maybe get my gas cut off. But when I thought about it, I remembered other things that had gone missing from that drawer, including money. Some time before Pandora came to live here, several notes I'd put in an envelope for paying a paper bill unaccountably disappeared. Only it wasn't unaccountable any longer, was it?

I sat down and wrote a cheque for the gas people. Then I wrote to the estate management people, the ones I pay my ground rent to, telling them I wouldn't have their window cleaner in my flat again. But I didn't send it. I started thinking about Stu. I started thinking what would have happened if I'd said all right and gone out for that drink with him. Looking back, I ask myself if any man has actually said those words to me before: you want to come out for a drink? I don't think anyone ever has. But I think, from what I've read and other girls have told me, that this is what men do say. Those are the first words they use when they want to start a *relationship* with you. The two lovers – if you can call them that – that I've had didn't ask me out for a drink. The married one started snogging me – horrible word but expressive of what he did – walking me to the bus stop after I'd been at his house having tea with his wife. I was feeling low after being out somewhere with Hebe when I met the single one on the top of a bus, so low and hopeless that when he wanted to come home with me I said yes. He came 'home with me' a couple more times, but I think that was just out of the kindness of his heart. He was ugly to look at but he had a nice nature.

Stu looked really hard at me, he *stared* at me, when he asked me to go out for a drink. That makes me wonder if he's a bit obsessed with me and he took the gas bill just to find out my name. He wouldn't have known it before, only the number of this flat and that he's supposed to come here once a month. I tear up the letter I've written. Then I have an idea. I pick up the phone, ask the enquiries people for a phone number for Tesham, Glanvill Street, Westminster, and they give it to me. I wait ten minutes and call them again. It's a different voice and this time I give the phone number and ask for Tesham's number in Glanvill Street. They give me that too.

Did I really see Sean Lynch in the street or was it my imagination? I've given him a German shepherd dog but I've never seen it. Perhaps it's not true and there's no dog. It's Callum who had the dog, the mastiff, but it's dead now and Callum is dead. I am looking out of the window but there is no one in the street, no men and no dogs.

25

Mummy has been mugged. She hasn't been hurt, though I expect she would have been if she hadn't given the man her handbag when he asked for it. I think immediately that the man must have been Sean Lynch.

'Was he wearing black leather? Was he a big thick-set man with long yellow hair, dirty hair?'

She clutches my arm. 'You know someone like that? Do you, Jane? You must tell me.'

I tell her his name and where he lives and I would have gone on to the rest of it, I think, but she cut me short. 'It wasn't a man,' she says. 'It was a boy. He was only about sixteen.'

She is so stupid she makes me angry. I wanted to hit her, claw at her the way I did at Pandora. But I turn away while she tells me she actually walked into a police station and told them what had happened. They took details from her and said an officer would come round here later in the day. But they won't catch him, of course they won't. A hundred pounds was in that handbag. I can't help thinking how much better it would have been if she'd given that money to me before she went out. Her Visa card was in there too – I am surprised she had one – and she wants me to ring them and tell them to cancel it and give her a new one, because she doesn't know how to. Can the sixteen-year-old buy a lot of expensive things and empty her bank account? I say, not if we are quick, and I get on the phone straight away.

She will never go out alone in London again, she says. How people can live here with that sort of threat around she doesn't know. I shall have to come with her to buy a new handbag, because the one that was stolen was the only bag she had with her. Then she remembers her keys. They have gone too and she has to phone her neighbour, the fat woman, who has a spare set. Is there any way the boy who took her bag can know the keys open the front and back doors of her house in Ongar?

'Not unless there was something in your bag with your address on it.'

'Let me think,' she says. She remembers the letter from her old schoolfriend in Scotland and not only the letter but also the envelope it came in.

'You'll have to have new locks put on your doors,' I tell her, hoping this will send her home fast.

But her mention of that envelope with her address on it reminds me of my gas bill which Stu must have taken. He knows my address already, though, so he must have taken that bill to have something of mine. No one has ever been in love with me but he might be. There's always a first time. I'm half wishing I hadn't been so hasty in saying no thanks when he asked me to have a drink with him. He's not good-looking but then nor am I. I used to think I was a cut above people like him because of my education and the way I speak. Because I've been to a university and he left school at sixteen. But if I do what Mummy wants, there won't be so much difference, will there, between a shop assistant and a window cleaner?

Only I won't do what she wants. I shall stay here and write to Ivor Tesham and get myself an income to live on comfortably. I have suddenly remembered something I haven't thought of for years. When Hebe had been married a few months she was at home alone in Irving Road and an electrician came round to fix something. She fancied him and he fancied her – well, all men did – and she went to bed with him. I mean they did it. I don't suppose a bed was involved. That makes me think that it wouldn't be all that out of the way for me to get together with Stu. At least I haven't got a husband. My mind might get better if I had a man. I might not have these dreams or say things to make people stare.

The police officer comes round. It is quite late and I am just getting something for our supper, as Mummy refuses to go out again. He repeats what they have said already, that it's not likely they will catch the thief, and adds that we must all be thankful Mrs Atherton wasn't hurt. She tells him about the letter from her friend in Scotland and he says that in that case she must have new locks put on. Then she asks him if he would like a cup of tea. He would.

'I'll just pop into the dining room to fetch the teapot,' she says to give him the impression this is a proper flat instead of a 'studio' with bath.

'Don't go to any trouble,' he says.

She goes into the bathroom and comes out empty-handed, saying the teapot must be in the kitchen after all. How pathetic can you get? Tea is made with teabags in mugs as usual. The policeman drinks his, eats a biscuit and says he'll be off, he'll 'leave you ladies in peace'. He's been gone about five minutes when Mummy says she has decided to go home on Sunday.

She has made such a fuss about having her handbag taken that I do something I meant not to do. I ask her what she would do if she were in my position and had been attacked as I was by Sean Lynch. I tell her all about going there (inventing my reason) and what happened, and in a way it's a relief to talk to someone about it, even to her. As I might have known she would be, she is shocked and horrified.

'London is no place for me, Jane. If I stayed here I'd never have a quiet moment. It's no place for you either. I shall be worried sick till you come. I think we've decided you're coming to live with me, haven't we?'

'*I've* decided I'm *not* coming,' I tell her.

That was yesterday. I was regretting that I told her and she was scolding me for worrying her. We had an argument, nothing unusual for her and me, ending in my going out for a walk on my own. I hadn't realized what a nice day it was. I walked up to West End Green, all the way to Child's Hill and up Pattison Road to the edge of the Heath. It was a Saturday, but even so it seemed to me there were more couples about than usual, people holding hands or walking with their arms round each other. I began to feel calmer and more peaceful (the policeman had said he would leave us in

226

peace) than I had for months, since I was turned out of Irving Road, in fact. And when I was on my way back, heading down the Finchley Road, I saw Stu. He was cleaning the ground-floor windows of a house in Weech Road and when he saw me he raised one hand in a sort of salute. It wasn't a bit like me, I don't do things like that, but I waved back and called out, 'Hi, Stu.'

He gave me a smile in return and shouted that he would see me on Monday. That is when he is next due to clean my windows. I thought, maybe he sleeps with my name and address under his pillow. People do that sort of thing, or some do. Mummy was packing when I got back to the flat. She folds her clothes like shop assistants do and puts sheets of tissue paper between them, shoes wrapped up in tissue and her toilet bag laid on the top. When she saw me she said she would take me out for dinner 'just once more'. Where would I like to go? There isn't all that wide a choice in Kilburn, to say the least, and I reminded her that she had been robbed of all the money she had with her and her credit card. We ended up going to a place in Fortune Green Road with me paying.

'It's the least you can do, Jane, considering I've been practically keeping you for the past year.'

I didn't mind all that much because I kept thinking that by the end of next week I'll be rich. Mummy said her 'dreadful experience' of Friday and being 'interrogated by the police' had worn her out. She went to bed ten minutes after we got back and fell asleep at once. I sat in the kitchen, planning a draft of a letter for Ivor Tesham. Once I have walked Mummy to the tube station in the morning (and bought her ticket and lent her money), I shall copy out what I shall have written neatly in my best handwriting and take it to the post. There's a post that goes on a Sunday at eleven in the morning and I shall aim to catch it, so he will get the letter on Monday. The hard part was deciding what to say. I thought I could just write baldly to him, tell him I knew exactly what he had done on 18 May 1990, and if he wanted it all kept dark, the way he has been keeping it dark for four years, he will have to pay me. But

I had to find the words and every word I thought of sounded so vulgar and low, the kind of words Hebe might have used but I couldn't. Yet my future depended on it. Well, on him or on Stu. Or both of them. I wish I could sometimes have nice dreams and then I do, a waking dream of me living with Stu and telling him I've got a private income. He doesn't even have to go on cleaning windows if he doesn't want to.

I stopped there and gave myself to the dream, sometimes glancing at Mummy fast asleep. I have just started again. My writing paper and envelopes and a couple of ballpoints I keep in the drawer under the one where all the bills and receipts are. I was getting out a sheet of paper and a pen when my mind rushed back to that day when I went to the Lynchs' and it all flashed before my eyes, the way they say it does when you're drowning. I felt like I was drowning, because I have remembered what happened to my gas bill. Stu hadn't taken it. The idea that he might have was stupid from the start – more signs of my mind not being quite right.

I had put the bill in my bag when I went to William Cross Court. That bill and the stuff which came with it were the papers I had taken out of my bag to glance at while I was pretending to be a social worker. Sean Lynch had snatched them out of my hand and thrown them on the floor. Maybe he hadn't looked at them again. They might have ended up in a waste bin. But I couldn't believe that. He would have looked at them and read my name and my address. He had my name and address. It was like one of those anonymous phone calls people get where the caller says, 'We know where you live.' Sean Lynch knew where I lived.

I could write in the diary but I couldn't write the letter. After staring at the blank paper like they say authors do when they've got writer's block, I went to the window and looked down, expecting to see Sean Lynch standing there under the street lamp, his head lifted and his eyes on the top floor of this house. No one was there but that didn't mean he hadn't been there earlier. Ought I to go to the police about him? If I had known about the gas bill earlier I would have said something about Sean to the officer who came. If I had he might have been arrested by now and locked up and not be out there, thinking up ways to get himself into this flat.

You would think he'd hate Tesham after he caused Dermot to be what he is now, but I don't think he hates him. His mother certainly doesn't. 'Mr Tesham's been very good to us,' is what she said. Tesham must be giving them money. So did Sean attack me because he sees me as Tesham's enemy? Would he *protect* him? And what does that say about my future once I've written this letter to Tesham and maybe he tells Sean? Another thing I've thought of – Sean didn't need the gas bill. Tesham could have told him where I live.

I don't know what to do. Now, at that moment, the only thing seemed to be to go to bed, not that I thought I would sleep. I did, though, and dreamed I was back in William Cross Court, but this time Sean was reading the name and address on my gas bill and I was trembling in fear. He seized me – as he always does, over and over – and pushed me at the wall, beating my head against the bleeding heart of Jesus. Something in his face tells me he means to rape me and I screamed. I really did scream aloud, waking Mummy, who sat up, put the light on and felt my wet nightdress and took hold of my shaking hands.

'The first thing I'll do when I get you to Ongar,' she said, 'is take you to my lovely GP.'

It was better in the morning but I still don't know what to do. I need someone to protect me and I begin to wonder if Stu would protect me. If we were going out together he would look after me and if he heard there was some man intent on doing me harm he would do harm to *him* before he got the chance. He belongs to the class of people who think that way. When I see him next, which will be tomorrow, I shall be very nice to him and then I'll ask him if that offer of a drink still holds good. He will say it does and soon we shall be going out together; we shall be an item. Thinking like this makes me feel better still and I'm wondering how it will be when I've got a man of my own. Quite different from anything that has ever been, I suppose.

I would really rather not go out at all today but I shall have to take Mummy to West Hampstead tube station. Not Kilburn, because it's rougher that way and I connect rough areas with Sean Lynch. Mummy and I hug and kiss in the station entrance, something we haven't done for years, and she says we must keep in touch every day and that she will expect me in Ongar in a week's time 'at the latest'.

The walk home on my own was rather scary. Everywhere is quiet on a Sunday morning and deserted streets always make you more nervous than when there are a lot of people about. I could hear a single set of footfalls behind me and I crossed the road, but when I looked back it was an old man wearing a hat and carrying an umbrella. Still, it was a relief to reach the house and get inside my flat. Being alone again is all right too.

But I am left with my ongoing problem. I had begun looking on my approach to Ivor Tesham rather like an application for a job. There would be the application to make, then the interview with the employer and after that his acceptance of me on his staff. A staff which perhaps included all those Lynchs and even Carmen, who used to be with Lloyd Freeman. Now I had to rethink this 'job'. I still wanted it, of course; I had to have it. It was my only hope, but I had to find a different approach if I wasn't to become the victim of a particular member of that staff.

One thing is plain. I can't write my letter today. I have to wait until that other side of my life is cleared up, until I know that I am no longer alone. I once read somewhere that twice one is not two, twice one is two thousand times two, and that this is why the world will always return to monogamy. That means it's always best to be in a partnership – for protection and company. I wonder if people ever go mad when they have got someone to be with; I don't think they do.

While Mummy was here I have been putting the diary in the shoebox under the floorboard. Force of habit makes me go on doing that. I thought of putting Hebe's things there too, but they may as well stay where they are, in the case I bought specially for them inside the cupboard.

I am spending a long time this evening looking at myself in the mirror and I think I can see now what it was that made Stu fall in love with me. All the time Mummy was here I couldn't put on Hebe's clothes, but now I get them out of the cupboard and start dressing myself in them, the black underwear, the boots, the dog collar. When I imagine Stu seeing me in them I feel excited but calm too and in peace, the way the policeman promised.

26

On my way to the tube at Mansion House, I bought the *Evening Standard* at the station entrance but I did no more than glance at the headline. Another murder was what registered with me, a woman in Kilburn this time. I'd got a seat and found myself next to a City acquaintance, someone I'd got to know quite well over the years, and we talked until he got out at Temple. It was several weeks since I'd seen Ivor. He'd called my office earlier and left a message for me, one of those bland messages which nevertheless seem to carry with them an undercurrent of urgency. Drinking with Ivor, or occasionally watching Ivor drink, was a commonplace in my life but this time I had a slight sense of foreboding. I got out of the train at Westminster, leaving the *Standard*, which might have told me what I should be worrying about, on the seat beside me.

He took me into the Pugin Room, a crowded place which is really just inside the Lords and which peers say the Commons stole from them about a hundred years ago and refuse to give back. Ivor got a table at the back overlooking the river, in spite of pretending to despise the view, which he said was all right if you like looking at St Thomas's Hospital, where parliamentarians go to die. The river was rolling along at a swift pace, black, glittering and choppy. It was cold out there and looked it. I said I'd have claret but Ivor didn't hesitate before ordering a double Scotch for himself.

'I shouldn't,' he said, 'but I need it.'

I asked him what was wrong.

'Have you seen the news or a paper?'

'I left my *Standard* in the train,' I said.

'You didn't recognize the murdered girl's name?'

I said I hadn't read it. These things were too horrible to dwell on.

Ivor looked round in a hunted way. He dropped his voice. 'The murdered girl is Jane Atherton. She was Hebe's friend. I used to call her the alibi lady.'

There was nothing to say.

'I'll get you the paper.'

He soon came back with it. Jane Atherton's body had been found in her own flat by her mother. Though they had made an arrangement to keep in touch every day, the mother hadn't heard from Jane since she left her the previous Sunday. Getting no reply to her phone calls and by then very anxious, she had come back to London on the Wednesday and got the police to force a way into the flat. Jane was lying on her bed with a knife in her back. She had been raped.

'It's disturbed me a bit, Rob.'

I thought for a moment – a very short moment – that he meant it had distressed him. She was a woman, she had met a dreadful death, she was only thirty-something. I should have known him better.

'I mean, has her death any connection with me? Anything to do with what happened to Hebe? I can't really see why it should have, but naturally I can't help being a bit disquieted. These things have a motive, don't they? Some thug doesn't just come up to a woman at random and bash her over the head. Or does he?'

It's fear of being a prig, being *seen* to be a prig, that stops a lot of us taking a moral stand. People haven't always been like this. Until well into the twentieth century men at least seemed to have no objection to telling a friend that he was a cad who infringed some unwritten code. But it's all gone now and though I told myself that was nearly the breaking-up-with-Ivor point for me, I said and did nothing. I might have thought of getting to my feet, saying that I couldn't stand any more of this and walking out, but I didn't. After all, I'd been there before. Several times. Besides, I wasn't sure if I could find my way out of the labyrinth which is the Palace of Westminster. I sat there very still and kept quiet. If he noticed he gave no sign of it.

'Unreasonable of me to think the way I'm thinking.'

I said in a tone I hoped was chilly but probably wasn't, 'Which way are you thinking?'

Ivor made a face. The room was full now, everyone talking at the tops of their voices. He edged his chair nearer mine. 'Well, if she told people about it. I mean friends of hers who were also friends of Hebe's. It's quite likely she did. She wouldn't have kept that to herself, but of course she didn't know that much. Be that as it may, Rob, and to be absolutely frank with you, what's worrying me is that the police may want to talk to me.'

I asked him why. Why would they?

'Look at it this way. They'll talk to her friends. They may talk to Gerry Furnal, he of the pearls, right? They'll certainly talk to her mother. Her mother found the body. If she was close to her mother, she'll have told her about me and Hebe.'

'It's four years ago,' I said. They'd have had better, more topical and pressing things to talk about. 'People in your sort of situation get paranoid. You're paranoid. Do you really think a woman whose daughter's been raped and stabbed to death is going to tell the police that she supplied an alibi to a friend who's been dead for four years? She's going to tell them that this friend was having an affair with you? And suppose she does – are they going to think you had a motive for *killing* her? Come on, Ivor.'

'Keep your voice down,' he said, very nervous. 'I didn't mean that – well, maybe I did. I just don't like any of it. Oh, God, there's a division. Don't go. I'll come back.'

The green bell had come up on the screen. Here, on the threshold of both Houses, the Commons division bell and the Lords division bell were equally audible. Those of us not summoned were left behind. Looking out at the black water, the lights, the disturbed curdy sky, I asked myself what was the worst that could happen and came up with nothing much. Jane Atherton's mother wouldn't blacken her dead daughter's name by telling anyone, let alone the police, that she supplied an alibi to help a friend commit adultery. In spite of this, if the police found out that Jane had once had a friend who was involved *four years ago* with a Conservative MP . . .

But no, it was too absurd to consider, too far-fetched, too much the product of what had become a neurosis.

'When you hear the division bell,' I said when Ivor came back, 'do you still think of the first time you saw Hebe?'

Once before he'd told me that ringing reminded him of her. He stared. 'That's not at all the sort of question I'd expect you to ask. It's not actually a man's question at all. Now if Iris had asked it . . .'

'Do you?'

'Rob, just think about it. How many times have I gone into the division lobby in the past four years? It wouldn't be possible. It wouldn't be in human nature. I was crazy about Hebe, as you know, but even so . . .'

'Don't worry about Jane Atherton,' I said. 'You won't hear any more about it.'

And for a while he didn't.

Five parliamentary by-elections back in June and simultaneous elections to the European Parliament had illustrated (I'm quoting a left-wing newspaper) the level of unpopularity of the Conservative government. The Liberal Democrats won in Eastleigh by more than nine thousand votes over Labour, with the Conservatives in third place. Bradford South and Barking were both held by Labour with much increased majorities, the Conservatives again in third place. On the crest of this wave, that autumn Aaron Hunter made a widely publicized speech at a Lib Dem rally in Imberwell, a most unusual thing for an Independent candidate to do.

He lashed out at sleaze, having, I suppose, its latest perpetrator or victim, an air marshal with an unsuitable girlfriend, in mind, but referring to people in public office generally and to Tory MPs in particular. There was the one who had committed perjury and the one who had committed adultery *and* perjury and another who had accidentally hanged himself during some masturbatory activity. He harked back to orgiastic house parties of thirty years before and pinpointed a three-in-a-bed drama of recent months. His tone throughout was sanctimonious. It's my contention that all political parties have their sleaziness. With the left-wing, Labour or Liberal, it's mostly versions of fraud, while with the Conservatives it's sex. Once, when I put this theory to Ivor, he laughed and said he knew which kind he'd prefer, and most sensible people would agree with him.

What view he took of Hunter's speech I don't know. We never discussed it. His view of the man was basically that politics was for professionals and those who had been trained in other disciplines shouldn't dabble in it, though where the dividing line between the amateur and people like himself came, he didn't say. One thing I was pleased to hear from him was that he and Juliet had 'phased out' (his phrase) their visits to the Lynchs.

'The difficulty,' he said to me, 'is the class difference. Always was, I suppose. I've pretended to myself that I can transcend all that, even that they enjoy my company and, God help us, I enjoy theirs. But it isn't so. They're not comfortable with me. I'm not comfortable with them. I can't take Sean's girlfriend calling me "Ive". It's a bit easier for Juliet, they get on better there.'

He paused. I thought for one uneasy moment that he was going to hint that Juliet was several rungs lower down the class ladder than he was, but he didn't. Maybe he recognized the danger in time and restrained himself.

'But the upshot of it is that we've had to put the brakes on.' Along with his increased pomposity, my brother-in-law had taken on a good many politician's clichés since he became a minister. 'I've had to face the fact that the important factor for them in our relationship, such as it was, is that I'm the source of a considerable chunk of their income. And why not? This way it's a good deal easier all round. It's no use thinking we can have a level playing field because we can't.'

I've no idea if Ivor was the first to use that particular metaphor but he was certainly one of the first. He may have invented it. I'm sure that was the first time I'd heard anyone say it, though now of course it seems to have become accepted politics-speak. No major speech can afford to be without it. But Iris and I were glad of the break with the Lynchs and told each other so, Iris adding that her brother seemed to be showing some sense at last. We were speaking too soon. Ivor's mistake was not so much that he had made contact with the whole Lynch family or that he had given them money, but rather that he had ever known them in the first place – that he had ever asked the man who serviced his car to drive the Mercedes that picked up Hebe.

It was a while before we experienced a déjà vu feeling. Newspapers almost weekly carry a paragraph saying that a man (a nameless man at that stage) is helping the police with their enquiries. We noted what the rest of the country did, that someone had been found for the murder of Jane Atherton. The poor girl with the frizzy hair, the girl lying on her own bed in her own blood. What the newspapers seldom tell you is that the police have let this particular nameless man go home because he is the wrong man.

This one, however, looked like the right man and he hadn't gone home. Not like he had once before, when suspected of IRA affiliations, which was where our we-have-been-here-before came in. His name was Sean Lynch and he'd been charged with Jane Atherton's murder.

27

We never knew how the connection was made, only possible ways in which it might have come about. But next day one single newspaper carried a short and apparently innocuous note: the arrested man was the elder brother of Dermot Lynch, driver of a kidnap car involved in a crash four years ago, in which two people had died. Now, once a man has appeared in court and been charged with an offence, the media are supposed to keep silent about him. His past, his antecedents, his family history, all this must not be touched upon in case public prejudice is created; it is from this public that a jury will later be drawn.

Mostly they don't touch upon it, but there are exceptions, which usually give rise to rebuke or even threats from the judiciary. Revealing these facts about Dermot Lynch (who had never been tried for anything, let alone kidnapping) was a breach of this rule but nothing was ever done about it. In the normal course of things, Ivor would see several daily newspapers every morning but not, I thought, that day. He had told me on the phone the evening before that he would be flying to Culdrose in Cornwall 'at the crack of dawn'. There's an RAF helicopter base at Culdrose and he was going there to view something or inspect something.

At the present day you can get hold of anyone anywhere and at any time. Everyone carries a mobile phone. Apparently, there are more mobiles in this country than people. There weren't thirteen years ago. I hadn't got one and Iris hadn't. Poor Jane Atherton had one but only for use in her car. Ivor had shown me his but I didn't know the number and doubted if anyone at the department would give it to me. Also, phoning him while at an important visit that was part of his job wasn't the way I'd choose to break this news to him.

Instead, I phoned Juliet.

*

Before I did so I realized something which was always slipping my mind, that Ivor's fiancée knew as much about events of May 1990 as we did, probably as much as Ivor himself did. Nothing need be kept dark from her. There was no need for even ordinary discretion.

She hadn't seen the paper but as soon as I read it out to her she said she'd come. No, we needn't arrange to meet somewhere, she'd come. She'd like an excuse to see the children. She arrived in Ivor's car, the big BMW. I don't know why, but if anyone had asked me or I'd asked myself I'd have said she was that rare creature, the person who can't drive. It's an absurd thing to say, and probably sexist too, but I'd seen her as ultra-feminine, too feminine to be a driver. Of course I was wrong. She steered the rather macho, cumbersome car between our gateposts with panache. Each time I saw her I'd forgotten how beautiful she was. The legs, which were the first thing about her to attract Ivor, descended from the driving seat in that most elegant way a woman can alight from a car, moving her body to the right in her seat and, with knees pressed together, setting both feet on the ground. It was autumn and she wore a black and white figured skirt with a pure white cardigan. I wondered if I had ever seen a lovelier woman, her black hair cut to fall just below her ears, a fringe coming to just above her eyebrows, her lips painted a deep pink and parting then in a wide smile. It's strange how I could admit her transcendent beauty and yet at the same know that I found my own wife far more attractive. Just as well, I suppose.

She had stopped on her way to buy the paper in question and read the paragraph. 'He'll read it some time today, you know. He's bound to. You think I ought to phone him, don't you?'

'I don't know, Juliet. I just think we all ought to be prepared for him to be in a state about this. It's going to be a blow to him.'

Iris came in then with Joe in her arms. He was trying to walk by this time, though in his case walking meant getting into everything, pulling everything down from its appointed place and generally making mayhem. Another man, if a little one, to be drawn to her beauty, he came over when she called him and sat on her knee. Iris had told me of Juliet's love for children but I'd never before seen it for myself quite as I did that day. I'd never before seen in her that characteristic of the woman who knows what children want, the bestowing on them of undivided absorbed attention. Nothing, not even Ivor's interests, would have distracted her from Joe, but within seconds he had found her handbag and begun trying to open it. Iris, of course, intervened, feebly expostulating, but Juliet wasn't having that. The handbag was opened, placed on the floor and abandoned to Joe's excavations.

'What do you think will happen?' Juliet said.

'Let's hope nothing. If the media find out that Sean was questioned four years ago about Sandy Caxton's murder, they can't use it. But they know that. The trouble is that I can't see any reason why they shouldn't go back into their archives and resuscitate the kidnap story.'

'Because that would be about Dermot and not about Sean?'

'That's right. But I do think the chances are they'd concentrate on a kidnap attempt on Kelly Mason rather than on Hebe Furnal. It's never been finally established which woman it was they meant to abduct, or whether it was a real kidnap or a joke. And remember, no one has connected Hebe with Ivor. Ivor hasn't been mentioned. There have been stories about Kelly Mason in the papers, that she was in a psychiatric hospital on some remote island, and there was an interview with her husband saying she hadn't been well since all those threats were made. He meant she hadn't been sane.'

'You mean they're more likely to concentrate on her,' Iris said, 'than on Hebe because the poor woman's gone bonkers? What utter shits they are.'

'Maybe, but that's how I think it would be.'

Nadine was at her infant school but Adam marched in then and, seeing his brother intent on removing notes, change and credit cards from Juliet's purse, snatched it from him, grabbing the handbag with his other hand. Screams and bellows followed from Joe, triumphant laughter from Adam, admonitions from Iris, until peace was restored by Juliet's producing from the plastic bag the newspaper was in a writing pad and case of coloured pencils. In spite of having several sets of pencils and infinite sheets of paper already, Adam fell on this gift with enthusiasm, while abandoning the handbag to Joe.

'You're really good with kids,' Iris said.

'If I am I expect it's because I like them.' Juliet smiled. It was always, I'd noticed, a rather shy smile for so beautiful a woman. One expected enormous self-confidence and got diffidence instead. 'Please don't say I ought to have some of my own,' she said. 'I know it. I'd love to.'

Iris is notoriously outspoken. I was afraid for a moment she might ask Juliet why she didn't have some of her own, but she didn't, said only that she'd go and make coffee. Like me, she knew the answer. Ivor wouldn't want to be a father without being married first. He was a Conservative and a landowner. He must have been one of the few people left even then who still referred to children whose parents weren't married as 'illegitimate'.

'So you think that may be the end of it?' Juliet said.

'Well, I do.' I'm not sure that I did. I was trying to comfort her, though I needed comfort myself. 'As I say, they can't publish anything about Sean's past, whether he has any convictions or things like that. There's no apparent link with Ivor in any of this.'

'I can't believe Sean would kill anyone. Why would he?'

I said I didn't know the man. I couldn't say. But I remembered his thuggish looks from Ivor's party, the brutality in his face, and I wasn't so sure.

'The difficulty is that Ivor is the link between Jane Atherton and Sean Lynch. Any possibility that Sean's some sort of psychopath who raped and killed a woman he saw in the street and followed home isn't on, is it? It would be too much of a coincidence.'

'Are you saying Sean killed her to *protect* Ivor?'

'I don't know. Did she threaten him in any way? If she did, he said nothing to us about it.'

'Nor to me,' Juliet said. 'I'm sure she didn't. But Sean – I know this sounds an exaggeration but it's not – Sean *loves* Ivor. I don't mean he just likes him or looks up to him. He said so to me once. "I really love that man," he said. He loves him, he worships him. It's not too much to say he'd do anything for him.'

'Well, I hope to God he hasn't.'

'People do love him, don't they? Dermot did in his way. The way Ivor talks about him, I'd say Sandy Caxton loved him too. I do. I do love him so much.' She looked at me and this time there was no smile, diffident or otherwise. The beautiful mouth trembled and she began to cry.

Iris had just come in with the coffee. She put the tray down, went to Juliet and threw her arms round her. 'Don't cry, darling, please don't. It'll be all right. It'll blow over. You'll see.'

'I don't see how it can.'

I was thinking, though I didn't say it aloud, that even if it blew over at the present time, when Sean came up for trial – nine months, ten, perhaps a year away – the man's motive must come out and there could be no other motive, it appeared, but saving Ivor from Jane Atherton's malice or greed. Or desperation or need, if I am to be fair.

'He'll be home by seven,' Juliet said. 'He's bound to know by then.' Neither of us had asked, it would have been too much of an intrusion, but it was as if we had. 'It sounds silly but it was love at first sight for me. The first time I saw him I thought, I want to marry that man. Well, not the first time, that was at a party, but the second. Whatever happens I'll never leave him. If he wants to get rid of me he'll have to throw me out.'

'He won't do that,' I said, though I was by no means sure he wouldn't. 'Get him to give us a ring when he comes in.' We kissed her and Iris hugged her, holding her tightly for a moment. We had our answer to the question we'd so often asked. Why? What was in it for her? Not for unspoken blackmail, not for a gourmet meal ticket, but love, just love.

'I was wrong,' Iris said when she'd gone, 'about her being unfaithful, wasn't I?'

*

Ivor didn't phone us that evening, though he knew. He'd seen the relevant newspaper in the plane on the return flight and there were a few lines in the evening paper, rather cunning subtle lines. They said only that Dermot Lynch, driver of 'a kidnap car' in which the intended victim had been Kelly Mason, having been in a 'protracted coma' for a long time, had made a partial recovery. (As if kidnap, crash and recovery were all recent history.) Juliet told us about it next morning. She called us after Ivor had gone in to the department. They had both also read the follow-up story in the right-wing daily newspaper Ivor had delivered.

This was just an account of Sean Lynch's arrest and his appearance in the magistrates' court, where he had pleaded not guilty to the charge of wilful murder. There had been, of course, nothing about what led the police to him and no details about him except that he was thirty-three years old (the heavenly number) and lived in Paddington, west London. But at the foot of this brief account of the proceedings, there appeared once again the two lines about Dermot, his involvement in a suspected kidnap attempt, his long period of unconsciousness and his 'limited recovery'. Not a word about any relationship between the two men, nothing to show they had an address in common.

'How is Ivor taking it?'

'All right. Not bad. He's tough, you know, Rob. He keeps saying, "There's no mention of me. They haven't made the connection and with luck they won't." He's got a statement to deliver to the House this afternoon and he'll do it. He won't only do it, he'll do it as if he hadn't got a care in the world.'

But I think he was already making preparations for the action he meant to take. If things got worse, that is, if the connection was made between himself and what three newspapers had called 'the kidnap car' and therefore between him and Sean Lynch. I don't mean he was resigned to his name coming into this; not at all, that mustn't be thought of. He hoped with all his strength that the media would stop there. What would happen when Sean came up for trial was a long way off; all sorts of things could happen between now and then. He had to think of the immediate future, the next few days in fact. He told us all this when the four of us met in the evening of the day after he came back from Culdrose.

He was an optimist, he always was, but a fatalist too, and I could hear it in his voice and, if it doesn't sound too melodramatic, see it in his eyes. It was a kind of foretaste of despair. Things which he had thought – had hoped – had passed away, buried themselves, had only been waiting before they were resurrected. Iris, who is the literary one of us, said it reminded her of a line from *Lear*: 'The gods are just and of our pleasant vices make instruments to plague us.' Well, Ivor had had his pleasant vices all right, but he really thought by now that he had got away from the wrath of the gods.

'If nothing more has happened by the end of the weekend,' he said across the dinner table, 'I've probably got away with it again. It's a funny thing,' he went on, 'but when I read that bit in the paper on the flight home last night I had that ghastly feeling of something falling out of me. As one does. Like being in a lift when it comes to a stop too fast. And then this morning I read it again and I was used to it. I could take it. It didn't seem so bad. And tonight's *Standard* – well, there it is again, with a quote from that guy Mason and a photograph of the car after it crashed, and all I thought was, what was I making such a fuss about on the plane last night? You get used to things. I suppose you can get used to anything.'

'Oh, darling.' Juliet took his hand in both hers. 'Nothing more will happen. You won't have to get used to it. I'm sure it's over.'

He wasn't sure and I doubt if she was either. When we say we're sure, we mean we doubt but we're hopeful. A look of grimness, of dark resolution, had come into his face and, with hindsight of course, I think, as I've said before, that he was making up his mind then what he would do. We said goodnight early. They went back to Westminster and we to our Barnet–Hertfordshire borders, where all three children had, for reasons best known to themselves, been giving my mother a hard time.

I don't know what Ivor and Juliet talked about that night, though it's hard to imagine it could have been anything very different from what we'd discussed over dinner. Iris and I lay awake a long time, trying to guess what the media's next move would be. Both of us thought that, having talked to Damian Mason, they would be naturally led to Gerry Furnal; much hung on what Furnal might disclose to them. Would he say anything? He never had, but that was before the pearls and his discovery that the wife he revered had had a lover. It really depended on whether Furnal wanted to expose himself as a cuckold (to use Ivor's word) and whether in fact he'd be audacious enough to make accusations against a Minister of the Crown. Iris was positive he would. I was more doubtful. He of all the people involved in this business must know the most.

'If he'll stand up to my brother in a crowded room at a party and practically chuck his present in his face,' Iris said, 'he'll have nerve enough for anything. He may want revenge. He may want more satisfaction than he got from giving back the pearls. And what's a Minister of the Crown these days? It's not the eighteenth century.'

Neither of us foresaw the direction from which discovery would come and I'm sure Ivor and Juliet didn't. Philomena Lynch perhaps or Gerry Furnal's wife, some witness to the pearls incident or Jane Atherton's mother – we thought of all those. The pathway which led one astute investigative journalist to Ivor never crossed our imaginations. We didn't know all the people; we didn't know the host of minor characters on the perimeter. It couldn't have crossed Ivor's mind either as he lay sleepless at Juliet's side through the long watches of the night.

28

Nothing happened for a while, not for several days. The first story about Dermot Lynch had appeared on the Thursday morning, the day Ivor went to Culdrose, and we had all dined together on the Friday evening. Saturday's papers were empty of all references to Jane Atherton's murder or to Sean Lynch, and so were Sunday's – those Sunday papers, the cradles of scandal. For Ivor, waiting and dreading and hoping, it must have been rather like the days after the crash, when he waited and hoped Dermot would never regain consciousness. Worse now, though. Accumulations had happened since then. He had advanced up the ladder, he had inherited money, bought a glamorous house, acquired a beautiful fiancée, made numerous successful speeches, even come to the edge of (I repeat again my wife's quotation) 'the fierce light that beats upon the high shore of the world'. It would be immeasurably worse for him now. But nothing happened. Not yet.

The journalist who brought things to light was a man called David Menhellion. Iris says it's a Cornish name. In the first piece he wrote, he remarked on the fact that Juliet Case, 35, fiancée of Ivor Tesham, MP for Morningford and a Minister of State at the Department of Defence, had once been the 'live-in girlfriend' of actor Lloyd Freeman, killed in an accident to the 'vehicle in which he was "allegedly" attempting to abduct Kelly Mason and demand a ransom from her husband, multi-millionaire Damian Mason'. You can't libel the dead, of course, so Menhellion was in the clear there. Dermot was mentioned only as the driver of the kidnap car. But all this was known already. When she first became engaged to him, Juliet had herself said in an interview that she had once been married to Aaron Hunter and later had a relationship with Lloyd Freeman.

She and Ivor had met through a mutual friend, the actress Nicola Ross. Very little comment had ever been made on this disclosure, but Menhellion made as much of it as he could. Had Mr Tesham perhaps known Lloyd Freeman himself? If he had, hadn't he some questions to answer? It would be unusual, to say the least, ought to be impossible, for a member of the government to have a friendship with a kidnapper and one who was very likely also the author of demands for money with menaces made to Mr Mason.

When I'd read this through twice I thought that on the whole it was pretty thin. It was scandal-sheet stuff. A rational reader would soon see that Ivor might well have known Lloyd Freeman as an actor only and have first encountered him in Juliet's company. Nor did it much worry Ivor.

'All that's already in the public domain,' was the way he put it, in the politician-speak he used when he was disturbed.

Next day, though, none of us could remain unconcerned. Menhellion's story, a lead in a tabloid, looked at first like a simple follow-up of the previous day's delving into Juliet's past. There was nothing new in the first three paragraphs. Then he asked his first rhetorical question: what was Ivor Tesham, Minister of State at the Defence Department, doing while his present-day fiancée was sharing her Queen's Park 'apartment' with her live-in lover Lloyd Freeman? Involved, Menhellion said, in a 'steamy' love affair with none other than Hebe Furnal, 27. Hebe had died in the kidnap car crash along with Lloyd Freeman.

I spoke to Ivor on the phone ten minutes after I read that. He was calm but very quiet.

'We've already had them phoning,' he said.

'What, journalists?'

'Someone called. I mean, not the American "called", came to the door. I slammed the door on him.'

'Will you go in?'

'To the department? Yes, of course. I must. Look, can Juliet come up to you? I don't want to leave her alone here. They're bound to come. That's for sure. I could get her out the back way before I have to go.'

I had an appointment. I was due to pay another visit to that client in Blomfield Road, Maida Vale. The last time I'd been there was when I saw Ivor and Juliet heading for Warwick Avenue tube station after they'd been to see the Lynchs in William Cross Court. They should never have gone near the place but I wouldn't allow myself, even to myself, to say I told you so.

Juliet spent the day with Iris and the children and was still there when I got home. She'd spoken to Ivor several times on the phone, but the last time she'd tried he was in the House of Commons with his mobile switched off. I'd brought the evening paper in with me and, as we'd all expected, they were carrying a portrait photograph of Hebe and the windblown one of her with Justin, both of them alongside Juliet in extravagant eighteenth-century comedy clothes. She looked about twenty.

I asked her where they got that from.

'I had a part in *The School for Scandal*. Apt, isn't it? I'd guess Aaron gave it to them.'

'Would he do that? I thought you and he were on good terms.'

'He hates this government. It's not Ivor in particular. He'd do the same if it was anyone in the government. It's all part of this anti-sleaze campaign of his.'

There had been nothing about Juliet's marriage to Hunter in the morning papers but there was by the evening. Apparently with enthusiasm, he had given them an interview as well as the photograph. Yes, he knew Ivor Tesham, he'd met him on several occasions. Lloyd Freeman too. He wasn't prepared to say (he said) that he and Juliet had been divorced on Freeman's account, there were many factors which led to their break-up, but Freeman had certainly 'appeared on the scene' very soon after their decree became absolute. He had moved in with her at her home in Queen's Park. Whether they were still together when the kidnap attempt was made in May 1990, he wouldn't care to say.

A double-page spread, sprinkled with photographs, was devoted to a biography of Hebe. As is usually the way with beautiful women, she had often had her picture taken. There was a wedding photograph, Hebe in clouds of white clinging to Gerry Furnal's arm. There was a postnatal photograph, Hebe in bed with her baby in her arms, and another of her in a black dress with pearls.

'*The* pearls, I suppose,' Iris said. 'Surely Gerry Furnal didn't give them those pictures. Surely he wouldn't, not her husband.'

'Come to that, who gave them the story? Who told them all that stuff?'

I drove Juliet home at about six. I was crawling slowly along through Westminster when we saw the crowd ahead of us. It was their spilling over into Marsham Street which was causing the traffic hold-up. We passed Ivor's house, necessarily slowly, and Juliet turned her head to look at them, the press pack, the media with movie cameras, the photographers. The house faced directly on to the street, with short pillars linked by a chain rather than a front garden separating it from the roadway. The reporters were inside the chain, pressed against the front wall and downstairs windows. They left only half the roadway accessible to traffic and one of them was sitting on top of a van illicitly standing on the yellow line.

'I can't go in there, Rob,' Juliet said in an unnaturally high voice.

I turned down the next street on the left, came out on to Millbank and found a place to park on the Embankment. She would have to come back with me, I said, and we'd better get hold of Ivor too. Would he be there for the evening vote? She said she was sure he would be. In the bar, probably. Her gentle, loving tone took away any sting there might have been.

'It must have been like this for Gerry Furnal,' she said, 'before they thought it was Kelly Mason that Lloyd and Dermot were after. I mean, the media outside like that, persecuting him.'

She had a mobile phone with her and from the car she called the Commons and left a message for Ivor to phone her urgently. He phoned and he turned up at our house at about eight, having taken a taxi all the way. The children, especially Nadine, enjoy having people to stay and were all over Juliet. Much as I love my daughter and my sons, I know this kind of attention can be irritating when you're anxious about something quite other, but Juliet was perfect. She behaved with them as if there was nothing she would like better than conversing with them to the exclusion of everyone else until bedtime came. Nadine insisted on taking her upstairs to see the bedroom where she and Ivor would sleep, instructing her in things she undoubtedly already knew, like how to turn on the bed lamps and which tap the hot water came out of.

Ivor and I went into the study, taking our drinks and the bottle with us. It's not really a study, at least in the sense that Iris and I do any studying in it or any work at all, but it's a quiet haven with appropriate leather armchairs and a desk of sorts, and the children aren't allowed beyond the doorway.

'No one's said a word to me in the House.'

'It's been more about Juliet than you,' I said. 'It's been more about Hebe.'

'So far. My biography will start tomorrow. We'll have to go home; there's no escape. We'll just brave those people and that's all there is to it.'

'Just out of interest, why did you get to know the Lynchs? You've never really told me.'

'Dermot – he was on my conscience. As soon as I knew he was going to survive. You didn't think I'd got a conscience, did you, Rob?'

That's not the sort of question I ever answer. 'Now tell me why *really*?'

He laughed. It wasn't much of a laugh, more a dry sort of barking sound. He closed his eyes for a moment and when he opened them he smiled. 'I wanted to know what sort of a state he was in, whether he could ever tell the police that I was the "mastermind" they were looking for. By the time I knew he couldn't I'd met Sean and his old mum, I was going to give them money and it was too fucking late.'

'There was a bit of conscience in it, then,' I said.

At that point he said something which may have been original, though it sounded like a quote: 'When a politician becomes "the story" he's no longer any use in politics.'

Ivor ordered a taxi and the two of them went back to Glanvill Street at six in the morning. The press weren't there but they had turned up by seven. They mobbed Ivor when at last he came out and made Juliet cry when she appeared at a window. She thought they were going to break the window, but they didn't; they took photographs of her through the glass.

Our morning paper came after Ivor and Juliet had gone. Not Gerry Furnal but Philomena Lynch and Sheila Atherton had both given interviews. Neither mentioned the kidnap attempt. The art-less Mrs Lynch, poor woman, mother of a probable criminal and murderer and of a disabled wreck of a man, all of which the paper exploited, said how Mr Tesham had been a friend of her son Dermot. When Mr Tesham heard that Dermot was 'a cripple' he'd come to see them with his fiancée, Miss Case, and offered Dermot a pension, which he'd been paying ever since. He was such a generous man and very good and kind, with no side to him. As for Miss Case, she was a lovely girl.

Sheila Atherton said that her daughter, the murdered girl, had worked as a children's nanny to Mr Gerald Furnal because he had lost his wife and needed someone to look after his small son, Justin. His wife, Hebe, had been a 'very close friend' of Jane's. They had been at university together. She had died in a car crash. Yes, she thought it was the car crash which took place somewhere in London on 18 May 1990 and she thought the driver was killed. But it may have been the other man who was in the car. 'A coloured man,' she called Lloyd, and I was surprised the newspaper printed those words.

If you scrutinized this as Iris and I did, you could see that the link between Ivor and all this was that he had taken up with Juliet Case after her ex-boyfriend Lloyd Freeman was dead and that he had paid an allowance (a sort of disability pension) to the driver of a crash car in which Lloyd Freeman had been a passenger. Did the media even know what they were looking for?

They kept it up through the Wednesday, mostly with repetition and a plethora of photographs. Ivor went into the department by day and into the House of Commons to vote. In the past he'd always walked to work and back, but that had become impossible. Thanks to the photographs, people recognized him; cameramen followed him, anxious for more shots to use next day, leaving enough of their number behind to catch Juliet if she dared emerge. Braving them was a frightening thing, because they crowded Juliet, thrusting their cameras into her face. Her being so beautiful and eminently photogenic didn't help. I suppose she hadn't been much of an actress or hadn't had the right agent, because surely if she had she would have somehow found her way to Hollywood. Perhaps she was just so nice and, oddly, so modest. Every photograph of her which appeared made her look perfect. There was no awkwardness in any of them, no lines of strain or *moue* of anger. In a single one she seemed distressed and had tears on her face and in that she looked only like the Tragic Muse.

But why did they persist? Why did they keep the story going? Nothing new came out and two days went by. Iris said she thought that perhaps they were working on someone, persuading someone to say more, to confirm what they knew but dared not divulge without confirmation.

On the Friday afternoon Ivor drove himself and Juliet to Ramburgh. It was a brave thing to do, first pushing through the reporters and photographers to get to the car. He told me afterwards that getting Juliet through was the hardest part.

He thought for a while, then, 'No,' he said, 'the hardest fucking part was not giving that *Sun* guy a sock on the jaw. Lovely expression that, don't you think? Does anyone say it any more?'

I said it was a very good thing he hadn't and felt like a prig. Braver, though, was facing his constituents in Morningford and this he did on Saturday. He held his surgery as usual. Someone asked him why he was paying a pension to a man whose injuries happened through his own careless driving. It wasn't the sort of question constituents should ask when they came to their MP for help, but Ivor answered it or, rather, he said that no charge had ever been brought against Dermot Lynch, so it was impossible to say if his driving had been careless or not. By that time he had seen Saturday's newspapers, or one of them, the relevant one.

It had a scoop. On its front page was an interview with a woman who called herself a friend of Hebe Furnal's but who wished to remain anonymous.

I say he had seen the newspaper but he hadn't read the story in the sense of perusing it. The paper which was regularly delivered to Ramburgh House, where my mother-in-law was, of course, living, was *The Times*, but the one which had scooped the rest Ivor picked up after he'd parked his car in the Market Square of Morningford. He saw the headline, the picture of Hebe, and he read the first line of one of the paragraphs in her account of things. Then his agent came down the steps to greet him and he had to run the gauntlet of the people waiting to see him.

Presumably, Gerry Furnal had refused to speak to them and so had his wife, Pandora. When I saw the paper and read the story, I found myself hoping against hope (in soppy-father mode) that Hebe's son, Justin, was too young to understand any of it and that no one would ever tell him of it.

Ivor went back to Ramburgh House. He had no local engagement that evening and none on the Sunday. Going home to London on the Sunday morning was an option and he decided to take it. By then he had read the anonymous woman's interview with a journalist twice while sitting in his car, parked in a farm gateway on a quiet stretch of lane. Much of what she said was untrue or, at best, half true. She talked of Hebe's promiscuity, her spending of her hard-working husband's money on 'other men'. Hebe had neglected her child, she said, in order to meet her lover 'two or three times a week' and had often not returned home until 'the small hours'. He had given her a pearl necklace worth seven thousand pounds which

253

she had told her husband came from the British Home Stores. Ivor's name wasn't mentioned – the anonymous woman didn't know it – only that Hebe's lover was 'an important man in government', which, at that time, he was not. Ivor read the interview a third time. When he came once more to the bit about how he was supposed to have met Hebe so often he said aloud, 'I should have been so lucky.'

It was a fine sunny day, warm for October. He could see the fields, not yet ploughed, white with camomile flowers where the barley had been. I'm not saying this to add colour to my narrative. This is the way he described things as he sat there reading and re-reading that paper.

He didn't show it to Juliet or his mother. He was an English gentleman, enough of the old school in spite of his *outré* sexual carryings-on, to feel it right to keep unpleasant things from women if he could. Of course they must know it and know it soon, but not yet, not on this glorious day. He ate his lunch, not drinking too much till the evening. He and Juliet went for a walk, through the grounds of Ramburgh House, across the fields to the river and back by the lanes and the village. I know it well; Iris and I have done it many times.

Some time that evening, in preparation for his departure next day, he must have gone into the room next to the boot room at the back of the house and fetched what he needed to take back to London with him in the morning.

While Ivor was sitting in his car on the way back from Morningford, Sheila Atherton, Jane's mother, was in her daughter's flat, where she found Jane's diary under the floorboards. I know it was at the precise time, or at any rate on the precise morning, because she told Juliet the date and the time of her discovery when she sent her a copy. She had been walking about the one-room flat when she noticed how a floorboard creaked as she crossed a certain point. Jane's flat wasn't carpeted but scattered with rugs. She moved one of these rugs, lifted a loose floorboard and found the diary, sheets of A4 paper clipped together.

If they ever knew about it, the press must have longed to get hold of the diary. They never did. Sheila Atherton handed it to the police, though not apparently for quite some time. After all, they had Jane's murderer in custody, which must have been the result of what she told them Jane told *her* about him and his attack on her. Why did she send the copy she made of the diary not to Ivor, but to Juliet? Malice? Revenge? I don't know. You will have seen by now Jane's hatred of Ivor and contempt for him and also the light it sheds on so many dark corners and imponderables. It was because she sent it to Juliet that I have been able to include it, or parts of it, in this account, having first secured Mrs Atherton's permission as holder of the copyright.

What happened to Hebe's clothes? Those presumably sexy, lap-dancer's, *embarrassing* clothes which poor Jane put on to see how she might entice the window cleaner. Was she wearing them when Sean Lynch made his way in? Perhaps her mother found them in the suitcase in the cupboard and threw them away out of shame.

29

Menhellion had cleverly never mentioned Sean Lynch, yet his name seemed to underlie every line. It was all there too, in an experienced journalist's synopsis. We left it to Ivor to get in touch with us, or we did so until the Sunday evening and we had heard nothing. At about seven he phoned us and, hastily getting hold of a babysitter, paying her double time, I drove us to Westminster.

His mother and Juliet had done what he asked and Ivor was alone. He'd aged ten years. His hair hadn't turned white overnight because, contrary to popular belief, that doesn't happen, but there seemed more grey in it than when I'd last seen him. He'd eaten nothing since he left Ramburgh at nine that morning but he'd put away a good deal of whisky and had moved on to red wine. Iris found the fridge well stocked with food by prudent Juliet and she made us sandwiches.

'Someone will ask a question in the House tomorrow,' Ivor said.

'And you'll be there?'

'Oh, yes,' he said, as if it were a foregone conclusion. 'It'll be that cliché about "we who are about to die salute thee" crap. I wonder why those poor old Christians bothered to say that. I wouldn't if I were about to be eaten by a lion. I'd tell the emperor to fuck off.'

'D'you think you'll be eaten?'

'Of course. It's the end of me, Rob. I've become the story. No secretaryship of state now. I'll never get into the Cabinet. No re-election. They won't like this in Morningford.'

I asked where Juliet was and he told us she'd stayed behind in Ramburgh. 'I considered just breaking things off with her, you know. Tell her it wasn't working out. It's been nice knowing you and please keep the ring.'

'You wouldn't do that,' Iris said, aghast.

'Well, I didn't. I only said I'd considered it.'

We ate the sandwiches, or Iris and I did. Ivor took one but didn't eat it. He opened another bottle of Burgundy and said he'd probably have a hangover in the morning.

'But that may be no bad thing. It will distract me.'

The expensive babysitter phoned then and said Adam was crying and complaining of pains in his stomach, so we had to go. We left at once, Iris already over-anxious. There was nothing wrong with Adam. He shut up when he saw us, so I suppose it was a ploy to fetch us home. But I wished we could have stayed longer with Ivor. I hated leaving him alone. He shook hands with me and kissed Iris, which were most unusual actions, but he was already half drunk and I thought that must account for it.

We didn't sleep much, either of us. After trying to get to sleep, I went downstairs and picked up a book I'd been reading all day, on and off, in an effort to distract myself from Ivor's troubles. I have often thought about English gentlemen in literature and the recourse to which certain authors drive them, and here in this Dorothy L. Sayers novel was a classic example of the very thing. It was *The Unpleasantness at the Bellona Club* and towards the end Dr Penberthy faces disgrace, a trial and, in those days, execution. I'm going to quote from it because it was extraordinarily apt, though of course I didn't know that at the time.

'Dr Penberthy,' said the old man, 'now that that paper is in Lord Peter Wimsey's hands, you understand that he can only take the course of communicating with the police. But as that would cause a great deal of unpleasantness to yourself and to other people, you may wish to take another way out of the situation . . . If not –'

He drew out from his jacket pocket the thing which he had fetched.

'If not, I happen to have brought this with me from my private locker. I am placing it here, in the table drawer, preparatory to taking it down to the country tomorrow. It is loaded.'

'Thank you,' said Penberthy.

I finished the book which, by the way, was what people who know about such things call 'a good read', and went back upstairs. Iris was still not asleep; a wakeful child – it was Adam – had joined her and very pretty they looked with their arms round each other. It was ten past four. I carried Adam back to his bed. Should we phone Ivor in the morning, I asked Iris, or would a call from us just be a nuisance to him? When someone close to you is in the sort of trouble he was in, you don't want to let him feel isolated or feel that you don't care. We phoned. He said he'd slept a bit, more than he'd expected, and the strange thing was he'd woken up feeling quite fresh and calm, not a trace of a hangover.

'I won't drink before I go into the chamber. I'll have a drink afterwards.'

'Is it certain it's going to happen?'

'Oh, yes,' he said. 'As luck will have it, I have a statement to make and once I've made it, while I'm still at the dispatch box, some Opposition backbencher will ask me if there's any truth in the Menhellion story. It goes without saying. That is what will happen.'

I asked him what he'd say.

'Christ knows. Well, I suppose I do know. I'll tell the truth. I have to. I'm not getting into that sort of shit, lying to the House of Commons. I'll tell the truth, but it won't necessarily be the whole truth.'

'Will the whole truth have to come out?'

'You know, Rob, I don't think it will. I really don't think it ever will.'

That should have alerted me, that should have rung an alarm, but it didn't. I listened to the *Today* programme on Radio Four. It devoted a full five minutes to the Lynchs, the Furnals and Jane Atherton, with an aside that Ivor Tesham, the Air Power Overseas Minister, would have some explaining to do and that, though invited, he had been unwilling to come on the programme. I listened to all that and then I went to work. When I got there I read a selection of the morning papers. They were full of follow-up stories, including life histories of the Lynch family and Sheila Atherton's account of her dead daughter's school and university days, a boyfriend called Callum and another who was the son of a wealthy glass manufacturer. Gerry Furnal maintained his dignified silence. What the point was in showing a large photograph of his new baby, I have no idea. I suppose Pandora, silent and otherwise reserved, gave it to the newspaper with pride.

I could easily have found out exactly what happened in the Commons that day but I didn't. By the time the paper came next day I couldn't bear any more. Did Ivor have notice of the question the Labour backbencher Mark Saddler intended to ask him? Do they have to table a question like that or can they just get up and ask it? I don't know. But I do know what Ivor said, because it was headlines. It was on television and radio; it was everywhere.

Saddler was a notorious anti-royalist and well known for his derisive wit. At each State Opening of Parliament, when Black Rod summoned the Commons 'to attend Her Majesty in the House of Peers', he regularly shouted out some ribald comment, insulting the Queen over her expenditure or the conduct of her children. He was notorious as a troublemaker and an *enfant terrible*.

It must have been known by the afternoon that something exciting and probably of political significance was about to happen. The House was packed, no room left on those ribbed green leather benches. After Ivor had read his statement – something pedestrian about the cost of an episode in the Balkan wars – Saddler got up and asked him if he had anything to say about the implications of a report in *The Times* of that morning. I suppose everyone thought Ivor would prevaricate, bluster perhaps or say he had no comment to make. He did neither.

The dispatch boxes in the Commons are of polished wood with dull brass fittings. Slightly to the right of them, on the table, lies the mace, symbol of royal authority. On his feet at the dispatch box, he said, 'The honourable gentleman is quite right to ask this question. The allegations are true. Certain details are incorrect but the account of what I did is substantially true. Hebe Furnal was my mistress. I did arrange her abduction, though not against her will. I am paying a pension to the driver of the car, Dermot Lynch, brother of Sean Lynch, at present on remand for the alleged murder of Jane Atherton.'

What happens in Parliament being privileged, Ivor could mention Sean Lynch with impunity. A gasp had gone up (according to the newspaper) from all sides of the House. It turned into a roar like that of hounds baying in pursuit of some hunted creature. But Ivor was no fox or hare and, in his peculiar way, I think he must have enjoyed it. Perhaps, then, he knew the answer to why those Christians gave their humble yet defiant salutation to the emperor. I imagine he looked round at the benches, at the ranked faces, the yelling mouths, with the same kind of panache. Then he sat down. I suppose there was some discussion, more questions perhaps, but when the Speaker moved on to the next business he walked out. His departure met with utter silence.

He walked home. It wasn't very far. According to his cleaner, who had left about an hour before, not a single reporter or photographer had been outside since Ivor had left for the House at lunchtime. They would be back, of course, in greater numbers than ever now, but when Ivor let himself into his house, none of them was there. The action was all happening inside the Palace of Westminster.

I wasn't there either. I was in my office in the City, unable to concentrate on anything much, wondering if the question Ivor had predicted would be asked, wondering what he'd say. Iris was at home with the children, or, rather, fetching Nadine from infant school, with one little boy on foot and the other in the pushchair. At Ramburgh House, Juliet was keeping my mother-in-law company.

Because we weren't there, I don't really know what happened, but there are things one can deduce. I'd say that the first thing Ivor did was take from his desk drawer the will he had made the previous week. Juliet told me later that he had had an appointment with his solicitor on the Friday, on the morning of the day they drove to

Ramburgh. This will, correctly signed and witnessed, he left on top of his desk, making sure it was the only item there. After that, he drank some whisky from a bottle of Jack Daniel's. I don't know why he drank Jack Daniel's. He once told me he didn't like it, he preferred Scotch, but perhaps that was all part of it. It didn't much matter what he did or what he liked at that point, though it had to be whisky because that is what a 'very important man' drinks when anaesthetizing himself for what lies ahead.

He went up to a spare bedroom, where he had hidden, on the Sunday night, the thing he had brought back from Norfolk. This was a twelve-bore shotgun. It wasn't loaded. Ivor would never have carried a loaded gun of any kind, not even when setting out to shoot something. Ammunition was in another desk drawer. He loaded the gun.

By this time, according to a neighbour, the media were back. Ivor could have seen them from one of his front windows and he probably did. If they hadn't been there, I believe he would have put the gun back into the boot of his car and driven off to some secluded place. He once said to me, years before, that if he wanted to kill himself he wouldn't do it at home because that would contaminate (that was the word he used) the house for future occupants. But he couldn't get out to his car. There was a reporter sitting on his doorstep. There was no help for it but to do it in this house and I think the fear of 'contaminating' the place was his reason for choosing a small room on the lower ground floor. This was part of a suite of bedroom, sitting room and bathroom intended for live-in help but which he and Juliet had never used. Ivor went into the bedroom, unfurnished but for an old sofa Juliet had brought with her from Queen's Park.

He didn't shut the door. I suppose he was anxious not to make it too difficult for his body to be found. He sat on the sofa, stuck the gun between his knees and, placing his head in the line of fire, pulled the trigger.

30

It's called the pathetic fallacy, isn't it, the tendency to credit nature with human emotions? The day was so mild, the autumn sky so blue, this sunny weather that I saw as indifference, as an affront to Ivor's downfall. I had read the evening paper in my office, called Iris and set off for Westminster. It was just after half past four.

Before I left I'd tried to phone Ivor but both his home phone and his mobile had been left on message. He'd be at home, I knew that. Where else would he have gone? I saw the reporters and the cameramen as I turned into Glanvill Street and when it was clear I meant to get into Ivor's house they crowded me. I told them I was Ivor Tesham's brother-in-law but I knew nothing. I didn't even know where he was.

'In there,' a woman said. 'The guy next door saw him go in.'

She actually held on to me, clutching my jacket, while I rang the bell. I rang and rang until it was pointless to keep on. That was when I cursed not having a key to this house, but why should I have had one? I pushed my way back through the crowd. Helen, his cleaner, worked at a place at the end of the street most after-noons. Juliet had told me that, I don't know why. The reporters followed me as, praying that this was one of Helen's afternoons, I rang the doorbell, but no one was at home. That was when I remembered Martin Trenant, the QC who lived next door.

He wouldn't be at home, of course. He'd be in court somewhere. And even if he was at home, why would he have a key? I battled back down the street, carried along by the press pack, one of the cameras actually knocking me on the head, while reporters asked me what I was doing and where I was going. On Trenant's doorstep I held my breath and thought I must be hallucinating when he opened the door.

Surveying the press calmly, letting me in and closing the door smartly on everyone else, he said, 'I think my wife has a key, only she's in Lisbon.' Was the woman never at home? 'I'm sure we can find it.'

It was hanging on a hook inside a clothes cupboard. We forced a passage through the reporters, Trenant shouting at them in a commanding voice to clear out of our way. We managed to get in and managed too not to let any of the media people in with us. The house seemed to be empty. It was insufferably stuffy, the air barely breathable. In that big open-plan living room where I'd met Sean Lynch at the house-warming party, I saw Ivor's will lying on top of the desk and read the first line: *I, Ivor Hamilton Tesham of Canning House, Glanvill Street, Westminster, London SW1, hereby revoke all other wills* . . .

Like a fist closing, my heart seemed to squeeze. I said to Trenant to try upstairs. He'd had the key, it had been very good of him to come, to struggle through that hell and push in here, but I didn't want him with me. I half knew what I should find and I wanted to find it alone. Full of dread, he as much as me, I think, we went upstairs. That was when I remembered what Ivor had said about contaminating a house, so he wouldn't have done it in his bedroom, not in that pretty bedroom Juliet had made into a boudoir of white lace and pale blue satin. He hadn't done it upstairs at all.

It was cooler down in the basement, cool and dim. This floor was never used. All the more reason for him to have used it and there we found him, lying sprawled across Juliet's old sofa in what he had called 'the maid's room'. Trenant glanced at him, cool as ever, and went back upstairs to phone the police, not hesitating, asking me nothing.

Ivor's head was a mass of blood and blood was still coming from a wound above his right ear. The shotgun he'd used was on the floor. I went up to him very slowly, terribly afraid I might vomit. The blood was coming, so he wasn't dead, he couldn't be. I touched his hand, warm still. I tried to find a pulse but had no idea where to locate it on his wrist. Still holding his hand, I turned away – I had to; I couldn't bear to look at that blood, leaking, dripping – and with his hand now held in both mine, I sat on the floor and heard myself sob. Then I began to cry like one of my own children stricken by some nursery tragedy.

I was helpless but I didn't know how I could have helped. Why the ambulance crew came first I don't know. Maybe Trenant phoned them as well, but however it was, medical help was there before the police arrived. They carried Ivor out on a stretcher and covered in a blanket, the feral reporters wild with excitement, one of them shouting at me that he'd heard the shot. I went in the ambulance with Ivor and they gave him blood on the way to hospital. A soon as we got there, I phoned Iris and told her to come as they might need next-of-kin. Sayers's Dr Penberthy had been more successful at killing himself but he had used a pistol while Ivor had used a shotgun, always a dodgy suicide weapon. That was the first time I'd used the word and at the same time I thought that the will he'd left was his own idea of a suicide note.

He lay unconscious and 'on the danger list' if there is such a thing. We were allowed to see him for a few minutes after they'd cleaned him up and put him on a transfusion of his own blood group. They didn't know if he'd live or die. When there was nothing more for us to do, we went home to our fidgety babysitter, who was desperate to get away and go out with her boyfriend. The next thing must be to call Louisa and Juliet or just Juliet and leave it to her to tell Louisa.

'I ought to go and tell Mother myself,' Iris said.

I said that even if she caught a train in the next hour she wouldn't get to Norwich before midnight. They would have to be told now, at once.

'I'll do it,' Iris said. 'I don't want to but it's the only way.'

Before she could, Juliet phoned us. She was worried, desperately worried. She'd tried to phone Ivor after she'd seen the BBC early-evening news. Proceedings in the Commons chamber had been televised since 1989 and when she saw Ivor standing at the dispatch box and answering Saddler she'd been stunned. She'd found it unbelievable, 'like an awful dream', the kind where exemplary people find themselves in situations of filth and squalor. All this came out before she could be told and Iris was crying so much that I took the phone from her.

'He's alive,' I said. 'Hold on to that. You must tell his mother.'

'Where did he do it?'

It was like the guy in *Macbeth* who says, 'By whom?' when he's told his father's been murdered. I used to think it an irrelevant remark to be made at that point but I didn't when Juliet asked where. Horrible as it was, appallingly distressing, she would want to see Ivor and this act of his in her mind's eye. I found out later the contents of that will. With the exception of Ramburgh House, in which his mother had a life interest, Ivor left everything he possessed to Juliet.

His convalescence was a close parallel to Dermot Lynch's case. Like him, Ivor lay unconscious for a long time but, as far as I know, no one was wishing him to die, as Ivor had wished for Dermot. His mother sat beside him for long hours, holding his hand. Juliet went every day and Iris and I nearly as often. I don't know exactly what he had done to himself when he pulled that shotgun trigger, only that he had damaged his brain. The consultant in charge of his case described it as being rather like the effect of a severe stroke but, he added, 'It might have been a lot worse.'

The fuss in the media might have been a lot worse too if Ivor hadn't made that suicide attempt. In part, it deflected the newspapers from any involvement he might have had in the kidnap–Jane Atherton–Lynch family–Furnal affair. Of course his action was inseparable from it, but for a few days his attempt to kill himself was predominant in every line. Then those articles by investigative journalists which news stories give rise to, particularly in the *Guardian*, began to concentrate on various aspects of the events: the kidnap (which most of the media now accepted was no kidnap), the Hebe Furnal–Jane Atherton friendship, the Lynch connection, the Freeman link with particular reference to Juliet and the incapacity pension which might be no pension but more likely was blackmail.

The prospective Independent candidate for Imberwell, Aaron Hunter, wrote a vitriolic piece, citing and condemning sleaze among the Conservatives. Ostensibly, it mentioned various culprits but it was essentially about Ivor, what he called 'the whiff of perversion' in the kidnap set-up occupying several paragraphs. Hunter said nothing about his marriage to Juliet but other newspapers took him up on it, some congratulating him on his courage and honesty, one censuring him with violence on his cowardice in failing to say that Ivor Tesham's fiancée had been his first wife. Then the cry went up for an inquiry. A commission of independent people with no government or Conservative Party connections must be appointed to look into 'the whole sorry affair'. And so it went on while Ivor lay insensible, linked to life by a series of tubes.

31

What would have been Sean Lynch's fate if the police hadn't read that diary? The mandatory life imprisonment, I suppose, maybe fifteen years. Jane's diary, which Sheila Atherton eventually gave them, saved him. Of course nothing was ever revealed to the public about its existence. There was no outcry, no shouts about wrongful imprisonment. All that the police did was release Sean to return home to his mother and his brain-damaged brother. He wasn't the man they were looking for. His arrest had been the cause of the revelations about Ivor and his suicide attempt, yet Sean had done nothing unless you count forcibly ejecting Jane from his home where she had made her way in under false pretences.

He came out of the prison where he had been on remand a happy man, basking in the prospect of a hundred-thousand-pound offer from a tabloid newspaper for his 'astoundingly frank and mind-blowing' story. If Ivor's condition had put an end to the Lynchs' pension, they would scarcely have missed it. Though, in fact, it hadn't. He went on paying it for the rest of Dermot's life.

Another thing I wondered about was if Ivor had inflicted that wound on himself knowing that it might well kill him, but if it didn't it would place him in a similar position to that of Dermot Lynch. He had a conscience, after all. He saw himself as the author of that poor man's sufferings and incapacity and the only thing for him to do about it was become like him. Iris said this was rubbish. It was sentimental, maudlin and utterly unlike Ivor. Anyway, only some medieval saint would behave like that. Perhaps she is right, I don't know.

An enormous fuss was made in the newspapers about the whole business of the birthday present, wild conjecture, surprisingly accurate assumptions, new revelations which were entirely the product of journalists' imaginations. But the inquiry which was always hinted at never happened, gradually it all died down and by the time Ivor came out of his coma it was seldom referred to. When it was, in feature articles about sleaze or news items revealing some other member's misdemeanour, he was always mentioned as 'the disgraced MP Ivor Tesham', a description he had once told us he dreaded. I doubt that he read these pieces. Having daily studied newspapers for years, he ceased even to glance at headlines. What the eye doesn't see the heart doesn't grieve over.

But how did David Menhellion know that it was Ivor who had been Hebe's lover? We never knew but, though the diary didn't tell us, there was a hint in its early pages. About five years after I read this I happened to glance at a review of one of the previous evening's television programmes. Menhellion, who had become a feature writer for a 'quality' Sunday, had been invited on it as a guest reviewer and in the piece he wrote he referred to his own weakness for costume serials. Cosy domestic asides were becoming fashionable, so there was nothing unusual in a columnist bringing in his wife and her preference for docu-dramas. What was unusual was her Christian name, very uncommon then and now. Jane mentions a Grania as one of Hebe's friends and as Gerry Furnal's helper. It's not too far-fetched to think that they are one and the same and that the Grania Jane met in Irving Road, if not then married to Menhellion, may soon have become his girlfriend, happy to pass on to him what she deduced as to the identity of Hebe's lover or what perhaps Hebe herself had told her.

It was a long time before Ivor recovered enough to go home. The wound to the side of his head, which had been covered in bandages while he lay unconscious, was at last exposed on a day in September when Iris and I visited the hospital. It was an ugly sight, enough to make you recoil and hope he hadn't seen. He has had several skin grafts since then but he still has a kind of furrow from his temple to his crown and no hair grows on it. As soon as he was back in Glanvill Street he applied for a special licence and he and Juliet were married, the bridegroom seated in an armchair, wearing an immaculate suit and a woolly hat to hide the scar.

Most newspapers carried a photograph from their archives of Ivor and Juliet taken when he first became a Minister of State. Variations on 'Disgraced MP weds' were the captions above these pictures, but since newspapers were no longer delivered to his home, Ivor saw none of them. Juliet had longed for this marriage and now she had got it. Did it make her happy? She said she was happy. At thirty-six she was more beautiful than ever and in the spring she told us she was pregnant. She adored Ivor and said the happiest day of her life was when she told him he was to be a father. According to her, he wept for joy. I wonder. It's well known that victims of stroke or similar blows to the brain often cry very easily. I can only say that in all the time I've known him, I've never seen tears in his eyes.

Was it the present Ivor or the memory of what he had been that Juliet loved? Though possibly not moved to tears, he was a changed man. Whether this change was due to the damage the shotgun had done to his brain, a straightforward trauma, or to the punishment he had suffered in the weeks and days before he tried to kill himself, I don't know. Recklessness was gone and panache and that callousness which had been so much a feature of his character, the indifference which had made him wish for Dermot's death and not grieve at all over Hebe's. He had done clever things and stupid things to save his skin and when it was stripped away he had become a little dull. Politics had been the breath of life to him and now he relinquished what he called 'all that' apparently without a qualm. Now there could be no question of infidelity to Juliet. And 'all that' included other indulgences.

'I haven't had a drink since I came round,' he said to me. 'I don't seem to fancy it.'

'Many would envy you,' I said.

'Would they?'

He gave me a long steady look but said no more. I regretted that remark I'd made, but it was too late. Still, it had provoked nothing but a wistful enquiry. It might, instead, have brought on one of his rages, paroxysms of uncontrolled anger when he would shout and roar, often breaking some ornament by hurling it against the wall. Juliet may have been the recipient of some of this noisy violence, but if she was she never said so. She was entirely loyal to him in word and deed and, I'm sure, in thought too.

One day, alone with Iris, he talked to her about his suicide attempt. 'I know a lot of people think I didn't mean to kill myself,' she told me he'd said to her. 'They're wrong. I did. I thought, I can't go on any more with all that stuff going round in my head. Nothingness would be preferable. I suppose all would-be suicides think like that. That's the essence of it.'

She asked him if he still felt like that. It was a *num* question, expecting the answer no, and that's what she got, but it wasn't unqualified. He answered her in that wistful way he often spoke in at that time. 'No,' he said. 'Oh, no. I have a lot of good things going for me now. And another thing, I've become an ostrich. I turn away and hide my head when unpleasant things happen. I turn off the radio and change TV channels. I shall never look at another newspaper. I *save* myself. I don't feel in the least tempted to know what's going on.'

Out in the world where Ivor never went, more precisely in the constituency of Imberwell, the prospective Labour and Liberal Democrat candidates stood down to ensure that Aaron Hunter won the seat as an Independent. I suppose no one thought the Conservative candidate was a threat to him and indeed she wasn't. In the 1997 general election, on his anti-sleaze ticket, Hunter gained Imberwell with a majority of over twenty thousand.

Long before that, in 1995, Ivor and Juliet sold the house in Glanvill Street and moved permanently to live at Ramburgh House. There was some question of their having a pied-à-terre in London but neither of them really wanted it and the house in Ivor's old constituency became their only home. Over the years Juliet has done wonders with the shabby gardens and now they are opened to the public on two days during May and June. Louisa and John never redecorated the place or refurbished the furniture but Juliet has done both, showing great taste and a flair for that sort of thing. A good many of the old portraits of ancestors whose names are long forgotten are gone and she and Ivor have replaced them with modern landscapes and a portrait of herself. She wears a full-length red silk gown and is seated, as some eighteenth-century lady might be, with her little daughter standing at her knee and her baby boy in her lap.

Ivor, who had never been self-conscious, still less felt insecure, was sensitive about being recognized in public, especially if he walked about Westminster, which he had once or twice tried doing. Louisa Tesham gave up the house to him and Juliet, as she had always said she would when Ivor married. She went to live in the lodge that Ivor, in the time of his prosperity, had sometimes called 'the dower house'; he did so no longer. He told me he felt quite differently about walking down to Ramburgh village stores or St Mary's Church from how it was in London. Everyone spoke to him and no one stared. It was the same in Morningford and when he met the woman who had replaced him as member in the by-election – and who lost the seat to Labour two years later – she was courteous and charming and made no reference to his previous incumbency or his subsequent downfall. Imagine the old Ivor caring about someone else's manners or attitude to himself!

Unlike certain other 'disgraced' MPs, he didn't throw himself heart and soul into charity work or adopt some cause to champion.

'I might run into Gerry Furnal again,' he said with a rare flash of his old sense of fun, 'and have to call him out.'

Something crazy like that was exactly the sort of thing he might have considered doing in his carefree days. More than anyone else I've ever known, I can picture him fighting a duel with swords. I'll correct that and say I can imagine the old Ivor in that role. In Ramburgh he embarked on what was to be a quiet life. He read a lot, began on the research for a life of Lord Palmerston and, in a modestly luxurious kind of way, entertained old friends at the weekends and in the holidays. Juliet's daughter – I call her that in the mode Ivor had said was used by Evelyn Waugh – was born in the autumn of their first year at Ramburgh and her son a year and a day after the general election in which Labour enjoyed such a huge landslide. We too had our fourth and last child that year, a girl called Isabel, while Ivor and Juliet gave their children Christian names of irreproachable Conservative credentials: Lucy and Robert.

There have been two coincidences over the years. If they are coincidences. Perhaps they should just be thought of as interesting happenings. My daughter Nadine's schoolfriend Hannah is going out with a boy called Justin Furnal, aged nineteen. It must be the same one. Philomena Lynch had a huge win on the National Lottery about five years ago and, according to the *Evening Standard*, bought with half the proceeds the house in Hampstead Garden Suburb once owned by Damian and Kelly Mason. Once more the *Standard* dug up all the dirt about Ivor and Hebe, the Masons and the birthday present, but Ivor up in Norfolk saw none of it.

Dermot died in that house, a year or so after his mother bought it, and then Ivor ceased to pay the pension. She and Sean had no need of it. Sean has got married and, as far as anyone knows, has become an exemplary citizen. Of the fates of Sheila Atherton, Erica Caxton and the Trenants I have no knowledge. Nicola Ross has married a Polish count and, like Ivor, has two children. But long before any of this, at the start of 1995, the police found the murderer of Jane Atherton.

Considering they had had Jane's diary for several months by then, they took their time. Perhaps they had too little evidence to proceed. But Jane had been raped, so I would have expected tests to show beyond a doubt that he was guilty. But I don't know. My ignorance on these matters is as profound as that of most law-abiding men, I suppose.

He was charged, appeared in the magistrates' court in February and his trial took place at the Central Criminal Court in the following December. No one even remotely connected with this whole business had ever heard of him unless they had read Jane's diary. He was Stuart Thomas Higgs, 28, a window cleaner of Kensal Rise.

At the trial details of his association with Jane came out. He had been employed by the managing agents of the building where her flat was to clean the residents' windows inside and out. His counsel suggested that she gave him great encouragement, which is not suggested by the diary. She seems, eventually, to have been attracted to him out of despair, out of resignation to her only hope of finding love and companionship. They went to a pub together, apparently drank a good deal, and she invited him back home with her afterwards. As far as they knew. Anyway, he must have been in the flat with her. His counsel told the court that she consented to sex with him, then changed her mind. Higgs had no memory of what happened after that. He said he found himself with one of her kitchen knives in his hand and the two of them there on her bed in a pool of her blood.

Higgs was sentenced to life imprisonment, as was mandatory, with a recommendation that he should serve a minimum of fifteen years. This means he should be out in three years' time.

Unanswered questions remain. Would Jane have attempted to blackmail Ivor? It must have been a large sum she meant to extract from him if she expected to live on it for the rest of her life. She seemed very determined. Would Ivor have agreed to what she asked? I have never mentioned that aspect of things to him. As far as I know, he isn't aware of the existence of the diary. Juliet has read it but she is even less likely than Iris and I are to tell him of it. Why did Dermot Lynch drive across that Hendon junction fast and against a red light? A suggestion was made when I told the tale to a psychiatrist friend of Iris's, heavily disguised and with the names changed, that Dermot, a single and perhaps celibate man, had been over-stimulated sexually by tying Hebe up and putting handcuffs and a gag on her while his own face was covered. This would perhaps have led to his total loss of control.

Having shown himself a master of drama in the handing back of the pearls, why did Gerry Furnal do nothing more? Why did he never speak to the media? Why did his wife never speak to them? Well, I have the impression he was always a quiet, reserved sort of man, the antithesis of what Ivor had been. As for her, no doubt she kept silent to please him.

What became of the pearls?

We spent last Christmas with Ivor and Juliet and their children at Ramburgh House. Over eighty by now, Louisa was there with her live-in carer and the Munros with their daughters. Some cousins of Iris and Ivor's came and Juliet's brother with his girlfriend, so we sat down twenty to Christmas dinner. Juliet, a little heavier than she had been – she always ate heartily – but as beautiful as ever, was in black with pearls. According to Ivor she had said she 'didn't do pearls', but here she was wearing a string of them, large flawless pearls.

'Is it the same one?' Iris whispered to me.

I don't know. If it was it is perhaps a sign of the perfect accord between Ivor and his wife.

He just wanted a decent book to read ...

Not too much to ask, is it? It was in 1935 when Allen Lane, Managing Director of Bodley Head Publishers, stood on a platform at Exeter railway station looking for something good to read on his journey back to London. His choice was limited to popular magazines and poor-quality paperbacks – the same choice faced every day by the vast majority of readers, few of whom could afford hardbacks. Lane's disappointment and subsequent anger at the range of books generally available led him to found a company – and change the world.

'We believed in the existence in this country of a vast reading public for intelligent books at a low price, and staked everything on it'
Sir Allen Lane, 1902–1970, founder of Penguin Books

The quality paperback had arrived – and not just in bookshops. Lane was adamant that his Penguins should appear in chain stores and tobacconists, and should cost no more than a packet of cigarettes.

Reading habits (and cigarette prices) have changed since 1935, but Penguin still believes in publishing the best books for everybody to enjoy. We still believe that good design costs no more than bad design, and we still believe that quality books published passionately and responsibly make the world a better place.

So wherever you see the little bird – whether it's on a piece of prize-winning literary fiction or a celebrity autobiography, political tour de force or historical masterpiece, a serial-killer thriller, reference book, world classic or a piece of pure escapism – you can bet that it represents the very best that the genre has to offer.

Whatever you like to read – trust Penguin.